OSSIE HOPKINS read Literature at Durham, and
rock climbing in a seventies comprehensive. He p
– apprentice to the chief education officer, pro
thought you were learning to write along ca
A Master's at Manchester helped the career, but not the writing.

As deputy director with Birmingham LEA he produced plenty of
sound-bites for the dailies, Central TV and Pebble Mill but somehow
never got round to 'real' writing.

Later he became throttlebottom-in-chief at Ribble Valley Council.
My, but it was cold up there. And lonely. Maybe if we turned things
upside down... Now we can see how many people we're there to support.
So leadership is just like teaching – helping people grow. Must get round
to writing some of this down. Whoops! Palace revolution! Ossie leaves the
same way he arrived: fired with enthusiasm!

Still, one door closes... And here's a brand new international
institute for customer service looking for advocacy in the public sector.
Further corridors-of-power to tramp, but again, more PowerPoint than
authorship!

At last... The opportunity! Supporting his son's haulage business with
eighteen-hour days on the road, Ossie can no longer avoid the challenge
of that first book in the series...

£5

CHALK for CHEESE

OSSIE HOPKINS

SilverWood

Published in 2015 by SilverWood Books

SilverWood Books Ltd
14 Small Street, Bristol, BS1 1DE
www.silverwoodbooks.co.uk

ISBN 978-1-78132-376-2 (paperback)
ISBN 978-1-78132-377-9 (ebook)

British Library Cataloguing in Publication Data
A CIP catalogue record for this book is available from
the British Library

Set in Bembo by SilverWood Books
Printed on responsibly sourced paper

One

Jill's earliest memory was the bonfire. Their pile of broken furniture and splintered boxes was almost complete when some gowks from Prudhoe Street burnt it down. So her brother, Rob, and some of the older lads decided to build a proper one and mount guard over it like their dads did with the leeks in the run-up to show time.

The new one had a centre pole: a railway timber that Rob, who was eight and dead strong, had dragged up from the side of the track that ran from Newcastle all the way to Tynemouth. He and his cousin Pete scooped out a waist-deep hole and buried the tar-brown sleeper in the gravelly soil. Then they shored it up so it stood six foot-proud: easy. First though, they hammered in some rusty nails found near the station-box to pile up smaller timbers and the last of the boughs from the fallen oak down the dell. A lot of the wood was wet, but with enough kindling and a dousing of petrol stolen from the rope works it'd go off a treat on the night. Then a whole gang of them brought the tinder – cardboard boxes, a garden gate, squares of discarded carpet, even a couple of broken creels that one of the mums who worked down the fish quay had donated. Stuffed with newspapers and magazines and soaked in fuel it would make the perfect fuse. 'Light the blue touch paper and retire,' as the warning on the fireworks said.

And there'd be loads of *them*! Not that anyone could afford owt fancy but they'd all been spending whatever they could scrimp at Billy Dixons. The corner shop at the end of Bewicke Street stocked Standard Fireworks from August onwards. Jill couldn't see the attraction herself and couldn't've afforded even sparklers. Aged four, she didn't get any pocket money, though occasionally Uncle Fred would give her threepence. But for that she had to sit on his knee and let him cuddle her; and in any case, Rob usually pinched the money. The first time she'd threatened to tell their mam; but Rob just laughed and said if she did he'd tell Mam how she got it. Rob didn't always know when she'd been given cuddle-money so she reckoned it was better to keep quiet.

The rule was that all the fireworks were pooled and kept under the watchful eye of Jimmy Seddon's mam. She supplied the trestle table on which they and the refreshments were kept. Jacket potatoes from the edge of the bonfire were retrieved once the embers had died down enough, and Aunt Lizzie provided a huge bowl of broth. You had to bring your own mug. The lads weren't interested in broth; only in the tin biscuit-boxes which housed a stack of fountains, mines, roman candles, Catharine wheels, jumping jacks and of course bangers. They were s'posed to be let off under Mrs Seddon's direction, but as the evening wore on the lads were able to pinch the jacks and bangers at will. Nor did they 'retire' after lighting the blue touch paper, preferring to grasp them until the last second before throwing them at some unfortunate victim. Rob was one of the worst. He'd just tossed a banger at Geordie Bertram who'd retaliated by loosing off a rocket. Rob ducked out of the way and the rocket whooshed through Jill's hair, singeing her temples and causing her to wail in anguish. She looked briefly round for comfort, although she knew none would be forthcoming, and fled. She tore all the way up the street to No. 40 where she burst through the front door and locked herself in the cupboard under the stairs.

It was pitch black, but that didn't worry Jill who was used to playing in the gloom of the air raid shelters. At least she was safe from the bangers whose explosions she could still hear dimly from down the street. After a while she dozed off, only to be woken by a crash as her dad staggered in from a session down the Club. She must've cried out, cause even though he was singing and laughing at the same time she heard something about: 'Hidin' under the stairs, eh! Well get these, hinny!' and the next thing Jill knew two lighted bangers were being shoved under the cupboard door. Terrified, she cowered in the corner, screaming as the enclosed space magnified first the sparks and then the detonations. With her ears ringing, Jill was still sobbing as her father's cackling disappeared into the kitchen. She didn't come out of the cupboard that night.

She didn't say owt to her mam though, partly as it would've felt like she was dobbing her dad, but mainly cause she was never there to tell anyway. Like most of the kids whose mams and dads were both working, Jill Walker brought herself up. She got dressed, grabbed whatever there was for breakfast, fed her little brother, Al, and then spent the day mucking about with Annie Robson and Denise Kerr. If it was fine they'd be on the slag heaps or out by the lake where they collected paper bags full of gravel and played sweetie shops. If it rained they'd be in the air raid shelters playing hide-and-seek and Cowboys and Indians. There were five shelters altogether and although they were dark and damp and musty they were a good place to play; except when some of the bigger lads ruined their games by joining in. They didn't join in properly though; they just hid in the nooks and crannies and jumped out screaming or tripped the girls up so they went sprawling in the clarts. The worst of them was Geordie Bertram.

One time he hid in the pitch black of the deepest shelter waiting for Jill to be chased down by one of the other lads. But as she helter-skeltered past he didn't scream or trip her up he just grabbed her round the waist, clapping his hand over her mouth and dragging her into the recess. Her pursuer went tearing by and as his footsteps died away Geordie hissed: 'Mak a soond and aa'll belt yer. Do as I say an yer won't get hurt. Alreet?' Jill nodded her submission and he removed his hand from her mouth. He still held her tight round her middle though. But before owt else happened, her erstwhile stalker came blundering back and taking advantage of Geordie's inattention she slipped from his grip, and ran. She knew the shelter better than they did and was able to hide in an alcove whilst they lumbered about in the blackness searching for her. After a spell they got bored and left, Geordie shouting into the gloom: 'Divn't worry, aall get yer next time, yer little slut!' Jill didn't know what a slut was but she had no intention of Geordie getting her then, or in the future.

Come the spring, when she just wanted peace and quiet Jill would walk past the allotments, down the burn and over the stream to the reedy pond. There she'd catch tadpoles and water boatmen in a little net. It wasn't hers and it wasn't a proper net. Rob had made it by twisting a thin metal coat hanger into a circle, covering it with muslin pinched from their nan's sewing box and jamming the 'net' into one of the canes their dad had borrowed from work for his vegetable patch. She put the pond life in a jam-jar. It was suspended on a piece of string and she dreamt of carrying it back home to show an admiring family. But Rob had grown out of pond fishing whilst Al was just a bairn. So when she'd tired of her sport she emptied the catch back into the pond and, fishnet and jar in hand, trudged home.

One time, however, she showed her haul to Bowly.

Everyone knew Bowly. He were 'safe enough but a bit sackless' and he used to hang around and talk to the youngsters. He could tell the different kinds of butterflies and birds. Especially birds: he knew loads about them and pointed out some of the common ones – spuggies, tits and blackies – to Jill. She liked him cause as well as teaching her about birds, he always seemed interested in what she'd caught in her special net.

One day Jill was specially happy. She'd a reet good haul in her jar, and was lying contentedly on the mossy bank by the pool catching cloud-shapes. She'd already spotted a whale, a castle and a hat like her dad wore on Sundays sometimes. She closed her eyes and smilingly imagined bottling the shapes in a separate jar and surprising her friends. Dozy Denise probably wouldn't be impressed but she reckoned Annie, who could make stories in her head, would be. She giggled at the prospect, only opening her eyes when she felt the presence of an intruder.

It were only Bowly.

She smiled lazily at him, expecting him to smile back. He did briefly, but then the smile was replaced by a funny look as he suggested, 'Let's see what you've caught, and I'll show yer summat.' And when she pointed proudly to the tadpoles and a tiny minnow he grabbed her hand and pulled her – gently enough – behind the bramble bushes. Jill was puzzled but not particularly worried. Then Bowly undid his belt and dropped his trousers to the ground. He had strange white underpants on which bulged at the front, like Uncle Fred when he gave Jill a cuddle. She wondered what he was going to do next, and then Bowly pulled them down and muttered huskily, 'Look at that, eh! Yer can touch it if yer wanna.' Jill was scared now, but she didn't show it. She muttered summat about her mam expecting her home and, eluding Bowly's grasp, legged it back past the pond. She didn't stop running 'til she reached the top of Bewicke Street.

Finally, the dawdling summer was over and it was time for Jill to go to St Kits, the primary school near the rope works. Rob had been there four years already and was a junior. Jill knew roughly how to get to the school. She'd have to go on her own, even though she'd heard her mam give Rob strict instructions to make sure his little sister got there safely on her first day. So she dressed quickly in the blue skirt and white blouse her mother had brought home from the stall that Saturday. Then she bolted down a slab of bread and strawberry jam and set off in good time.

It was cool and cloudy, with rain in the air. Jill glanced upwards anxiously in case her new clothes got wet. She took one wrong turn and, for a minute or two, worried that she was going to get lost; but she could see the cranes at Swann's towering over the houses so she couldn't be far out. Soon she was back on familiar territory and turned into Collingwood Street where the school was sited. When she got there, however, the gates were closed and padlocked and no one else was about. She sat down on the wall to wait. After maybe a quarter of an hour she began to panic that she'd somehow missed the beginning of school. And by the time the bin men stopped by she was crying. One of them came across to ask her what the matter was. Sobbing, Jill explained that she'd been locked out of school for being late. The man laughed and, putting his arm round her shoulder, explained, 'Why hinny, yer not late. It's only just past seven. School won't be open for another hour!' And when he'd established where she lived, 'Howay, hop aboard and we can drop you off at the top of Bewicke Street on our way past!'

Jill didn't recall much else about her first day.

Two

The playroom was the first thing Jay could remember.

It was large and square and the floor was covered in rubber mats with green and black streaks. You could barely see the cracks. If you got a good run with your socks on you could slide for miles.

The room was almost bare today, apart from some wooden staging along the wall that overlooked the driveway between Ivy Bank and the house next door. On the staging a marvellously-contrived model railway was laid out. It had two stations and the tracks wound through tunnels below green and brown papier mâché mountains. In each station was a Hornby train: one a dark maroon steam locomotive with its tender and five chocolate and white carriages, the other a grimy black goods train with a string of freight wagons. They belonged to his big brother, Chris, and Jay wasn't normally allowed to touch them, let alone play with them. But this being his birthday he and his friends had been given a special treat. His father's demonstration, and the chance for each youngster to propel one or other train a little way round the track, had been the highlight of the party so far.

The other feature in the playroom was Jay's fifth birthday present – a merry-go-round. It was painted bright red and yellow, with the maker's name 'Triang' in gloss black; and had two seats opposite each other, one on each metal spine. Apart from one shy boy, they'd taken it in turns to ride round faster and faster and had ended up thoroughly dizzy by the time the birthday tea was due.

Tea was set around a low, round table surrounded by bright mauve and green plush cushions. His mum was about to go through to the kitchen when Jay realised that the boy who had been too timid to risk the perils of the merry-go-round was holding her hand; as he had been for most of the afternoon. Jay didn't really know Malcolm very well and was sure he didn't want the other boy to be the centre of anyone's attention. However, as he pondered this prospect he noticed his mum whisper something to his dad and deftly transfer Malcolm's hand to his before departing for the kitchen. Jay was relieved.

Shortly afterwards his mother reappeared pushing a dark brown Bakelite trolley. She parked it in the centre of the expectant ring and resumed hand-holding duties as his father vanished to his study. The two shelves of the trolley bore an array of sandwiches, sausage rolls, meat pies, cakes, jellies, strawberry sundaes, custard flips and blancmanges; and Jay – determined to regain everyone's attention – began to announce the menu in the manner of Ratty from one of his favourite stories: 'there's coldtonguecoldhamcoldbeefpickledgherkinssaladfrenchrollscresssandwich-espottedmeatgingerbeerlemonadesodawater—'

Jay recited this menu on every family picnic but now he had an audience of five bemused but delighted guests, who promptly implored him to repeat it. He needed no encouragement (usually his big brother stifled any repetition) and would've embarked on a reprise had not his mother intervened with a kindly but firm, 'That's enough, darling. It's time to eat now.' Thwarted, the birthday-boy had just time to show off further by proclaiming: 'I could tell you lots more about food. I'm gonna be like Autolycus, who went around snapping up unconsidered trifles!'

This was met by blank stares, much to Jay's disappointment.

Autolycus had been Jay's favourite hero since his father told him about *The Winter's Tale* over breakfast one morning. He'd remembered him because he was a 'rogue' (Jay knew what that was cause his dad called him one sometimes), a likeable rogue, and apparently taking after *his* father was 'a snapper up of unconsidered trifles.' This sounded pretty good to Jay, who was clear that snapping up trifles was the thing to do, especially if they were those red-jelly ones with the coloured sugar sprinkled on top.

Like the one his mother had just set down at the centre of his birthday tea. The boys tucked in and all was quietly intent for some minutes. Then, without warning, Malcolm scrambled up from the cushions and marched to the far corner of the playroom. He stood up straight, pausing momentarily to get his balance and proceeded to turn head over heels repeatedly right across the skiddy-rubber tiles. Then, after colliding with the opposite skirting board, he turned around and repeated the gymnastic feat. His audience was stunned, but clapped their hands wildly, delighted by this unexpected display from their previously subdued friend. The train set, merry-go-round and trifle paled into insignificance. This was definitely the highlight of the party.

And, for once, Jay didn't mind at all.

That night, as a final treat, Jay's dad recounted his own version of *The Winter's Tale*. Jay loved the old story and its diverse characters: Mamillius, the young prince who seemed a bit of a nit; and his sister, Perdita, who didn't count cause she was a girl; Polixenes, King of Bohemia and his son, Florizel; and, of course, Autolycus, who became the hero of Jay's Ivy Bank imagination.

The winter's tale became spring, and then summer. It was late July and not long light. Jay climbed onto the ottoman that contained his bed linen and stood up to pull open the curtains. From here he could see much of the known world.

Immediately below were the burnt-red ridge tiles and grey slates of the washhouse, accessed from the stone-flagged yard across which stretched his mother's white plastic washing line. It was currently occupied by two, four, eight no less, young house martins. Jay knew they were martins not swallows because their tails had no streamers and they were all dark brown and white – no splashes of red under their chins. They had recently fledged and their grey mud nests lay empty under the gutters. Jay knew the difference between house sparrows and tree sparrows too and for this and other avian knowledge he had his mum to thank.

Beyond the martins lay the back garden; and curving around the house was the beige-flecked, black tarmac drive, swinging right to negotiate the tumble of millstone-grit boulders where nasturtiums grew. Jay loved the bright orange, yellow and red flowers and had not been put off them even when his brother had suggested they were good to eat; the pungent taste of the leaves being far outweighed by the flashes of colour amongst the boulders. The latter abutted a stout wooden trellis fixed to the stunted oak tree. Chris had explained that it was *stunted* 'cause if it wasn't stunted it would be taller than the house.' Underneath the oak tree was a sandpit.

The tarmac continued for thirty yards or so to a block of blackened-stone buildings housing a workshop and a garage. The garage had a wooden and glass door which slid on rails round to the side, but Jay always liked it open so he could see his father's prize possession: a 1948 Flying Standard. It was maroon with black wings and chrome bumpers and its registration number – the first Jay memorised – was BG 9835. Fixed to the grill was an 'AA' badge. Chris said 'AA' stood for 'Automobile Association' which was a bit of a mouthful but sounded good. The AA had been around for yonks, but it was only recently that their motorbikes and bright yellow sidecars had become widespread. The drivers wore brown uniforms and when they saw Dad they saluted. Chris said this was cause Dad worked for 'Her Majesty' and was important; but Malcolm's elder brother, Hugh, whose father's Jaguar Mark VII Saloon also sported the badge, said they saluted his dad, too. So Jay wasn't sure. Either way, it gave him a thrill.

In between the garage block and the trellis lay the vegetable garden, and a greenhouse where Jay's father grew tomatoes. When you cautiously opened the glass door you were met by a warm, horticultural smell. Jay was in two minds about the garden. His bad memory was of being caught by his father having a sneaky pee. Piled up against the wall by the greenhouse was a heap of rubble out of which sprung a luxurious growth of rosebay willowherb. The plants were so dense you could hide behind them: almost... His father didn't spank him (indeed he couldn't remember receiving any physical punishment from his father – ever) but he rebuked him in sharp enough tones for Jay not to forget. And he never told anyone either. It was best not: that way you knew it was a secret. And no one but Autolycus could snap it up!

His good memory more than made up for this misdemeanour. Some Saturday mornings when his father was playing golf he would receive a commission – weeding. The one plant which grew better even than the willowherb and seemed to thrive in between the serried ranks of potatoes was groundsel; it was so prolific that even at the going rate of a penny-per-twenty he could easily make sixpence, which more than supplemented his pocket money. The sixpences went into his money box, which was fashioned like a metal book on whose cover were painted scenes of Noddy and Big Ears. When he'd saved up two-and-sixpence he'd be allowed to go into town with Dad on a Saturday morning and buy a Dinky toy to add to his collection.

Jay's favourites were the racing cars. He had six altogether and, if a rainy weekend forced them indoors, he and his friend Michael would play 'farthests.' Michael was exotic. He could speak French and lived, appropriately, in 'Parris.' Jay knew that Paris was the capital of France and an advert in his mother's weekly Picture Post promised that BEA would fly you there for '...as little as £9.15 RETURN!' Even though his mum had explained that 'Parris' was the name of the street where Michael lived, Jay preferred to believe that he flew over specially to see him; particularly as he visited only rarely and it was a mystery how he got there. Sometimes Michael would be 'Michel' and teach Jay French words, but not when they were playing farthest, cause that was Jay's game so he had to be in charge. First, you chose your cars – three each – in turns. As they were his cars Jay baggsied first turn and always got the bright red Ferrari which had the best wheels. That was the key to winning.

The cars were lined up on the staging where the train set ran and the trick was to run them down a six-inch-wide plank onto the rubber mats. If you managed to keep your car on the plank and it got to the mat, it could go right across the room. If you reached the far wall you got ten points. If not, you just got two points for going farthest. Jay kept the scores in his head – in English. The Ferrari's wheels being the best it often made it to the wall opposite and so was Jay's banker. Gradually, Michael – who was not slow to spot the best performers – learned to take the Alfa Romeo as his first pick. It was yellow and blue and went almost as straight as Jay's Ferrari, so if the latter failed to get down the plank (a not-infrequent occurrence) then he had a good chance of a ten-point lead. After that there was not much to choose between the Lotus (which Jay tended to pick because it was English and painted in British Racing Green), the BMW, the Maserati and the Porsche. According to how many rounds they played the game could go on for hours; or until Jay's mum said it was time for Michael to go. 'Au revoir,' he would announce grandly and sweep out to board the afternoon plane.

Beyond the back garden lay a narrow strip of recently planted woodland – saplings, really, mostly ash. However, inspired by Ratty, it assumed the proportions of the 'Wild Wood' and naturally beyond the wild wood was the 'Wide World' – although actually it was the golf course on which his father played so regularly that he was the current course champion, off a handicap of three. Jay didn't know what that meant except that it was good; though it was confusing too as normally a little number like three wouldn't count for much. Especially as it was an odd number. Jay preferred even numbers – you could double them better and get bigger ones.

The ashlings in the Wild Wood swayed slightly in the early-morning breeze, making them difficult to count. Counting was another of Jay's passions: a considered trifle that he snapped up whenever he could. He tried computing the trees, first in ones, then in twos, and then fours. He wondered what would happen if you *kept* doubling the number one and started to do so in his head. Later that day when his father appeared to tell him a bedtime story Jay asked, 'Do you know what happens if you keep doubling one?'

His father twinkled: 'No, d'you want to tell me?'

Jay smiled confidently and began with a rush: '1-2-4-8-16-32-64-128-256-512-1,024-2,048-4,196.' He paused for a moment and then continued in a more measured fashion, concentrating hard: '8,392-16,784-33,568-67,136-134,272-268,544-537,088-1,074,176. There,' he concluded triumphantly, 'see, Dad, it only takes twenty goes to get to a million!' He subsided onto his pillow exhausted by the mental effort and his eyelids began to flutter with sleep. But not before he'd registered the surprise and admiration on his dad's face and squirreled away his: 'That's excellent, son…very well done!'

Three

Jill soon settled in at St Kits and with help from Miss Charlton, the student teacher, she learned to read quickly – surprisingly quickly; it wasn't as if she had a head start over most of the kids. There weren't any books at home, just the occasional newspaper or magazine. Mostly they were for adults; but there were a couple of old *Rupert Bear* and *Roy of the Rovers* annuals and sometimes Rob brought a copy of *The Beano* or *The Dandy* home. He'd rapidly tire of it and when he threw it out Jill would retrieve it. Soon she had quite a stack and although she couldn't read many of the words she liked looking at the pictures. Her favourite cartoon was Minnie the Minx, who seemed to get into the sort of trouble that stalked Jill and her friends. She mentioned this one Saturday when Annie and her older sister, Liz, were round.

Liz was seven and could read really well. She offered to recount some of the Minnie stories and, whilst Annie showed no interest and wandered off outside, Jill sat on the older girl's knee, transfixed by the tales of Minnie's battles with Dennis the Menace and the scrapes they both got into. Liz seemed pleased that Jill wanted to hear the stories and promised she could go round to their flat in Ridley Avenue where Liz had her own collection of comics. These included *Girl*, which had only recently come out and had stories as well as puzzles and activities like making baskets and things. Liz said it was super! And so it became a routine – once every fortnight or so Jill would go round to the Robsons' flat. At first Liz would just read the stories out loud, but she soon found that Jill's questions were so persistent it was easier to explain the story and teach her the odd word.

Miss Charlton's family came from Jedburgh, just into Scotland, and she could trace her ancestry back to people called the Border Reivers. She talked a bit funny but she was always on the lookout for keen learners and when she found one – like Jill – she would go to great lengths to help her. In class, once they had mastered the rudiments, the beginners started with Janet & John. *Here We Go* and *Off to Play* were the first two. Jill didn't think much of the little blond girl and the red-haired lad:

dead smartly dressed and nowt like anyone she knew. But she liked being able to master the stories, so she'd soon read the whole series and Miss Charlton was encouraging her onto the Noddy books and little stories by someone called Dr Suess about cats and a turtle, named Yertle. She didn't like the drawings in those; but it didn't matter as she soon got on to the Ladybird Books which didn't just tell you stories but included loads of useful snippets as well. And she discovered a series of Observer books; she liked the ones on trees and birds especially. There weren't too many trees near home, only down the burn, but she soon learned to recognise some of the commoner birds which perched on poles and rooftops around Bewicke Street. She already knew some of them – spuggies and blackies, for starters – but *they* stirred disagreeable memories of Bowly so she took against them a bit. Meanwhile, there was the highlight of each day: their teacher reading a chapter from *My Friend Flicka*.

Miss Charlton encouraged Jill to take a book home at the weekends. What Jill really wanted was to read to her mam, but she was never there or, when she was, didn't seem interested. So instead she would trek round to the Robsons and read to Liz, who was mightily impressed with Jill's progress and claimed it as her own.

Now that she'd found something she could do well, Jill was enjoying school. By the following Easter she was the best reader in the infants and already there was talk of her joining the junior reading set. So it was an unwelcome shock when later that term their dad, George, who was a driller, lost his job at the shipyard and announced that the whole Walker family was moving to somewhere called Aberdare. Apparently it was in South Wales – which left Jill no wiser – and one of their dad's brothers lived there with his family. Like him they'd moved to find work – down the mines.

Jill remembered little of the journey except sitting on numb-cold iron benches in freezing stations waiting for connexions which her dad swore would be along any minute but always seemed to take hours. The first leg – into Newcastle Central – was okay as it only took twenty minutes; but then the long haul to York was followed by an even more dismal drag to Birmingham; and then to Cardiff, where they had to wait for a connexion to Aberdare. They travelled Third Class and could get no seats for much of the way so that Jill's principal memory – apart from the draughty platforms – was perching on the battered suitcases they'd borrowed from Granny Johnson, trying to get off to sleep. By the time they finally reached Aberdare she, along with the rest of the family, was exhausted.

They were to stop with Aunt Florrie and Uncle Arthur who had two sons, Mathew and Colin. They lived in a three-bedroom semi in Castle Road and instead of a number it had a name: 'Dunromin' (Uncle Arthur had been a Petty Officer in the Royal Navy and the family had lived abroad, as well as all over the place in Britain). It was going to be a bit of a squeeze and not for the first time Jill found herself sharing a big bed with her brothers. She didn't mind that, and in any case it was insignificant compared with the best bit about Dunromin – it had a front garden with a lawn and a small pond. Jill had never lived in a house with a garden and thought it wonderful. Even their mother, who apparently disliked Aunt Florrie with a vengeance, conceded that it was 'a step up.' The house was also right opposite the infants' school which Jill would attend, so there wasn't any danger of her getting lost this time.

Aunt Florrie was very tall and thin, with a mass of short, white permed hair. She ruled the house with a rod of iron. And she was stingy. At tea, if you had a biscuit you couldn't have a piece of cake; and when she made sandwiches she cut the thinnest slices of tomato possible. When you were hungry it was hard luck – the larder was kept locked and only Aunt Florrie had the key. Uncle Arthur, though, was a jolly man always laughing and making jokes. Maybe that was his way of coping with Florrie, but Jill liked him for it and took to him from the start.

St David's school was okay, and being a quick learner as well as sociable Jill soon settled in, even though it was awkward starting halfway through the term. The way they talked was funny and Jill might have found herself ragged for her Geordie accent except that quite a few of the kids spoke in the same way; their dads having come from the Northumberland pits to find work in South Wales villages. What remained of the term went smoothly, the only glitch occurring in December when Jill was chosen to play the Virgin Mary in the Nativity Play. That didn't go down well at all with the locals – although, so far as Jill could tell, it was more the girls' mothers than the kids.

Still it spoilt the school festivities a bit, which was a shame as they'd have been the highlight for Jill, an Aunt Florrie Christmas being a very dour affair indeed. There was no Christmas tree – though that was nothing new since their Bewicke Street flat never ran to one either – and no decorations apart from a small crib with hand-painted wooden figures. There was a goose on Christmas Day itself but as usual the portions were so small that even stoking up with vegetables Jill was still hungry afterwards. Goodness knows how Rob and her dad managed with their appetites. And there were no presents.

Though nothing like as severe as they were used to on Tyneside winter dragged on and spring was damp and wearisome, too. But summer was better and the promise of a holiday – the family's first – kept them all going. It wouldn't be exactly a holiday, and it wasn't until September, but it would be a new experience and therefore exciting. And it got them away from Dunromin; in Jill's case, for good.

Four

Robin Wakefield lived next door but one and since East Bank was on the same side of the main road as Ivy Bank they could play at each other's houses without having to get parental permission. Today Jay would risk Mr Earnshaw's wrath by crawling through the gap in the hawthorn hedge and then belting across his front lawn (Robin negotiating the slightly trickier reverse journey, where he was in hawthorn-view for longer). But if their irascible neighbour were out gardening or washing his Hillman Minx then Jay had to use the slightly longer route via the green wooden door in the back garden wall and the grassy path on the edge of the Wild Wood. Robin didn't know the Wood was Wild and was therefore impervious to its myriad perils. And Jay had no intention of letting him in on the secret. Apart from being a bedtime treat and therefore not something you vouchsafed to anyone else, revealing the fantasy would mean populating it with Mole and Ratty and Toad and Mr Badger. Jay wasn't about to share *them* with his friend.

Robin had two older brothers – William and Walter.

'Bet you wish you'd been called Wilfred,' Jay had told his friend, after some reflection.

'Huh? Why?'

''Cause then your initials would've been double-W, too!'

Robin gave him a nonplussed look and Jay decided it was pointless explaining.

Unbelievably ancient, Walter Wakefield was rumoured to be off to university that very autumn; but William and Chris were the same age and best friends. Nearly twelve, the pair were free to roam across the road and down to the railway line (though with pointed instructions never to go on the track) or up over the golf course onto the moors behind, from where, if you had long enough and were strong enough, you could climb Pendle Hill. Chris and William claimed to have done so earlier that summer but Pendle was so far beyond the Wide World that even Jay's graphic imagination could not encompass it.

Today was one of those rare occasions when the two older friends allowed Jay and Robin to play 'grown-up' games. So no chase, or den-building today – but summat called 'parachuting.' Chris explained the rules: 'You have to go up over the boulders and climb the trellis until you can step across onto the trunk of the oak. Then you've to shin up as far as that smooth horizontal bough and shuffle along until you're over the sandpit. Then you parachute down.'

Apart from not understanding (and certainly not asking) what 'horizontal' was, Jay remembered that the oak tree was stunted, otherwise it would've been taller than the house. It still looked awfully big to him though. He tried to work out how high it was – 2-4-8-16 feet at least – maybe 32; but the jumping-off point didn't look too bad: p'raps three times as high as him. What he didn't understand, however, was where the para-thingy came in; although he was sure that if Chris and William each had one then somehow it would help. The puzzle was soon solved. Both the older boys were wearing their corduroy jackets, even though it was a warm morning. William's had five buttons down the front whilst Chris's sported a zip. Neither was done up. His brother rummaged in his pockets and produced two large safety-pins. Taking off the jacket he pinned the bottom of each front to the inside of the sleeve-end and put it back on. When he stretched out his arms the jacket became a cape or, as Chris asserted, a parachute.

Jay watched carefully as his brother climbed towards the launching pad, noting exactly where he put his feet. Although each of the boulders was higher than Jay they were easy – he played on them frequently, ascending them like the peaks whose names the principal ones assumed. His dad was a mountaineer and had promised that as soon as he was old enough they would all go up to the Lakes and climb the Langdale Pikes. They weren't the highest mountains in the Lake District but they were amongst the most famous and probably the best to tackle first. Whilst satisfied with his father's advice, Jay nevertheless wanted to know which mountains *were* the highest then? And how high were they? Then he made an immediate mental note: Scafell Pike 3,210 feet; Scafell 3,162; Helvellyn 3,118; Skiddaw 3,053. His favourite boulder was Scafell because even though it didn't symbolise the highest peak it was the toughest, especially if you went 'from Scafell Pike down to Mickledore and then skirted the great crags of the Central Buttress and scrambled up to the summit via Lord's Rake and the West Wall Traverse.' Jay liked the sound of his father's description and forthwith set himself the challenge of climbing the real thing, once a successful family ascent of the Langdales – Harrison

Stickle (2,403) and Pike O' Stickle (2,323) – had proved he was ready. Meanwhile, however, he clambered over 'Scafell' and the other grit-stone boulders in his pumps, his dad having told him stories of pioneers like OG ('the only genuine') Jones and the Abraham brothers who, when it was too wet and greasy to don hob-nailed boots, would put on plimsolls and wear their socks on the outside. Scampering about like a Goa calf he was unaware that he was honing the very techniques that would later equip him for real climbing.

The first part of the ascent then, over Scafell and Skiddaw, he knew was easy; and the trellis, though vertical seemed to have lots of holds. The move onto the tree might be awkward and Jay was a bit worried about shuffling along the snake-bough, as his brother was doing now. But all in all he was confident about the climb, though less so about getting down. That was obviously the tricky bit, cause otherwise they wouldn't need the para...jackets. He'd have to watch that bit really carefully... Then suddenly Chris seemed to swing under the wotsit limb and float down to the sand. He must've landed on his feet but toppled over as the next moment he was rolling forward out of the front of the sandpit. Anyway, his para-thingy clearly worked; as did William's when he repeated the jump a minute or two later.

There then threatened to be a wrangle between the two younger boys about who went first, Robin as usual pulling rank because he was two months older, which was stupid, thought Jay, as *he* was a much better climber. Robin, moreover, had no jacket and therefore no parachute but William assured him that it wouldn't matter: being younger and lighter he would float down safely without one. So Jay watched enviously as his friend scrambled clumsily over the boulders (no names for him, thought Jay, spitefully) and pulled himself up the trellis onto the oak tree. Robin struggled awkwardly up the trunk and seemed to be making a poor job of the anaconda-bough-crawling when, without warning, he fell. He shrieked, his left arm caught the sandpit's retaining wall and there was a sickening snap as his wrist broke.

In the kerfuffle that followed Jay did feel concern for his friend, who was obviously in pain, but he was mainly furious that the need to get Robin some treatment meant an end to proceedings. There was no chance for Jay to show how much better he would have been at both climbing and jumping. Moreover, the imbroglio of parents and the trip to the cottage hospital led to a subsequent ban on all stunted-oak-parachuting or related activity. Silent fury far outweighed any sympathy for Robin's ordeal.

Five

It was Uncle Arthur who'd put their dad onto it. Soon after the war he'd been stationed in the dockyard at Chatham and had come across 'hop-picker specials' on their way from London to the Kent hop gardens. Apparently it was a tradition that each September poor families from London's East End – but also from Kent, Sussex and as far afield as East Anglia – would take a 'holiday' picking hops. Normally they had to be invited by local farmers but Uncle Arthur still had friends in the area and had been able to arrange for the Walkers to spend September at Town Farm, near Tonbridge.

It meant more long train journeys – back to Cardiff and then all the way to London Paddington – but Jill was more used to the routine by now and what with their parents treating the trip as a jaunt it all seemed a lot pleasanter. For one thing, they didn't have anything like as much luggage cause Rob and their dad were returning to Aberdare and the delights of Aunt Florrie's hospitality. Mary Walker and the two youngest would go back to the north-east. When they got to Paddington they had to use the Underground. Jill had never heard of a train going under the ground. They had to change stations, and lines, at somewhere called King's Cross but since they never emerged into the light Jill saw neither the King nor his Cross. Then they were onto something called the Northern Line which brought them out at Waterloo. From there they embarked on a hop-picker special to Tonbridge; and finally, by farm trailer, pulled by an ancient, faded-orange Ferguson tractor to Town Farm, just outside Chidborough. It had been a long haul but Jill was too elated to be tired – she'd never been to the country before.

On the farms they had passed most of the families were housed in tin shacks built in a block around a courtyard where they shared cooking, washing and toilet facilities. Others, whom Jill noticed were scruffier and dirtier, lived in abandoned cattle sheds and pigsties. Town Farm's hop-picking business had been so successful over the last few years that the farmer had pressed into use some of the derelict outhouses. Gaffer

Headcorn was a big man, though his shoulders were bowed through years of farm work. He welcomed them warmly enough, though Jill noticed he spoke only to their dad: 'So how's me ole mate Arfur? Given up wandering the world at last?'

'Why ay, man. He's proper settled now. Said you'd look out fer us like. Thanks!'

'Thas nuffin. Be hard work, mind: no special favours. But I've given you decent quarters.' And the Gaffer showed the Walkers round the stable. It was actually a much sought-after billet. True it had a corrugated-iron roof, just like the shacks, so when it rained it sounded like gunfire (according to Rob); but it had thick stone walls and was otherwise quiet. Moreover, since its usual incumbents had stopped there for many seasons it had been improved year by year so that – although it boasted only two 'rooms' – it had its own cooking stove and was snug and dry with patchwork quilts on the walls. In one room there was a fagot bed made of logs which Jill's little brother Al shared with their mam and dad. In the living area there was a bunk bed up against the far wall. Rob bagged the top berth; and although Jill fancied sleeping aloft she was happy to have her own spec.

At seven o'clock the next morning, when the whistle went, it was time to start work. Rob, who was sturdy and strong and nearly eleven, was expected to labour full-time alongside their parents, whilst Jill was supposed to look after Al. To begin with though, they all trooped out to the hop garden and with the enthusiasm of novelty even the two youngsters contributed to stripping the first few plants of their fruit. In no time the family had filled a bushel and their dad was enthusing: 'Why man, we're gonna make a fortune!' (Apparently, the going rate for a bushel was a shilling so if they filled one every half-hour their dad calculated they could make six pounds in a week.) However, they'd struck lucky with the first few clusters, many of the cones being the size of pears; further down the row where the soil must've been less fertile, some of the cones had shrunk to broad-bean size and their mam was counselling, 'See, George, divn't jump to conclusions; I reckon there's more to this pickin business than meets the eye. Whas more we ont be paid owt til the end of the month, so don't yer go spending aall our savings doon The Shovel.'

Moreover, after the first flush of success Jill and Al were more hindrance than help and their mam sent them off to play with instructions to return at dinner when they could go to the shop to get provisions. 'Divn't go too far away and listen for the whistle,' she advised them 'then yer'll know when t' come back.'

And off they'd sped; back out of the hop garden to the stable and then down the track to the main road. Across the road was a small stream and beyond – after a running jump – an apple orchard. The harvest was in full swing here, too, but the pickers were up the far end so Jill reckoned they'd be safe enough scrumping a few hereabouts. First, though, they needed something to store their plunder in – Jill seeing a chance to make a bob or two if they could get enough, rather than simply filling their own stomachs. 'You stay here, our Al,' she commanded, 'and if anyone comes jus pretend yer lost. Aa'll be back soon.' And she tore off to the stable block to find some sacks. She found a wooden barn and gazed up at the massive double doors held closed by a huge iron clasp. With difficulty she managed to undo it and haul one of the doors open. It smelt musty inside and was dark. After a moment or two Jill's eyes became used to the gloom and she could make out a mountain of sacks – all of them full – but also a pile of disused ones. Most of them were made of hessian and looked very large – far too big for her and Al to handle. Then she noticed some plastic ones labelled 'Corn Feed – 56 lbs' which she calculated were small enough, even half-full of apples, for them to drag back to their would-be store. It hadn't yet occurred to her how they were going to hide the apples until she'd worked out how to sell them. She just grabbed a couple of the smaller sacks, stuffed them in her blue-and-white-striped plastic duffel bag and set off triumphantly to re-join her little brother.

But when she reached the orchard Al was nowhere to be seen. Jill was not one to panic; besides, her little brother was always wandering at home and invariably came back without anyone organising a search party. So she decided to give him a few minutes before looking for him, and sat down on a dead bough under a gnarled oak tree on the fringe of the orchard. She picked up a fallen apple and polished it on her sleeve. Then, as she started to munch on it, she was joined by a plump Robin Redbreast.

Where she came from they called them ruddocks and before he'd scared her Bowly had told her stories about how tame they were and some of the places they nested in. She flicked this one a bit of apple and it hopped along the bough to within two feet of her. She wondered where its nest was and recalled Bowly's list of unlikely places – tins and saucepans, peg bags, gardeners' jackets, even in the bodies of dead animals. But her favourite was the weird story of the ruddock which had made its nest in the skull of a man who'd been hung for highway robbery. Bowly said it had been hundreds of years ago but so famous they'd made up a rhyme about it:

24

'There he swings for robbin' mail
But his brain of robin female
Still is quite full...'

There was more, summat about passion; but Jill hadn't understood that bit and had forgotten it. Then she remembered the other thing Bowly had told her about ruddocks – unlike robins from places like France, they were brave as well as friendly and that's why they'd come up so close to you. She was just about to see if this one would eat out of her hand when Al came scampering between the apple-trees and English-bold or not it flew away. 'Bum, our Al, yer scared me ruddock! Where've you bin?'

Al sniggered and muttered something about 'spyin...' but Jill was used to his tales and couldn't be bothered to pursue this one.

'Well never mind bout that,' she said dismissively, pulling the plastic sacks out of her duffel bag, 'less get these filled 'fore anyone comes. Aa'll pull 'em doon an you stick 'em in the sack.'

Jill was a good climber, though a lot of the boughs were close to the ground so she didn't have far to reach. Quickly, she was bombarding her little brother with large, firm, bright red apples; and just as swiftly he was stuffing them into the first bag. 'Don't fill it too full,' counselled Jill, 'else we'll not be able to drag it back.' Al took no notice so judging the first sack already to be heavy enough, she instructed him to start filling the next one. She'd moved onto a higher tree now and was a good ten feet off the ground when she saw people approaching down the orchard, maybe fifty yards away. 'Quick!' she hissed down to Al, 'someone's coming. We'll have to leg it.' And sliding down the trunk so fast she barked a shin and both forearms Jill landed beside him and gathered in the heavier of the two sacks.

'Thass what I were telling yer, sis. I were spyin on 'em before,' muttered Al knowingly, before they scurried towards the stream at the bottom of the orchard, stooping low and hauling their booty over the lush grass. They listened for the anticipated cries of pursuit but hearing none, slowed to a standstill beside the beck. Jill just managed to swing the lighter of the two sacks across the water and Al retrieved it; but the other sack was too heavy for her and landed with a resounding splosh on a small mud-bank in the middle of the stream. There its neck unfurled and the sack started to spill its apple load agonisingly into the fast-flowing water. Jill, loathe to lose the entire booty, waded into the beck and caught as many apples as she could, lobbing them out to Al who collected them in a pile on the mossy bank. She'd maybe lost half of them, she figured, but she hung onto the rest and they rapidly transferred the remains into the second sack. It wasn't much heavier than the first now, but Jill still opted to pull it along herself.

Without the expected hue and cry they reached their stable safely. Jill didn't think their mam and dad would be fussed by the scrumping of a few apples. On the other hand she didn't want them, or anyone else, taking credit – and the bounty. Then whilst she and Al glanced round the hut for a suitable hiding place they heard the whistle go in the distance; the rest of the family would be back soon. For want of anywhere safer they spread the apples as flat as they could within the sacks and Al – who was just skinny enough – squirmed underneath their parents' fagot bed and stowed their treasure up against the far wall. He had just wriggled free when Rob puffed in from the hop garden. He looked knackered.

Six

The ennui of the slowcoach summer holiday was over. Though towards the end of August there had been a spike of expectation. Chris had passed his 11 plus and was to go to the grammar school. Their mother had taken him into Blackburn to buy his new uniform – black, full-length trousers, a white shirt, a blue, red and yellow striped tie and a royal blue blazer with three silver buttons and a badge on the breast pocket. This was topped – literally and splendidly – by a peaked cap in the same colours with the same badge and the motto 'In saxo condita,' which Chris joked meant 'Pass the salt' although their mother said it was actually Latin for 'founded on rock.' Chris would have to learn Latin at grammar; apparently when the school was founded in the sixteenth century that was its purpose. But as William, who was also proceeding to the grammar school, had claimed it was a 'dead language' Jay couldn't really see the point. Presumably there were also 'alive languages' but since he couldn't picture what a language might look like he was none the wiser. 'Grammar' was eight miles away so the boys would catch the school bus and their days would suddenly become much longer, even without homework heaped on them every night. All in all, it didn't seem much of a prospect.

Jay far preferred St Peter's, not least because he could walk to it. Until now he'd been in his big brother's charge, although that had frequently meant being accompanied until they were across the road and out of sight of the house and then abandoned. But since Chris was no longer available for escort duties, and Robin and Malcolm went to other schools, there was only one solution. Now he'd become a junior he would tackle the one-mile walk on his own. Mostly, this made him feel grown-up and independent, but for a couple of quandaries.

Once you turned right off Somerset Avenue and carried on down the narrow, sunken track that came out by the railway bridge, the route plunged into deep woodland for around 200 yards. The trees formed a dense archway above you and even on a sunny morning or afternoon it was quite dark and damp. Ordinarily, that wouldn't have worried Jay who routinely conquered the challenges of the Wild Wood. But his brother had warned him, 'It's okay mostly, but if it's dark or rainy you have to run the whole way. Otherwise Rumpelstiltskin'll get you. And whatever you do, don't get caught in the boggy bit near the end or he'll suck you into the morass and you'll never be seen again.' Jay didn't know what a morass was, but it sounded nasty. He was fairly sure Rumpelstiltskin was just another character in Grimm's fairy tales but, just to be on the safe side, if conditions were inclement he ran full pelt the whole length of the grotto.

The other peril was the orphanage girls. They'd been the bane of Jay's life since the incident in the school garden. The garden was the opposite side of Lovely Hall Lane behind a high dry-stone wall. One sunny Thursday afternoon in September two of the older girls – Estelle and Barbara – had accompanied Jay on a gardening expedition. It was hot and their enthusiasm for weeding having languished they were sprawled on the bench next to the shed where the tools were stored. Without any warning Barbara suddenly announced, 'Hey, Jay, we'll show you ours if you show us yours?' Not having the slightest idea what they were on about but aware that if you didn't understand it was better to agree than admit it, Jay replied tentatively, 'Yeah, awright.' Whereupon the girl unhooked her grey serge skirt, slid down the zip and pulled it apart to reveal her navy-blue knickers. Then she raised her bum from the seat and pulled the knickers all the way down her legs, finally shuffling them off over her white plastic sandals. 'There!' she announced triumphantly: 'you can look if you like.' And she parted her legs to give the bemused boy a better view. Not knowing what he was expected to do, Jay gazed attentively at Barbara's outstretched thighs confused by the lack of anything between them. 'You can touch it if you want,' promised the girl, stroking herself indicatively and looking a little flushed, 'but only after you've shown us yours. Fair's fair, ain't it, Estelle?' The younger girl – who seemed disinclined to remove her own knickers – nodded in submissive agreement.

Jay became flustered. He didn't know what he was supposed to do next; and the girls, taking his lack of co-operation as refusal, grew aggressive. 'Come on, get your pants off and show us your willy,' urged Estelle. When Jay still declined: 'Okay, if that's the way you want it, we'll see for ourselves,' threatened Barbara. 'Estelle, you hold his arms whilst I undo his pants.' The prospect sounded appalling but before he was completely trapped Jay found the strength of panic. He jumped to his feet, sprinted through the garden gate, slammed it after him and tore up the road for all he was worth. With lunchtime still in full swing he didn't fancy going back into the playground so he kept running past the school, and the church that gave it its name, along the meadow by the cricket ground and over Vicarage Lane.

He could hear the girls in the distance. They'd freed themselves from the garden and set off in pursuit. Even so he was a good 200 yards ahead of them before he reached Rumpelstiltskin's wood where, for once, the morass and its promise of deadly immersion never even crossed his mind. Kenching right at the railway bridge he tore up the path, into Somerset Avenue, and almost ran into the traffic without looking. He sensed the girls were still after him but by now he was over Whalley Road and into his drive. Safe!

Seven

That evening Jill was sent down to Spenser's, the village shop that served Chidborough and the surrounding farms. The order was simple – a loaf, a greaseproof pack of Stork, a small jar of marmalade, half a pound of streaky bacon and a dozen eggs. Jill was nervous. The woman at the counter seemed unfriendly and all the supplies were behind wire screens, not like at home where they were just piled up for you to take and pay for. However, she became less hostile as soon as she saw the voucher that Jill held out. Her mam had been given it by Gaffer Headcorn, who was prepared to extend the Walkers' credit because of his friendship with Uncle Arthur. (Their mam had come prepared with savings from the pit wages so she hadn't mentioned the credit to George – even though he'd find out soon enough – otherwise he'd be down The Shovel that very night.)

As it turned out it was nearly a fortnight before George Walker rumbled the system and when he did it was without rancour. He merely announced that, the following day being Sunday and the hop-pickers' day off, they would all go down the pub for their dinner.

The Malt Shovel was no different from most pubs in the hop fields: they were happy to take the pickers' money but nevertheless treated them like dirt. The pub was divided into two, one bar for the locals and the 'home dwellers' and another – much rougher – for the pickers. Their bar had no carpet, cheap wooden tables and chairs and the men had to drink not from proper glasses but from cut-down beer bottles. Women and children were not allowed in the bar but could eat and drink in the garden outside, which was furnished with trestle tables and benches. They had to bring their own beakers and a jug if they wanted beer. The kids could have ginger beer or lemonade – or shandygaff, if their parents deemed them old enough.

Sunday dawned sunny and warm and the Walker children were looking forward to their treat. Their dad was invariably generous with someone else's money so even Jill and Al ended up with a beaker or two of weak shandy. And since The Shovel, like all the local pubs, also catered for summer visitors, there was a ready market for both farm goods and luxuries that passing salesmen knew they could offload of a boozy lunchtime. Jill quickly twigged this was the chance she'd been looking for and, with bags that Mrs Spenser's supplies had come in, she set up a little 'stall' selling the apples at a penny a bag. In no time she had two shillings for which, she calculated, she'd have had to endure a couple of months perched on Uncle Fred's weekend knee.

'How're you finding it then?' The query came from Brian, a gnarled little picker who was sat at their table. 'Hard work, eh, ten hours a day?'

'Nah! It's aall reet, man Brian,' rejoined their dad, 'it's a lot easier than a twelve-hour shift doon the pit. Better money an aall, I reckon. Or would be if it weren't for how they work oot what ye've picked, like!'

'Aye, and you hadna bin so puffed up in the first place,' said their mam snidely.

Brian chose to ignore that and merely added sympathetically, 'Ah, you mean the measurers.'

The measurers and the tallyman were the bane of the Walkers' and all other 'foreign' pickers' lives (though not so if you were a home dweller and that caused more resentment). The hops were measured two or three times a day and, especially after rainy days when they were still wet, some of the measurers deliberately crammed them into the baskets and then squashed them down again when they went into the tallyman's bushels.

'Aye, ah reckon by the time them beggars've done we're getting aboot half what we should be, man! An if they doon't pay us 'til we've finished how the hell are we s'posed to remember what we've done?'

'Divn't worry aboot that,' chipped in their mam. 'Ah've got me oon tally.'

'Well that's as maybe,' warned Brian, 'but you doan wanna be causin trouble with the tallyman. He'll blacklist you. Then you can't come back next year.'

The Walkers had no idea whether they'd be back again but since they'd got the break courtesy of Uncle Arthur they didn't want to blot their copybook. So Dad grumbled; and Mam blamed not the tallyman but him, as usual. Jill hated that.

Mostly, the Walkers enjoyed their holiday. If Mam moaned there was nowt new in that, whilst Dad still insisted it was easy money and the kids just liked being out in the country. Especially Jill, who marvelled at trees and birds she'd previously encountered only in her Observer books, and whose joy was unbridled when her dad announced he was going to take her to 'the show' that very next Sunday. Slyly, Mam had said she was busy. Rob apparently preferred to play with his summer mates and Al was judged too young for all the traipsing about. So Jill would get her father all to herself, an occurrence sufficiently rare for her to treasure the prospect.

The 'show' turned out to be the Tonbridge Agricultural Show – though it was actually held just outside Chidborough on the Tonbridge road. Farmer Headcorn had offered to take a wagonload of pickers – mostly home dwellers but one or two grace-and-favour families like the Walkers. They were to pay sixpence each which would cover both the transport and farmer-subsidised entrance to the show. It would last all day.

Entrance was via a large field where numerous wagons, carts, tractors and the odd motor car were already drawn up when they arrived. The site was huge but organised on an open-square so it didn't take long for Jill to get her bearings even though she clung to her father's hand for as long as possible, pretending that she was afraid of getting lost. Not that her dad minded: he was proud to show off his pretty young daughter and if he spent so little time with her normally it was just that the shifts he worked and the counter-attractions of pub and club left few hours to spare. They navigated the whole site taking in the traction engine show, a shire horse competition, vegetable and flower stands and a small fairground with coconut shies, a shooting gallery, slot machines and a carousel with ponies, zebras and tigers to ride. At the far end of the fairground was a row of eight red and yellow shuggy boats. They were free so her dad was happy for them to have a go. She shouted, 'Higher, Dad, higher!' as her father propelled them ever more precipitously into the blue-sky air. It was magic!

As the morning grew old they finally drifted off from the fairground. Jill could've remained there whilst her dad was with her but once he'd announced he was just slipping into the big tent for a beer she knew she would have to amuse herself for the rest of the day. And fun as the rides were, she could get them down the burn of an Eastertime. Here, though, were loads of animals she'd only read about in books, and she was gonna make the most of them. There were ducks and chickens, pigs, sheep and goats, cattle, ponies and horses.

Her attention was caught by two big pens: one full of cows, the other sheep. The cows were mostly black and white, like the ones in her Observer book – Friesians; although in a smaller enclosure next door were some browny-red ones which she hadn't seen before, even in a book. She'd seen Friesians in the fields between Wallsend and Tynemouth when she took the train down to Cullercoats once with Annie and Liz. And the sheep didn't look particularly interesting, especially as there didn't seem to be any dogs about so they couldn't be going to have any sheep-dog trials. That was a pity. She'd heard about them from Miss Charlton cause they had them out Rothbury way. They were good fun to watch. The dogs and their handlers were really skilful.

The red cows caught Jill's attention again as she saw a sign attached to the fencing. They were Sussex cattle, apparently, and descended from oxen which used to pull the farm carts hereabouts. Then she noticed that next door to the cattle pen was a much smaller enclosure in which just one animal was confined. She looked through the bars and saw him – a massive, humpy-shouldered, red and white bull with a ring through his nose. It wasn't a very big pen and he seemed free to roam around it. When Jill put her head through the bars he came up to them quite slowly and not at all threateningly. He leant his head down towards the girl and she saw that his nose glistened a purply colour. Unafraid, she rubbed her nose against his. It smelt lovely. It was a moment of quietness amongst the lonely noise of the fair. Jill treasured it and vowed she'd 'collect' bulls from then on.

It was late afternoon before the wagon set off back to Town Farm. The Sunday sun had dipped below the ridge of the Downs and it was just starting to get chilly. Jill snuggled up to her dad. His coarse-linen shirt smelt of cigarettes and his breath of beer, but he cuddled her and the journey back was lovely, even when he fell asleep. As they got back to the stable, Jill anticipated her mother's usual coolness, so she was agreeably surprised to find her in a sunny mood and keen to learn what her daughter had been up to. She even gave her husband a hug, and later that evening, as Jill awoke momentarily and was drifting off to sleep again she distantly heard not her mother's usual, 'Ooh, for Chrissake get on with it,' but a much friendlier: 'Howay, man, if yer wanna bit...'

The next morning, as she was wolfing down her bread and marmalade Jill vaguely remembered what she'd overheard. It puzzled her, Mam being nice to Dad for a change. But it soon went out of her head, replaced by the warm memory of the Show, and the smell of the bull's nose.

Eight

'Jay, what're you doing home at this time?' demanded his mum sternly. 'What's the matter?'

'Nothing, Mum, I just...' and he burst into tears. His mother gave him a hug, but when he'd calmed down and she repeated her question, he just started sobbing again.

Loath to press the point but determined that Jay should understand he still had to give an account of himself, his mum continued, 'Well, if you can't tell me, you'll have to explain to your father when he comes home.'

His dad was working away for the Thursday and Friday of that week, so it was the weekend before the matter could be broached again. Since there'd been no repercussions from school, his father deemed it unnecessary to prolong the incident and quietly let it drop.

That autumn and winter were the happiest of Jay's time at Ivy Bank. He'd exorcised Rumpelstiltskin by the simple ruse of asking his dad to read him some of Grimm's *Children's and Household Tales*. And after an initially unpleasant period when Barbara and Estelle had chased him home whenever they could, he'd reached an uneasy truce with them by solemnly promising never to reveal the events in the school garden. Not that he'd any difficulty with that as he'd not mentioned it to anyone anyway and didn't intend to. (Another secret snapped up tight!)

Moreover, with his two worst fears behind him and his big brother preoccupied with settling in at grammar, Jay found himself able to monopolise his parents' – and particularly his father's – attention. When his brother had claimed that the AA patrolmen saluted their father because he was important and worked for 'Her Majesty,' the second part, at least, was true. In addition to his academic qualifications, Raymond Fincher was entitled to add 'HMI' after his name since he was a member of Her Majesty's Inspectorate of Schools. Quite how he'd secured such an exalted position was a source of amazement to nobody but Raymond himself. His own father had sold flowers from a handcart in Sparkhill; and Raymond had only succeeded by securing a scholarship to the local secondary school. Instead of going into the Austin factory like his older brothers he'd gone on to Birmingham University where he'd gained a First in Geography and met Muriel Hughes.

Muriel's background could not have been more different. She and her younger sister, Gwendolyn (both good Celtic names, she'd been told) had Methodist parents. Their father, Robert, had graduated from Liverpool University via Chester College, where he'd been Captain of Boats. He'd become a secondary teacher and, in due course, a much-respected headmaster in Southport. He'd married Amy Stanley who, as well as bearing him two daughters, looked after their home, and her husband's career. Muriel had progressed from her girls' grammar school in Lancashire to Birmingham, and found herself in the university's very first Geography school, as well as the hockey team, along with her future husband – of whom her parents initially disapproved because of his lack of social standing. Muriel had no such misgivings; her only reservation being that she spent all her spare time when she wasn't with Raymond studying, whilst he spent his playing snooker. So she was a little miffed when he got a First and she received only an Upper Second. Both became teachers: he in Birmingham, she in Lancashire.

Though it took Raymond a little time to win over Muriel's parents, they relented when his undoubted talent was rewarded with successive promotions. Five years later the couple were married, at which point iniquitous education law obliged Muriel to give up her teaching career. When the war came Raymond could have avoided action as he was in a 'Reserved Occupation.' But perverseness propelled him into the RAF and in due course he became a Flight Sergeant. Their first son was born at the height of El Alamein; their second a year or so after the war finished. After demobilisation Raymond was advised to become a college lecturer and within a year he'd found himself invited to become an HMI – not bad for a barrow-boy's son he thought privately. His in-laws' reaction was a mixture of envy and pride – mostly the latter – and Muriel particularly noted how eager her mother now was to introduce Raymond with his full title whenever a social occasion permitted.

They made a handsome couple. Muriel was slim and dark-haired with flashing brown eyes that were attractively framed by laughter lines. Raymond, with what his wife liked to describe as a fighter-pilot's dashing looks (even though he'd served in bombers) had a more solemn mien, but one which easily relaxed to exhibit a lively sense of humour.

Once he'd finished his probation Raymond had a considerable

measure of autonomy – plus help with buying a car, still very much a luxury. But whilst he was expected to travel both to the divisional office in Manchester and to the inspection of any secondary school on his patch, he also had leeway to work at home, and for that he required a study.

Ivy Bank had two downstairs rooms looking over the front lawn towards Whalley Road. The first was the 'best room' and the boys were only allowed in on Sundays for tea (when their father wasn't playing golf) or on other special occasions. That certainly didn't include today! His mum was out shopping so Jay had ushered Malcolm in proprietorially, 'This is the lounge. Look, we've got a piano. And a bookcase so tall it almost reaches the ceiling.'

'Huh!' exclaimed Malc dismissively. 'We've got a *grand* piano. And a TV set. Where's yer TV?'

Jay was mortified. 'Mum says she prefers the radio,' he salvaged. 'So we don't have one. Bet you haven't got any of these!' he ventured, pointing out the serried ranks of *The National Encyclopaedia*.

Jay wasn't forbidden to examine them, but he wasn't encouraged to either. They were old, bound in deep olive and black buckram with a gold crown on the front and the letters 'VR' inscribed.

'Chris says that stands for "Vic...Victoria Regina".' Malcolm looked gratifyingly bemused and Jay pressed home his advantage, 'Yeah, she died in 1901 so the books could be even older than Mum and Dad.'

Neither of them had any idea how old their parents were but Malcolm looked impressed. 'Bet you don't know what the first and last entries are.' And when his friend shrugged as much as to say how could he, Jay proclaimed triumphantly, '"A" and "Zygo...Zygophyll...phylleae".' Jay hoped Malc wouldn't ask what the Zygo-thingies were cause even though his father had explained that they were an order of plant found in the tropics, he wasn't any wiser. He knew where the tropics were but couldn't see how you could order a plant.

Thoroughly deflated by the encyclopaedic encounter Malcolm switched his attention to the piano. 'Can you play it? My dad can – he's brilliant!'

Jay was only momentarily defensive, 'Nah, not the boring bit. But look at this.'

At the bottom of the black façade was a small panel which you slid sideways to reveal two large paddles. These could be pulled outwards and down and when the music roll was placed behind a similar panel in the top of the piano the foot-bellows produced classics to order – a Pianola that anyone could play! Jay inserted a roll of Chopin and proceeded to blast out a mazurka. This time Malc looked confused as well as intrigued. Jay knew he had the upper hand and sensed he could afford to be generous. 'D'you wanna go?'

But in the brief silence as they exchanged places Jay heard the back door open. 'Heck! Mum's back. C'mon!' And they dashed out of the lounge, along the hall and up the 2-4-8-16 stairs to his bedroom. There they lay low until it was safe for Malc to go home.

The other room which was out-of-bounds if unaccompanied was his dad's study. It was small: as deep as the lounge but much narrower; and it contained another tall bookcase, a desk, chair and filing cabinet. The first and last were full of official Ministry of Education documents; whilst the desk was a sturdy oak affair with green leather inlay, facing the window with a view out over the lawn to the sticky-leaved sycamore trees which separated Ivy Bank from the main road. On the desk stood a grey angle-poise lamp and a black telephone. Sometimes, the 'phone would ring when Jay was there and he thrilled to the sound of his father's deep voice responding: '48672.' His dad needed a 'phone in case Her Majesty called him with some important task. Most of his friends' parents didn't have one. The only exceptions were Malcolm's dad who was a dental surgeon and Michael's who was a doctor (though not theirs). He knew their numbers, too – 48078, and 48911 – which was more than either of his friends did; but then Jay was pretty sure they couldn't get to a million in twenty goes either.

The only other piece of furniture was a wicker wastepaper basket which was fourteen inches high and twelve inches in diameter. Jay had measured it with one of his dad's rulers. They were wooden, and each one had a crown with the letters 'HMSO' printed on it in black. Jay knew that meant they were Her Majesty's rulers although what the 'SO' stood for stumped him. Whatever it meant he was impressed by the stock of rulers the Queen must possess if she could afford to lend his dad so many. Usually the wastepaper basket was in the well of the desk but when his father was filing it retreated to the far corner of the room, just inside the door. His dad's forte – which he claimed mysteriously improved his putting – was to scrunch up any unwanted sheet of foolscap paper into a tight ball and throw it backward over his shoulder into the basket some fifteen feet away. Whether it was practice or the funnelling effect of the right-angle of the walls Jay didn't know, but his father very rarely missed and, if he did, he would mutter some explanation like 'damn wind!' Jay looked forward most of all to Saturday mornings helping his father with the filing. He would sit on a leather stool brought in specially from the playroom, waiting to receive any paper designated 'Rubbish!' and then attempt to crunch the paper up just like his dad did and hurl it across the room towards the basket. Occasionally, it went in.

Nine

It was early October and the Walkers were coming to the end of their hop-picking adventure. George was due to go back to Aberdare and the delights of Dunromin and would take Rob with him; Mary would return with the youngsters to Wallsend. There was room for the three of them with Granny Johnson, who lived in Lumley Road. Jill was not happy at the prospect: Mam and Gran under the same roof!

The house was bigger than their old one in Bewicke Street and although she had to share a bedroom with Al at least they had their own beds. There was a proper kitchen with running water and a range and, best of all, it was opposite Simpsons Hotel. The hotel was not very grand, more of a men's hostel really, but it was run by her Uncle Bill. He was Dad's eldest brother, very tall and ramrod-upright but with a kindly manner and a generous nature. He was Jill's favourite uncle.

Jill also found herself back at her old school and although she'd not maintained her initial progress she was still well ahead of most of the other girls. Al was soon old enough for school, which meant she had to take him, but that was okay and unlike Rob she didn't abandon him. In any case, their new home was closer to St Kits so it wasn't long before he could find his own way there and back.

The best thing though was the library on Ferndale Avenue. Jill had passed it often on her way to and from school but didn't know what it was. Before the year was out, however, her teacher, Miss Charlton, had escorted her into the building and made her known to Miss Lambton, a young trainee-librarian and friend. It was a special privilege, they explained, as junior membership didn't normally start until you were ten but as she was so keen they would make an exception. Jill nearly let herself down straightaway as she couldn't help laughing when she clocked the librarian's name. The only Lambton she'd heard of before was the one in the song: 'Whist! Lads, haad yer gobbs I'll tell yers aall an aaful story,' was how the famous *Lambton Worm* song began. It told how the dragon slayer Sir John Lambton slew the notorious Lambton worm somewhere in the middle of the River Wear in the days of the Crusades and it was one of Jill's favourites cause her dad had taught it her. At first she'd been spooked but he'd explained she wasn't to worry cause you'd only come across the dragon if you were unlucky enough to find yourself down Sunderland way – which, for a Magpies supporter, was not likely!

Miss Lambton scarcely looked old enough to have left school. She was tall and skinny and wore glasses. But she had lustrous long blond hair which hung straight down over her shoulders. Jill always resented the tendency to curliness of her own thick black locks and was envious but impressed. More importantly, however, Miss Lambton was kind. Jill couldn't tell whether that was because, like Miss Charlton, she had a natural fondness for avid learners, or whether she was just kind to Jill because Miss Charlton had asked her to be. Either way it encouraged Jill to stop by Ferndale Avenue on a Saturday morning whenever she could.

Although not every Saturday morning. Once a month she and the Robson sisters went to The Pearl. If you took two jam-jars you could get in free for the Saturday matinee. You just handed them to the lady in the booth and got your ticket in exchange. Jill had asked her mam about the arrangement and been rewarded by an unusually full explanation, 'Why thass simple, our Jill. They go to Craggies. Yer kna, the jam factory. They're aalways shorta glass.'

So the three of them turned up with their half-dozen jars to see *Lady and the Tramp*. The cinema was old-fashioned and when you first went in you were greeted by the sound of Mr Dobson playing the organ in front of the stage. Everyone called it a Wurlitzer even though it was just a cheap imitation; it really came into its own when the Saturday evening shows were on and the young lads competed in skiffle bands. Her brother Rob was in a group – he played the washboard – and occasionally she'd be allowed to go and watch him. It wasn't much fun really as she didn't like the music and as soon as they arrived at The Pearl her brother disowned her. Worse, she had to find her own way back in the dark as Rob and his mates repaired to the chippy and wouldn't take her.

As the organ faded out and disappeared into the pit, the cockerel announcing the Pathé News crowed out and grainy black and white features flashed up, accompanied by a presenter with a very posh voice that made the kids laugh. Then there were some short cartoons – *Tom and Jerry*, and *Mr Magoo* – and the cinema went quiet before the main event.

Jill loved *Lady and the Tramp* with the fancy-pants cocker spaniel falling for the street urchin mongrel. That, and the trouble-making Siamese cats. She and Liz liked the songs too, particularly the ones with Peggy Lee. Liz's grandparents, who were posh and lived in Whitley Bay along from the Spanish City, had given her a brand new Dansette for her tenth birthday. Jill didn't know anyone as young as Liz who had their own record player and one of the first records she'd acquired was the album from *Lady and the Tramp* with Peggy Lee singing all their favourites – *He's a Tramp*, *Peace on Earth* and, best of all, *The Siamese Cat Story*. It was great; so when they went to The Pearl that Saturday they felt like the best-rehearsed girls in the audience and sang along to their favourite tunes until an usherette told them to shut up or she'd throw them out! Luckily she didn't really mean it. They knew Maureen and at the start of the interval were first in the queue to buy little greased white-and-orange cartons of Kiora and twopenny ice cream wafers from her. That's when they could tell she wasn't really going to throw them out cause she laughed and admitted she'd enjoyed their sing-along.

Mostly, though, Jill liked the westerns. Just released that spring was a Walt Disney adventure film of Davy Crocket based on the TV series. Jill had seen them because of Mrs Smellie. Although they all laughed about her name, Mrs Smellie, who was related in some distant way that Jill didn't understand to Granny Johnson, was a kind old lady who lived in a detached house on the open land between Lumley Road and Bewicke Street. She'd been the first person in the neighbourhood to own a television and Jill could remember being taken with Rob to watch the Queen's Coronation. Apart from thinking the young Queen looked very pretty and the Duke of Edinburgh (the only other person she recognised) very distinguished, Jill found the novelty of the experience was soon overtaken by the boring nature of the event. But she had remembered to thank Mrs Smellie very much for letting her see the programme. None of the other kids had thought to do the same and Mrs Smellie had told Jill that she was very welcome to come and watch anytime she wanted.

So had developed a most unlikely friendship: Jill being not quite seven and Mrs Smellie in her sixties. Jill had thought no more about her whilst the family had been away but they had become reacquainted since Mrs Smellie occasionally came round for a cuppa with her grandma. Her original invitation was reissued and once a fortnight Jill would go round at the weekend and watch the latest American TV series. But first they 'took tea.' Mrs Smellie had been in service as a girl and had later married 'way above her station,' as her jealous neighbours used to complain (though never to her face). She'd long since been widowed but had retained what the same neighbours termed her 'airs and graces,' but Louisa Smellie preferred to think of as 'refinement.'

Pondering it Jill decided there was a lot about Aunt Louisa (as she was now encouraged to call her) that was refined. Her house had large, wrought-iron gates painted a glossy black and hung between stone pillars. On the right-hand post was a large brass plaque with the address 'Delaval Lodge' which Jill thought was very natty. She imagined herself sweeping up the drive and parking outside the front door in a carriage which, when Lousia originally married Mr Smellie before the First World War, was indeed how their house guests arrived. The front door had an electric bell which Jill used to like pressing to announce her arrival, if Aunt Louisa hadn't already spotted her and opened it first. The Smellies had never had children and the whole house – or at least the rooms Jill was allowed in – had a fusty, grown-up feel to them.

Not that Jill minded. The very fact of being in a 'Lodge' with a dining room as well as a kitchen and a separate drawing room was impressive enough; and she knew that although her friends used to mock her for 'havin tea with Mrs Smellie' they were secretly as jealous as hell. High tea on a Saturday was Aunt Louisa's principal refinement. Initially she prepared everything herself, but once it was established how careful and reliable Jill was she was permitted to take the crockery out of the corner cupboard (another novelty) and lay the table. The 'crockery' was posh. It was made of translucent, glazed white porcelain ringed with a gold and cobalt blue pattern and on the base of each cup and saucer and side plate was a gold crown with the words 'Royal Doulton' and an individual number in black. Jill made sure she always got '48672' as, by the sort of coincidence that she knew was significant, it was the number of the first steam train she'd been on with her dad from Howden Station.

She laid out the crockery in the way Aunt Louisa had instructed her, placing a delicate, ivory-handled cake knife on each plate; and then she helped carry the other accoutrements (as her aunt termed them) in from the kitchen. Louisa bore a large circular tray with a silver-plated teapot and hot-water jug; whilst Jill was entrusted with two oval platters on which were laid a variety of crustless sandwiches and a chocolate cake, respectively. Then the two companions tucked in. Only after they had taken their fill and the tea things had all been washed-up and dried did Aunt Louisa announce, 'Time for your programmes now, dear.' And they sat down to what she termed rather snootily, 'A basinful of Yankee pap!' Nevertheless, noted Jill, she always watched with her.

They were three episodes into *Davy Crockett, King of the Wild Frontier* when Aunt Louisa intrigued her protégée by producing a slightly shabby copy of *Go Ahead – Davy Crockett's ALMANAC, Of Wild Sports in the*

West, And Life in the Backwoods. Calculated for all the States in the Union.
She handed it to Jill. It was dated 1836 and had a picture of the Colonel, his frontiersman's rifle strapped to his back, wading the Mississippi on extended crutches with a barrel-light suspended between his feet. In the background you could see a paddle steamer. Jill examined it more closely. The paper felt quite brittle and smelt musty, sooty almost.

Aunt Louisa explained, 'Mr Smellie worked on the Eastern Seaboard between the wars. He collected old volumes. This one was published in the year Crockett died as a hero at the siege of The Alamo.' She paused to check Jill was still listening and continued, 'Crockett grew up in the Appalachian backwoods. That's where he'd learned his native craft. He didn't have much education but his heroics with the Tennessee militia got him known. He ended up serving two terms in the U.S. House of Representatives. As a Democrat,' added Aunt Louisa with some emphasis, just in case Jill should suppose otherwise. Jill didn't know what a Democrat was but she warmed to anyone who'd succeeded in spite of not having had much schooling.

Jill admired George 'Georgie' Russell who was played by Buddy Ebson. He was Davy Crockett's friend. But, of course, her favourite was Davy himself, played by Fess Parker. She particularly liked his racoon hat and thought she'd look rather fetching in one herself. She confided as much to Aunt Louisa who smiled encouragingly; but she didn't mention it to the Robson sisters. Back in The Pearl the following month, she was content to keep up a running commentary most of the way through the film, based on her superior knowledge from the TV series. Once again Maureen's torch sought them out in the gloom and there was the renewed threat of eviction, which merely served to give them all a fit of the giggles.

Ten

Some Saturdays, if Chris was not at school and their father was neither working nor golfing the family would 'go for a run out.' This was a treat for everyone, not least Dad. The Standard Vanguard had now made way for a Ford Consul Mk1. It was shiny black and its chrome grill bore the transplanted AA badge. Its number plate was 'MXJ 365.'

'That's really easy to remember,' said Mum – 'Mixed Jam!'

To which Jay almost too obviously added '+ the number of days in a year.'

And Chris trumped with, 'Yeah, but not this one clever clogs. It's a leap year!'

On which harmonious note they would depart for a picnic (but without any recitation of 'coldhamcoldtonguecoldbeef...' which was temporarily forgotten by Jay, if not by his doting parents).

Sometimes the destination would be known – Pen-y-Ghent (2,255 feet, computed Autolycus) or Ingleborough (2,350) – but what Jay liked best was when their father, in answer to their queries, would vouchsafe only, 'It's a mystery tour!' In practice, there was little difference as Jay, especially, would not know where they were going even if the route were announced in advance. But it did seem to reduce the irritating frequency with which he enquired, 'Are we there yet? Are we there yet?' What it didn't prevent, though, was an even more annoying habit of Jay's.

The Ford Consul had scarlet upholstery and a bench front seat trimmed in PVC. Jay's seat was behind his dad, though by standing up he had a better view. He could also reach over the back of the bench seat and slide his hands down the space between the seat front and his father's back – often when enquiring simultaneously about the proximity of their destination. For some reason this seemed to irritate his mother more than her husband-driver. So much so that on more than one occasion, exasperated by her younger son's need to be the centre of attention, she would exclaim, 'Raymond, I don't know why you let him do that,' or even, if she were really exasperated, 'Stop the car, Ray, and put him out!' The first time she'd been driven to such lengths, Jay was stunned enough to cease immediately and park himself on his own seat. But he couldn't see much from there so the urge to stand up was irresistible; and from there the hands-down-Dad's-back routine was equally automatic. Moreover, once he'd worked out – from his father's good-natured response – that the car wouldn't be halted and Jay left at the roadside, then the ritual became entrenched as part of family-run-out folklore. It didn't irk Muriel any less though.

Occasionally, the run out and picnic would embrace the Armstrongs, who lived opposite in the Croft whose lounge encompassed both a bay window and the grand piano that Malc boasted about. Neville's dental practice was extremely successful and supported a lifestyle which was 'lavish' (according to a remark of his mum's that Jay had overheard). This included a succession of Jaguars: the current model, the Mark VII Saloon, being the one that also sported a bright yellow-and-silver AA badge. The Jag was battleship-grey with a lot of chrome – which Malcolm kept clean – and had fog lights that were almost as big as the headlamps. It had very racy lines and was fast. 'Much faster than your dad's Consul. It can do a hundred.' What Jay admired most about it though were the 'white-wall' tyres. They gave it the sporty look which Jaguar promoted in their advertising slogan – 'Grace, Space, Pace' – and Malc and his brother Hugh were nauseatingly conscious that it was the most desirable car on the whole of Whalley Road.

Their mother, Marjorie, was Jay's favourite. He'd been in love with her ever since he'd slipped on the rocks in the Croft's back garden. He'd grazed both knees and before Marjorie patched him up she'd cuddled him and kissed it better. She was wearing a downy white jumper which was so soft it soothed Jay's troubles immediately, and he associated it and a fragrant smell with her ever afterwards. He'd already decided that, if he didn't become an Eskimo, he would marry her when he grew up. Or maybe he could do both, he wasn't sure if Eskimos had wives…

In spite of the difference in their financial status, the two families had become friends, and one sunny Saturday in the summer holidays found the Jag and the Consul parked side by side on a grassy river bank (nothing like Ratty's) in the Yorkshire Dales. All four boys were playing together damning the stream and had managed to create a lake large enough to splash about in. Their parents were sitting sunning themselves in striped deckchairs. After a lot of horseplay and shrieking the older boys got bored, leaving the two youngsters to go exploring. As earnest prospectors they were hopeful that the stream would contain gold, or at the very least silver, and Jay drew on his father's geological expertise to take charge of proceedings. He'd noticed in amongst the limestone slabs a large number of spiky white rocks and taking a piece for inspection by his father he was informed it was quartz and was 'worth a fortune.' Jay was aware that his dad sometimes had him on so he took this with a pinch of salt. However, he didn't see why Malc should be let in on the secret. So he returned to advise his co-prospector that the sharp white rocks were 'kworts' and worth loads; whereupon Malcolm, who was always desperate to impress his father announced gravely that he was going to make a collection for his dad.

Over the ensuing half-hour Jay took great delight in pointing out the choicest rocks which seemed to be in deeper and deeper water so that quite soon Malc was soaked. Nevertheless, he'd amassed a pile of rocks by the grassy bank, after which he set about transporting them to his father's deckchair. Each trip was accompanied by the announcement, 'Hecky, Dad, look at this one!' oblivious to the singular lack of interest exhibited by his father. All went well until the last chunk of quartz. It had taken their combined efforts to extract it from the stream and Malc could only just carry it. Staggering up to his recumbent father he announced his prize proudly once again but, unable to grasp it any longer, dropped it: right on his dad's sandal.

Neville woke with an anguished cry, leapt up and placed his uninjured foot under his younger son's backside to lift him clean into the river several feet away. The two older boys laughed uproariously; but Jay and his parents looked on with astonishment as Malcolm landed in the lake he'd helped construct earlier. It had now swelled considerably both in extent and depth and it was rapidly apparent that Malcolm, who could not swim, was in difficulties. Things got worse. Coughing and spluttering he was carried over the dam and into the main river – where the swift-flowing current swirled him around and smashed him into the boulders. He was in imminent danger of drowning and, as Neville was still growling about his injured toes, Ray plunged into the maelstrom and pulled the distraught boy to safety.

Jay expected everything to calm down; but he'd reckoned without a mother's wrath. Now that Malcolm was safe Marjorie was livid – partly out of the relief that had overtaken her alarm, but mainly at Neville.

'What on earth d'you think you're doing?' she shrieked. 'You'd no business kicking Malc like that!'

'Well...er... I didn't mean to...kick him, complained Neville defensively. 'He just got in the way!' he attempted, half grinning at Ray.

'Got in the way!' shouted Marjorie furiously. '*You're* in the way! You haven't a clue how to behave!'

This was too much for Neville. His own anger boiled over as he barked, 'Right! That's it! Get in the car! We're going home!'

The picnic thus ended at a rather low ebb (unlike the river, thought Jay, wickedly unsympathetic as was his wont) and although he wasn't about to take any responsibility publicly Jay had an uneasy feeling that he was partly to blame.

Later that summer came unwelcome news. Their father was being moved. Her Majesty required his expertise in somewhere called Norfolk. Jay was eight, settled at home and school and not looking forward to it. But at least it meant another journey to see his nana and grandpa. They lived in Southport, more than thirty miles away and parts of the route along both the A59 and A565 were along dual carriageways. The Consul had just been superseded by another Ford – a Zephyr Zodiac Mark 1: NVU 256. It was blue with cream leather upholstery and a three-speed gear change mounted on the steering column. At the front was a magnificent chrome grill, shaped like a mouth with an arch on top. On one side was the AA badge – still smartly saluted – and on the other a red, black and silver badge. The black bit at the bottom had silver writing which proclaimed it was a Ford product, 'Made in England.' The top part was red and had a silver lion and three torches on. The lion was standing up on his back legs and waving.

But the best thing about the Zodiac, as his dad called it, was its speed. It wasn't quite as fast as a Jag but it could easily do eighty and, urged on by the boys, their father usually succumbed on whichever bit of dual carriageway was quietest. There was always a race when they got to Duke Street to see who would tell Grandpa Dad's latest exploits. Usually the Zodiac had to negotiate the narrow driveway forward which meant Jay was closest to the lawn and the paved pathway to the front door, with Chris having to slide across the bench seat.

So it was a triumphant Jay who burst into the hall shouting, 'Gramps, gramps you'll never guess how fast we went on the way – seventy!!' His grandpa's, 'well, I never!' sounded impressed; although Jay wondered if maybe he wasn't a bit jealous, too, cause his old Ford Popular would only do fifty-five and Jay had heard his dad remark one time that he bet he wasn't allowed to do that when 'your mother's in the car...' This seemed borne out by his nana invariably tut-tutting and suggesting that their father was not setting a very good example. Since their dad hadn't broken any speed limit and both the boys would've loved to go even faster, Jay thought his grandma's point a weak one.

Their grandparents' house was a lot smaller than Ivy Bank and for some reason it was all on one floor, so Jay couldn't check whether they had the regulation fourteen stairs, rather than the superior-sixteen at home. It had two bedrooms and if the family stopped the night – which happened only very occasionally – the boys were put up on camp 'Army beds' in a back lounge which was otherwise never used. This was exciting, not just cause of the beds which were khaki-coloured and had to be assembled specially but because there was a French window which you could sneak through when you were supposed to be asleep. The window-door led directly to a long narrow garden with two sheds.

The top shed was where gramps kept his tools: all clean and polished, along with a Panther lawnmower that you had to push. It wasn't as hard work as it sounded cause Grandpa had lived at Duke Street for a long time and the lawns were well tended and kept short cropped. The lower shed was close to a high wall. It was made of red-brick and had broken glass in the top to stop anyone from the public house next door climbing into the garden. Gramps used to go to the pub at one time but as Nana strongly disapproved he gradually went less and less until he stopped going altogether. That, Nana had informed their mother, was 'a triumph of superior counsel which you would do well to ensure Raymond emulates.' Jay didn't know what that meant but the way his nana spoke, it didn't sound much fun. After six years in the RAF and a war that had stretched from Birmingham to Berlin their dad 'liked a pint' when he could find time for one.

The bottom shed was where gramps smoked his pipe, which Nana also disapproved of and which had long since been banished from the house. Occasionally, when they were down there on their own, Grandpa would seat Jay on his knee, select his favourite briar from the circular pipe stand and light up. Then, when he'd got it going properly, he'd say in a theatrical whisper, 'There you are, my lad: three puffs and a spit out!' It didn't taste very nice but Jay didn't let on, and he never told his nana.

Back in the house two objects held a special fascination for Jay. One was above the fireplace – a large sepia photograph of Watergate Row in Chester. It was framed in dark teak and had a brass plaque at the bottom, inscribed, 'Chester College RC To: H. Hughes [CAPT Boats] 1905.' As well as the rows you could see in the foreground a set of wooden steps (five with a half landing, then five again, noted Autolycus-the-numerate) towards the bottom of which was an elegant young woman in an Edwardian dress shepherding a little girl, who clung tightly to her hand, down to the street. His grandpa had told Jay they were his nana and mum, but that must've been a fib cause he knew that, old as she was, his mother wasn't born until 1911. Gramps was fond of stories and insisted that the Hughes family could trace their lineage back to Llywelyn ap Seisyll, the King of Gynedd some 900 years earlier and that he – and therefore Jay – were directly descended from a line of Welsh princes! Jay knew from his dad that he was a good Lancastrian so he wasn't too sure about the Welsh bit; though he quite fancied the line of princes.

The second object was scary. At the back of the gloomy entrance hall from which the other rooms opened was a tall mahogany wardrobe on top of which stood a bust maybe fifteen inches tall. The figure was wrapped in a deep-green cloak; its face was dark, with a black moustache and on its head was a cream turban. Grandpa said it was given to him by a lashkar whose life he'd saved in the Third Afghan War; but Jay had never seen a dark-skinned man in real life and just found it frightening in the semi-darkness of the hall. And as far as the lashkar was concerned, he wondered whether it was just another Welsh-princes yarn. If he'd checked with his father he'd have realised that gramps was too old to have fought in 1919; but he wouldn't have dreamt of doing that for, like the lady-on-the-steps and the three-puffs-and-a-spit-out, this was a secret between his grandfather and him.

Eleven

As spring blossomed into summer and Jill's tenth birthday approached she had more freedom than ever. Her mother had two jobs now: a daytime one in a butcher's on North Shields high street (most unusual for a woman) and an afternoon/evening one at the Tunnel Club. Not that she ever seemed to have much time for Jill anyway, which suited the girl as she didn't get on with her mother and couldn't wait for her dad to return from South Wales. Granny Johnson ran a relaxed regime. Provided you kept your room tidy and did your share of the chores she didn't much mind your comings and goings. So once the summer holidays arrived, Jill was pretty free to do what she wanted and that included helping Aunt Elsie across at Simpsons Hotel. In return for washing and drying in the kitchen and cleaning the ground-floor rooms – she wasn't allowed anywhere near the men's sleeping quarters – her aunt gave her a shilling a week. This was regularly supplemented by her Uncle Bill's indulgently enquiring how she was with a, 'there's sixpence, pet, for next time you go down the coast.' Since her brother Rob wasn't around to pinch it off her and no one else knew which floorboard she kept her cash under, Jill was gradually able to amass a canny sum.

She was still mates with the Robsons; but Annie seemed to have developed a circle of younger companions so Liz, who'd had a soft spot for Jill since she helped teach her to read, gradually became her best friend. Jill was mature for her age – mentally and physically – and gravitated naturally towards older girls. That summer the two of them were off to sea!

They walked down to Howden Station and stood on the bridge waiting for the Newcastle train to pass underneath. They heard the heavy pulse of the belching steam before it was in sight and within seconds they'd stuck their heads over the parapet to see who could get the sootiest face. Then they headed down to the Ladies and washed it off under the cold tap before presenting themselves at the ticket office: pictures of innocence. It was threepence return to Tynemouth but Jill had her Simpsons savings and Liz never seemed short of a bob or two so it wasn't a problem.

The train stopped four times and took twenty minutes. At Tynemouth Station they had a strip machine. For twopence you could dial your name into it — a maximum of twelve letters — and then pull the lever which printed the letters onto a little metal strip about three inches long. For another penny you could get a leather strap to attach it to so that you could each have a wrist band. Jill wore: 'L-I-Z-R-O-B-S-O-N' and Liz: 'J-I-L-L-W-A-L-K-E-R.' They were tin sisters!

Their destination was Cullercoats, about a mile's walk away. It was tempting to dawdle all down Front Street and call at the chippy, but Liz knew a shortcut down Hotspur Street. This brought them out past the Grand, just by Longsands, and 200 yards further on — opposite the boating pool — was The Plaza. Jill had been once before on a rare outing with her dad; Liz claimed airily that she'd been 'loadsa times.' The complex would be the first port of call for the two buccaneers. It was a huge art deco building with a ballroom for weekend dances and an ice rink. The girls weren't interested in the former and couldn't afford the latter. What they enjoyed was the penny arcade.

Before you got to it, just inside the front swing-doors, was the Laughing Clown. Jill and her dad had found it a right giggle on their previous encounter and the girl was quick to slip a penny into the slot this time. The grotesquely-rotund figure in his blue-buttoned suit immediately started to heave and guffaw which he was programmed to do for upwards of half a minute. Jill began to laugh, remembering how much her father had, too, when she realised that Liz wasn't laughing at all. The younger girl paused, anxious not to commit some indiscretion; but it was too late. Liz remarked haughtily, 'Why man, thass just for kids, c'mon let's get on the machines whilst it's still quiet.'

Jill felt herself going red in the face, but didn't saying anything, and by now they were through the vestibule and into the long hall where the serried ranks of slot machines stood to metallic attention against the walls. In the middle were the prize devices: the one with the metal grappling hook suspended on wires just above a floor of assorted goodies, and the other one with the bar. Her Laughing Clown faux pas warned Jill that these were childish contraptions and that Liz was intent on more serious challenges.

On her previous visit, Jill hadn't been allowed on the fruit machines — or 'one-armed bandits' as her parents called them. It was typical of her mam, Jill had mused resentfully. She couldn't be bothered to come herself but instructed her husband to ban any chance their daughter might have of making her fortune. The fact that her invariably unlucky father had fed in two-shillings-worth of pennies to no avail assuaged Jill's jaundice not one jot. *She'd* have won if she'd been allowed…

This time, though, there was nothing to stop her. And the best thing was they were still on their own. Somehow that seemed to make it more exciting. So after watching Liz's technique, Jill slid her first penny into the slot on the bandit and pulled down the handle assertively. The reels rapidly spun round, each slowing to a halt in turn from the left: Cherry-Apple-Pear. She grasped the handle of the next machine (Liz was moving purposefully along her row) and yanked it down forcefully: Cherry-Cherry-Banana. There was a clatter and three lucky pennies cascaded into the steel scallop at the base of her bandit. Jill let out a triumphant shriek and was rewarded with a nodded-smile of approval from her friend. This time she stayed on the same bandit ('Stick with the lucky ones,' Liz had counselled) and promptly lost the three pennies.

Inveterate gamblers by now, the two girls persevered, and although they didn't have any big wins they didn't lose anything either. They'd each keep picking up threepence here, sixpence there which would tide them over the next few goes. They were just about to move on to the farther hall when Jill heard a screech of delight from her friend and crossed the hall just in time to see the three yellow bells lined up and pennies clink-clunking into the winnings tray. It took some time for 120 coppers to rattle down, but no time at all for the two girls to bear them along gleefully-baggaged in their t-shirts to the cash kiosk where they exchanged them for four bright silver half-crowns. Jill was mightily impressed with her friend's dexterity but even more impressed – no, staggered – when Liz smilingly gave her two of the coins, remarking, 'There yar, hinnie – half-share winnings!'

Jill had never owned a half-crown before and she scrutinised the coin avidly. It sparkled, reflecting the flashing neon lights of the arcade. On the one side was a sort of shield with a crown on top and in capital letters round the rim the words: 'FID. DEF. HALF-CROWN 1957.' It was brand new then. Holding it gingerly between her thumb and forefinger, she flipped it over and read the other side: 'REGINA ELIZABETH II. DEI GRATIA.' She knew how much it was worth – two of her saved-up shiny shillings plus sixpence – and also that it portrayed the head of the current queen – 'Regina.' But she didn't understand the 'Dei Gratia,' nor twisting it back over, the 'Fid Def' and when she asked Liz neither did she. Jill made a mental note to ask Miss Menzies who taught the top juniors if she knew, always assuming she'd seen a half-crown herself of course. It was a lot of money, even for a teacher. Then she remembered her manners

('Next stop, Newcastle!'), giving Liz a big hug and enthusing, 'thanks, hin, thanks a load!'

She was gratified when Liz hugged her back and murmured, 'Yer reet welcome, pet,' and bending slightly, planted a kiss on the middle of Jill's forehead. 'There's plenty more where that came from.' Jill expected that to be it, but with one arm still round her waist Liz ran the other one up her back until her hand cupped her friend's neck. Then she leaned forward again and kissed her full on the lips. No one had ever done that before – certainly neither of her parents – so Jill didn't know how to react. It seemed nice though, so she just mumbled, 'hmm,' and cuddled her friend back. Liz seemed disinclined to let go and they remained in a close embrace for a few seconds more. Then, as some other kids emerged noisily from the inner hall Liz loosened her grip and let her friend go – slowly and without any embarrassment, as if it had been the most natural thing in the world, which, for both of them, it had been. Just before she was released from the older girl's embrace, however, Jill couldn't help noticing that Liz's breasts, which had been pressed just underneath Jill's collar bones, seemed to have gone all hard at the tips.

She'd have to ask Liz about it when the time seemed right.

Twelve

The day Jay had been dreading arrived. The big navy blue and white Pickfords removal van had left first thing and a couple of hours later they'd followed. Jay didn't remember much about the journey, except that it was long and he kept falling asleep.

Just before they reached Ditchingham the Zodiac turned right off the A144 into the long drive that led to The Lodge. The first 200 yards were paved in oblong slabs of concrete over which the Ford proceeded with regular rubber-clicks. Then the track became gravel and arrived at a curious, round tin house. Jay was concerned that this was their destination cause Chris had explained that a lodge was a little cottage in the grounds of a big house. He needn't have worried though. Dad swung the Zodiac sharply to the right under dense, giant rhododendron bushes and in another 100 yards they came to a glossy, black, five-barred gate. This gave access to wide meadows bordered on the left side by the distant River Waveney and on the right by a range of low, sandy hills. And low they were, as far as Jay was concerned – maybe 200 feet at most, hardly a Scafell or a Skiddaw he thought contemptuously!

The drive from Lancashire had taken eight hours and the summer evening was starting to draw in. They were all tired, especially Jay whose first comment as the track dipped under a tall elm tree and The Lodge came into view was, 'Oh! What a horrible house!'

He was exhausted and crabby and unconvinced by his father's tolerant response, 'Oh well, you'll probably feel better after a good night's sleep.' (His mother would definitely have had him put out of the car.)

There was no excuse for Jay's reaction. It wasn't horrible at all; it was a fine Georgian mansion which had been in the Kirkstead family for generations. Its current owner was a naval captain whose prolonged overseas postings necessitated The Lodge being let for extended periods – in this case, six years; years which Jay later realised had been the most idyllic of his childhood.

And predictably, his father had been right. The next morning everything seemed different.

The front door was bright blue. It had a big brass doorknob and stood between black columns with a shell window above. That's good, thought Jay: 'You can be sure of Shell.' It was his dad's preferred petrol and Jay liked the yellow pumps and the red and yellow shell sign on the garages. So it was a good start, with better to follow as the door opened onto a huge hallway with beige flagstones and three doors leading off it. To the left was the lounge where, mysteriously, the giant bookcase from Ivy Bank was already in residence; and to the right the dining room which, similarly, housed their upright piano. The two rooms and the hall between them stretched the whole breadth of the house and were much bigger than anything Jay was used to. He just about preferred the dining room, partly because it was half-panelled in dark pine (hmm, matches the piano, he thought) but mainly because it gave onto to the kitchen which was spacious too and led to its own pantry. It also housed a Frigidaire. They'd never owned one before (although the Armstrongs' kitchen had boasted one for years). Romping on in a circle the boys came to the best surprise of all – a games room with a three-quarter size snooker table surrounded on two sides by toy cupboards built into the walls. Several doors led off this gem, including one to his dad's new study and another to a downstairs lavatory reached, intriguingly, via first an outer then a baize door, about six inches apart (must've been some smelly crappers, sniggered Jay). But if you ignored them for now and chose the last door then you came full circle (past the eight steps down to the shallow cellar), back into the entrance hall.

The best bit of the entrance hall was the staircase. The shallow steps swept round in a splendid semicircle and Jay had already counted them – ten to a small landing from which an archway appeared to give access to another landing; then eight more to the main landing. Smashing, thought Jay: two more than their previous house with the promise of more to come up to the third storey. May as well check them now, he thought, even though Chris had already staked his claim up there. Through the arch a long, narrow landing led to a cramped servants' bathroom; whilst up another six stairs to the right was yet another small landing with a door to a massive bathroom which must easily have been as big as his old playroom. Then up curved the bare wooden tread again – six, turn left through the stairwell, with a weird little cupboard off to the right, and a final eight to the top landing. Brilliant! six-six-eight plus the eighteen below = thirty-eight. Easily a new record!

On this top storey were a couple of large junk rooms, then Chris's bedroom and a further three empty bedrooms beyond. To Jay they seemed cavernous, an impression magnified by the bare floorboards and empty casements. He could see why his brother had chosen this eyrie. It had the best view back over the drive and the meadows. And it had a fire escape. Not a stepladder – a rope, on a large aluminium cylinder which was stowed away just now but unwound to drop the thirty-odd feet to the driveway. Their father explained, 'if there's a fire you can shin down the rope. You'll have to learn to abseil. But it's handy for rock climbing. I was going to teach you anyway.' That sounded exciting, thought Jay. The top storey possessed one further discovery.

In the junk room next door they'd previously missed a small entrance into a tiny box room where a flight of open-steel steps (2-4-6-9 – can't be right, furrowed Jay: stair-counts are always even) led to an enormous loft stretching out to the eaves and covering the whole area of the floors below. It took them a while to get used to the gloom as the only light was that filtering under the eaves. Initially they felt their way forward, taking care to balance only on the wooden joists; otherwise, as Chris cautioned, 'You'll go straight through the ceiling!'

After a while they could see more light coming from a square door at the far end of the loft, and making their way cautiously to it they found only a rusty metal bolt separating them from whatever lay outside.

Chris drew it back and pushed at the creaking door which opened to reveal a large bay-shaped, lead-covered flat roof. Clambering out, they found themselves level with the pine trees on the wooded slope to the north of the house. But most enticing of all, leading off round to the right above the main façade of the house was a lead-faced parapet which ran as far as they could see. It was a foot or so wide and although over a drop of perhaps forty feet held no terrors for the brothers, who had each inherited from their father a good head for heights. Without debate, they set off in single file, hoping that no one, especially their mother, would see them from the driveway or garden far below. After less than a minute of foot-before-foot traversing they reached the far end of the roof where a similar deck-in-the-sky looked south over the side garden to the marshes and the River Waveney.

'Strewth, little brother,' gasped Chris, 'this is some crow's nest! What say we keep it to ourselves though? Dad wouldn't mind, but he'd probably tell Mum and she'd ban us – well, you anyway!' Jay was content to follow his big brother's advice. He wondered whether keeping it secret included their friends. Then he remembered they hadn't any here. At least not yet. He wondered whether Malcolm or Robin would be able to visit but concluded it was probably too far.

Back on terra firma they realised they still had one whole floor to explore. On the way past the stairwell cupboard Chris halted, 'Don't wanna put you off, kid,' he whispered, glancing around dramatically, 'but they say the ghost of the Lodge lives in there. It's shapeless and they call it "The Thing". Only comes out at night, of course…' Then, leaving his little brother wide-eyed with alarm he hurtled down the remaining stairs to the half landing and on up to the middle storey.

Here an ornate balustrade protected the drop to the entrance hall. A door off to the left led to the master bedroom – Mum and Dad's. But the one to the right gave way to another large bedroom, beyond which was a secluded, smaller room with a huge picture window looking south towards the river. 'Bags I!' shouted Jay, forgetting that Chris had already made his choice; *he* might be able to abseil out of his window, but Jay could see the river. Or rather, as Ratty had put it, '*The* River.' And Jay dredged up the passage where Mole had '…learned to swim (well he could do that already – his grandpa had taught him at Belper Street baths) and to row and entered into the joy of running water (though maybe not like Malc); and with his ear to the reed-stems he caught, at intervals, something of what the wind went whispering so constantly amongst them.' He wasn't sure about the last bit cause even though Autolycus had schooled him to memorise it, he didn't really understand what it meant. But as for the swimming and rowing and having fun on the water, he resolved silently that he would be master of all those things.

A fortnight later, Jay was out exploring. He had ridden proprietorially down the drive on his Raleigh Rudge. He'd been given it shortly before they left Ivy Bank and, painted lustrous maroon it featured a Sturmey Archer three-gear control. When he reached the tin house he stopped, and leaning his bike against the rusted ring-fence, ventured into the garden. He glanced through dusty windows at the scruffy interior and was about to knock on the door when a voice behind him croaked, 'You the new bor at the big 'ouse?' Startled, he turned round to face a boy not much older than himself. He was taller and thinner, though, and had dark, olive skin. He was Ennio, he announced, and would Jay like to play? He would show him the 'mill 'ouse' and he could meet Rufus. And so they set off.

At first they retraced Jay's cycle ride up the drive to The Lodge (although not by bike – Ennio didn't have one so it seemed only fair that Jay should walk too). Then, after a couple of hundred yards they swung left past a big gravel pit. It had been flooded and a painted sign proclaimed 'Cherry Tree Angling Club: Members Only.' But they went past this, too, and down a hushed woody lane that reminded Jay momentarily of Rumpelstiltskin's lair. He didn't say anything; he'd have to explain who Rumpelstiltskin was and besides, he felt he'd left him behind. This was a new adventure in fresh surroundings.

Soon they came to the River Waveney ('The River,' Jay reminded himself, although of course he said nothing to Ennio), which hereabouts was divided into two streams by an island. The island was reached by a narrow, steeply-arched bridge made of metal and painted white, and as they stepped cautiously down the far side Jay saw that the ground was covered in thick undergrowth. Armed with his mum's intelligence he could identify willowherb (good place for a pee then, he recalled ambivalently), purple loosestrife and comfrey. There were elder bushes and sweeping above them, entwined with ivy, tall willows with their rough green bark – just like in the book. Clearly this was a continuation of the Wild Wood. They pushed on through the bushes into a clearing where a ramshackle hut stood. 'Thass mill 'ouse' announced Ennio. 'Less see if Rufus is 'ome.'

He wasn't, but Jay had time to take in his surroundings – the place was squalid, far worse than Ennio's, and looked as if a tramp lived there. It smelt of damp blankets and dog-poo. Unperturbed Ennio announced, 'Never mine, bor, we'll find 'im 'nother time. C'mon, I'll show you Sandy.'

They clambered over a second white-painted metal bridge. This one was much bigger and the river below wider, deeper and faster-flowing: altogether a more serious proposition, thought Jay, who liked to log future challenges and rank them in order of severity from one to ten. Swimming across here would rate a six, he reckoned and even then you'd finish up well down the opposite bank – probably where those thick reeds sheltered a little bay. Yeah, if you could climb out there then six…maybe seven; but if you couldn't and you were washed further downstream to where that ash bough had toppled into the water, then more like eight. He wondered whether Ennio could swim; and, if so, what he'd rate it. As if reading his mind Ennio observed: 'you can't swim 'ere. It's too fast and those weeds ud drag you down. C'mon and I'll show you where.'

One hundred and fifty yards upstream they came to where the river divided. This was Sandy. Across the water was the island where the ground was largely bare underneath tall beeches and river-elms. Up the trunk of the one closest to the bank were nailed little planks. If you climbed them you'd come to a large bough overhanging the pool where someone had built a rickety platform for jumping off. This could be even better than parachuting: Jay couldn't wait.

It hadn't crossed his mind earlier in the day that he would be going swimming and he remarked to Ennio that he hadn't got any trunks. 'Cor,' scoffed the lad, 'we doan worry bout that round 'ere; 'sides I ain't got any at all,' and he stripped off and launched himself across the sandy-bottomed bay. There was no one about and Jay couldn't see how it could get him into trouble, so he did the same. They waded across the stream to where, in the bank opposite, someone had fixed an iron ladder. If you looked down you could see the underwater-rungs wavering slightly in the current. They hauled themselves onto the bank where the mossy grass was embedded with the empty husks of last year's beech nuts. Keen to show his climbing prowess, and anxious to establish his primacy at the same time, Jay shinned rapidly up the rungs (two-four-six-eight) and along onto the platform before pausing just long enough to make sure Ennio was watching. Then he let out a whoop of 'Geronimo!' and launched himself into the shimmering water ten feet below.

He surfaced and cried out, 'Brill! That was brillante,' and struck out strongly for the ladder. 'C'mon, your turn,' he urged a reluctant-seeming Ennio who, muttering something that sounded like 'durstn't,' danced away from Jay as he tried to push him towards the jumping-tree.

'Nah, nah... I'm not doing it,' panicked the older boy and as Jay tried once again to wrestle him towards the trunk he wriggled out of his grip, only to stagger backward and overbalance into the deepest part of the pool. It was then that Jay realised his new-found friend couldn't swim. Ennio came up spluttering and as he went down for a second time it was apparent Jay needed to act quickly. He dived in and, grabbing the boy under his arm and across his chest in the way his grandpa had taught him, he swam with Ennio back to the ladder, where they clambered onto the bank. When he'd stopped coughing and choking Ennio gave Jay a weak smile and muttered, 'Thanks, bor, you saved me life.'

'It was nowt,' grunted Jay and, figuring that since it was his fault that Ennio ended up in the river to start with and it was probably best not to advertise the incident, he added, 'Don't say owt about it, eh...' Anyway, even without the last bit there would be plenty to brag about to his big brother later. After all, he'd chalked up the river (not 'The River' as far as telling Chris was concerned, of course), the island, Sandy and the diving platform. Surely he'd be impressed with that?

Later in the day, however, he was crestfallen at his big brother's response. 'Oh, Sandy,' Chris jeered, 'that's pretty tame. It's where the kids who can't swim properly go; it's not half as good as Finches. That's really hard to get to, there's a rope swing as well as a diving board and the river's so deep there, it's bottomless!' Then, seeing how downcast his little brother was he relented, 'Anyway if you're lucky, after tea I'll show you.'

And so, as the early September evening began to draw in Jay found himself on the second adventure of the day: and the best bit was it was him and Chris! They went out the back way, past the woodshed and the stable yard where the Zodiac was already safely garaged, and set off down a grassy cart track. The marshy fields to the left led down towards the now-much-closer Waveney, but to the right the wood sloped up steeply and looked impenetrable and definitely 'Wild,' thought Jay, with its brambles and sprawling, bushy undergrowth. After a quarter of a mile (according to Chris who was a Boy Scout and could measure distance by time) they came to a long flinty-chalk wall on their left. Walking on for a further forty paces (by Jay's count) they reached the middle of the wall where an arched doorway led to a huge vegetable patch. 'That's the kitchen garden,' explained Chris authoritatively, which puzzled Jay as it was a really long way from the kitchen. Moreover, when you pushed through the ancient green door it didn't look anything like a garden, being largely overgrown with tangled bine-stems, nettles and briars. Although down the middle lay an arched lattice-way with some sort of vine growing up and over it. Even here, though, were ferns and heavy brush.

They struggled through the undergrowth and emerged briar-scratched at a rusty iron gate which swung open onto the riverbank. Jay was entranced and expected at any moment to encounter not only Ratty but quite possibly Otter as well. There was yet more to come. Just twenty yards downriver was a somewhat dilapidated boathouse and moored to the decrepit staging a two-man kayak called *Tarka*. Now it was Jay's turn to parade his knowledge.

'Cootaheck!' he exclaimed (an expression learned earlier from Ennio). 'Tarka's the name of the otter in that book by Henry Williamson. You know: the bloke who wrote *The Peregrine's Saga*!'

'Yeah, I know,' rejoined Chris. 'According to Mum he used to live nearby. Maybe still does.'

Jay filed this away, aware that his just thinking about Otter and their coming across Tarka was obviously not a coincidence, more an omen…

However, before he could puzzle out what it all meant Chris was urging, 'C'mon: I said I'd show you Finches. Jump aboard,' and to Jay's unbounded delight he was allowed to slide into the front of the kayak whilst his big brother took the double-bladed ash paddle and propelled them smoothly into the main current. Within minutes they came to a huge bend in the river and there, round the corner, was Finches. It was getting dusk and remembering what Chris had said about the pit being bottomless Jay was apprehensive, as well as mightily impressed. Chris manoeuvred the kayak to a landing place on the steep bank and they clambered up the dark soil to a grassy sward. Soon the ground became marshy and criss-crossed by deep, narrow dykes that they had to jump. And all the while the dusk gathered round them and the willow trees' fingery branches tugged at their clothes as they fought their way through to the swath around Finches. It was eerie; Jay felt scared.

Salvation arrived with a sudden spark of inspiration, courtesy of Autolycus. It had dawned on Jay increasingly throughout his adventurous day that although its central theme had been The River his imagination was populated by characters – Ratty, Mole, Otter and so on – who were essentially part of a childhood left behind at Ivy Bank. He would not desert them but, as the mist began to swirl around the far edge of Finches, he needed new heroes.

And then he saw it, thrusting high into the dark blue of the evening sky and right on the edge of the bottomless pool – Old Man Willow! Of course, fizzed Jay's associations, this was Tom Bombadil country! With Tom to look after him like he'd looked after the four hobbits in the story he and his dad had recently begun, Jay would be quite safe, even without his big brother around.

Tom was a master ('*The* Master') of the marshlands and the thickets and the river-undergrowth – just like Jay would become. For now, though, he was relieved Chris was there as well. And his day was complete when, on their way back to The Lodge in the pitch black of the autumn night, his brother advised him in conspiratorial tones not to say owt to their parents!

Jay slept in a tomb of contentment that night.

Thirteen

The noisy intruders who had disturbed the girls' embrace had been playing the pinball machines. Jill had watched her dad have a couple of goes, but before she'd been able to beg a turn herself he'd announced that it was time they were getting back (which Jill knew meant simply that the Tunnel Club opened in an hour and as her mam was on the bar there might be a free pint or two coming his way). Pinball was expensive, threepence a play, but they were flush after their fruit-machine triumph and promised each other 'as many goes as we want.' Liz had played before, natch, but Jill was a quick learner and after watching her friend for a couple of games, she was ready to try her hand. Although the room was empty once more and there were several machines they took turns on the same one so it could be a together-tournament.

Just tall enough to handle the controls properly, Jill was fascinated by the machine. The base stood on four chrome legs slanting upwards with the playfield under the glass-covered cabinet and a vertical tableau at the back. It was called 'Coronation' and the painting on the rear wall was of a young beauty queen sitting on a shell-encrusted, seaside throne. She certainly didn't look much like the queen who'd been crowned on Mrs Smellie's black and white telly all those years ago: nor the one on her newly-acquired half-crowns. This one was clad in a glittery silver bikini and a purple cape which hung down over the edge of her marine throne. She had sparkling high-heeled shoes and a gold crown. The bikini top was so skimpy you could see her boobs bulging over the top of it.

You pressed a button to obtain the first of five large, silver ball bearings and pulled back the spring-loaded rubber knob. Jill had noted that Liz pulled it back just enough to send the ball as far as the middle – and highest-scoring – channel. She tried to do the same; but her first ball only dribbled up to the lowest-scoring gate. It then began to ricochet off the various bumpers which lit up their respective scores with loud pings as the ball moved down the table towards the hole at the bottom. Once it went through there that go was over, but skilful manipulation of the two flippers on either side of the casing could keep the ball, and your go, in play for some time. She'd already sussed that the trick was to be vigorous enough to ensure the flipper made contact with the ball but not so violent that a 'TILT' came up and you lost that go. Liz seemed adept at getting the balance right, but again Jill discovered it was trickier than it looked.

After their first full turns – including Liz getting an extra ball once she got to 5,000 – Jill had scored 2,040 whilst her mentor had racked up 9,460. 'Divn't worry,' she said kindly, 'you'll soon get the hang of it, pet.' True: on each of the succeeding goes Jill's score was closer to Liz's, although still a good way short. Only on the turn they agreed should be the final one – the tournament having taken well over half an hour and most of one of their half-crowns – did Jill threaten her friend's supremacy. Liz had notched up a respectable 13,750, but Jill managed to get an extra go at 5,000 and then, on her last ball another one at 10,000! For a moment she harboured prospects of overtaking Liz's high score (which instinct told her might not go down too well) but then she lost concentration, flipped despairingly hard at the disappearing ball and incurred the dreaded 'TILT.' 'Uh oh, hard luck, hinnie,' cried Liz, sympathy concealing relief.

They'd had enough of the arcade and decided to head for their original destination – Cullercoats. It was a beautiful little bay, with a sweep of sand that gave good safe swimming, fringed by rocky pools on either side. These filled and emptied with the tide, leaving masses of small crabs, mussels and periwinkles – their particular quarry, to be taken home in plastic bags and then boiled with salt. Extracted with the little wooden cocktail-sticks which Jill's mam pinched from the Club, they were delicious. They didn't find any crabs large enough to take home but within an hour they'd harvested loads of winkles.

Wandering across the rocks they came upon a secluded bay and Liz declared it was time for a swim. She pulled out a couple of stripy towels from her duffel bag and was just about to extract her swimsuit when Jill wailed, 'But I haven't got a cossie!'

Swiftly Liz stuffed hers back into the bag and announced decisively, 'Divn't worry, pet, we'll skinny dip. There's no one around.' And she started to strip off. Jill was unfazed by the sight of her friend's rapidly unclothed body although she contained a small gasp when Liz took off her blouse to reveal a skimpy cotton bra. She'd seen bras before, of course, but only on a washing line or on the generous proportions of her mam when she came home from an afternoon stint at the Club a little the worse for wear and decided to take a bath without bothering to close the door. As she got undressed her boobs swung free and to Jill's eyes they were massive.

Far too big, she thought spitefully – you'll fall into the bath with 'em one of these days. But she couldn't help being a bit envious too, wondering whether she'd ever have ones like that. Jill didn't wear a bra yet, although of late her chest had begun to swell a little. But Liz was nearly thirteen and already well-developed for her age. Judging by the cheeky grin she gave her young friend as she unclipped the bra, she knew it. Jill tried not to make it obvious but couldn't help gazing at her friend's rounded breasts and her dark-pink nipples. Liz twigged and enquired pointedly, 'like 'em hinny?' Then when Jill nodded shyly she just laughed.

By now Jill had unpeeled her clothes as well and they were running, naked, towards the sea. There was only a gentle swell and they splashed quickly through the shallows into water deep enough to swim in. Both girls were proficient. It was one thing Jill could thank Rob for; he was a really good swimmer and had taught her the previous summer in the municipal baths. Now the girls revelled in the sensations of fluid-strength and freedom. Jill had never swum nude before and the feeling of the water flowing over her was wonderful.

She told Liz so as they bumped into each other in the deep surf. 'Yeah, it's great,' agreed her friend, 'feel's brill. Almost as nice as this feels,' she declared, deliberately bumping up against Jill and wrapping her arms round the younger girl's waist. She rubbed her hands up and down Jill's back and then, without warning, kissed her on the lips again. The waves lapped over their faces and they spluttered and laughed but didn't break their embrace. Jill decided she liked being kissed by another girl and drew her mouth away just long enough to tell Liz. Whereupon the latter surprised Jill even further by sticking her tongue out and licking her friend's lips. 'Open your mouth,' she instructed, and when Jill did so she felt Liz's tongue slide between her lips and into her mouth.

'Oh, oh,' she gasped unable to say any more. But it was nice and she wanted Liz to know it so she squeezed her friend more tightly. Their bodies seemed to intertwine in the ebb and flow of the sea and somehow her knee became stuck between Liz's legs.

The older girl withdrew her tongue from Jill's mouth just long enough to implore, 'Ooh, move your leg up,' and when she did, 'Yeah, that's it, rub it up and down.' Then, just before she gently slid her tongue back between Jill's lips, she suggested, 'Put *your* tongue in, pet. See if you like it!'

Jill did. It was nice, especially when their tongues touched. For some reason she didn't understand it made her go all hot, even though the sea was cold, and her whole body felt tingly. She felt Liz's tummy thrusting forward so that her thigh rubbed up and down between her friend's legs, right at the top where her thingy was. Jill could feel it now even though the sea swelled between them. It was covered in little hairs but felt slippery as well. Liz was panting a bit, what with the vigorous kissing and the water splashing over their faces, but most of all she seemed to be enjoying Jill sliding up and down against her. Again she disengaged just long enough to tell her friend, 'hmm that's lovely, pet, keep rubbing.'

Jill was still following instructions when the swirling surf momentarily submerged them both. They emerged spluttering but not before Jill felt her friend shudder all over and cry out something she didn't catch. She hoped Liz hadn't got cold but then her friend kissed her one last time and headed for the shore. That were aall reet, thought Jill. I liked that.

She told Liz as much as they emerged, goose-pimply-tingling-with-pleasure and ran back to their towels. Jill couldn't fail to notice her friend's nipples and asked her why they were sticking out so. 'Why, hinny, it's the cold. That, and when you get excited,' she added calculatedly.

Jill took the hint. 'So when we were in the arcade…yer know…and they were hard was that cause you were cold?' she enquired archly. 'Or did that kiss make 'em go hard?'

'Whaddya think, yer minx!' rejoined the older girl. 'Now let's get dry before we freeze.' She swept both towels up from the sand and shook them clean, handing one to Jill. The other she threw over Jill's shoulders and started to rub her back and buttocks vigorously with it. Jill assumed she should do the same, so she threaded the towel round Liz's waist and began rather clumsily to rub her friend up and down. The towelling drew them closer together and with no clothes to impede them this time Jill could feel her friend's nipples hard against her upper chest. They were as stiff as little hat-pegs, she thought and murmured something to that effect as Liz giggled, 'I'm not surprised, yer sod, now I'm cold *and* excited! Don't stop,' she added hastily, as Jill's movements threatened to cease.

Their mutual towelling continued until Liz gasped, 'I'm pretty much dry everywhere 'cept one place. Shall I show yer?' However, just as Jill was nodding, pretty sure she knew now what Liz was talking about, a pair of elderly rock pool hunters stepped gingerly down onto the far side of 'their' beach. 'Damn!' exclaimed Liz with disappointment 'now we'll have to get dressed. Another time, hinny, promise…'

Fourteen

Merton Bright was a year older than Jay. He was stocky and strong but timid, and content to take Jay's lead whether at home or school. St Mary's, like his old school, was more than a mile from his house but he was allowed to cycle as far as the end of their drive, cross the main road and then park his bike at Merton's. The Bright's whitewashed semi was just across the Woodton Road, sore-thumbed in a small row of cottages between the Women's Institute and the Duke of York. Most days over the next year they would walk together through the village, cutting down Baldry's Walk and along Hollow Hill Road and back again. They were best friends at school, but for some reason Jay couldn't understand, they scarcely ever met up at weekends or during the holidays.

Instead, the Fincher family got to know the local farmers – the Hoods. Felicity and Roger had three sons: Peter, the eldest, was the same age as Chris whilst Tom, the youngest, was a year older than Jay. In between came James, the odd one out. Their farm, Brooklands, was nearly three miles away by road, back towards Woodton, up Hollow Hill and past Ditchingham House. However, you could strike steeply (for Norfolk, that was, hardly Helvellyn!) up through the woodland above The Lodge until you came to a sunken pathway running between the wood and the open farmland beyond. If you followed this for a mile or so, kicking through the leaves which seemed to pile up regardless of the season, you came to the cottage where Henry Williamson used to live. It was now apparently occupied only by his wife who was a bit of a recluse. Jay didn't know what a recluse was but it sounded remote and slightly strange.

Continuing along the increasingly overgrown track above Target Hill, where you could still find the blunt lead remnants of bullets shot across the river during Army practice before the war, you came eventually to Bath House. Here lived Lady Veronica – ultimately, as Sir Reeve Kirkstead's heir, their landlord. She was a fascinating old biddy whose stories about the estate and its houses, including The Lodge, Jay enjoyed. Even though she talked terribly posh!

Or soon after Target Hill you could veer off on a cart track which skirted the headlands of several arable fields to reach the road once more at Thwaite Farm, where Tom's grandfather lived. A half-mile further and you swung left into the driveway to Brooklands. By the following spring Jay was a regular visitor and although unintentionally, his growing friendship with Tom adopted precisely the opposite pattern to that with Ennio and Merton. Merton he saw every day at school but infrequently thereafter, whilst Ennio rarely attended school but was a stand-by if Jay had no one else to play with. Tom attended prep school as a weekly border so they would occasionally catch up at weekends and during holidays. Tom's older brothers were already at public school.

Jay could easily have been lonely, but secretly enjoyed being different. He knew he was unlike either bunch of friends and sensed that knowing both set him apart from either. And if he experienced occasional isolation – when he'd inadvertently set each coterie against him, for example – it was a small price to pay for what would pave the way for a lifetime of independence.

Meanwhile, in the first year or two at The Lodge the Finchers' lives were changing. It seemed that Jay's mum and dad were different too: living in a grand house. Well it had once been grand, and after decades of neglect had recently been restored to much of its former glory, although Lady Veronica had described the transformation in less glowing terms, according to Muriel.

'Listen to this piece in the press,' she said to Jay's father over Sunday breakfast. Jay was preoccupied dragging strips of bacon in and out of his fried egg, but switched on when his mother announced, 'It's by Veronica, entitled *The Ghost of a House*. "Prospective tenants in perfectly-creased trousers and with spotless hands, accompanied by equally exquisite wives, became increasingly pained and silent as one processed through the endless back quarters and threw open the door of yet another cavernous cellar. One particularly spruce husband positively shuddered when I remarked it was a lovely house for a family, *if* they were prepared to find all their amusements in the place, as there was always a great deal to do".'

'You don't think she included us in that do you?' Muriel queried, a little indignantly it seemed to Jay, now busy scoffing his egg-soaked bacon.

Their father was relaxed as usual, 'Hardly, darling. That refers to before we moved in. Anyway, she's intimated since that we were exactly the tenants she was looking for – "different"!'

Jay's attention drifted as the alterations from the sixteenth-century original were listed in detail, but his ears pricked up again as he heard his mother exclaim, 'Listen to this bit, Ray: "I walk back round the front

of the house, past the place where a giant hornbeam used to stand..."
I wonder if the one in the courtyard was seeded from it.'

Jay didn't need to hear his father's reply, he was already off his breakfast stool, through the games room and out of the back door to the side courtyard. Sure enough there was the hornbeam – tall, slender and awkward to climb. He'd already been inclined to add it to the list of 'special trees' the first of which had been, of course, the parachute-oak in the back garden at Ivy Bank. The list had been enhanced by 'Langdon's Express,' as Jay who couldn't pronounce 'Cypressus' had dubbed the magnificent lone conifer on the edge of the hill a furlong or so (an Autolyclean measurement he'd snapped up from Old Farmer Hood) from the house. The Express was a great tree to climb. After a running jump and a wild swing brought the lowest, upside-down limb within reach, the branches formed a perfect V-runged stepladder whose bough-treads gradually grew thinner and more challenging towards the top, some seventy feet above the buttercup meadow. Jay had already established himself as its champion, since no one else was either bold enough or light enough to get as close to its pinnacle as he'd achieved. Even Chris and his new friends Smir and Humph had been impressed. His mother had been horrified, however, and forbidden him ever to climb it again, though his father had murmured, 'well done, son,' in tones not unlike those he'd used to applaud Jay's getting-to-a-million-in-twenty-goes.

Could the hornbeam match that, wondered Jay, developing a crick in his neck as he traced the smooth, boughless start and studied the most feasible route to its topmost branches? Only if it were so difficult that no one else could get up it.

He wandered back into the kitchen as his mother concluded her recitation '...she goes on: "Through the door into the stable yard, I make my way homewards. It is many a year since the horses clattered out down the long drive to the main road and I walk down a couple of hundred yards of path to the kitchen garden. One prospective tenant, struggling along in the rain, her high-heeled shoes sucking in and out of the mud, remarked that it seemed a long way to go for a lettuce." (Well, puzzled Jay, I can see her point) "...now the broken door opens onto a wilderness of weeds and un-pruned and dying fruit trees. Yet this garden, so skilfully sheltered and carefully sloped to the south that the sun is hardly ever off it, used to be famous for its vegetables, which were a fortnight earlier than anywhere else. They say its day is done, that no one will walk all that way..." Well, *we* will, Veronica!' declared Muriel with some spirit. 'It'll be my labour of love to restore that garden!'

Fifteen

The following summer excitement was building at Granny Johnson's. Jill's dad and her big brother Rob were due back from South Wales, the pit where George had been working having closed down. Swann's were taking on drillers again and he'd secured a job there from September. The same month Jill would start at Marsden Secondary Modern, just a few days after she turned eleven.

Miss Menzies had been furious. Just because no one from St Kits had made it to grammar school for some years, neither the school nor the girl's indifferent mother had been prepared to let her sit the 11-plus.

'It's an absolute travesty,' she complained to the junior school head-master, 'the youngster's easily bright enough to benefit from a grammar school education. But what with her mother's fecklessness and your intransigence she's not going to get it. How are girls like her – bright and diligent – ever to get to university if the education system lets them down as badly as their parents?'

Mr Parker shook his head sympathetically but was unable to come up with a response before the redoubtable Miss Menzies launched forth once more, 'I don't blame the father. If there's no work here then he's got no alternative but to find some elsewhere. But that mother of hers needs a good shaking. She'd sooner spend time in that Tunnel Club than looking out for her only daughter. She's no better than she should be...'

It had never occurred to Jill that she'd go anywhere other than Marsden's. It was where they all went. But Miss Menzies sought her out deliberately on the day they left, wishing her all the best for the future and declaring quite sternly, 'You're a bright girl, Jill Walker, and don't you forget it. Keep up your reading whatever anyone says. Work hard and there's no reason why you shouldn't make something special of yourself.' Jill had never heard her teacher praise anyone like that. From then on, whenever she needed a bit of reassurance she would whisper to herself, 'You're a bright girl, Jill Walker, and don't you forget it!'

The reuniting of the family and the prospect of big school were only part of the excitement though. Her mother might be 'no better than she should be' but she was a hard worker and had quite a bit put by against George's expected unemployment. Also whatever anyone else might think Jill's grandmother had a soft spot for Mary so they'd been living rent-free, which considerably augmented their savings. So George's coming back to a job meant they could move into a new home – a council terrace on Engine Inn Place. Jill would still have to share with Al, but Rob would now have his own bedroom. They would move out of Lumley Road towards the end of August and the best news of all was that they would go off on holiday for the week prior, which meant they'd be away for Jill's birthday. Now that was a treat!

Apart from the hop-picking adventure down in Kent when she'd seen precious little of the family apart from Al, Jill had never been on holiday. Anticipation rose throughout August. First, there was the joyful return of her dad and brother. For once everyone really did appear pleased to be back together – even their mother, who seemed genuinely grateful to have a permanent husband (as opposed to a series of temporary 'uncles') once again. And for the first time Jill could remember they seemed to be 'in the money.' What with her mother's savings and her father's severance pay they could afford to stop in a caravan up at Seahouses for the week.

They were to travel by coach on Thursday morning. That meant a half-mile walk to the terminus at Percy Main, but since they were accustomed to travelling light it was no great burden. After that they had comfortable seats all the way – no waiting about on draughty platforms – and a good view of all the sights. The first bit was familiar as they skirted Shields and went down Tynemouth's Front Street before cruising left along the coast past the Grand and The Plaza and Cullercoats and the Spanish City. They could see St Mary's Lighthouse, which Rob had once swum around, and then it was on towards the chimneys and pit-wheels of Blyth, where they made their first stop. The coach was now jam packed, but after they'd dropped more people at Newbiggin, Amble and Alnwick there was enough space for all three children to bag a window seat on the coast-side of the bus.

Just in time, too, as the coach now took the scenic route. This was the bit Jill had been looking forward to. Although she no longer saw her infant teacher at the school, Miss Charlton was often at Ferndale Avenue when Jill called to see Miss Lambton of a Saturday morning. When they heard the family was off to Seahouses they made sure Jill knew what to look out for on the way.

'The first interesting place you'll stop at will be Alnwick,' advised

70

Miss Charlton, 'so make sure you look out for the Market Place. It's really old. And especially don't miss the Castle. It's belonged to the Percy family for about 700 years. The Dukes of Northumberland live there. The road goes quite close. You can see the battlements across the lake. You'll love it. Just a pity you can't stay there.'

'And after Alnwick,' took up Miss Lambton, 'you'll come to the coast at Boulmer. They pronounce it Boomer, but it actually comes from the Anglo-Saxon (she'd had to explain what that was) for Bulemer or bulls mere. Oh, and your brother Rob'll be interested in the RAF base.'

And here they were, swinging onto the seafront near Seaton Point and over the headland to Boulmer. 'You wanna look out in a minute, our Rob, cause yer'll see summat yer'll like,' remarked Jill knowingly; and before she could be subjected to his usual sarcasm there it was: 'RAF Boulmer.'

For once Rob, who aspired to join the Air Force, really was impressed. 'Eh, well done, sis, thass brilliant!' He would've liked to shout to the coach driver to slow down, but he didn't have to. Driver Thomson knew exactly what would catch his passengers' attention and always slowed down both here and at several points over the remaining ten miles or so. It was built into the schedule of the 'Seahouses Special.'

So Rob, able to spot numerous aircraft, offered a rapid inventory: 'There look, see that biggun on its own? Thass a mothballed Avro Shackleton and those four in a row are Fairy Gannets. Dunno what they're doin here, mind, they're usually out at sea. And the two next to them,' he rattled, 'are Supermarine Attackers. They're used by the Navy too, but they're not much cop. Oh, and over there by the fence – they're Sea Hawks. They're made by the same firm as makes Hawker Hunters.' And so he chunnered on, until they swung round the corner and lost sight of the base.

Rob's enthusiasm shone through his commentary, which became loud enough for most of the remaining passengers to hear. As he finished there was a smattering of applause, and although he blushed bright red, Jill could tell he was chuffed. She was impressed herself and wondered how when he seemed to have no interest in or mastery of his school subjects he could remember all these details about the aircraft. She murmured something along those lines and Rob rejoined, 'Thanks, our Jill, I'd probably have missed 'em altogether if it hadn't been for you.' It made Jill's day.

They veered inland after that but were back on the coastline at Craster. In contrast to Boulmer, there was a spectacular little harbour. Jill remembered what Miss Lambton had told her – it had been built in memory of Capt. John Craster who'd been killed in action in India around the turn of the century. The Craster family had been there for nearly 700

71

years. At the sight of Craster their mam finally showed some interest, having had her head buried in successive copies of *Woman's Own* for most of the journey. 'You wanna look out here, our Jill. They've the best kippers and crabs in Northumberland. We sell 'em at Watsons – Robson's kippers, they are. They used to supply them to the Royal Family.'

This amazed Jill. She couldn't remember her mother passing on that much information about anything before!

Across a flat stretch of headland they could see the ruins of Dunstanburgh Castle and, beyond it, Embleton Bay. Miss Charlton – the reiver expert – had been the tour guide for this stretch. 'Look out for Holy Trinity Church: it goes back to Norman times. I've family from Embleton as well. In days gone by the farmers used to pay the Castle sixpence a year to drive their stock inside when the reivers came. Oh, and when you get to Beadnell see if you can spot Ebb's Neuk Point – Oswald, King of Northumbria built a house there for his sister St Ebba.'

Jill had recounted this last bit to no one in particular, concluding that St Ebba's house probably dated from around AD 640. 'That's Anno Domini,' she explained proudly, 'it means "In the year of our Lord" cause our calendars count time from the birth of Christ.'

If she'd expected a reception like Rob's she was disappointed. The only reaction to Jill's intelligence was a shrug of the shoulders from her mother who sniffed, 'Where on earth d'you get this stuff from? Them two at the library I s'pose.'

Jill felt cowed. She didn't know what to reply. Her disappointment didn't last long though. A few more minutes brought the coach to its destination just off Seahouses' main street and in the thrill of arriving Jill almost forgot Miss Lambton's words of wisdom: '"To travel hopefully is a better thing than to arrive" – that's Robert Louis Stevenson,' she'd cautioned. 'It comes from a book called *Virginibus Puerisque* – for boys and girls, published a couple of years after *Treasure Island*. And that, Jill Walker, is what I've selected for you to read on holiday.'

In truth, Miss Lambton's cautionary quotation was only partly to introduce Stevenson to her avid young reader. It also reflected the view that she and her friend, Joyce Charlton, held of Seahouses. In their opinion the richness of a journey that included Alnwick, Craster and Dunstanburgh was poorly complemented by a destination built less than seventy years earlier whose chief claims to fame were a row of fish and chip shops and Coxon's ice cream. Oh, and Horton's caravan park where they were about to reside for the next week.

Fortunately, Miss Charlton's view was not shared by the Walkers.

Sixteen

It didn't strike Jay that he lived in a Georgian mansion. He did notice though, that other boys called it 'the big house' – just like Ennio had done when they'd first met. It seemed a bit odd when they all went to fancy schools, but then their dads were mostly farmers, or connected to the land. No one else's dad worked for 'Her Majesty,' had offices in Norwich where several of his new friends had never been (it was fifteen miles away, after all), and was responsible for inspecting schools across a region stretching from Thetford to Lowestoft and Cromer to Ipswich. Neither did anyone else's dad drive a Zephyr Zodiac, they mostly seemed to own beaten-up old Morrises. So when the other boys talked about Jay's dad it was in tones of awe which Jay deemed entirely appropriate.

On the other hand, his weekend friends belonged to the Pony Club and their fathers went hunting and shooting. The Finchers had no aspirations in that direction and Raymond's sporting activities were restricted to golf. He'd joined the local club which featured a flat, sandy course enclosed by a big loop of the River Waveney, and although he didn't seem to play anywhere near as often as he had done at Ivy Bank, he still found time for a couple of rounds at the weekends and one on Wednesday evenings in the summer. Although his dad never said so, the boys discovered via Chris's friend Humph – who lived just by the club gates and whose father, the local bank manager, also played there – that their dad had the lowest handicap at the club. He and Humph's dad soon started playing together and Raymond was introduced to most of the people who 'mattered.'

By the following summer he'd won the Club Championship and was in a regular Sunday four-ball with the Hedham brothers. This apparently caused him some amusement. 'It's not bad for a Brummie Staff Sergeant, eh Mu?' he joked one lunchtime. 'This foursome, y'know, the other three are an RAF Commodore, a Brigadier and a Naval captain, and their family owns half the neighbourhood!' But what most tickled him was the initiation ceremony. They'd been playing together for some months, and had proceeded beyond surnames when Ray's partner, the Brigadier – James – had paused after they'd just holed out on the ninth.

'Bit of a tradition we Hedhams have, Ray, now that you're a regular,' he smiled, rummaging about in his golf bag to produce four bottles of Guinness, which he proceeded to open and hand round: 'Cheerio, all!'

To begin with, Ray swore, it tasted awful and he partook out of sheer politeness. But as the ritual was repeated on a weekly basis he gradually acquired a liking for the stuff. It wasn't too long before a crate began to appear in the cellar beyond the games room and an occasional bottle or two would be taken of a Friday evening. Despite her mother's teetotal advice, Muriel chose to ignore it, deciding that something which clearly gave her husband pleasure was to be welcomed not forbidden.

The other Guinness ritual was after gardening. As the article in the *Eastern Daily Press* had intimated The Lodge's grounds had been sadly neglected and whilst she had no doubt her new tenants were keen to do their bit, Lady Veronica was quick to assign an estate gardener to Lodge duties. Buck was a jovial giant – always smiling, ruddy-faced and as strong as a shire horse. He didn't have any set hours and his remuneration was initially a mystery as whenever Raymond tried to broach the subject he would murmur that, 'th'estate look arter that...' He also resisted all attempts to address him by anything other than his surname (their parents insisted the boys call him *Mr* Buck, even though their weekend friends all called him Buck). Whilst he smilingly declined any reward, he was partial to a Guinness. 'Doan mind if I do, Mr Fincher,' he enthused on the first occasion. And ever afterwards of a week's-end evening he and Jay's dad would lean on the iron railings at the far end of the front lawn they were gradually restoring and chew the fat. Again, it was clear to Muriel's astute eye that far more good than harm came of it. 'He's a real genelman, that husband of yourn, Missus Fincher,' Buck would remark in appreciation.

In truth, Ray enjoyed the exercise. It made a nice change after the intellectual but essentially sedentary manner by which he made his living. At his office in Gentleman's Walk his every need was met by the efficient but redoubtable Miss Jenkins; whilst his frequent excursions around the secondary schools of East Anglia were, of necessity, by car. Only the weekend golf and gardening were antidotes. Until the fishing, that was...

It was Humph's dad, banker Ray Clarke, who'd put him onto it. 'Perfect relaxation after the office,' he'd advised. 'That pit of yours would be ideal.'

'Marchlands' was the former gravel pit Jay had noticed on his very first excursion with Ennio. It was owned by Cherry Tree Angling Club and its secretary worked at Barclays as one of Mr Clarke's tellers. Being a bit off the beaten track and on private land it was little frequented and Ray would often find himself the sole angler. Initially, he'd been inclined to scoff at the 'sport' it provided. His only previous experience was of game fishing on the streams of the Lake District and in the Welsh Marches, where he participated in an annual summer camping course run by the Ministry of Education. Apart from the prospect of consuming the catch, fly fishing for trout and salmon on fast-flowing, often picturesque upland waters was exciting. The calm expanse of Marchlands looked a little tame as did the potential take of uneatable roach, tench and bream. Whilst he conceded that watching the badger-quill float meander slowly across the placid green surface was a tranquil enough pursuit, it hardly got the blood racing. Then, one mid-week evening he had company – a young man from Barclays who, it turned out, lived close by in Ditchingham. Ray watched him alternately casting and reeling in, and was intrigued. He'd decided to introduce himself, when the bank clerk approached him.

'Hart. Ben Hart, Mr Fincher. Glad to make yer acquaintance, sir,' he said deferentially, almost doffing his flat, angler's cap. 'I see you're arter the dozies, sir,' he said smiling. 'Meself, I likes a bit more action,' and he indicated his line at the end of which glittered a silver and red lure revolving jauntily on its swivel. 'Would you like to try, sir?' he enquired, offering Ray his rod. 'Just cast out past that reed bed over towards the elders; there's often a jack pike there lying in wait for gudgeon.'

'Well, thank you, Hart; I'll certainly give it a try.' And taking the rod with care he endeavoured to master the unfamiliar action of the spinning reel. He was conscious that as well as being a generous offer on the part of the younger man, it was probably something of a rite too. Clarke would doubtless have mentioned Ray's trout-fishing prowess and the locals were always keen to take anyone who might think he was a cut above them down a peg or two.

After little more than a dozen casts Hart's prediction proved correct. Ray's line went taut as his spinner was taken and he struck hard to hook the fish, which immediately kenched sharply towards the reed bed. He was about to reel it in when he thought better of it. 'Reckon I might lose this in the reeds. D'you want to bring it in?' he said with a carefully pitched mix of anxiety and respect, handing the rod over to his mentor.

He watched in genuine admiration as Hart let the fish run out line towards the reeds, slowing its escape just before it reached them and then gradually dragging it back in. Several more times he let it run, each time hauling the tiring fish closer until finally he motioned Ray to get the landing net under it. They laid it out on the grass bank, disentangled the fish and cautiously removed the spinner from its long narrow jaws. Hart produced a small metal weighing scale with a large hook which he inserted under the fish's gills and lifted it triumphantly aloft. 'Just under foive pound! Thass about as big a jack pike as'll grow in this pit. Any bigger and you can bet it's a female. Good though, ain't it? Beats your half-pound trout any day!'

The following Monday Ray went out at lunchtime to Crabtree's fishing shop near the River Wensum and bought himself a spinning rod, a reel and a plastic box of assorted plugs and spinners. And from that day on, whenever the kitchen clock ticked towards seven Jay's mother remarked sympathetically, 'Oh, your poor father, working late at the office again,' they all knew the likelihood was different! Far from being miffed, Muriel recognised that it was much better for him to be home late and relaxed than early and tense from administering Her Majesty's business.

Seventeen

The caravan site was on the outskirts of Seahouses, a ten-minute walk from the coach terminus. The younger children were excited, but Rob was blasé, 'Why man, caravans are for softies. Give me a tent anytime!'

It was an orange Good Companion and as soon as she saw it Jill wished she were sleeping in that instead of sharing the cramped quarters of the van. The latter was one of four which had been dragged to the bottom of the home-croft by tractor and now squatted there permanently. The site itself was just a large grassy field with a makeshift toilet block. But their caravan overlooked the bay and in the distance you could see the Farne Islands. Jill knew they were the Farnes, cause Miss Charlton had said they were the best thing about Seahouses and that she must take a trip out to them if possible. Accordingly, that became her principal ambition for the week.

When they arrived, Mrs Horton, the wife of the farmer who owned the site, was still cleaning the van after the departure of its previous occupants just an hour before. She was a plump, rosy-faced woman with thick, black curls that suited her. Jill took to her straightaway. She was volunteered to help her, a move that proved shrewder than she realised on her mother's part as they were 'in her good books' from that moment on and helping Mrs Horton around the farm meant getting free eggs into the bargain. The cleaning didn't take long and her parents were soon installing themselves whilst Rob pitched his tent a few yards off, closer to the sea.

Jill asked to help and was chuffed when Rob agreed. She held the A-poles still, with the tent trailing underneath them from the large aluminium hook, whilst he banged the pegs into the firm ground with a wooden mallet and attached the guy ropes to them. Rob had been in the Scouts for a few months until there was a row after the Scoutmaster had been too friendly. Rob had taken exception with a hot-headed right hook, and been asked to leave. It only took them ten minutes now, to pitch and trim the tent. It was shaped a bit like the tepees she'd seen in the Davy Crockett films. They looked inside. There was loads of room – easily enough for two, noted Jill, wondering how she could persuade Rob to let her sleep there one night.

The caravan was pretty small for four people, but Jill was used to that. Her parents had a separate compartment for sleeping whilst the two bench seats either side of the plastic table converted into bunk beds for the night. There was a little sink with a tap through which you could pump up cold water and a stove connected to a bottle of Calor Gas under the van. And there were gaslights which they lit once it got to about nine o'clock at night (even Al was allowed to stop up on holiday). They looked brill, and there was easily enough light to read by, if the opportunity ever arose. That seemed unlikely, however. Each evening after they'd consumed the fish and chips or sausages wrapped in the *Northumberland Gazette*, their mother would make two cups of instant coffee. Then their father would enquire, 'summat to keep the cold out, Mary?' and pour in two large slugs from a bottle of dark rum generously provided as a holiday treat by Uncle Bill. For some reason, their father kept up the pretence that it was the same bottle all week even though Jill knew her uncle had given them two, to make sure they 'had enough.'

Come Saturday morning their mam said they should use the holiday to do more together as a family; which was pretty rich coming from her since she was the one who was hardly ever there. It turned out that what Mary actually meant, however, was that the kids should amuse each other more, especially in the afternoons when she and George would sample the numerous pubs along the high street. That afternoon, when they'd gone off to the Red Lion at the bottom end of the village, Rob had redeemed a long-standing promise and taken Al off to the open-air pool to teach him to swim. Jill reached for *Treasure Island* immediately.

Just before they'd left for Seahouses, her literary mentors – the 'lit twins,' as she'd now christened the two women – handed Jill the 1946 Rainbow edition of *Treasure Island*, with its Introduction by May Lamberton Becker. Mrs Becker had died just that April and Miss Lambton had written a tribute to her in the *Whitley Bay Guardian*. Amongst more recondite literary references, she'd explained how pro-British Mrs Becker had been. At the start of World War Two when many Americans had been neutral at best, she'd donated the royalties from *Introducing Charles Dickens* to finance a Charles Dickens Ambulance in London. The lit twins' enthusiasm fired their charge's imagination as well, and she was only too grateful to follow their recommendation. 'Be sure to read Mrs Becker's Introduction, pet,' Miss Lambton had instructed, 'it'll explain a lot about the book.'

So dwelling only briefly on the double-page 'Map of Treasure Island – July 1784' and the full-colour portrait of a villainous-looking Captain Flint, Jill rifled quickly through until she arrived at page eleven: '*Treasure Island* – most critics call it the best boys' book written in English,' she read and immediately understood why she'd been told not to overlook it. The lit twins were stalwart supporters of equal rights for women and were determined that no book should be a closed-one to Jill simply because it was normally regarded as appealing only to boys.

Jill read on, absorbed. She met Lloyd Osborne, Stevenson's stepson who had insisted, 'there should not be a woman in it.' She sat with Lloyd and Stevenson's father listening to a fresh chapter each evening. And she marvelled at the author's determination to finish *The Sea Cook* (as it had been called when serialised in *Young Folks*) even after continued deterioration of his health necessitated his recuperating in Switzerland. Mrs Becker summed it up: 'If ever you find life hard and need courage to carry it like a banner, try reading a life of Robert Louis Stevenson.' Hmmm, and don't you forget it, Jill Walker, she mused. And she hadn't even started the novel proper!

'I can swim, sis, I can swim!' blurted Al as he tripped up the metal step at the caravan door and sprawled across the first bunk, making expansive frog-strokes with his arms. 'Rob showed me how and I didn't sink once. Not even when he took his arms away. And now I can do a whole length! And Rob says we can swim in the sea t'morra, if you wanna come.' It was the longest speech she'd ever heard their Al make and Jill couldn't help but smile, especially when she saw Rob's expression of pride.

Their dad was impressed an all, when he wove a slightly unsteady path down the Croft to the van, later that afternoon. 'Howay man: a whole length? Well done, kidda. And you, Rob! Thass aall of us can swim now. Well barring yer mam, of course!'

The latter seemed, as usual, less than overwhelmed, and rewarded her youngest with, 'Well, good, our Al. Now hie along to Mrs Horton and ask her for some eggs. As many as she can spare. I'm gonna make some sarnies. We're off on a picnic to the Farnes t'morra.'

Even Rob looked excited and Jill figured that with him still feeling proud of inculcating his swimming skills now would be a good time to ask if she could sleep in the Good Companion that night. She sidled up to him and whispered the request, anxious not to get rebuffed in front of everyone. Unexpectedly he didn't hesitate, 'why aye, sis, it's yer birthday t'morra after aall.'

Jill was pleased as Punch (although why someone who'd strangled their own child should be pleased had always puzzled her, from the time when Miss Menzies had first recounted the fable).

Once inside the Good Companion they rolled the flaps up and Rob showed her how to tie the thin orange tapes in half-square knots. He had chosen the site well. It was a still, clear evening and sitting by the open flap they could see the dark shape of the Inner Farne against the calm slate sea. It would be their first port of call in the morning.

Soon it was dewdrop-cold in the tent and they were glad of blankets strewn across the groundsheet. Jill hoped Rob might tell her a story – she would've recounted what she'd read of *Treasure Island* if she'd thought he'd be interested – but it presumably didn't occur to him. And since she was too timid to ask she had to accede to his direction – 'Time for bed, sis. Get in yer sleeping bag' – and to slither down inside fully clothed. She watched the tent darken as Rob loosed the tapes and slid down the zip. They didn't have a torch so she felt rather than saw her brother struggle into the snugness of his bag. She could hear the tide lapping softly on the shore, no more than twenty yards away, and before she could discover whether Rob snored Jill was fast asleep.

Eighteen

They'd finished school the day before and Jay was looking forward to the long holiday. It was also the Summer Fayre, traditionally held on the last Friday before St Bartholomew's in the village hall. It was one of the few occasions (Christmas and Easter being the others) when 'high' and 'low' village met socially. High village went to St Mary's which, on account of The Plague, was actually nowhere near the village. Jay sang in the choir there every Sunday at matins. Low village went to All Hallows, which was closer to the main population but not really in the centre of the village either. Jay sang there, too, at evensong, though not every week. Merton and some of the other older boys and girls from school sang there, whilst the Hood brothers sang at St Mary's. Only Jay sang at both.

The village hall had been decorated. There were red, blue and yellow paper chains and a large beech bush on the corner of the stage. On top of the piano was an assortment of brightly-wrapped gifts and small, garish flags. Around the outside of the rectangular, wood-block floor stood three rows of trestle tables laden with painted-wooden toys, puzzles in gaudy boxes, food and drink and more gifts. In the centre were refreshment booths which would later be replaced by chairs for the concert itself. Most of the turns were pop tunes, sung by three of four members of the rival choirs or instrumental performances – an accordion player, a violinist and a lad with a mouth organ. All the acts were short.

Raymond had found the illustrated edition of *Old Possum's Book of Practical Cats* in a second-hand bookshop on Elm Hill, not far from Norwich Cathedral. He'd intended it for both boys, expecting Chris to espouse Eliot's whimsical collection of cat-tales and Jay the striking colour drawings by Nicholas Bentley. In fact, it was his younger son who took to the poems, chunks of which – with his acquisitive proclivities – he soon incorporated into his recitative canon. The 'Rum Tum Tugger' was a family favourite as it seemed to delineate perfectly their own pet: a jet-black stray his mother had christened Satan. (It was a source of family amusement that she would call him from the wood above the house as night fell. Even Muriel smiled at 'what the neighbours might think' – a somewhat redundant concern as the nearest ones were half-a-mile distant.) Jay liked several cats in particular. There was *Skimbleshanks* who was easy to learn because of his rhythmical cadences; *Mungojerrie and Rumpleteazer*, whose antics were the most mischievous; and …*The Pekes and the Pollicles* which was the best yarn.

But tonight he was to regale the assembled masses with *Growltiger's Last Stand*, all fourteen verses and 590 words (that was if you counted the hyphenated words as one each). He'd persuaded his mum to draw on his face what he specified as 'ferocious feline features' (Autolycus liked alliteration) in black eyeliner. Then he'd practised hissing and snarling in front of the bathroom mirror until he was satisfied he was sufficiently Growltigerish. He employed this to what he hoped was good effect, scowling upon a hostile world (his audience) in a suitably aggressive manner. He conveyed his distaste for foreign cats – especially Siamese – with such bristling contempt that when he paused to stress the point some of the younger members of the audience, who didn't understand the poem anyway, thought he'd finished and broke into half-hearted applause.

Growltiger glared at them and continued undeterred, finally ending on a note of snarling contempt!

This time the applause was loud and prolonged, even if some of it represented relief that the saga was over. The youngsters, especially, weren't used to having to concentrate on unfamiliar topics for so long and Jay's performance whilst memorable was also puzzling. The consensus amongst his fellow choristers was, 'Cootaheck! He's a rum un!'

Academic prowess had already led to his promotion from Standard Five, to which his age had initially allocated him, to Standard Seven, which represented preparation for secondary school. A few months before the Growltiger episode his headmaster, Mr Beech, suggested Jay be entered for early selection. The arrangement was sufficiently unusual for it to raise a few eyebrows and when Jay passed with flying colours there were mutterings about favouritism. That was unfair. The two principal requirements – Maths and English – happened to be Jay's strong suits. Nevertheless, his final few months at St Mary's as the school swot were uncomfortable ones and worse was to follow.

That September he progressed to Wyndhams, the local grammar school. After a four-mile bike ride which took him through the centre of town, Jay swung into an imposing avenue of lime trees leading to the main building. It seemed huge. Six classrooms were ranged either side of a central hall. Jay parked the ancient Raleigh in the sheds at the back, where a lot of bikes were padlocked onto the rails. Anxious already, he loitered nervously until a hand-bell summoned the school to assembly. He'd never seen so many uniforms.

No one else from St Mary's had come up that year and it didn't help being small for his age and upwards of a year younger than the rest of his class. Every day for the first fortnight he was picked on. The second Saturday he and Chris were playing snooker, 'Yer a bit quiet, little brother. Whassa matter?'

'Nowt! I jus can't seem to pot a ball.'

Chris took a second look at Jay's pale face and lowered head. He was close to tears. 'Yeah, well jus cause yer losing forty-nil doesn't mean it's the end of the world! Wassup really?'

'Promise not to say owt?'

'Yeah, course.'

'I keep getting picked on. Cause I'm the smallest in the class. Sparks – he's the worst.'

'Oh...right... Well, next time he tries it on, challenge him. Properly. There's a fight most Fridays up by the air raid shelters. Get him up there and when he comes for you... Sodit! Here comes Dad... Tell you after!'

And he had.

A week later Jay followed his big brother's advice and there they were, surrounded by most of Form One in the quad that constituted the 'ring.' As Chris had forecast, Sparks came running at him trying to barge him over. Jay stepped easily under his assault and kneed him as hard as he could in the nuts. (Just like Chris had told him.) Then as Sparks doubled up in pain Jay punched him violently in the face. Sparks went down and Jay, vaguely aware of raucous cheering, jumped on him. He pinned his arms to the grass and landed him another hefty smash. Sparks's nose was bleeding and the baying rose in a crescendo of lust. But before Jay could wallop him again his arm was held and a furious adult voice roared. 'That's enough, Fincher! Get off him! Now!'

But the damage had been done – certainly to the Sparks hooter, reflected Jay vindictively. His own punishment – three strokes of the headmaster's cane – was a small price to pay. Besides, Jay's instinct ensured that Dr Hevitt's admonition that he'd never before had to cane a boy in his first month became common knowledge which, of course, further cemented his standing. True to their fraternal code of silence, his brother never said anything about it at home. And Jay never got bullied again.

Nineteen

Jill awoke to a birthday bonus. Rob was already up, crouching at the front of the tent and hunched over a primus stove. The smell of a fry-up pricked her nostrils and by the time Rob had conjured up bacon butties their dad had shuffled across from the van with two palm-warming mugs of tea: 'There y'are, hinnie: Happy Birthday!' Jill was delighted: she was special!

It got better. When their mam had announced the trip to the Farnes, Jill assumed they'd go with the Seahouses tour operator. She recalled seeing the sign: 'Billy Shiels – Farne Islands Boats – Est. 1918,' and the big blue motor vessel with its three-quarter white cabin and open rear, moored in North Sunderland harbour. She'd already decided that if they did get the chance to go on it she was sitting out the back in the open. True it would be too high to trail her hand in the sea (like Jim Hawkins row-boating around the *Hispaniola*) but she'd be able to watch the engines churning up the water and the herring gulls swooping for scraps. It was the stuff of her '*Island*' imagination.

The reality was even more exciting. They weren't going with a crowd of other sightseers on a regular tour they were to sail on Mr Horton's fishing smack and combine a pleasure trip to the islands with the work-a-day business of checking his catches. The only drawback was that by the time Mr Horton and his two kids, Morag and Jamie, were aboard there would only be space for three more. Jill was momentarily downcast. Five into three usually meant the 'Walker men' (no matter that Al was only eight). However, it was her day and their dad must've already explained to Al, who didn't kick off at all when it was announced that Jill would be going 'as her birthday treat,' along with Rob and their dad. Their mam hardly seemed distraught either.

Jill watched keenly as Mr Horton's venerable, once-blue tractor hauled the clinker-built coble over the damp field, across the wet, firm sand of the narrow bank and into the shallows. It had a steep, high bow and a flattish, russet-coloured keel; its upper timbers were painted a brilliant white. Around twenty feet long according to Rob, it had a squat, glass-windowed cabin amidships and space for fishing gear and four or five sailors fore and aft. In bright red letters on either side of the bows was painted 'BK 56,' which Morag explained meant that like most boats in Seahouses it had been registered up the coast in Berwick-upon-Tweed. But what really grabbed Jill's attention was the boat's name – again in red letters, above the cabin window – *The Spyglass*. Jeez! Some coincidence! *Spyglass Hill* overlooked the site where Captain Flint's booty had been buried on Treasure Island. Maybe today's crew wouldn't see the significance, but the lit twins would. Jill must remember to tell them.

The Spyglass chugged steadily towards the Inner Farne across the glassy millpond of the Sound. 'By, you've chosen the right day for it, hinnie,' smiled Morag, 'I've never seen the Sound so calm. There'll be some great views an I'll tell you all about the islands. Yer gonna have a canny day, pet,' she promised. Morag had a strange accent – Geordie, of course, but quite like Miss Charlton's, a bit posh, courtesy of The Duchess's Grammar School in Alnwick. She was a year younger than Rob so wouldn't be fourteen until Christmas but she was due to enter the fourth year in a week's time and had already got GCE 'O' Levels in English Literature and English Language. Jill was amazed, and Morag embarrassed, by her father's proud biography. Even Rob, never easily overawed, gazed at Morag admiringly; though Jill suspected that was cause she was really pretty as well.

Jamie was the same age as Jill, and very quiet.

It turned out that Morag was also keen on geography and was close to completing her holiday project – on the Farne, and Holy Islands! She was the ideal guide and was in tour mode even before they reached their first stop. 'There's twenty-six islands altogether but some of them are just bare rock. And besides they're covered at high tide. We're gonna land on Inner Farne; then, if there's time, we'll go across the far sound to Staple Island. There are absolutely loads of birds there. Then maybe even to Longstone so you can see the lighthouse where Grace Darling lived.'

They were nearly at the landing cove; and Morag was rattling on about saints. The others had clearly lost interest, but Jill was fascinated. 'If you look way up north there you can just see Lindisfarne. It was where Christianity started round here in the seventh century. Its Bishop was Saint Aidan. He used to come here to meditate. But the best known was Saint Cuthbert – he retired here; I can show you his chapel.'

'I've heard of him!' exclaimed Jill. 'He converted King Oswin. He's buried at our priory in Tynemouth. Or so they say,' she concluded lamely, hoping she hadn't overstepped the mark.

It was Morag's turn to be impressed and she looked at Jill, as if she'd just spotted some exotic bird lurking beneath the drab feathers of a cormorant. 'Hey, well done, hin, he did, that's right. Then later he died here – probably about 687 AD. D'you know what that stands for?'

'Anno Domini,' said Jill proudly, 'In the year of our Lord,' to demonstrate she really did know what it stood for and wasn't just reciting it 'parrot-fashion,' as Miss Menzies would've said.

'Good on yer, pet' smiled Morag, raising her eyebrows in mock surprise. 'Later they moved his remains to Durham. That's where I'm hoping to go to university,' she confided. 'I went to the cathedral on a school trip once. It's brilliant. Cuthbert's buried under a black marble slab behind the altar. There are four massive candlesticks, one at each corner. And on the great north door there's a knocker with a demon on it. It's supposed to be one of a troop that Cuthbert happened on here – riding on goats with their faces covered in black cowls. He scared 'em away with a wooden cross.'

They beached the coble in St Cuthbert's Cove and the two girls set off for the chapel. Morag regaled her young listener with a heady diet of ecclesiastical history and, as they reached the restored-ruined church, its architectural features. Then suddenly, just as they entered the courtyard, she pointed to the masonry: 'Look there, those titchy orange-yellow flowers. The light keepers are supposed to have brought them here in poultry food. "Amsinkia intermedia" – they come all the way from California!' Jill half expected to be quizzed on her geography of the States and wondered whether knowing that Davy Crockett grew up in the Appalachians would suffice.

Meanwhile, Mr Horton – who by now had become 'Alex' – was showing George and their respective sons the best place to fish for mackerel. Normally, you'd cast your lines from the boat but there was a little headland just along from the cove where the current from Staple Sound funnelled through the kettle and brought the fish close to the rocks. Within the hour designated for the return of the girls the combined rods of the 'Horton and Walker boys' had landed over twenty fish – mostly mackerel, but a smattering of cod and herring too, and a lone and highly prized wolf fish. Their expiring, silvery-blue bodies were slapping about in a large metal bucket. Rob's primus was going to be busy later.

'We'll skirt Staple close enough for yer aall to see the birds,' promised Mr Horton.

'There's seals, too' offered Jamie. It was the first time he'd spoken and Jill felt obliged to acknowledge this clearly special bit of information with a smile. Jamie blushed and said no more.

But he was right. As they neared the rocky coastline there they were

– upwards of twenty grey seals bobbing up and down in the deep, greenish water with their doe-eyes and narrow nostrils. The Walker kids had never seen seals before and Jill was fascinated. They seemed really tame and hovered so close to the boat you could almost touch them if you leaned over the side. Jill did, and was only saved from falling in by Jamie swiftly grabbing her legs as she threatened to overbalance. She collapsed back into the boat full of apologies, and gratitude. Jamie blushed even more deeply.

'Well no harm done,' exclaimed Mr Horton, laughing. 'I daresay you can swim okay, and if need be one of us would've pulled you out! Anyhow they wouldn't have hurt you – though *he* might,' he warned, pointing to a large, dark brown bull which was basking on a low promontory about thirty yards away. 'Best not lean over t'side again, just in case.'

Perhaps emboldened by his rescue act, Jamie suddenly burst into a running commentary on the birdlife. 'This here's Kittiwake Gully. You can see where aall the nests were. Most of 'em have gone now, though. The kitts are the real sea gulls. They're ace fliers even in storms. But a lot of 'em get killed by bonxies.'

'Skuas' explained Morag, and for the first time Rob joined the conversation.

'The RAF's got Skuas. And the Navy. *Blackburn Skuas*. They flew a sortie to Norway soon after the start of the War. Sank a German cruiser. Funny name. Summat like *Konigsberg*. It were first time a warship had been sunk by dive bombers.'

Jill was pleased her brother had been able to show off some of the stuff he knew. She could tell he was keen to impress Morag and until now he hadn't really had the chance. She seemed to give him a different look an all – sort of surprised and admiring. But she didn't say owt, which was a shame.

Jamie hadn't finished though. 'See them black and white uns with the thin necks? And web feet. They're guillemots. There's thousans of 'em. You can eat their eggs, an aall – tho yer not s'posed to. And them other black 'n' white uns with the swordy beaks – they're razorbills.' Jamie pointed out other sorts of gulls, as well as shags and cormorants ('brilliant fishers – d'you get 'em on the Tyne?') until Jill finally clocked a small black and white bird about as big as a milk bottle. It had a bright red, yellow and grey triangular beak and she recognised it as a puffin. (They were story books an all, she reflected.) She vaguely recalled someone telling her about them – and lots of other birds – when she were a kid; but there was something unpleasant associated with the memory and she was relieved when Jamie broke in once again.

'If yer look up on that peaty bank yer can see their burras. They used to snare 'em for food. And their feathers. They'd stuff pillows with 'em. Me gran told me. Best thing's their nickname, though: they call 'em "Londoners". D'you know why?' Jill shook her head. 'Cause they stand on the cliffs looking out to sea, aall sackless like!' They all laughed; Jamie grinned triumphantly and went scarlet.

It was past dinner now and high time for the sarnies Jill's mam had made. They were mostly egg and some cheese and pickle. And crisps. Jill rummaged in her packet until she found the little blue greaseproof sachet of salt. Then she opened up each of her two egg sandwiches and tipped most of it on, shaking the rest onto the crisps. There were bottles of lemonade, too – it were a real picnic!

Fortunately conditions remained benign, with only a slight swell that increased as they approached Longstone and the open sea. Otherwise, announced Mr Horton, they probably wouldn't've risked going all the way out to Longstone. Apart from Knivestone, it was the farthest out to sea and caught any bad weather first.

'That's why they built the lighthouse here,' resumed Morag. 'Ships were getting wrecked before they could spot the lights on Brownsman and Inner Farne. Longstone was where Grace Darling lived with her parents. It's a 120 years next week since the wreck of the *Forfarshire*. There's all sorts of tales, mind. This island we're passing now – the Big Harcar – is the one Capt. Humble drove the *Forfarshire* onto. Grace spotted it from her bedroom window. The legend says she persuaded her dad to let her help rescue the sailors. They rowed more than a mile in massive seas twice to save the survivors. She were a national heroine afterwards. She even got a gift from Queen Victoria. But she died four years later and she were only twenty-six.'

Jill was spellbound and asked if she could find out more when they got back. 'Sure,' promised Morag, 'the Grace Darling museum is just up at Bamburgh. It's only about four miles. We can cycle up there tomorrow, if you want?' she added without considering that Jill might not be able to ride a bike.

Jill wasn't worried, though – it was unlikely her mam would let her out two days on the trot and she was having such a good time today that it hardly seemed to matter. So she just smiled her thanks. Besides, they were on their way back now – just one more call to make at the Wideopens to check the lobster pots. Normally Mr Horton would do that first thing but he hadn't wanted to clutter an already busy boat up all day with what he hoped would be a hefty catch.

They were back in millpond waters again and the boys were trailing lines from the back of *The Spyglass*. To help attract their quarry they hurled in handfuls of live bait and it wasn't long before they had a sky-full of gulls and terns for company. Their catch was less successful. Unlike Mr Horton's whose haul of crabs was prodigious. Most would go to market next morning but he selected the best half-dozen and keeping three for Mrs Horton's salad table presented George with the others. How could he have known they were me dad's favourite, wondered Jill? The prospect of dressed crab for tea — and maybe a glass of cider — rounded off a perfect birthday!

Twenty

As Jay's second year at Wyndhams drew to a close his mother was admitted to the Norfolk and Norwich Hospital. Their father was uncharacteristically reticent about the reason so neither boy enquired; but it had to be fairly serious as, after tests and the initial diagnosis, she was expected to be confined for a month. The first fortnight caused few problems – both boys were at school and capable of looking after themselves at home. However, the onset of the holidays coincided with their mother's recuperation when, since there had been 'complications' she would apparently need complete rest – and peace and quiet, no visitors. When Dad announced he was taking them to the Lakes and Scotland it never occurred to Jay that his mum might be lonely, merely that they would get to climb some serious mountains. The tables were still clearly fixed in his memory: Scafell Pike, 3,210; Scafell 3,162; Helvellyn 3,118; Skiddaw 3,053.

Their father had let slip that he might have a surprise for them and Jay assumed it was something to do with their destination. Maybe they were going via Fort William to take in Ben Nevis (4,406 – heckythump!). Then, the day before they were due to depart the surprise arrived – a brand new Zephyr Zodiac Mk II. It was all white with a chrome strip down each side and an imposing chrome grill, which Jay calculated would take a bit of polishing. Like their previous model it had a three-speed gearbox with a column-mounted change. According to Chris it had a top speed of almost ninety and accelerated from 0-60 in 17.1 seconds. The only bad news, conceded their father, was its fuel consumption – 21.5 MPG – and with petrol having recently gone over four shillings a gallon, 'I'll not have to be putting my foot to the boards too often! Still the trip should give us a chance to see what she's got.' Its registration, noted Jay, was WAH 672.

They didn't drive direct to Scotland or even the Lakes; they were to stop over with the Armstrongs first. This was partly to break the journey. It would take them eight hours just to get back to Lancashire. Then they'd pick up Malc and Hugh who were to accompany them on the first leg of their adventure. Jay was chuffed, but a bit apprehensive too; except for one brief visit the Armstrongs had made to The Lodge, he hadn't seen his erstwhile best friend for nearly five years. Maybe he'd changed, maybe they wouldn't get on.

He needn't've worried. Apart from the Armstrong boys' tendency to show off about their father's latest Jag – which irritatingly topped the new Zodiac in every key respect – they all got on splendidly. The plan was for their dad to take the four boys up to a chalet Neville Armstrong rented on an estate in Langdale and then for him to join them at the weekend. Mrs Armstrong would remain at the Croft. Jay was a bit disappointed about that – especially with his own mum not there – but he didn't say anything, of course. In any case, when he thought some more it became obvious. This was a men's trip!

Chris sat up front with their dad and the three younger boys squeezed onto the bench seat in the back. The journey was sixty-four miles Malc informed them authoritatively, and would take less than two hours. Jay would've regarded that as a challenge if he'd been driving and maybe his dad did too cause they arrived at the estate just outside Elterwater in an hour and a half. The Zodiac swung through the main entrance and past The Gatehouse where you could have meals, apparently, but where they were 'a bit snotty' according to Hugh. Then they edged circumspectly down a narrow, grey-shard track between high slate walls. It opened out onto a small tarn; on its gravel-shore was a large chalet with a polished wooden name-plate which read 'Wetherlam.'

'One of the Coniston Fells – 2,502,' pounced Jay, keen to regain some of the ground already ceded to the Armstrong boys' familiarity with their surroundings.

'Yeah, but I bet you don't know what the tarn's called,' crowed Malc. And pausing just long enough to register Fincher ignorance, '"Harrisons."'

'Be after Harrison Stickle, then,' countered Jay, '2,403!'

'Okay, that's enough you two,' warned Raymond cheerfully, 'let's go and see our living quarters. They're certainly well named – see the olive-green hue in the stonework? That's Tilberthwaite slate – there's a lot of it in the Coniston Fells. You'll see for yourselves if the weather stays okay. I'm planning to take you all up the Old Man on Friday. And before you mention it Jay: 2,633!'

Raymond produced a heavy, metal key on a silvery chain and, climbing the three wooden steps, unlocked the front door. It gave into a spacious living area ('commodious?' supplied Jay) with mountain prints he recognised as Heaton Coopers on the birch-beam walls and off to the rear, a generously-proportioned kitchen with all mod cons. Also at the back were the master bedroom and a bathroom; whilst up a short, steel ladder that hung from the ceiling were two bunk rooms built into the roof, each with its own skylight. They quickly unpacked the grips and rucksacks, bagged their respective bunks and tore off to explore. The grounds were extensive and criss-crossed by narrow, fast-flowing waterways which were just begging to be jumped across. Since they were deep and lined with sharp slate it was the one thing Raymond advised them against. They didn't want any broken ankles to spoil the planned ascents.

The first of these was scheduled for the next day which Jay, on the top bunk and closest to the skylight, rapidly established was fine and dry. They were headed for the Old Dungeon Ghyll Hotel and the Langdale Pikes; but not before bacon and beans and a gear-check. The Fincher boys were well equipped and Raymond – aware of Neville's habit of ensuring his family had the best of everything – expected Hugh and Malc would be too. Their waterproofs were indeed new and expensive – Barbour waxed jackets and over-trousers; but he was taken aback to discover that Neville had interpreted 'boots' not as climbing, but Wellington-boots. Not just any old boots, naturally, but green Hunters of the sort worn amongst the Norfolk country set. Raymond couldn't help smiling (he hoped to himself) and whilst he had reservations about scaling either Langdale breccia or, especially, Coniston slate in wellies he was confident the boys would manage – provided, ironically, it stayed dry.

The Zodiac stood out amongst the assorted Prefects and Morris Minors, Jay noted snobbishly, and he wasn't at all frustrated when it took some time to organise the gear – and the hardtack their dad had assembled in lieu of sandwiches. He surreptitiously garnered a few envious glances from other youngsters; then they were off out of the car park and back along the gated path towards Mill Gill. It would have been more direct to go up from the Hotel but Raymond wanted to reconnoitre a new route on Middlefell Buttress: 'It's reckoned to be one of the hardest lines on the crag,' he explained. 'It was only put up a couple of months back by two mates of mine. It's called Mendes traverse. It's Hard VS,' he added. The Armstrong boys looked completely blank; but Jay knew what his dad meant. After the scrambly grades of Easy and Moderate, rock climbs were graded Diff (for Difficult), V Diff, Severe and Very Severe. He remembered his dad telling him they'd recently started adding 'Hard' to VS in the Lakes (although in Wales, apparently, they'd had that grade and an even harder one – Extreme – for about ten years now). He didn't feel like explaining though and his father went on: 'There, look, at the right-hand end of the face. See that groove with a holly in it. You start up there, I think, and then traverse left. The crux is that flake in the middle, it's supposed to be really dodgy.'

Their own traverse eastwards into Mill Gill was far less demanding and they were soon scrambling up the bed of the unusually dry stream until, suddenly, they broached a low ridge and there it was: the shimmering blue Stickle Tarn across which Pavey Ark rose like a brooding black whale-crag. Their dad pointed out a major line – another traverse rising steadily from right base to left skyline – Jack's Rake. 'It's not a rock climb. It's a tough scramble, though. We'll see how you go on through the week and maybe give it a go before we head north.' Jay knew he meant just Chris and him as the Armstrongs would be gone by then. And in any case, they were much less experienced and he doubted either of them could manage it.

'Stickle Tarn's about 1,500 feet, so we've around 900 to go. You boys ok?' The question appeared to be aimed at him and Malc but since Jay had already climbed Harrison Stickle he suspected it was meant for the Armstrong boys. They did too cause they both nodded their heads confidently. And so it proved: the steep grass and sandstone outcrops could've been tricky in the wet but in the dry the wellies coped and the whole party arrived on the craggy summit about forty minutes later. They were all pretty puffed, but the view was superb. It was dominated by the rhino-back ridge up to Bowfell where the sheer crags gleamed wetly in the bright sun. Closer by cloud-shadows chased each other back to the precipitous face of Pavey Ark. Yeah, thought Jay we'll do that an all. But for now he was pleasantly tired. Like the rest of them, it seemed, as they slumped contentedly on the angled, sheep-cropped sward of the summit.

'Well done everyone! Who'd like some mint cake and raisins?' Then when they'd all tucked in: 'You can see Pike O' Stickle. Just over there, look. It's only half-a-mile away: take about ten minutes. Then if you're all up for it there's a scree run which'll get us down to Mickleden in double-quick time. It's steep, though; see what you think when we get there.'

The summit of the second pike was a perfect dome reached only after a rocky ascent. The drops to the south were precipitous and Raymond could tell that neither Hugh nor Malc fancied the scree run. Nor were their fashionable wellies suitable for the rough, loose rock. On the other hand his own two, he knew, were itching to plunge down the vertiginous gully and doubtless see just how quickly they could be in Mickleden 1,900 feet below. He settled on a compromise: 'why don't the three of us head along to Troughton Beck and follow the zigzags down to the valley, whilst you two take the stone shoot?' Two relieved faces and two excited ones told him he'd got it right. 'You two'll be down first, so you can stroll along and rendezvous.'

Half an hour later they all met up on the smooth green swath of Mickleden, Jay bubbling over with the triumph that it had taken him and Chris just eight minutes to 'rorse down the scree run,' whilst the Armstrong boys were equally relieved to have completed the climb without mishap. The reward for all was the promise that the following day they would tackle Coniston Old Man.

Twenty-One

Margaret Jackson was nearly two years older than Jill. Everyone called her Marge. Jill met her at the Tunnel Club. She was on an errand to her mam and there was Marge, washing glasses in the kitchen. They got talking whilst Jill waited for her mam's shift to end. Jill took to her straight away and she was dead chuffed when Marge asked if she wanted to meet up outside the coffee bar that Friday. They'd got on so well Jill was invited round the following weekend when they'd 'have the place to worsels!' They seemed to be kindred spirits and it wasn't long before Jill had a standing invitation.

Marge was very smart for her age – too much so according to some of the old ducks who warned: 'too sharp for her own good that one; she'll get herself into trouble one of these days!' Jill didn't know what sort of trouble they meant but she guessed it had something to do with boys. They were usually trouble, if *her* brothers were anything to go by.

Marge wasn't just bright, she was an early developer physically as well, and along with Liz, had been the first of Jill's friends to wear a bra. Very proud of it she was; although since it was still for Sunday best, most of the time she just wore a cotton vest. One afternoon when she and Jill were alone in Marge's front room she enquired archly, 'D'you wanna see 'em, hinny?' And without waiting for a response, she unbuttoned her blouse and pulled up her vest. Jill gazed at her friend's nascent breasts, vaguely comparing them to Liz's. They were smaller, she reckoned. 'You can touch 'em if you like; if you scratch the ends it makes the nipps grow. It's nice.' Jill was shy. Apart from the time down at Cullercoats she hadn't touched anyone else's body. But Marge grabbed her hand and rubbed her middle fingers over her nipples. Sure enough they soon became stiff and Marge sighed slightly muttering to her friend, 'divn't stop, pet, it's lovely...'

However, before either of them could get carried away there was a loud crash from the front door as Marge's elder brother Carr arrived home. Reluctantly Marge pushed Jill's fingers away, pulled down her vest and began rapidly to do up her buttons. Unfortunately, Carr barged in before she'd finished and swiftly taking in the prospect of his little sister with her blouse half undone grinned impishly: 'Just up to a bit of titting, eh sis? Why man it's wicked at your age!'

Marge was unfazed and merely rejoined, 'sod off, Carr, it's nowt to what you get up to,' which puzzled Jill who made a mental note to ask her friend to explain at an early opportunity.

Jill knew about willies, of course – bath time at Bewicke Street had meant the copper filled to the brim with steaming water and each sibling in turn plunging in before it could get cold. So she was used to seeing her brothers naked and thought no more about it other than that they were different from her 'down there.' But that wasn't what Marge was talking about.

Mr Jackson was a foreman at Swann's and the family had recently been able to afford a better house than the end-terrace they'd lived in since Marge was born. So they'd moved to a semi on St Paul's Road where the children had their own bedrooms. Jill was very envious but it was nice to mess about in Marge's bedroom or 'den' as she called it. One Saturday both girls were up there dressed in their weekend 'uniform' – bright shirts and equally lurid Capri pants from the market in Shields. They were sprawled across her bed and had been talking about boys they knew and what a pain their brothers were. Jill had tried to sound grown-up by bringing up the bathing arrangements but Marge countered, 'Nah, I'm not talking about a willy like you've seen at bath time; I'm talking about when it changes.' Marge glanced at her friend's expression and noting it was suitably puzzled went on, 'Yeah, like our Carr's. He's got a dirty magazine under his mattress and when he thinks no one's about he gets it out. Not to read, mind, just to look at the pictures. One Saturday a bit past when he thought I'd gone to help our mam on the stall I noticed his door were slightly ajar. I crept up, parked meself on the landing and spied through the gap.' And there Marge paused keen to assess what effect she was having on her younger friend.

Jill was dry-mouthed in anticipation: 'What yer stopped for, Marge?' she blurted. 'Go on. What happened then?'

'Well then I saw him,' said Marge, lowering her voice conspiratorially even though no one else was around. 'He were sitting up in bed with just his jeans on and no shirt looking at his Playboy magazine. He admitted later he'd pinched it from our dad's stash. It felt funny watching him, but exciting too cause I knew I shouldn't be. But then, if he did catch me what could he do? I'd already planned to say I'd tell Mam and I didn't think he'd want that so I figured he wouldn't do owt. Anyway, I wasn't gonna get caught cause no one else was in and Carr looked far too interested in what he was doing to notice me. So long as I kept quiet.'

'So what next?' interrupted Jill, her attention hooked on Marge's suspended words.

'Howay, pet, I'm coming to the good bit. He stopped turning the pages when he reached the picture in the middle – the centrefold, it's called,' explained Marge knowingly. 'Then he propped the magazine up so he could hold it with just one hand and undid his belt with the other. He'd got white boxers on underneath and you could see the bulge inside them. I sort of knew what he was going to do cause Christine Anderson – y'know, my cousin who's in the fourth year now – told me she'd seen her brother Don "tossing off". She didn't go into any detail mind, so she could've been making it up. Anyway, he held the magazine in one hand and started stroking his willy through his boxers with the other. (Except Carr says it's not a willy – they're for kids – all the lads call it a cock.) It were weird cause as he seemed to be getting excited, I was too. I was holding my breath to see what he did next, then when I couldn't hold it any longer it would come out in a big pant which I was afraid he'd hear. And another thing, I could feel myself getting flushed like what Carr was up to was making me hot, too!'

Jill shoved her friend in the shoulder impatiently, 'So what *was* he getting up to?' she enquired, half innocently, but sensing that her friend was getting to the 'good bit.' She also noticed that Marge seemed to be a bit flushed herself, though it wasn't specially hot in the den. So she asked as casually as she could: 'Is that how it's making you feel now, Marge? Hot? Cause you're going a bit red in the face.'

'Yes, hinny, it is,' and pausing, she added teasingly, 'you know it is, you little madam!' Then, smiling at her friend, Marge did her blouse trick. 'Time for some titting, pet,' she murmured, as she undid the buttons revealing that this time she didn't have a vest on but was naked under the vivid yellow shirt. Jill wondered whether she'd forgotten to put her vest on when she got up. 'D'ye not think they're getting bigger?' she enquired, running her hands underneath them and arching her back so that her boobs showed to best effect. Then, as she resumed her story, Marge began almost absent-mindedly stroking her nipples with her thumbs.

'Now,' she crooned, 'where was I up to? Oh yeah: *What Carr-ty Did Next*,' she giggled. 'Well it was pretty peppy, I can tell you.' And still holding her nipples between her thumbs and forefingers, she rolled over onto her tummy. 'And it really did make me hot watching him – just like now, telling you about it,' she confided. She lifted her hips and wriggled into a more comfortable position.

'Yeah, but what *was* it he did?' asked Jill impatiently, worried that Marge was deliberately spinning her account out and anxious lest her friend suddenly curtailed the story and announced: nothing, she was just making it up!

'He tossed himself off,' blurted out Marge, as if that were an end of it.

'Whaddya mean "he tossed himself off"?'

'Ooh, yer want the gory details do you, little minx? Well okay then... He'd been stroking himself through his boxers, right. But then he undid his buttons, stuck his hand inside and pulled out his cock. It weren't owt like yer willy-at-bath-time. It were long and stiff and it shone. Bright red, and purple. I nearly gave meself away, but he must've been too far gone to notice and he were breathing aall hoarse like...'

Marge was dying to take her Capris off but she didn't want to alarm her friend. So she just kneaded the bedclothes rhythmically and returned to the culmination of her tale. 'He were panting now, and I figured he was close to 'coming,' as Christine calls it. I didn't know about him but I reckoned I might be gonna come as well cause I had a lovely feeling up here where I'd been rubbing meself against the door jamb.'

'So what happened then? Did the nice feeling carry on?' But before Marge could continue, Jill added, 'Is it happening now? Yer know...that feeling?'

'Hmm, yeah,' murmured Marge, which prompted Jill to inquire why she didn't rub herself then? 'Yeah, if thass alreet. Yeah...'

'So when you stuck yer hand down yer jarmies what did yer thingy feel like?'

'Well it were getting moist – yer know like a bit wet.'

'So first yer thingy gets moist, then it gets wet. Is that reet?' And when Marge nodded breathlessly, Jill persisted: 'So is it moist now? Or wet?'

'Oh, it's wet alreet,' gasped Marge. 'Why pet, it's that wet me knickers are soaked,' she exclaimed, and was delighted to hear Jill ask to see. 'Ooh, hinny,' she sighed, gripping Jill's hand firmly in her own and guiding it between her legs: 'There! Are they soaking, or what!'

Jill felt them tentatively. Blimey! If Marge's knickers were that wet, what was her thingy like? She soon found out as Marge pulled up her waistband and slid both their hands inside, delighted when Jill began to rub her fingers up and down without even asking: 'Oh, strewth, hin...go on...thass brill.'

Jill was chuffed. She'd done the right thing without needing to be told. Maybe she were cut out for this – what had Christine called it – yeah, frigging. Maybe she were a natural. P'raps that meant she'd be good at coming herself. That'd be the big test. But first she had to make sure she made a good job of helping Marge. She seemed to be doing okay so far. Marge was panting, and her bum was writhing around on the bedspread so it was hard to keep rubbing her properly. But that didn't seem to matter as her friend were getting that carried away Jill figured she must be close. She wondered briefly how she'd know...

But she needn't've worried. Jill had been so preoccupied with her own thoughts she'd unconsciously rubbed her friend faster and faster and Marge, inflamed by the novelty of their situation and unprepared for Jill's vigorous enthusiasm was on the brink in no time. All thoughts of schooling Jill evaporated under the latter's frenzied onslaught. She came in a huge rush and subsided on the counterpane.

Twenty-Two

The Old Man day dawned bright and Jay was in his element on the trip round to Coniston. They'd crossed Skelwith Bridge and passed the turn to Tarn Hows. Jay was sitting between Malc and Hugh with an Ordnance Survey 'Map of The Lake District' unfurled on his knees. Instead of the usual cream-and-red cover and OS insignia with the name and number of the sheet and its title ('like "Sheet 126 Norwich", he'd explained') this was a 'Tourist Map' and had a sepia photo of Loweswater on the front 'by Mr Alfred Furness.' And it cost four-and-six net instead of the regular three shillings. 'This map's on a scale of One Inch to One Mile – that's 63,360 inches,' explained Jay patronisingly, hoping that they wouldn't know what he was talking about, but they'd still be impressed – well Malc, anyway, it didn't matter what Hugh thought, he was Chris's friend. 'We're here look – on the A593 just between Holme Fell and Tarn Hows. In a minute we'll be able to see Coniston Water. That's where Arthur Ransome set *Swallows and Amazons*, though some of the books describe the Broads. You know, near where we live in Norfolk.'

Sometimes even Raymond wondered where his younger son acquired his esoterica as they didn't have any Ransome at home. But Jay was in full flight now: 'and it's where Malcolm Campbell set the world water speed record just before the War – 141 MPH. His son Donald's trying to do 300 though,' he added, before resuming Ransome. 'The second book, *Swallowdale*, has got loads about the Old Man in. Only he calls it Kanchenjunga to disguise it. Bit of a funny disguise, if you ask me. The Old Man's 2,633 feet and Kanchenjunga's 28,168. It's the third highest mountain in the world. It was only climbed five years ago: by Band and Brown. Is that the same Brown who's done all those hard routes in Wales, Dad?'

His father nodded, 'the very same. He and his mate Don Whillans. They're the two best rock climbers in the world. They don't only climb in Wales though. Where we were yesterday, Mill Gill – if you go up the next stream along, White Ghyll, Brown put up two of the hardest routes in Langdale there. "Laugh Not" and "Eliminot" he called them – both Extremes! But don't worry, we're not going to be doing anything like that today,' he reassured them, lest the Armstrong boys be put off before they'd even started.

He need've had no concerns about the ascent, however. After a hard slog up the steep, winding slate path, with a brief stop to view Low Water and the beetling, water-streaked slabs of Buckbarrow Crag, the party reached the summit in good order, though in the company of a large party of Boy Scouts, much to Jay's disgust. Like his latest hero, Alfred Wainwright, Jay preferred solitude. Wainwright was in the middle of producing *A Pictorial Guide to the Lakeland Fells* and Jay had just acquired his latest prize *Book Four: The Southern Fells*, which had only come out a few months earlier. Twelve and sixpence it cost. The reward was because he'd not made any fuss when Chris had been bought a brand new pair of leather climbing boots: 'Scafells.' Jay reckoned it was pretty big of him considering they cost six pounds ten!

He was pleased to see that Wainwright recognised Coniston Old man as important. Its chapter had eighteen pages – more than Scafell, though fewer than Bowfell and the Crinkles. Very properly Scafell Pike had the most – a stonking thirty pages. He'd read the whole Coniston chapter the previous evening and had memorised large chunks – about the route they'd taken from Coniston, the Coppermines and, especially 'the Summit.' This last had two whole pages devoted to it and at the top of the first was one of Wainwright's trademark drawings of the summit itself. He'd smiled when he'd seen the two sets of figures – tourists gawping at Blackpool Tower and a bunch of Boy Scouts – but now he remembered the "Solitary fell-walker...looking north to the hills." Unobtrusively, to make sure he wasn't accompanied Jay detached himself from the others and took up station where he calculated the figure in the drawing had been. He didn't recognise most of the peaks but solemnly noted for his journal the ones he did – Crinkle Crags and Bowfell quite close, and the distinctive shapes of Skiddaw and Blencathra way up to the north.

The following day the Armstrong boys went home with their father, whilst the Finchers headed north. No time for Jack's Rake on this outing. They were to camp just south of Oban on the shores of Loch Nell. Jay's memory of that leg of the trip was jaundiced. They broke down near Dumbarton and had to be rescued by the AA; he was carsick; and when they did finally pitch camp on the dusky shoreline they were eaten alive by midges.

Next morning was better, though, as Jay awoke to early-morning sun streaming in through the tent flaps with a sparkling blue loch just a few paces away. From the gravel outside came the aroma of sizzling bacon grill. Whilst that cooked he swiftly checked out their neighbours. There was only one other tent and it was occupied by a pair of Brummies who were preparing a whopping-great breakfast: 'chips-chops-sausages-fried bread-fried-eggs-peas-and-trout' they informed Jay heartily, stirring inchoate memories of Ratty's picnic.

Then onwards! To the ferry from the Kyle of Lochalsh across a choppy sound to the Isle of Skye. Once there they marvelled at the precipitous Cuillin Hills and headed north through the capital, Portree, picking up the A856 to the Trotternish Peninsular and their destination: Uig. The majestic sweep of the Bay came into view and Raymond guided the Zodiac carefully down the narrow track, past the church and Youth Hostel and over the River Ryd to 'Duntulm,' their home for the next ten days. It was a picturesque, whitewashed fisherman's cottage with two small bedrooms belonging to one Mrs McKilmer. The boys weren't used to sharing but would doubtless manage. Mr McKilmer had been lost at sea a decade since and she'd never remarried. But she was a cheerful soul, and a 'creature of habit,' as their mother would've dubbed her. The boys soon learned to conceal their mirth when for the third breakfast running she announced, 'I've made you some rhubarb jam, by way of a change.' They had rhubarb jam every morning and developed such a taste for it that they demanded their mother make some with the sticks that grew by the side of the path through the middle of the kitchen garden. (True to her word Muriel was reclaiming it bit-by-bit!)

The cottage was perfectly situated for exploring the upper reaches of the island. The first three days were spent touring the ruins of Duntulm Castle; on the craggy sea-cliffs round the northernmost tip of Trotternish; and down to Flodigarry where, as their father explained, the road needed repairing most years as the landslip of the Quiraing was still moving thereabouts. On the second excursion they parked the Zodiac on a grassy lay-by near Staffin Youth Hostel and set off up a gently-rising path across the moor in search of the Prison. Set amidst a bizarre lunar landscape was the rocky peak that Raymond had decreed would be a useful warm-up for sterner tests farther south in the Cuillins. It was quite a scramble, but caused them no problem. Then they headed north past the 120-foot high Needle to the Table itself, which was a flat springy-turfed plateau that had slipped down from the summit. Across the Sound of Raasay they could see the Torridon Hills dominated by Liathach which was apparently 3,456 feet: really easy to remember and higher than anything in England, thought Jay. It attracted his father's attention as it was on his target list for the following summer when he was due to lead a Ministry of Education mountaineering course to the area. 'Pretty good job, you've got, Dad,' Chris remarked, 'getting paid to climb mountains!' Their father laughed appreciatively.

The third expedition was to The Storr whose shattered, basaltic Old Man poked up like a skeletal finger, minatory in the misty distance.

And then the rain set in.

It was a whole week before it relented. Between trips to Portree and Dunvegan Castle their dad taught them poker – 'it'll come in handy, you'll see.' Then just one fine day remained to venture into the Cuillins. Raymond would've liked to give the boys some practice on the gentler slopes of the Red Cuillin before venturing onto the vertiginous gabbro of the black peaks. But there wasn't enough time and all three were set on Sgurr Nan Gillean – Gaelic for 'Mountain of the young men.' Just five feet higher than Scafell, at 3,167, the peak had a reputation for verticality and exposure. Even the 'Tourist Route' was for tourists only in the sense that it didn't require ropes and rock climbing.

They'd driven south from Uig the evening before and pitched camp – a three-man ridge, courtesy of the MOE's Camping Panel – in a field near the Sligachan Hotel, their father having promised them a stay there the following night on the successful completion of the Gillean. They struck camp and crossed the burn which led to the heathery slopes of the moorland before the ascent proper. The Pinnacle Ridge loomed above them, a classic rock climb: '1800 foot Diff,' advised their dad, 'too tall an order for today, even if we had the kit; but maybe next time, eh? No, we go over the Allt Dearg Beag – the stream straight ahead – and then all the way up the Coire Riabhaich. That's the massive corrie above us – you know, what they call a cwm in Wales. After that the hard collar work really starts!'

For nearly two hours they climbed steadily, speaking little, conserving their energy, until they reached the foot of the peak where the final ascent began. 'Don't be afraid to use your hands whenever you need to, boys. Watch out for the gabbro though. It's great rock but it's really abrasive.' They paused, panting, at the foot of the steep wall, guarding the last 100 feet or so. But wisely their dad pushed on, before either boy – and he anticipated it might be Chris – could get too anxious contemplating what lay ahead. Within minutes they were perched side by side on the summit. It was so isolated that they couldn't see any part of the buttresses below and the sense of exposure was immense.

It was a stunning vista. To the north reared up the Knight's Peak on the Pinnacle Ridge and beyond it the Skye coastline stretching from Loch Sligachan to the furthest tip of Trotternish. 'Look, that's The Storr, intit?' spotted Jay excitedly. To the west and south the Cuillin Ridge curved away to Sgurr Alasdair, the highest point at 3,251 feet; whilst to the east the red, hippopotamus bulk of Marsco and Glamaig dominated the skyline.

Stunning! But they still had to get down!

The trickiest part of the descent was near the summit, but twenty-minutes swift though circumspect manoeuvring overcame the worst of it. Thereafter, they were making steady progress over the sharp, black gabbro until Jay spotted the eagle. His exclamation distracted his brother who, screwing his eyes up against the sun behind the swooping wings lost his footing and fell from the knife-edge ridge. His anguished cry of 'Shi…ii…t!!' was the only warning they had before the steep slab which Chris had been traversing lay ominously empty. Fearing the worst they peered over the edge of the abyss. With enormous good fortune, Chris had slithered down to a sloping ledge maybe twelve feet below. But his body was contorted and it wasn't clear how badly hurt he was.

'You okay, son?' Raymond called down.

'Yeah, think so. Aah! Bugger! My ankle!'

'Right. Stay still. Don't look down. Keep looking at me.'

Raymond wasted no time in handing the rucksack to Jay and clambering cautiously down to his elder son's side. Hauling him upright, as they both tried not to gaze into the void, he shoved him precariously back up to the ridge where Jay helped pull him unsteadily onto it. He was paper-white and badly shaken; his left ankle was starting to swell alarmingly. From the perilous stance on the ridge they shuffled down to the sanctuary of a partially enclosed platform about forty feet below.

'Unlace his boot and get his sock down,' instructed their dad, producing a length of crepe bandage and a tube of ointment from his bag. 'Arnica montana, it'll help reduce the swelling as well as the pain once we've got you strapped up.' Chris was soon expertly bandaged and ready to resume the still-lengthy descent. Fortified by three aspirins washed down by the now tepid thermos tea, he set off, supported by Raymond with Jay revelling in his role of pathfinder and obstacle-spotter. After a few cautious minutes pointing out particularly tricky sections, it occurred to

Jay that the fall was probably his fault. 'Sorry 'bout the shoutin out. Made you fall, didn't it.'

'Nah! It was my own fault. Shoulda been more careful.'

'Does it hurt much?'

'Not too bad,' Chris reassured him cheerfully, 'I'll live!'

The ascent of a couple of hours in the early-morning cool now took twice as long to descend, with their dad doing most of the crutch-work and Jay supporting from time to time The sun had already sunk below the Pinnacle Ridge as they made their way wearily across the intervening heather-moor to the Sligachan Hotel. Thank goodness he'd had the foresight to book them in for the night, thought Raymond gratefully. Chris limped painfully upstairs to their bunk-room; whilst Jay was tired but thoroughly content. He'd conquered the mountain of the young men and helped rescue his big brother into the bargain.

Good day's work, eh...

Twenty-Three

At first it had seemed strange, learning subjects with different teachers and having to move to *their* classrooms. Maybe it was part of growing up – you had to learn the world didn't revolve around you as it used to at primary school. There, it seemed like you were at the heart of things. Here it was the other way round. It didn't matter that much as most of the teachers were okay and some were dead keen on their subjects. Not Miss Sharples, though. She was a sour-faced spinster and, unfortunately, she taught English, Jill's favourite subject. Miss Sharples acted like she was only there under sufferance and English was just a discipline. And you weren't supposed to enjoy discipline.

To be fair, it wasn't only Jill; she didn't seem to like any of her pupils. But she appeared to positively resent Jill's enthusiasm, along with the girl's continued pilgrimage to Ferndale Avenue. And if Jill had devoured not just the set book by, say, Eric Leyland, but the rest of the series as well it seemed to incense her. Just published was *Flame and the League of Fire*, and for once Miss Sharples seemed proud of securing thirty-five copies for the class. Intent on mocking Jill's avid reading habits she announced, 'You'll enjoy this Year One,' and then added sarcastically, 'though I expect you know Leyland from your precious library, Walker. No doubt you've read *Flame Takes Command* already.'

'Yes, Miss, smiled Jill proudly, and falling headlong into her teacher's trap, she added. 'And *Flame Sets the Pace* and *Flame of the Sahara*.'

'Hmm, quite the Miss-Smarty-Pants aren't we!' she remarked snidely, to a few titters from Jill's detractors. Jill compressed her lips sensing Miss Sharples had succeeded in showing her up in front of her classmates. If there was one thing her friends disliked about Jill, it was her being a bit of a know-all. She vowed to keep quiet in future. It was one thing remembering Miss Menzies's compliment in private, quite another demonstrating it in public.

But Miss Sharples's continued sniping failed to extinguish Jill's love of books. Nor did it curtail her visits to Ferndale Avenue. She'd heard her English teacher refer to the lit twins as a 'pair of dykes,' but since she neither knew what it meant nor set much store by Miss Sharples' opinions, it didn't dissuade her. She was far more impressed by the lit twins' scholarship – especially that of Miss Lambton, who seemed to know not just about the stories themselves but also loads about their authors.

One Saturday morning towards the end of her first year at Marsden's, Jill was cloistered in the stockroom with Miss Lambton. She was unpacking a stout box full of adventure tales, principally by Enid Blyton, who Jill had heard of, and Will Scott, who she hadn't. 'Not to be confused with Will Scott, the footballer,' laughed Miss Lambton. 'He used to play for South Shields; born in Willington Quay, just down from where you live. The *author* Will Scott came from Leeds. You enjoyed Enid Blyton's *Secret 7* series, didn't you? Well Scott's written a similar set called *The Cherrys*.' The librarian slit the Sellotape on a small cardboard box and tipped out a pile of brightly-coloured hardback novels. The design looked familiar and her guru, noticing Jill's interest, remarked, 'You'll find lots of similarities, pet. They're illustrated by Lillian Buchanan – she did the drawings for Enid Blyton as well. With your penchant for the briny you could start with this one,' and she held out a copy of *The Cherrys by the Sea*. 'It's one of his early ones so if you like it you could try the *Galleon* next, and then *Indoor Island*. And here, look, this'll remind you of your Farnes trip; it's called *The Cherrys' Mystery Holiday*.'

So Jill trouped off with the four books in a brown-paper-bag and was entertained by Capt. Cherry for the rest of term. She read them at home and didn't mention them at school. She'd like to have told Liz about her latest find, but her one-time tutor had lost interest in literature. She was fourteen now, and seeing a lad in her year. Apparently boys were more exciting than books; a view shared by Marge.

Jill never discovered why Marge had to go. She announced suddenly that she was going to live with her aunt in Liverpool, but not before they'd promised to keep in touch and sworn never to divulge their secret. There'd been an initial exchange of letters whilst Marge was living in somewhere called Toxteth but after she'd moved across the city to Bootle one of Jill's came back 'Returned to Sender: not known at this address.'

The loss of both mentors might have crushed the spirit of a weaker-willed youngster, but Jill was resilient. She had to be – with her mam, who had no time for her, always favouring her brothers.

Jill had very different relationships with them. The elder, Rob, she'd idolised as a kid until the incident with the poker almost put her left eye out. Rob swore it was an accident, that he was just pretending to be Errol

Flynn, and she'd got in the way. But Jill wasn't convinced and afterwards they tended to be a bit wary of each other. Her little brother, Al, adored her and, in the frequent absences of their mother, Jill looked after him. She would get him ready for school, walk with him in the mornings, look out for him when they'd finished, and prepare his tea. Although Rob now had his own room, the two youngsters had to share the box room, where the three-quarter bed took up almost all the space.

Usually Al, nearly two years younger, would go up first; occasionally they'd go together. This seemed to be happening more frequently of late. Jill overheard her mam remarking on it one evening she was actually there and not working down the Club. 'George, how long's our Jill been going up to bed with Al? You don't think it's time we separated those two do you?'

And she'd been relieved to hear her dad respond dismissively, 'Don't be daft, Mary. They're just kids. Besides, where would we put 'em?'

Rob had left school and was apprenticed at Brydons' rope works. He was nearly sixteen and spent every spare hour down the pool. He'd always been a good swimmer but latterly under Mr Gibson's iron discipline he'd improved dramatically. He was now well past the stage where other gala entrants, on hearing, 'Rob Walker's racing, mind,' would drop out. He'd been swimming for Northumberland for some months and there was talk of an Olympic trial. He'd been selected for a training camp that August. Fortunately most of the trip to Blackpool where they had an Olympic-sized facility coincided with the holiday shutdown and the three days that didn't were waived by his supervisor: 'Yer'll do us proud, lad. You get yersel chose!'

Their coach had picked up in Newcastle, in Whitley Bay and in Shields and by the time it arrived in Wallsend quite a crowd had gathered to see Rob off. Not their mam – she was too busy at work – but the rest of the family, several aunts, uncles and cousins and a few of the lads from the works. They might not be close, but Jill was prouder of her brother that morning than she'd ever been.

When the elation of waving him off had dissipated, however, she felt flat, almost downcast. There was no one to share her gloom so she took herself off on a walk. After an hour wandering around the drizzle-damp streets and down the sodden burn, she found herself near the station and, on a whim, boarded the next train to Tynemouth.

She didn't feel sorry for herself, but she couldn't help sighing nostalgically as she trudged past the wristband machine and down Front Street. She reached the Plaza and took a peek in the foyer for old-time's sake. The Laughing Clown had disappeared and she wasn't in slot-machine mode so she meandered along until she reached Cullercoats. It was mizzling and her jeans and jumper were getting all soggy; but the weather mirrored her dejection and she took little notice. The bay was deserted and she sat on the low rocks letting the foam roll over her sandals. Her friendships with Liz and with Marge flooded her mind and she couldn't help wondering why she only seemed to make friends with girls older than her. Maybe it was the flipside of being 'bright' – you frightened off your peers. P'raps it was better to be a bit thick and have loadsa mates, like Rob.

Her reverie was shattered by a barrage of screeches that sounded like Rob's bike when he hadn't oiled it properly. Jill looked up just in time to clock a gaggle of pickies. There seemed to be several different sorts and she vaguely remembered from her trip to the Farnes that the ones with the bright red bills and feet were terns. Arctic Terns. And the ones with the plain black heads were a different type. Summat to do with bread, she recalled, struggling to recollect what Jamie Horton had told her. Then she had it. Yeah: Sandwich Terns. Her pleasure at recognising them was short-lived. They dive-bombed her curly hair and threatened to scratch her face. Bummer, she cried: I thought it was only tourists they attacked when they got too close to their nests. Having no stick to fend them off she whirled her arms like a windmill and, as quickly as they'd descended the sea-swallows sheered off.

Maybe they were angry? P'raps they'd bin just about to set off for Africa and she'd disturbed their preparations? Jamie had explained the terns travelled great distances. One had been ringed in Greenland and was found dead in a harbour in South Africa less than three months later. So it'd flown nearly 9,000 miles. Jill wondered whether they got separated from their friends – like her and Liz. And Marge. Then, sensing her melancholy was getting the better of her, she murmured grimly, 'Hey, just give o'er. Yer not a bairn any more, Jill Walker and don't you forget it.'

She shook off the accumulated droplets, and her mood, and set off back to the station with an expression of fierce determination.

Twenty-Four

Jay had seen *The Vikings* at the cinema in Bungay the year before. The Mayfair was their local flea-pit. Entrance was one and six except for the back four rows which comprised the 'three-and-sixpenny doubles' with room enough for two and no arm-rest in between. Jay didn't have three and six to spare and wouldn't've wasted it on a double seat if he had. Why would you spend that much being cramped by some girl snuggling up to you spoiling your view and probably interrupting all the best bits? Mind you, Chris reckoned they were all right. He'd overheard him telling his mate, Humph, about the time he'd taken Monica Johnson to see *Psycho*, calculating that she'd be dead scared and want to be cuddled. Chris had regaled his all-ears mate with the success of this ploy, but Jay had got bored and wandered off. He stuck to the 'one-and-sixpennies.'

Besides, what would a girl make of a good, gory battle? Jay enjoyed those scenes in *The Vikings*, but his favourite was the one where Einar, played by Kirk Douglas, led the assault on the English castle. They'd hauled up the drawbridge but the Viking warriors ran forward one-by-one and hurled their axes into the wooden door until they formed a ladder all the way up. Einar had climbed up the axes, even though one came loose and he nearly fell to his death, and scaling the drawbridge which he promptly let down, enabled his compatriots to swarm into the castle. Victorious!

Merton still came up to The Lodge occasionally, and when he did 'Vikings' was their usual game. At the back of the house, en route to the stable yard, was the woodshed. It was a large square outhouse with an ill-fitting but solid oak door at one side and a broad, windowless, waist-high opening at the other. Inside were heaps of beech and oak logs – some already cut for the fires – and a trestle bench where Raymond and Buck used to lay the branches which they sawed up with the cross-cut. Sometimes he'd help his dad, or occasionally his brother, but he wasn't supposed to be in the shed on his own. In addition to the cross-cut there were two Bushmans with curved, tubular-metal handles, one red the other green. Jay preferred the green one – it was easier to cut with – and besides green was *his* colour, Chris long since having bagged blue. Sometimes the logs were too big to cut and had to be split first. Buck would knock a couple of iron wedges into the log and then, with a seven-pound hammer, split it right down the middle. Finally, there was an assortment of axes – two hand adzes, a machete and a large ash-handled splitting axe.

The game began when Jay roared, 'The favourite weapon of a Viking was his axe,' and they each grabbed one of the adzes. Jay always had first go which meant Mert leapt through the window and was pursued out through the stable yard, under the entrance arch and back around to the woodhouse. He had to hare back into the shed and get the door shut before Jay hurled his axe into it. Then they'd repeat the process but this time with Merton getting to play Einar. Jay always felt Mert made a poor Einar. His battle cry was unconvincing and his throw unskilled so that half the time his axe fell to the ground, unlike Jay's which usually stood proudly quivering in the increasingly-scarred oak door. If your axe fell out you forfeited a go; so frequently Jay would get two or three throws in succession. Consequently, he grew more accurate and stronger, and enjoyed the game more. Mert, on the other hand, seemed to get fed up with it after a while and would suggest playing something else like 'Army.'

Jay had nothing against Army – he had built up an enviable collection of camouflaged vehicles which they would arrange in rival forces swarming over the pea-gravel-hillsides of the front drive. However, rising thirteen he felt he'd outgrown Dinky toys – no matter how sophisticated their deployment – and 'Vikings' remained favourite.

It was the last weekend of the summer holidays. Jay had persuaded Merton to embark on one final rampage but his seldom-covetable prowess had faltered even as Jay's had burgeoned, resulting in Jay's Einar getting four outings in succession. His enthusiasm waxed with each chase and on the fourth attack Jay hurled his adze with such vigour that Mert had no time to slam the door. Instead, he collapsed to the ground just as the axe flew past where his head would've been, hurtled straight through the woodhouse and out of the opposite window. Ignoring his friend's whingeing, Jay was in full Norse cry when Buck emerged from the stable yard slightly redder-faced than usual and with blood streaming from a nick in his right ear. He was carrying Jay's axe. 'Maybes you need t' be a bit steadier with yer aim, Master Jay,' he remarked mildly, slipping the offending adze into his leather belt and closing the woodshed door firmly enough to indicate that the game was over for that day.

In fact, it was over for good. Jay was forbidden – on pain of pocket money – to play 'Vikings' in future. And Merton never came up to The Lodge again.

Jay became steadily more solitary. No one at school ever went to someone else's house. As far as he knew. Many of them were weekly boarders and amongst the day-boys Jay's four-mile bicycle ride to and from school each day constituted one of the shorter commutes. Most travelled by bus. A few lived in town and gathered at the caff after school. He was reluctant to join them but when it transpired that he usually had enough shillings to feed the jukebox his popularity seemed to grow proportionately. The shillings – not to mention the florins and half-crowns – came from the poker school.

Their father had been shrewd, teaching them poker whilst they waited for the skies to clear above Sgurr Nan Gillean. 'I'll teach you bridge later – it'll stand you in good stead at university – but poker's easier and it'll be more use just now.' Both boys were quick learners; Jay had the better memory. Not as good as his dad's – *he* compounded his knowledge of the odds by memorising the cards played and consequently knowing exactly which were coming up. He'd made a regular income in the RAF apparently, and had no qualms about his boys doing the same in school. Jay relished the odds. It appealed to his mathematical bent to know the statistical difference between filling an inside straight or a flush, and embellishing three-of-a-kind by a pair to make a full house. And you were playing not against the fixed odds of say a roulette wheel (not that they had one of those, although the Armstrong boys had acquired one the previous Christmas) but against the other players in the school. If you knew the odds and could remember the cards better than they did you were pretty much guaranteed to win.

Jay's poker school met on Wednesdays in the Michaelmas and Lent terms; and on Fridays as well during Trinity, when the cricket pavilion was available. In the autumn and winter they had to play wherever was 'safe.' Gambling was not expressly forbidden in the 'School Rules, 1948' but a framed table of 'Punishments' in the Library dated 1822 detailed:

Punishment	Birch strokes
1. Fighting at School	Five
12. Drinking Spiritous Liquors at School	Eight
14. Gambling or Betting at School	Four
15. Playing cards at School	Ten

The 'Pokists' as they called themselves (Jay's invention, naturally: Autolycus approved of innuendo) weren't sure whether such punishments would still be administered and they thought it most unfair that cards was singled out for the gravest retribution. But knowing their headmaster's predilection for a beating it seemed unlikely he would miss out on such an opportunity. For Jay – whose pugnacity and tendency to shout his mouth off led to regular punishment – that would merely mean burnishing his reputation as the second most-caned boy in the school. (Only Fullerton in the Upper Fifth had received more strokes and he was due to leave that year.) Other Pokists were less sanguine, however, and the fact that his treasured set of Bicycle Cards would undoubtedly be confiscated persuaded Jay not to take undue risks either. Accordingly, the safe-house moved from classroom to library to dining hall, unless Professor Hastings left the lab open, in which case the ante-room at the back provided the most favoured venue of all.

Participants varied. Usually there were five or six players. All were taught by Jay, who was the one constant, not least because they were *his* cards. Harter and Johnston were maths swots and posed the greatest challenge to Jay's hegemony; but neither possessed the temperament to beat him consistently. Harter was too timid; whilst Johnston's excitability invariably betrayed any hand above three-of-a-kind. Besides, whilst both of them gradually learned the odds – which the rest never mastered – neither of them could tell when Jay was bluffing with a king-high or when he had a straight-flush. As a result his income grew steadily, and since some of those who might have resented his success were jukebox beneficiaries no one complained.

Adam Faith, Cliff Richard (still backed by The Drifters at the beginning of the year but superseded by The Shadows during Michaelmas Term to the general approval of the Pokists), and Bobby Darin got the most plays. By the end of Lent *Running Bear* and *My Old Man's a Dustman* held sway. Jay couldn't stand the latter but had sussed that there was a correlation, no matter how tenuous, between his willingness to provide free music and continued attendance at his poker school. In any case, the fad for Lonnie Donegan would pass quickly; and sure enough Trinity brought American relief in the form of the Everley Brothers and Eddie Cochrane (though know-it-all Johnston reckoned the latter was already dead, killed in a car crash).

Jay's other, more solitary pastime was his Friday night date at the Mayfair; with a film that was, the three-and-sixpenny doubles still held no appeal. His proudly-gotten gambling gains easily paid for his cinematic addiction, along with a ten-pack of Senior Service, which he espoused partly because all the other lads smoked Woodbines and it made him feel superior, and partly because Chris had explained the senior service was the Royal Navy. (His brother had already confided in him that he intended to join the Navy, not go to university, and it gave Jay great satisfaction that he'd been told to keep it to himself!)

Whilst Cliff was travellin light and Adam Faith was enquiring what he wanted, Jay helped John Wayne sober up Dean Martin in *Rio Bravo* (released earlier that summer) and raced chariots with Charlton Heston just before Christmas. Then – a teenager at last – he managed to talk his way into the X-Certificate *A Summer Place*, bored by the psychologising but lusting after Sandra Dee's Molly with a vengeance. And by the time Ricky Valance was telling everyone how much he loved Laura, his new-found confidence had infiltrated *The Apartment*. The plot tried his patience but he sympathised with Bud Baxter's perseverance in wooing Fran Kubelik, admiring especially his card-playing prowess. Unashamedly, he incorporated Fran's final advice into many a Pokist session subsequently: 'shut up and deal,' he'd drawl.

Back at the caff The Shadows belted out *Apache*…

Twenty-Five

A single-storey, red-brick building next to St Catherine's housed the Catholic Club. On a Friday evening, however, the alliance of religion, bingo and dominoes gave way to table tennis as Father Dominic opened his doors to boys and girls aged thirteen to sixteen. A small porch led directly to what the youngsters had grandiosely christened the ballroom and the ping pong and snooker rooms were at the far end. Jill didn't care for ping pong.

It wasn't a full-sized snooker table and it only had ten red balls instead of fifteen so when you racked them you had to assemble them awkwardly in the top section of the wooden triangle. Few of the cues had tips and it was a struggle to secure a decent one, but it was good fun when you could get a game. You had to put your initials up on a slate board fixed to the wall and then, if you didn't want to watch a succession of cocky lads proclaiming their skill, wander back into the main room and check from time to time to see how many names above yours were now crossed out. Occasionally, someone would try and cheat but mostly it worked okay and if you'd only just joined the club and didn't know many people it was a way of meeting someone new – the winner of the previous game. At first, Jill only ever got one game at a time but as her skill improved she was soon able to hold her own with quite a few of the lads. None of the other girls played, so initially she was the object of both disbelief and scorn. This morphed into muted respect as she won more and more frequently.

On their own most of the lads were all right. Some crowed a bit when they won, others sulked when they lost. But they talked to you (a bit) as if you were a real person – provided, of course, you were fluent in footie. With two brothers and a Magpie-mad father Jill was. And recently she'd been allowed to go to St James' with her dad and stand on the partly-covered terraces at the Leazes End.

It was her thirteenth birthday treat and the Black and Whites were playing Fulham. Her dad had bought her a programme and she'd devoured it, absorbing the potted history of the club from the time when Newcastle East End and Newcastle West End had amalgamated in 1892 to the development of the major stands which now gave it a capacity of 60,000. Jill had no idea how many were in the crowd that day but it was more people than she'd ever seen. The first time their line surged forward when Newcastle scored they carried her down six or seven rows and back again, but she'd held tight to her dad's hand and he'd assured her she was quite safe. Just as well, she reflected, cause it happened six more times as the Magpies beat Fulham 7–2!

George proclaimed he was 'over the moon' and promptly extended the birthday treat to a visit to the Town Moor Fair. It wasn't the main fair – the Hoppings were held the last week in June – but some of the smaller rides and freak shows had carried on that summer so they spent a happy, riotous hour together before the call of the pint grew too strong and they repaired to the Strawberry. It seemed a funny name for a pub but apparently it came from the strawberry gardens that the St Bartholomew nuns tended. According to her dad – a good Catholic when it came to the tenets that mattered – they'd been threatened with excommunication (which sounded a bit like being banished by Miss Sharples) but still carried on selling strawberry wine and kept their nunnery going until Victorian times. Jill loved it when her dad told her things and although at the time she wondered which conversation she'd be able to insert her new-won alcoholic knowledge into she knew it would come in handy at some stage. 'Alcoholic' was right, too. God knows what her mam would say! Her dad had six large bottles of Newcastle Brown and, after the third of them he bought her a half of cider each time. A merry pair boarded the North Shields railway and although her dad remembered to take the Riverside Branch he'd nodded off by the time they reached Willington Quay so they ended up at Percy Main and had to walk back. Neither minded; and to cap a perfect birthday, Jill's mam was out when they teetered tipsily into the house.

Her outing stood Jill in good stead sooner than she expected and helped to cement her credentials on the snooker table. That Friday the only lad waiting for a game was Jimmy Wardle. They had three frames uninterrupted. Jimmy came from Durham and was proud of knowing the derivation of his surname: 'It means I come from Weardale and you can trace it back from the time of Magna Carta!' he boasted. In spite of her irritation at not knowing what Magna Carta was, nor what her own surname meant, Jill was impressed. However, when it transpired that he supported Sunderland and his dad had a season ticket at Roker Park she saw her chance. After all it was only two years since the Mackems had been relegated to Division Two, a fate which any good Magpies fan exulted in. Accordingly, it was Jimmy's turn to be dazzled, especially as Jill's recounting of her birthday treat could well have given him the impression that she was at St James' Park on a regular basis. This was compounded by her description of their most recent victory over Blackburn Rovers (her dad had told her all about it) which could easily have sounded like a first-hand account. Before he knew it Jimmy was two-nil down and only stayed on the table by winning the last frame just as a most objectionable lad (whom she wouldn't've wanted to play anyway) chalked his name on the challenge board. Still, he was alreet was Jimmy. For a lad.

It was just when they got in a crowd that they were stupid, decided Jill. Dance time for example. The ballroom was square and all around the outside were the chairs. They had brass frames and legs with plush crimson seats and backs: a bit like at The Pearl, except that you could move these around. The choice of tunes was determined by one of three music-monitors: older members authorised by the priest. Most of the music was to jive to, although the Twist was becoming popular recently. It had begun to catch on the year before when the B-side of Hank Ballard's single *Teardrops on your Letter* had been a hit. Mostly though, the girls still preferred to dance to rock and roll. But that was it − the *girls*. The boys just sat round the perimeter of the room looking like lemons and making puerile remarks about female movement or, worse, anatomy. The latter mostly revolved around 'tits!' which Jill, who was strikingly pretty but still not well endowed in that department, found especially galling. It didn't stop her dancing though, and she soon found she was making new friends.

'Why aye,' asserted her newest confidante, Gina, 'they're just being lads, man: stoopid!' Gina was fifteen and most definitely not modest in the 'tits' department. She knew it, too, and wore tight, low-cut sweaters which, had any of the boys had the nous to dance with her, gave a most inviting view of her beautifully-shaped breasts. Jill, not so backward in coming forward these days told her so and Gina laughed appreciatively. 'Thanks, hinnie, I'm well named then int I. Gina Lollobrigida's famous for her boobs, too; though she's getting on a bit now. She's in her thirties accordin to me mam. She says she's past it but me dad just says: "phwoar!"' Then, realising Jill was looking a bit blank she added, 'Yer know, her that made that film last year with that bald guy. Yul Brynner. *Solomon and Sheba* it were called. I saw it at The Pearl. There's an orgy in it, an' all.'

'What's an orgy?' enquired Jill, always keen to learn.

'Why man, it's when they're *aall* at it! Though you don't actually get to see that bit: just a load of sexy dancing. Yer know, like this,' and Gina swayed her hips in time to *Cathy's Clown*. When she rolled her shoulders as

117

well her boobs practically fell out of her stretched green jersey, and when Jill said as much, Gina giggled, 'Just make sure Father Dominic doesn't see us, thasall!'

'Will he tell us off?' queried Jill.

'More likely ogle us and then summon us for a talking to in private. Not so much a telling off, more a dressing-doon. Or an un-dressing-doon, if you get me meaning,' panted Gina, beginning to tire of her Lolla-gyrations. The dance petered out and they returned to their corner, Jill all agog.

'Well yer know he likes a drop. Thass not communion wine in that chalice. It's Scotch! And when he's taken a nip or two it's not your soul he's interested in, I can tell yer!'

Responding to Jill's wide-eyed attention, Gina warmed to her story. 'He called me in one time bout a month ago. Said he'd noticed me dancing a bit, yer know Sheba-like, and claimed he needed to counsel me. I should've realised there were summat up straightaway. When he ushered me in and sat me down he smelt like a distillery! At first he just talked to me, all solemn like, about "the temptations of the flesh". But being as he was the one who was getting red in the face I reckon his sermon shoulda been to hisself not me. Anyway, after a bit he stood up and walked round the back of me chair. I swear it was just so he could look down me jumper.'

'Did he do owt else?' interrupted Jill, speculating furiously about what the priest might have done to her friend.

'Nah, not really. He just put his hands on my shoulders and went on about the "purity of my soul" and how it was aall precious like. I'd decided to make some excuse to leave so he'd stop touching me. I'm sure he was working up to putting his hands down me jersey. I don't mind the right lad feeling me tits but not a soddin priest! Anyway, I told him I'd to get home to babysit. I'm not sure he'd have actually done owt but he was in a right state!'

'How d'you mean?' prompted the younger girl.

'Well he were wearing a long black cassock. Yer know like a gown that comes doon to your feet. And it were obvious, man. The cassock were sticking out; he'd got a hard-on like a lad gets when you dance up close to him.' Jill hadn't danced with any lads up close or otherwise so she had to take Gina's word for it. Besides that seemed to be the end of the tale; Gina was pulling Jill to her feet as the strains of *Apache* twanged out from the club record player.

Jill liked the tune: it was the first time Cliff's backing group had gone solo and it had been No. 1 earlier that year – on her birthday, in fact. She preferred The Shadows on their own as she wasn't keen on Cliff Richard. Jill was an Elvis fan and if you liked Elvis, you didn't like Cliff.

They were sitting down again and it was Gina's turn to interrogate. 'So have you not danced up close with a lad, hinnie?' and when Jill shook her head, anxious to avoid admitting she hadn't danced with a boy at all: 'Ah well we can soon sort that oot for you. See that lad over there, the tall one with the mop of black hair. That's Archie Dodd. "Hardun" Dodd some of us call him. He's a mate of mine. I'll have a word and next slow dance as comes up you can have it with him.'

And in spite of her misgivings, she had. He'd lived up to his nickname. Jill was quite sorry – and not a little aroused – when Ricky Vallence's dulcet tones faded away and their entwinement ended. It was nifty! Hardun made a change from snooker…

Twenty-Six

Both Cutters and Greene charged threepence.

They were Cutters and Greene only when it came to the class register. In the queue they were 'Oak-Tree' and 'Beechen.' The former's nickname emanated from Henley, the class zit, who'd claimed it was part of a medieval jingle:

> 'Now summere's gone
> And autumne fires want
> Oak-tree cutters'

Jay was quite irritated as he regarded it as his prerogative to come up with lexical witticisms; so when word was first getting round that Greene was equally well endowed he capped Henley's effort with 'Beechen.' When challenged he explained loftily, 'Huh! I thought you'd've known that, Henley, it's Keats:

> 'In some melodious plot
> Of beechen green, and shadows numberless'

'Ode to a Nightingale' he added superciliously. The name had stuck, partly because Greene was more popular than Cutters; the more so, it was rumoured, because he possessed the finer organ.

Each of them had snipped off the bottom of his pocket so that he could bend his cock up far enough for it to be seen, never mind felt, when they were queuing outside Mrs Hunt's fortnightly art class. The school rule was you had to queue in alphabetical order and since there was only Davis between Cutters and himself, and Greene was next behind him, Jay got an enviable view of proceedings. Indeed, as Davis was a sickly lad and often absent, he frequently found himself in pole position when it came to observing the paying customers. Accordingly, 'Rich-as' Vincent whose father owned the print works had offered him sixpence every time he'd swap places.

He remembered how riveted he'd been the first feel he'd witnessed; and it wasn't long before he was itching to have a go himself. For now, though, he noted the procedure punctiliously: you gave them the money and then you could put your hand in their pocket and give them a feel. If you were one of the favoured – i.e. you paid on a regular basis, not just as a one-off thrill or a dare – you were allowed to pull it up and down a few times. There were even, it was rumoured, a couple of lads who paid sixpence and were allowed to keep going until just before Cutters or Greene announced they were to stop now cause they were 'getting close.'

Sometimes Mrs Hunt was pretty late (mysteriously it could take her quite some time to emerge perky and bright-eyed from the staffroom) so that they could be standing around for six or seven minutes. That meant several threepences and, of course, repeated fondlings of the C & G tackle. More than once the pair were so agitated by the time they got into class that they couldn't wait for the usual routine – whereby one distracted their teacher's attention and the other jacked off behind the desk whilst gazing down Mrs H's generous and carelessly-concealed cleavage – but headed straight for the back row and relieved themselves immediately.

The most celebrated instance, however, was when Cutters was absent and Mrs Hunt even later than usual. By unintended coincidence almost all Greene's income that afternoon had come from regulars. They'd included Rich-as who'd paid his sixpence for Jay's grandstand position and was prepared to pay a further sixpence for an extended feel. For once Jay hadn't swapped places with Vincent but had remained where he was with an intimate view of proceedings. He'd noticed that several of Beechen's supplicants seemed to be getting more than just a few pulls and of course in Cutters's absence there was no one to share the load. Not that Greene appeared to mind. He was making heaps and, in any case, enjoyed his work! Jay did notice, however, that after three or four boys had given him substantially more than a perfunctory shake Beechen was getting quite red in the face and, to Jay's now-practised eye, more aroused than usual. He watched intently as first Denham, then Moat, then Power and finally Thomas sidled up, proffered their threepenny bit and slipped their hand into Greene's business pocket. He wasn't mistaken – each boy was taking longer than the previous one, and Beechen was definitely becoming inflamed.

And then Jay saw the bright flash of silver as Vincent pressed the coin meaningfully into Beechen's hand muttering: 'That's sixpence, Greene: I want my money's worth.' The latter nodded vigorously and, puzzlingly, almost with an air of resignation. Jay suspected Vincent might be going to break the rules and wondered what would happen if he didn't stop before

Beechen was 'getting close.' Then he realised the unusual features of the event – Mrs H later than ever/Cutters absent/the unduly protracted nature of the earlier feels – had affected not just Greene. Jay, too, felt excited. He registered dimly that his hand had slithered through the slit in the trouser lining he'd cut with his sheaf knife (in order to imitate his idols). He seemed much harder than he usually got when he masturbated in his bedroom or the woodshed. Still concentrating on the increasingly rapid movement inside Greene's trousers he began stroking himself. It was nice. He knew all eyes close enough to notice anything would be on Vincent and whether he was going to get his sixpenn'orth. He was tempted to carry on jerking off until the feeling came, but was scared of giving himself away.

Just as he was willing himself to stop, however, Jay realised that Vincent *was* cheating. Beechen's eyes were shut and he was murmuring, just audibly enough for Jay, so certainly loud enough for his tormentor to hear, 'No, no, stop!' But Vincent wouldn't stop. On the contrary, Jay could see his hand speed up and seconds later Greene was groaning as he twitched in Vincent's grasp and began to spew out a stream of viscous white liquid. A fair bit of it shot out of his pocket and onto the corridor-floor. Jay was stoked. When *he* masturbated, although he got a lovely feeling after a while, that was it (unless he felt like doing it a second time, which he frequently did). He didn't spurt out anything; though maybe it was only a matter of practice. Greene looked knackered and just as the stricken boy slumped against the wall Mrs H finally arrived.

Seeing him apparently the worse for wear she paused by the group. She looked even friskier than usual and Jay noticed the top buttons of her blouse were undone. He could see her bra and stared blatantly at the swelling of her breasts. Then, as she smiled at him, intercepting his gaze but making no attempt to fasten the buttons, he moved his foot surreptitiously over the thick creamy stain on the varnished floorboards. She looked knowingly at the chagrined victim and enquired brightly, 'feeling a little over*come*, are we, Greene?'

The latter sighed weakly but managed a smile: 'Just for a moment, Miss, I'm all right now.' Then, whilst Rich-as melted away behind them and the queue started to move, Beechen leaned across to Jay and said gratefully, 'Thanks, Finch, I owe you one.' Henceforth Jay had vowed to become a participant rather than an observer.

Initially, Greene had suspended operations because, it was alleged, he'd felt Vincent had taken advantage and he'd looked stupid in front of Mrs H who clearly sussed what was going on. However, within a month or so his funds were low and the feeling of humiliation had

122

been superseded by a mixture of avarice and prurience.

By this time Jay was acting as their agent collecting the money – there'd been the odd instance of a penny not a threepenny bit turning up in Greene's pocket – and negotiating higher rates for special privileges. Greene seemed pleased Jay was involved and was happy to resume normal service. Whilst Cutters made his reportedly knobbly prick available solely for the money, Beechen apparently relished feeling other boys' hands on his member. Well some, anyway; the others Jay now charged more.

Greene was a simple soul, though, and had not forgotten what he regarded as Jay's generosity in looking out for him when Vincent had left him vulnerable. He therefore counted Jay amongst those who were still favoured. Indeed he went further, perhaps because he was a bit sweet on the smaller, younger boy. A mainly-unspoken friendship developed between the two and Beechen promised him covertly, 'You can have a feel for free, Finch.'

Mrs Hunt was later than ever and Cutters had been plying a lucrative trade – 'one-and-six already,' he gloated.

It turned out that Vincent had been unpopular and no one objected to his being barred. However, one of the other rich kids had just offered Greene a shilling, 'if you let me do you properly, but only 'til you say stop,' he'd promised. Dubious about his ability to exercise such self-control, Beechen was nevertheless unable to resist the money. Jay pocketed it for now and watched in fascination as Lovatt vigorously manipulated his friend. As he looked on Jay could tell Beechen was beginning to enjoy it which made him both unaccountably jealous and excited (he could feel his own hard-on developing). Part of him wanted Lovatt to stop – was it because he wanted to do Beechen himself? But another part of him wanted to see the expression on the latter's face when he suddenly realised he was going to 'come' (as he now knew it was called); and to witness again the spunk erupting out of his pocket.

In the event he got a taste of his first wish. Greene signalled to Lovatt to stop and the latter who did not want to suffer Vincent's ostracism complied reluctantly and returned to his place behind Johnston. Jay could see that Beechen remained fired up but it was still a surprise when he leaned across and muttered, 'I promised you a free feel, Finch. You can do me for nothing. Yer know…all the way!'

Jay was all a-tremble and withdrawing his hot fingers from inside his pants he immediately plunged them into his friend's pocket. So soon after his own modest proportions the shock was palpable: Greene felt huge! His tool was smooth and warm and, like Jay's, circumcised. Even so he was able to pull the foreskin right over the end before rippling it back down, to his own delight and B's evident enjoyment. 'Lovely, bor,' he whispered, 'it won't be long.' Jay redoubled his efforts.

Unfortunately Greene had no sooner forecast his imminent climax than Mrs H hove into sight and they had to suspend proceedings. He just had time to promise 'later Finch after school in the cloakrooms...' Bad luck struck twice, however. The cloakrooms were crowded with a visiting eleven. The term ended with Jay unfulfilled.

In the New Year, Jay started dancing classes. They were held in Oulton High, the secondary modern which Merton attended. He'd never been there before and felt out of place. He wasn't much good either. He was a climber, a mountaineer not a dancer; even after four sessions he still couldn't remember the different sequences. The quickstep he'd more or less mastered; the foxtrot remained a complete mystery. The waltz was okay, but so slow – who would he want to dance that slowly with?

He'd spotted her the second week but had feigned indifference, being too shy to speak to her. Then that night, during the fourth session, their tutor had paired them up. He'd just about managed the quickstep and it was when they were revolving gently to the waltz music that it dawned on him. First, she was very pretty. And second – excruciatingly embarrassing – he was getting aroused. He tried to pull away from her so she wouldn't notice but she clasped him closer, probably expecting him to fall over. He was less than competent, after all. He caught her eye and blushed furiously but she just smiled and carried on whisking him over the polished boards of the gym floor. Her name was Janice Lumsden; she was in the fourth year at Oulton.

After that Jay's dancing began to improve. He only ever met Janice at the classes and didn't always get the opportunity to dance with her, but now he found himself looking forward to the Wednesday evenings. And it had nothing, he discerned, to do with the dancing. He didn't suppose she counted as a girlfriend but since he'd never had one he had no way of telling. The prospect of the Hunt Ball, which he'd been dreading, began to assume more manageable proportions. And the thought that he might invite Janice took shape.

Meanwhile, the news broke that they were to leave The Lodge that summer. The sailor was home from the sea and wanted his hammock back. They would move to another estate property: The Gatehouse. By now the whole family had grown to love The Lodge and everyone wanted to make the most of the last few months.

For Jay, who spent much of his life in the future – when he'd be old enough, or big enough, or strong enough to fulfil his latest fantasy – the summer meant meeting up with Malc again. They hadn't seen each other since the trip to the Lakes two years earlier and they hadn't kept in touch. So Jay was surprised to receive a letter postmarked Blackburn. He tore it open and, once he'd deciphered his friend's ungainly scrawl, twigged it was an invitation. To Loch Lomond – where Neville Armstrong's latest acquisition was a chalet right by the lake. Sounded brilliant, he couldn't wait! And as luck would have it his dad had to attend a conference in Manchester that July and promised to drop Jay off at the Armstrong's.

For Jay's parents the remaining months at The Lodge meant an even more active social life. They seemed to be invited to a dinner party almost every Friday, usually in town. Jay got to know the various participants: a bank manager, the local GP, a solicitor, the town's pharmacist...and so on. It occurred to Jay that the pairings were defined by the job the husband did; none of the wives worked. But then neither did his mum, although he knew she used to before he and his brother were born. And there was talk from time to time of her 'going back to teaching.'

Every two months or so, it was the Finchers' turn. The pine-panelled dining room would be arranged with five small tables. The best china and cutlery were deployed and Jay would be commissioned as a waiter. He would serve sherry and cocktails in what he these days termed the drawing room and then summon the guests with a portentous, 'dinner is served!' Thereafter he would wait on table, under the watchful eye of his mother and serve wine, as schooled by his father. Most of the guests were old – even older than his parents – but the pharmacist and his wife were much younger and had developed a racy reputation in their rural circle for their risqué outfits. James McDonald donned his kilt and his wife, Jackie wore shorter and shorter dresses with lower and lower necklines until, on this particular evening she had slipped off her stole to reveal a topless creation. The husbands were most attentive; the wives outraged; Jay agog. He'd never seen bare breasts before (although like Oak and Beechen he'd often imagined what Mrs Hunt's ample bosom looked like). The MacDonald table enjoyed excellent service and his undivided attention before Muriel twigged what was going on and instructed Ray to dismiss his sommelier! Disappointed and relieved simultaneously, Jay had legged it up to his bedroom with a raging stalker. He hadn't even reached a 100.

The Hunt Ball loomed. There were two old coaching houses in town – The Four Tuns and The Queen's Arms – and both boasted ballrooms. Formal dances tended to alternate; this year it was the Tuns' turn. The dance floor was rectangular, with aisles on either side, and larger carpeted areas at each end were set for the buffet. You collected this at 'half-time' (as the footballers liked to term it) from a separate room up half a dozen stairs at the rear of the ballroom. The bar was there, too, and most of the older boys reckoned they could get served.

Jay was not so confident. He was a young-looking fourteen and had only just started going down to The White Horse, or The Morgue as the locals called it, on account of its sepulchral atmosphere and undertaker-barman. Francis was small and hunchbacked. Whether he'd read any Shakespeare or whether it was just his way of taking the mickey when summoned from the tap room to draw the ale he would cry, 'anon, anon!' just like the Ostler in *Henry IV Part I*, which he and his father had read over Christmas. Jay had gone in with his brother and not tried to buy a drink himself. But he'd supped four pints of mild – at a frugal shilling-a-pint – and had fallen off his bike on the way home, prompting Chris to advise him: 'You'd better stick with me, kid, for the time being, in case you end up in the ditch again. Besides, Francis wouldn't serve you on your own. Smir and I were fifteen before we went in.' Considerately he didn't add, 'and we looked much older than you,' for which Jay, anticipating the put-down, was duly grateful.

Anyway that was a concern for half-time; bigger obstacles were imminent. After several weeks' cajoling, Janice had finally agreed to go to the dance with him, though he hadn't told her it was a 'ball' for fear she'd fight shy. She would meet him in the foyer at 7.45 and they could go in together.

His big brother had passed his driving test the year before and had access to their mother's Standard Eight. It was steel-grey, ten years old and called 'Chug.' Its number plate was LAH 262. However, on this Saturday he and Humph had commandeered it for a trip to the cinema in Norwich with two girls from St Augustine's College. Jay would have to ride in and leave his bike at the Mayfair cycle-stand. Janice's parents had no car and, in any case, she lived in town. She would walk.

Exonerating himself subsequently, Jay blamed unlucky timing. He arrived in his best (only) suit outside the Tuns just as two cars pulled up and eight of the County set tumbled noisily out, most of them in coveted DJs with their girls in evening dresses. A couple of them signalled him to join them. 'Where's your partner, Jay?' enquired Freddie Maidstone, in a tone that seemed to convey a mixture of genuine interest and incipient condescension.

'Oh,' rejoined Jay as casually as he could, 'her father's dropping her off at eight.'

'Right. Well c'mon everyone. Let's go and get some drinks,' and Freddie led the party up the steps into the foyer.

They were queuing at the cloakroom desk waiting to check in their overcoats, and there was Janice, standing just across the lobby. Her auburn hair was piled up in a beehive and she wore heavy make-up. A crimson blouse accentuated her buxom figure but was nipped in tightly at the waist to a flared skirt. It was cream and matched her high-heels. Jay thought she looked stunning. He was just about to go across to her when Freddie remarked brashly, 'God, what a scrubber! Where does she think she is: down the Tute?' His partner and the other two girls laughed derisively, just as Janice gave him a shy wave.

'Who's she waving at?' snorted Freddie. 'Christ! *You* don't know her, do you, Finch?'

Jay gulped, the Iscariot moment overwhelming him. 'Hardly,' he drawled, at his most dismissive, 'not my type, old boy!' and turned towards the desk, though not in time to miss Janice bursting into tears and scurrying awkwardly across the foyer to the exit. By the time he'd checked in his unfashionable duffle coat she'd gone. He knew he was blushing but remarked as insouciantly as he could. 'Hmm, nearly eight. Think I'll just slip out and see if Barbara's here.'

He strolled out and down the steps to the street and then broke into a run as he saw her already on the far side of the Buttercross. He caught up with her halfway up St Mary's Street but before he could work out what to say she turned on him and snarled, 'You're a bloody snob, Jay Fincher. Don't ever speak to me again.' And as Jay sought in vain to retrieve the situation she stalked off, as haughtily as she knew how, her high-heels clicking accusingly on the stone flags.

Jay trudged back, distraught. The evening was ruined. What was he going to say to Freddie Maidstone and his party? Crestfallen, he decided not to return to the ball but to explain later, if challenged, that Barbara's father had arrived but only to convey the sad news of her indisposition. (That would be the phrase that the mythical, but rather distinguished Mr Chilcott – he silently acknowledged the invention of Autolycus on that one – would have employed.) He didn't risk trying to reclaim his duffle coat but marched back to the bicycle stand and set off in a flushed fury. By the time he reached the driveway he was freezing and wondering what explanation he could offer for being home so early. Then he remembered his parents were at the MacDonald's that evening so the house would be empty. He meandered miserably in, bemoaning his misfortune.

Twenty-Seven

Jill was rising fourteen when she found herself running the Walker household. Not that she wasn't prepared for it; she'd looked after Al since he was small. It was just how things were: if you were five you looked after kids who were four. And so on. Cause your parents were working. Her mam was still doing two jobs and both had assumed more responsibility. She was now the only fully-qualified, female butcher in the Watson chain: assistant manager at the shop on Shields High Street. It meant more money but also entailed working Saturday mornings.

Meanwhile, she was also duty manager in the evenings at the Tunnel Club. That involved starting at seven when she'd often only got back from Watson's at six. So she expected a meal on the table, which was just about the only time she saw Jill. Her dad, too, demanded his tea when he got back from Swann's – often via the East End Club – about the same time. Jill and Al, who was eleven now, and a cheeky little sod, had their evening meal at five.

One Sunday in four – when their mam wasn't at the Club and their dad foreswore his usual visit to the Labour – they all sat down to a roast dinner together. But Jill had to cook that, as well.

So when the invitation came that Christmas holiday, Jill jumped at the chance.

Her favourite uncle, Bill, had decamped to Glasgow and was running Atlantic House, a hotel for merchant seamen. Jill was very welcome to come and stay any time, and in exchange for her keep, help Aunt Elsie. Her cousin, Rick, would be company. That was the only drawback: being an only son with doting parents Rick was spoilt rotten, and a pain in the arse. But Jill figured the advantages of a break from doing all the household chores for nothing – not even the occasional thank you – more than outweighed the presence of her tiresome cousin.

The hotel was vast, by comparison with Simpsons. Its façade was stone, blackened by years of Glasgow grime, and the glass in the windows was smeared a yellowy-white. It covered three floors with long, gloomy corridors,

Jill's abiding impression of which was Sunday and Monday mornings when outside almost every room was a tin waste bin, each with its quota of empty Whyte & MacKay bottles. It was the local whisky and the only brand the hotel's owners allowed to be sold over the bar – usually at closing time on Saturday. Scotland was dry on Sunday. It was her job to clear away the empties, and Jill was soon thoroughly, almost literally, sick – as the smell was rancid and turned her stomach – of Whyte & MacKay's finest. It was almost a relief to encounter an empty flask of the company's recently-acquired single malt, Dalmore, outside the room of a better-off guest. Unlike the blandness of the ubiquitous (good word that, Jill Walker, the lit twins'd be proud of you!) red lions, the Dalmore bottle featured an altogether classier label which proudly proclaimed its twelve-year age and showed a picturesque row of cottages beside the sea. Jill asked her uncle about them and he claimed it was where the whisky was distilled, way up north on the Black Isle, and the cottages portrayed stood beside Cromarty Firth.

Bottle duty was as close as she was allowed to the seamen's quarters and, even then, she had to be on the lookout for the occasional incumbent whose drunken state meant he couldn't distinguish between an adult cleaner and a fourteen-year-old schoolgirl. Mostly though, the corridors were safe enough in the mornings when she and Rick would race kitchen trolleys down them. It was only after closing time that they became hazardous and Jill was forbidden to venture along them.

Instead, she'd spend the afternoons out with Rick and the evenings playing records in the staff flat. The vinyl featured Rick's stock of Cliff Richard 45s which Jill suffered in barely-acquiescent silence. The trips out were to the Gorbals where most of Rick's mates seemed to live. The flats there were an eye-opener even for Jill. They were fourteen to eighteen storeys high and the lift was invariably broken. Not that you'd want to ride it alone anyway but the stairs were just as bad – steep, dark (even of an afternoon) and smelling of stale urine. Whole families of five and six lived in just two rooms and it seemed to Jill that what she could remember of Bewicke Street was palatial by comparison. Rick's two best mates had left school and hung around the estate looking for mischief rather than a job. As if there were any! Hardly anyone in the flats worked, although the men all seemed to find enough to smoke and drink and the Roseburn – a right-rough dive just past Eglinton Street – was a magnet for undesirables and the hub of the local drugs-trade, according to Dan and Bolger, both of whom claimed to indulge when they could afford to.

Jill didn't feel particularly safe in their company, even though Rick swore they were 'aall reet!' and she took care never to be alone with either of them. Whenever the weather allowed she'd persuade them to get out from the flats and down the Barrows: the gigantic market on the edge of the Gorbals which seemed to sell just about anything. There were fruit stalls with bananas, peaches, pineapples and pomegranates all fresh off the freighters which tied up on the Clyde; and tinned-goods specials where you could get owt from pilchards to Fray Bentos corned beef. Mostly Jill just window-shopped; they didn't need food or drink as both were plentiful at the hotel. But the jewellery and ironware stalls were fascinating as long as she didn't reveal a hankering for a particular item. She soon learned not to do that when, admiring a silver bracelet (which actually turned out to be plate) led to its being presented to her five minutes later by a jubilant Bolger. Another time she'd betrayed an interest in a bead-necklace only for it to be clasped round her neck by Dan as a rival token for her affection. After that, her enthusiasm for the Barrows waned, particularly as her Aunt Elsie quizzed her about her newly-acquired ornaments and, anxious not to drop Rick or his friends in it, she was compelled to lie. Jill didn't like lying. She encountered it too frequently when a parental excuse for a late return from the Tunnel Club or the Maurie was deemed necessary.

The trips grew more ambitious in the summer when the weather was better and the ferries were running. In the interim, Rick had badgered his indulgent parents into buying him the motorbike he'd set his heart on. Jill disapproved. Not because she'd anything against motorbikes – she'd never been on one – but because it was yet another instance when her kingpin-cousin who could do no wrong got his own way. Still, it did have one advantage: whenever he wasn't working at Atlantic House, Rick was off exploring, which left Jill free to do the same in her more sedate manner.

Glasgow Central was a ten-minute walk from the hotel. Jill liked stations. Glasgow was another matter entirely from Newcastle Central. It was much bigger and had a fine, oval ticket office with a storey above where you could get tea and cakes. She longed to treat herself to a coffee at the Central Hotel which Uncle Bill told her had once served both Winston Churchill and Frank Sinatra. But it was a bit too posh and she didn't fancy being turned away. Besides, the platform café did cheap coffee as well – you could get a beaker and a chocolate éclair for a shilling. And, as usual, her uncle had been generous in subbing her holiday outings with a surreptitious fiver that more than covered both her rail and ferry fares.

The trains to Wemyss Bay ran every hour. They took just fifty minutes to the little loch-side resort on the Firth of Clyde where the station had a wonderfully fluted roof – all glass and steel curves. Jill immediately added it to her box of treasures before plunging into a little tunnel which led straight to the pier where you boarded the ferry across to Rothesay. It was only a thirty-five-minute sail away on the Isle of Bute. She didn't have long to wait before the MV *Isle of Mull* chugged into harbour topped by its red and black funnel featuring yet another red lion in a yellow roundel. It was apparently the badge of the Caledonian MacBrayne steamship company whose headquarters were just up the Clyde. Jill intended crossing from Wemyss Bay to Dunoon and then onto Gourock where she would say farewell to MacBrayne. Hers was an 'Isles' ticket so she could disembark wherever she wanted to and resume her journey whenever the next ferry arrived. What she really fancied was a trip to Arran, but it was too far to get there and back in a day and there was no regular crossing to Brodick anyway. So she headed north.

With a mixed group of fishermen and holidaymakers, Jill boarded the much smaller MV *Carrick Castle*. The fishermen were mostly going home for the weekend whilst the tourists were in a tightly-knit party of six. After twenty minutes ploughing uneventfully across the widest stretch of the Firth, Jill felt a bit isolated and was starting to regret her independent journey until a young, tousle-haired Highlander from north of Ullapool (wherever that was) spotted her predicament and called her across to the snug wheelhouse. He turned out to be the skipper – 'Sandy McGregor, captain of the good ship *Carrick Castle*,' he smiled, 'at your service, miss.'

Jill shook his outstretched hand gratefully and installed herself beside him: the recipient thereafter of a running commentary on noteworthy sights the rest of the voyagers would overlook. The shores of the sea-loch gradually converged, the western side being heavily forested right down to the water's edge, whilst the eastern bank was flatter and populated by a number of tiny villages. Roughly halfway along, they came to a dropping-off pier below the slightly more substantial settlement of Gairlochead. Three of the fishermen disembarked and whilst they were tied up Sandy pointed out two Royal Navy frigates and a much larger American ship, USS *Idaho*. On the opposite side of what was now Loch Long they could see the subsidiary Loch Goil and sited at one of the few open stretches of coast the black-stone Castle Carrick after which their vessel was named. Jill was hoping for some bloodthirsty tales of its incumbents and was disappointed when her guide knew nothing about it.

What he did know about were the mountains which were increasingly hemming them in on both sides as the loch grew steadily narrower. Only having the Northumberland hills to compare they looked huge when a change of direction brought their destination, Arrochar, into view, and behind it even higher and more dramatic peaks. Before she could ask,

Sandy launched into his travelogue: 'Aye, those are the real peaks, lassie. The knobbly one with the steep crags is the Cobbler and the higher peak behind it Ben Ime. Thass over 3,000 feet so they say.'

Then they were chugging slowly into the bay below Arrochar village, where the remaining fishermen lived. The tourists, too, were disembarking for the next stage of their journey, by mini-coach all the way down the western banks of Loch Lomond and back to Glasgow. Jill wondered aloud whether she might hitch a lift. Luck smiled. The driver was another McGregor, a distant cousin of Sandy's who announced that whilst it was strictly against company policy as her ticket didn't extend to coaches, he didn't give a monkey's and, besides, he'd several spare seats. There being no luggage to load, the day-trippers were soon on their way to Tarbet where they'd get their first glimpse of Scotland's most famous loch. 'Be sure to look back roond aboot Inverbeg,' Sandy had advised as a parting shot, 'yer'll get a rare view of Ben Lomond.'

They stopped at Luss, where the lake began to widen considerably. Most of the tourists were 'oohing' and 'aahing' over the vista of multicoloured sails on the myriad yachts weaving their way in and out of the picturesque, wooded Inch Islands, but Jill's eyes were drawn to the north. There, as Sandy had promised, the spectacular bulk of Ben Lomond loomed, its topmost peak wreathed in wispy white clouds against an otherwise clear blue sky. Jill had no ambitions to climb the mountain but she couldn't help being impressed. For the tourists Luss meant lunch, and Jill realised with dismay that she'd brought nothing other than a banana and an apple which she'd wolfed down earlier on the train to Wemyss Bay. Realising her situation, an elderly English couple offered to share their more-than-ample packed lunch. When Jill tasted smoked salmon sandwiches for the first time she silently revised the Menzies mantra: 'you're a *lucky* girl, Jill Walker – and don't let anyone tell you otherwise!'

But what was really lucky was the village shop! Jill spotted the Walls Ice Cream sign as the mini-coach drew up. As she crossed from the lakeside car park she noticed a couple of lads skimming stones over the mirrored water. The older of the two followed her into the shop. He was quite small with mousy hair, but he had an intelligent face and a friendly smile. They reached the ice cream freezer together. He slid open the lid and gestured to her to go first. Jill spotted there was only one jumbo lolly left and extricating it, offered, 'It's the only one. You can have it if you like,' hoping he'd play the gentleman and demur.

'Thanks a lot,' he grinned to her chagrin, but then added, 'you can share it if you want.'

Jill laughed. Then she bought some sherbet drops and followed him out. The other boy had disappeared and they sat down on a bench. He offered her 'a lick' and she accepted gracefully. They sat in silence. She was going to have to take the lead.

'D'you live round here then?'

Silence!

Oh no! Don't say he was like the lads doon the Catholic Club: sole topic of conversation football. Then it struck her he might be shy. She tried another tack. 'Aam on a trip meself. From Glasgow. Me uncle's got a hotel there. But aam from Tyneside really. How aboot you?'

'Um… I'm from Lancashire. But I um…live in Norfolk.' Jill looked puzzled so he went on, 'Yeah, I'm on a trip an all. My mate's dad's got a chalet. It's right on the shore.'

'Can you see the hills from it?' Jill searched for something the lad might like and was rewarded with a sudden rush of enthusiasm.

'Sure can! There's a brilliant view of Ben Lomond. We climbed it yesterday. By the Ptarmigan Ridge. It's 3,195 feet high. That's only fifteen feet lower than Scafell Pike!'

Jill hadn't heard of Scafell Pike, but she looked suitably impressed. And the boy continued, 'Yeah, it's a Munro – yer know, over 3,000 feet. There's loads of 'em – 'bout 300. We're gonna climb them all,' he added proudly.

He paused long enough to proffer the communal lolly and Jill enquired, 'so how long yer here for?'

'Rest of the week. Then back home. Well, Norfolk anyway. Then we're going to Switzerland.'

Not especially interested in his grand-sounding holiday plans, Jill sought to steer the conversation back to him when she realised the coach was getting ready to leave, 'Damn!' she exclaimed, scrambling from the bench and tearing across the gravel car park, 'Aam gonna miss me bus. See ya!' Then just as she resumed her seat she slid open the window and shouted: 'Aam Jill. What're you called?'

The noise of the engine and the breeze rushing by almost obscured the reply and all she caught was a 'J…'

She whiled away the hour back to Glasgow with speculation. Something about the lad had intrigued her and she wondered what the 'J' stood for. 'James?' (he was too posh for 'Jim'!) 'John?' 'Julian?' Nah! Then she got it: 'Jeremy' which to reflect his fancy accent she pronounced 'Jewemy.' Yeah that'd be him, she smiled.

The coach dropped them off at Gordon Square – the trippers for a conducted tour of the City Chambers, Jill to skip happily along the two blocks to Atlantic House. Regaling her uncle and aunt with carefully edited highlights of her trip gave her almost as much satisfaction as the day itself had. For once, Cousin Rick took a back seat.

Twenty-Eight

The move to The Gatehouse was a tad shorter than their journey from Lancashire. As the crow flew over Earlham Wood it wasn't much more than a mile. Even by road, turning left out of the drive and up Hollow Hill past March Farm, in a couple of miles you came to the sweeping drive which led to the Hall; at the far end of the semicircle stood The Gatehouse. With his eye for numbers Jay noticed the date immediately: 1613. The year a small canon featuring in a new production of Shakespeare's *Henry VIII* set fire to the roof and The Globe burned down. He hoped it wasn't an omen.

It was a lot smaller than The Lodge, but just as intriguing. The side porch, where the iron numbers of the date were fixed, led straight into an oak-panelled drawing room from which a narrow corridor at the back of the house gave access to a large square study on the left and an intimate, elegant dining room on the right. There was also access to a loggia, with its own wood-store which led into a walled garden. Then you came to the hallway and another entrance. So perhaps, like The Lodge, it had been more than one dwelling. Beyond the hallway a small scullery led out left to the kitchen garden. No half-mile walk this time, thought a relieved Muriel, although true to her asseveration she really had transformed the garden by the river and restored it almost to the lost glory Lady Veronica had lamented. To the right lay the roomy kitchen with a large, green range and a view out over the lawns and flowerbeds of the front garden towards the sweeping driveway.

Upstairs – and there were two sets, one at each end – were three small bedrooms, a bathroom and a master bedroom. The stair which led to the latter then spiralled up to a fifth bedroom which Jay thought looked more like Horatio Hornblower's cabin than anything else. Naturally, Chris bagged it.

However, when he found that the two bedrooms at the far end were to be his – one to sleep in and the other as a study – Jay felt more than recompensed. And when he discovered that the door behind his bed accessed yet another spiral staircase which led directly to the kitchen he was delighted. His own private suite!

The gardens were far better kept than at The Lodge and the house was surrounded by three separate lawns. The one at the back, which you reached by the loggia, led into a large but unkempt orchard, at the far end of which were some decrepit, black barns – very promising! And, more promising still, for Acquisitive Autolycus, lawn-cutting duties on behalf of his busy father would mean additional income for him!

However, hardly had they moved in than they were off to Switzerland. It had been booked for ages – long before the date of their removal. They were to drive, taking the ferry from Dover to Calais and then staying at pensions in St Quentin and Belfort prior to crossing the Swiss border at Basle. After that they'd climb over the Jura mountains and head south through the capital, Berne, before driving along the south side of Lake Thun and through Interlaken to Iseltwald, where their hotel stood perched on the banks of Lake Brienz.

The hotel was like a miniature castle and with the lake just a few yards away it was very picturesque. But it was just a lake! Characteristically, Jay regarded the first week as merely a prelude and in spite of trips on the Lakes and to Interlaken he was starting to get bored. Then Monika arrived. She was small, flaxen-haired and attractive, from Munich. Unfortunately she spoke no English and Jay no German so when he'd plucked up the courage to speak to her on the stairs after breakfast they had to make do with French. Thereafter they conducted snatched and fragmentary conversations whenever they met in the hotel and on the second evening Monika's parents agreed she could dine at the Finchers' table.

Afterwards they strolled out to the jetty. It was a cool, clear night and the lake was cobalt-blue calm. In the distance they could see the lights of a pleasure cruiser which, on reflection, Jay realised had sailed this way every evening around nine. There was a small band on board and the combination of the beautiful setting and a most haunting melody drifting across the Brienzersee, as Monika called it, was powerfully romantic. Jay was nervous. The disaster of the Hunt Ball still haunted him, and he was fearful of making a fool of himself again. He couldn't think what to say.

'*Elle est une belle harmonie, n'est-ce-pas?*' whispered Monika, slipping her arm into his as they reached the end of the pier.

'*Oui, c'est très belle,*' returned Jay shakily, the inadequacy of his response being nothing compared to the weakness of his knees. He was stuck for further words, French or otherwise.

Happily, Monika took the initiative: '*Elle s'appelle "Muss I Denn".*

C'est très romantique.' She kissed him softly on the cheek and then, when he betrayed a lack of endeavour, more firmly on the lips. It promised to be his first proper kiss but before he could decide what you did next Monika's parents hove into view and she drew gently away from him. Jay didn't know whether to be frustrated or relieved. The following morning they left for Lauterbrunnen.

The chalet was imposingly positioned at the top of the village, directly opposite the beetling cliffs which closed off the south side of the valley. Above them loomed the three peaks Jay had researched back in England: the Jungfrau (highest at 13,669 feet), with the Monch (13,468) and the Eiger (13,025) with its infamous North Face were the heart of the Bernese Alps, and what the whole family had come to savour. Any regrets about leaving Monika were quickly dispelled – although he was intrigued to hear the beautiful melody back home on the jukebox that autumn. In English it was called *Wooden Heart* and had apparently been yet another No. 1 for Elvis earlier in the year. What a let-down!

Initially, they explored the valley – a glaciated U-shaped cleft with vertical limestone walls up to 3,000 feet high. They marvelled at the cascades that gave the defile its name and enjoyed the spray-soaking Staubbach Falls which were less than half-a-mile from their chalet. The water plummeted in an unbroken arc for almost a thousand feet – one of the highest falls in Europe, apparently. Then they took a train up to Murren (at more than 5,000 feet the highest Jay had been) and walked the Alpine meadows replete with buttercups, saxifrage and edelweiss. Jay, ahead of the rest of the party as usual, breasted a spur to disturb a pair of grazing chamois, but since they'd vamoosed by the time the others arrived there was some doubt about his sighting. He was prepared to sulk over it when he happened upon a knife lying in the thick grass by the side of their rocky path. After axes, knives were Jay's favourites – he had two sheaf knives which featured in frequent games of 'Stretch' both in the back garden and, especially, on climbing holidays with Malc. This one was a real corker – a red-enamel Swiss Army Knife with the crest of the Bernese Oberland imprinted in gold and black. It had two blades, a tiny serrated saw, a bottle opener, a screwdriver, a pair of scissors and a smooth, needle-sharp spike. 'That's for getting Boy Scouts out of horses' hooves,' joked Chris. It made Jay's day and became one of his most prized possessions, not least because it proved he was a true Autolyclean: no one else would've snapped up a trifle like that!

On the fourth day they took the Wengener Alp Bahn ('WAB,' recorded Jay in his holiday diary) to Grindelwald, a picturesque village perched on a plateau directly below the Bernese Alps. Jay was tickled to discover its population was the same as its height above sea level: 3,392' – so higher than anywhere in England, but not Wales, he logged. His geographer mother was well prepared as usual and informed them there'd been a 'Grindelwalt' as far back as 1146. But, of course, the boys and their dad had eyes only for the brooding presence, directly above them, of the North Face of the Eiger – all 5,900 vertical feet of it!

Raymond took up the story: 'Two early attempts both ended tragically. Don't know much about the first except that two young Germans, I think, were killed. Frozen overnight in Death Bivouac. It's about two-thirds of the way up. Here, look I'll show you the main features through the telescope.' And he proceeded to trace the route for them from the pillars at the base up past the Difficult Crack to the Hinterstoisser Traverse and across the two ice fields to Death Bivouac. 'Then it slants left up the ramp and back right across the Traverse of the Gods into that big snowfield. That's the Spider: the feature that struck Heinrich Harrer so much he named his book after it: *The White Spider.* From the Spider it's up through the Exit Cracks and over the Summit Ice-field to the top.'

The boys took it in turns to pick out the route – Jay memorising it by telescopic sections – as their father continued his narrative: 'The second failure's the one I remember best. It was just a couple of months before your mum and I were married. Two Austrians, whose names I forget, and two Bavarians: Anderl Hinterstoisser – he's the one they named the traverse after – and Toni Kurz. The account of his death at the end of a rope dangling upside down and agonisingly close to his rescuers, is supposed to be the most harrowing bit of the book.'

'S'pose his rescuers staggered into Base Camp and announced "Mistah Kurtz – he dead",' sniggered Jay.

'You what?' enquired Chris.

'Sorry, son, you've lost me there,' added his father, a tad caustically.

'Conrad: *Heart of Darkness!*' explained Jay, 'clever, eh!'

'Clever maybe, but uncalled for,' admonished his father in as harsh a tone as he ever employed to either son.

Jay tried to look suitably chastened, imagining himself instead as the heroic Kurz, meeting his death on the notorious 'Nordwand' as his dad resumed: 'It was two years later in '38 that Harrer along with Heckmair, Vorg and...' he hesitated, trying to recall the name of the fourth climber, 'oh yes, Franz Kasparek, made the first successful ascent. I think there've been about twenty more since then but no British one yet. That could change, though. I heard Bonnington and Whillans have got their eyes on it.'

Jay had thought Eiger-watching would be the highlight of their holiday, but an even more exciting treat loomed: they were to ascend the Jungfraujoch! Initially, they'd embark on the WAB once more, this time forking right and up to Kleine Scheidegg; then it was a rack railway – the Jungfraubahn – for the nine kilometres up to the pass itself. (Jay was content to measure in kilometres: it sounded longer.) The ascent would take them about an hour, the descent not much over half an hour. The views would be from the top as most of the journey through the Eiger and Monch massifs was in tunnels. Some French passengers expressed disappointment at that, but for him that was one of the best bits.

He liked tunnels and although he'd never been through much of one on a train he and Malc had often played in the one by Rumpelstilskin's wood, especially after they'd been told it was out-of-bounds. At first, they'd only venture in a few yards but as they got bolder the dare was to go in far enough for it to be dark and then when you spotted the lights of the engine approximately half-a-mile away, to run like hell. The danger, and therefore excitement, lay not in failing to make the most of your 800-yard head start but in tripping on a sleeper and sprawling headlong into the path of the steaming monster! Not that either of them ever did, nor anyone else as far as they knew...

Just under halfway the train slowed as a tourist guide attached to the French party explained that this was 'la fenêtre gallérie.'

'Of course,' interjected their father, 'this was where the guides who tried to rescue Kurz got out onto the face. Imagine it: stepping out onto a near-vertical ice-wall and then traversing diagonally upwards until they got within 300 feet of him; then having to abandon him for the night, before returning in appalling conditions the next day. And finally, getting to within a few feet before his rope jammed and he couldn't go any further. Apparently, one of the guides...Arnold Glatthard, I think it was... reckoned it was the saddest moment of his life.'

Jay began to understand why his dad had failed to appreciate his quip about "Mistah Kurtz".

The tourist guide was speaking again, but too quickly for Jay to catch much except that there were apparently plans to install panoramic windows at some stage. Then they were off again for another half-hour's darkness before they emerged into the blinding sunlight beyond the station hall. They couldn't go far as the tourist area was restricted to easy slopes within a few hundred feet of the viewing galleries. The azure sky, white snow and black rock were the most intense colours any of them had ever experienced. It was cold, too – below zero even in late August. Jay kicked happily through the snow, relishing the much more immediate views he now had of the Jungfrau and Monch. The Great Aletsch Glacier swept away beneath them whilst directly above was the Sphinx Observatory.

There seemed to be some disagreement about the height of the Jungfraujoch, with three different figures on display, so Jay plumped for 11,333. Easiest to remember, he decided: 11-x-3 = 33: 11,333 feet! That *was* the highlight of the holiday!

The return journey two days later was memorable for a breakdown, and a storm. The former happened just outside Bethune with the consequences that it incurred additional expense with an overnight stay in a pension and it decided Raymond that WAH 672 would have to go. The storm was at sea. Instead of taking two hours, the crossing from Calais took eight, including an hour and a half manoeuvring outside Dover harbour before the captain judged it safe to attempt the entrance. Everyone was copiously seasick except Jay, who contrary to instructions marched up and down the deck in the bracing gale eating apples.

The week after their return to The Gatehouse Jay began his GCE year, whilst his recently seasick brother left for Dartmouth Royal Naval College.

Twenty-Nine

By dint of her birth date Jill was still fourteen when she left Marsden's. Miss Menzies would've been furious all over again. Not only had 'good grammar-school material' slipped through The Establishment cracks but the girl wouldn't even get to sit her GCEs. Well, not at school, anyway.

That September, a proud fifteen-year-old Jill enrolled at Ashington Tech for a pre-nursing course. It would be two years and as well as covering subjects which she might have studied at school had specialist classes in Human Biology and Anatomy. After the increasingly oppressive atmosphere of school the freer regime at college suited Jill. She was outgoing and vivacious and got on well with students and lecturers alike. The only drawback to the new arrangement was the travelling.

Earlier that year the Walkers had moved again. With both her dad and mam in regular work and Rob no longer at home they'd been able to afford the council rent on a semi in Holy Cross. For the first time Jill revelled in having her own room, or 'den,' as she'd determined to christen it!

Holy Cross was nice but a long way to college. First, you had to walk up St Peter's Road to catch one of Lynemouth's antiquated, yellow charas along the Coast Road to the Haymarket where you changed for a red double-decker. This headed initially up the A1 to Wide Open and Seaton Burn before plunging into the countryside and winding its way through Bedlington ('where the terriers come from,' Aunt Louisa had told her) and finally depositing you in Ashington. It was only a short walk from the bus terminus to the college but the whole journey took well over an hour. Morning and afternoon. Five days a week.

In spite of the dispiritingly negative influence of Miss Sharples, Jill had retained her love of reading. She even found time to make the longer journey back to Ferndale Avenue where the Misses Lambton and Charlton, whom these days she was invited to address as Sue and Joyce, ran a literary circle once a month. She didn't tell her parents. Even her dad would've scoffed at his daughter joining something that sounded so high-brow. Attendance varied from eight or ten to just Jill. She was by far the youngest, most of the women being as old as her mam and it was clear to anyone who cared to notice that Jill was the favourite. There was the occasional sly gibe about this, and about their tutors. Jill knew what 'dykes' were now and thought as a derogatory term it said far more about her erstwhile English teacher than it did about the lit twins.

She still gravitated back to Cullercoats when she wanted to be on her own or the Spanish City when she wanted company. She was too old for most of the rides but the gang she went with were a laugh and some of the sideshows were entertaining: particularly when you were the centre of attention. Nat Turner and Alex Staighton had been apprenticed with her brother at Brydons and had assumed a kind of proprietorial, we'll-look-after-you attitude towards her. Or at least, that's the impression they liked to give. Jill was cuter than that; what they actually wanted was to get in her knickers. Being lads, they fondly imagined she'd be swayed by receiving the biggest cuddly toy from the rifle range or an ornamental ashtray from the hoopla. Admittedly, the latter was a handy extra in the den when she entertained on a Saturday night. Both her parents smoked: her mam Embassy and her dad Woodbines or, if he got them as a present off his brother at Christmas, Capstan Full Strength. Partly influenced by Sue and Joyce, neither of whom indulged, Jill had vowed not to take up the disgusting habit.

Along with Nat and Alex there'd frequently be three or four of her college friends who came from the Wallsend area. She was getting on a little better with her mam these days, and if she was in she'd make them steak-and-onion butties which they'd consume in the den to the accompaniment of pints of Newcastle Amber and her dad bashing on the ceiling below with the broom-handle to warn them to, 'Keep that bloody racket down!'

That autumn she went swimming a lot. Rob had fulfilled his long-term ambition of joining the RAF and was stationed back in England for six months, not far down the A1 at Catterick. Several weekends in September and October he managed to get home. He spent most nights out with his mates down the club but provided he wasn't too hung-over he liked to go up to St Mary's Lighthouse in the afternoons. Jill didn't know whether it was a case of absence making the heart grow fonder but she got on a lot better with her elder brother these days. At high tide the circuit of the lighthouse was taxing. Jill probably wouldn't have attempted it alone but had no such qualms in Rob's company. Although the Olympic Trial had come to nothing – he'd been homesick in Blackpool and had come home after three days – he now swam not only for the RAF but for the

United Services Team as well. Occasionally, Nat or Alex, or both, would try and muscle in on the outings, which was both frustrating and amusing. Having spent so little time with him as they grew up, Jill now wanted Rob to herself. On the other hand it was entertaining to witness their feeble efforts to impress her in the sea by comparison with her brother's dolphin-like prowess.

When it was just the two of them she'd quiz him about the Air Force, in which she had little interest, and the girls he'd been with, whose details were far more intriguing. He'd grown into a fine-looking man and his athletic accomplishments made him an attractive proposition. He'd been promoted rapidly and was now a dashing young sergeant who would have been even more of an asset to his unit had he not got the wrong side of his CO.

They were sitting over a warming cup of hot chocolate in St Mary's Café when Rob finally opened up. 'The CO's pretty young for a Squadron Leader. Maybes thirty, summat like that. Fancies hissel an aall.'

'What, gay yer mean?'

'Nah! Fancies hissel as a sportsman. Guess he divn't like the competition. Real problem's his wife like. She's a reet stunner. An she knaas it.'

'So d'ye fancy her?'

'Well I wouldn't say nah, like. But that weren't the point. It were her. She'd come on reet strong if we were alone and then ignore me if anyone else were around.'

'So what happened?'

'Well rumours got around that she fancied me and the next thing aam summoned to his office. No one else there. Gives me a reet bollockin, like. Says aah've aalways bin insubordinate, or summat.'

'And then?'

'Well, aam grittin me teeth like. Sayin nowt. And he starts slagging 'er off, callin her a slut an aall sorts and pushin me an aall. I says ter lay off but he just pushes me again, only harder. So I decks 'im!'

Jill's eyes were wide with concern. 'Strewth, our Rob, yer divn't oughta have done that. What happened?'

'The bugger rings for help an next thing aam in the glasshouse for two weeks. An when I come oot aah've lost me stripes!'

Jill was welling up with a mixture of sympathy and fury, 'The bastard!! So what happens now?'

'Start aall over again, I reckon.'

The 'starting over' was worse than Jill feared. She got the news just after Christmas: Rob was being posted to RAF Lubeck just north of Hamburg for eighteen months. Once again Jill found herself bereft.

The rest of her time at college shuffled interminably through the worst winter since the war. Even when snow had been cleared from the roads on the way to Ashington it was piled either side to a depth level with the top windows of the double-decker bus. Footpaths were impassable, and fields were an unbroken white desert. The college never closed though; and Jill didn't miss a single day. And, for once, she got her reward: she passed all eight 'O' Levels with the Merits she needed in Human Biology and Anatomy. What she was most proud of though were her English results – a Merit in Language and a Distinction in Literature. She couldn't wait to tell the lit twins!

Thirty

Raymond had fallen out with WAH 672, but his love affair with Fords continued. Habitually he bought his cars locally and second-hand, preferring someone else to suffer the first year's depreciation. That way, he reckoned, he kept his capital costs at a modest £100 per annum. This time was different.

Periodically, he would be summoned, or directed, by 'Curzon Street' as he, and his colleagues called the headquarters of the Ministry of Education. Usually that meant a trip to London; less frequently an 'FI,' or Full Inspection. These could take him anywhere and involved his leaving on a Sunday night, much to Muriel's disgust as it broke up the weekend so, and returning the following Friday. The actual inspection lasted four days, involved a number of subject specialists and was visited upon a leading grammar school. On this occasion he left in the white Zodiac soon after Sunday lunch, bound for Bournemouth. On the following Saturday he cruised slowly across the pea-gravel drive as Jay hurtled out of the front door to herald the brand new, two-tone-grey elegance of 5513 EL. That would be one in the eye for the public school Genevieves. 'First over Westminster Bridge' – most of 'em wouldn't make it to Norwich and back!

Other changes were afoot. The summer term had ended with the retirement of their formidable but much-respected headmaster, 'Scruff.' Dr Hevitt could not face the prospect of co-education and the move from the old grammar school to spanking new buildings on the outskirts of town. In future he would employ the backswing so meticulously honed on countless boys' bottoms to healthier effect on the golf course.

They'd given him a good send-off. Unlike the rest of the teachers whose cars were parked at the front of the school, Scruff had his own spot at the rear, close to where his study was situated. On the last day of term there was to be a special service of thanksgiving (for the head's departure, according to the wags) at Holy Trinity Church. Normally, the boys only trooped through the town for the Founders' Day service in November, and then reluctantly as it always seemed to be raining. This time there was a buzz in the warm summer air as most of the senior school and some of the more easy-going teachers knew what was planned. Half the Upper Sixth, including Chris and his mates Humph and Smir, absented themselves from the service. By the time the whole school packed into the library for the boys' own farewell there it was: the conspirators had removed the doors of the library which led onto the back schoolyard and lifted the head's brand new retirement gift into the back of the capacious room. The island stacks had been pushed against the walls and in the space created stood the bright blue Riley Elf. There was a nasty moment when Scruff appeared on the verge of apoplexy but then he burst out laughing and the whole school sang 'For he's a jolly good fellow,' several times!

The Upper Fifth were studiously ambivalent about the new arrangements. On the plus side the facilities were infinitely superior. There were specialist labs, instead of just one for General Science. Plus there was a proper gymnasium whereas PT at the old school had been conducted in the backyard by their history master. If it was fine, Dr Hunt would lounge against the library wall languidly issuing directions. If it was raining or snowing he would drive his black Zephyr round to the yard and shout instructions from inside. Dr Hunt smoked, like most of the teachers, and the clouds of tobacco-smoke billowing from their PT instructor's pipe very soon obscured his commands so that he was obliged to wind down the window to prolong their collective misery. Initially, Jay couldn't understand how Don – who must have been on far less than his dad – could afford a car of similar status, albeit several years older. But then it dawned on him that since both he and their art mistress, Knockers Hunt (whose prominent features were so appreciated by Oak-Tree and Beechen), could pool their salaries and apparently had no children, a decent car was within their means.

Nobody liked PT. Nor was it much fun getting changed in the cloakrooms. The showers were in a block with the outside lavatories and were cold and reserved for the cricket/athletics season. The new school, Fielden Avenue, not only had a gym but proper changing rooms – with showers. Although that didn't mean Jay enjoyed sports any more. At the old school, they'd played football in the Michaelmas Term, hockey in Lent and cricket in Trinity. Jay was poor at the first two and mediocre at the third. Being crap at football he could understand: he'd no great interest in it and had never been to a League match. Hockey was more of a puzzle. Both his mum and dad had played for Birmingham University and his mother had gone on to play for Lancashire and had had an unsuccessful trial for England; Chris was in the school first team. Jay was useless.

146

So, with twenty-five boys in his year he was invariably one of the three who remained un-chosen by the team captains and condemned to kick a ball or defend triangular short corners in a makeshift goal on a substitute pitch. It was humiliating enough in itself, especially at pick-time as the teams got gradually larger and the pool smaller until there were just the three of them; plus it was invariably cold and always seemed to be wet. If, very occasionally there were enough absences to ensure his participation, he spent the whole game desperately hoping the ball wouldn't come to him. If it did he usually missed it altogether or miscued it out of play.

Occasionally he got picked for one of the two cricket teams but that was mainly, he suspected, because both captains were Pokists and he took care to ensure that if there were a fixture coming up he actually fancied playing in they seemed to have a good run of the cards. (Not that he cheated, of course: he simply deployed his administrative skills to the full.) Once he got to play against Hailsham College where the Hoods went. It seemed distinctly odd. Jay felt he should be doing his best for Wyndhams, but there was his best friend, Tom, playing for the opposite side. He was puzzled as to how it would affect his social standing outside school and wondered if it mattered who won.

Jay had never bowled in a match, only in the nets. So when Moat tossed the ball to him he was instantly agitated. He needn't have worried. For once luck was with him. After a nervous wide he promptly took three wickets for two runs in that over to the increasing applause of first his team-mates and then the spectators. When Moat clapped him on the back announcing loudly: 'Well done, Finch!' he swelled with unaccustomed, cricketing pride. Retiring for the next over to his more-usual position at square leg he was daydreaming about mopping up the Hailsham tail when their number five hooked powerfully. Fast enough to get down but too slow to stop the shot properly, Jay was rapped viciously on the kneecap. He rolled aside in agony as the ball sped past to the boundary and then tried to stand up. He fell over; and was so obviously in real pain that the normal rule of 'Gerronwivit!' was waived. As square-leg umpire, Dr Hunt was only yards away, scooping up the recumbent Fincher and carrying him to the pavilion. There was a ripple of sympathetic clapping before twelfth man came on. Jay took no further part in the match but found, curiously, that his standing both at school and with the Hailsham crowd was enhanced.

The only other success had been on the athletics track. Once again he'd not been picked for his House – Popeson – but a last-minute withdrawal found him lined up at the start of the 880, along with fifteen other hopefuls, four from each House. He set off tentatively, anticipating he'd be as pathetic as at most events and, sure enough, at the halfway stage he trailed the field. Then he noticed that some of them seemed to be slowing down. First he caught a large bunch of maybe seven or eight and cruised past them as they seemed to be stuttering to a walk. The next group of three were only a few yards ahead and they, too, seemed to find the going heavy as he went through them on the inside. He was gaining on the next three who were strung out with maybe five or six yards between them; then, as he rounded the final bend he realised he was third. Only the red bands of Emmanuel and the yellow of Throckmorton quartered the white shirts ahead of him. Both of them staggered to a halt on what they thought was the finishing line but voices urged him: 'Keep going! Keep going!!' His rivals had mistaken the finish and stopped too soon: he'd won!

Jay celebrated this one-off victory with a little too much enthusiasm, and became the butt of some fairly good-natured humour. Todd, their new but ancient classics teacher and Popeson's unlikely Housemaster even graced him with a, 'well done young Hermes!' Most of the other comments were of the 'accidental victor' variety and were directed as well as taken with good grace. Only his beaten rivals took the outcome seriously. The Emmanuel boy, Prior, who should've been second was already in the Upper Fifth and was due to leave Wyndhams that month; he did so without speaking to Jay. But Power, the Throckmorton athletics captain, fellow Pokist and nearly-mate was more forthcoming, 'You shouldn't've won that, Fincher, you do know that, don't you!' Then, when Jay had looked suitably embarrassed: 'even so, you've never run before have you? Maybe you should think about cross-country next year. Remind me.'

Thirty-One

It was the monthly book circle that Saturday. Jill looked forward to it for intellectual stimulus, and for companionship. Often she'd stop behind after everyone else had left and help Sue and Joyce catalogue new books and sort out old ones. Not once did either of them demonstrate any feelings towards Jill other than respect and affection although, secretly, she wouldn't've minded if Sue had. Jill found her not only instructive but also increasingly attractive, and her experiences with Liz and with Marge had left her with no hang-ups about same-sex relationships. Most of the boys she'd met, on the other hand, had been immature and insensitive – and most definitely nowhere near as alluring!

The lit twins were jubilant about her GCE successes. 'Always knew you had it in you,' announced Joyce. 'I'll let Sally Menzies know, if it's ok? She'll be delighted for you.'

Sue added, 'This calls for a celebration! Let's all have a drink tonight and you can tell us your plans. How about the Engine Inn Tavern at seven? Or is that a bit close to home?' she concluded, alive to the fact that strictly speaking Jill was still underage.

'Nah, the Engine's fine. Me mam and dad don't go in there and they've been serving me in the lounge for months.'

When it came to getting ready Jill realised how nervous she was. She'd only ever met the two women at the library and one of them had once been her teacher (although that was a really long time ago). She wondered what she should wear, and how much older than her they actually were. She knew there was five or six years' difference between them because although they'd both been to the same university Joyce had left well before Sue had arrived. They'd only met subsequently at a college reunion. Also she vaguely remembered a good-humoured exchange they'd once had about how youthful Joyce appeared and how it'd been a good job she'd taught primary not secondary or she'd've been mistaken for one of the pupils. She also knew Joyce had only just started as a student teacher at St Kits when Jill first went. So...she'd be eighteen when

I was five…and…let's see…twelve years on…she'll be about thirty. A lot younger than Gina Lollobrigida, giggled Jill. And, at that rate, Sue must be about twenty-four or twenty-five. Not *that* much older than me, she concluded happily. Somehow, what to wear no longer seemed an issue.

But that didn't mean she'd just throw any old rags on. After all the twins were both professional women and had standards to maintain. They'd be smart, she reckoned; so she should be, too. She donned her only pair of fashionable black slacks and decided on her lacy purple blouse to go on top. It was 'svelte and diaphanous,' according to Aunt Louisa who'd given it Jill as a birthday present. She worried it might be a bit over the top. Then because it was partially see-through she agonised over what to wear underneath. Reasoning that if the blouse was designed to show off your assets she might as well allow it to she considered nothing at all then panicked and selected a half-cup satin bra which she hoped looked demure and sexy at the same time. Why was she worrying? Probably no one would notice – except Trev, the cheeky Cockney barman, and she really ought not to encourage his ogling; he was bad enough when she was dressed in her scruff.

She was glad she'd agreed to the Engine. Familiarity bred confidence, and she strode into the lounge with none of the nervousness she'd've felt in, say, The Rose or The Maurie which her parents frequented. Sue was already there and instantly Jill was glad she taken the trouble she had in dressing. Her friend looked more like a model than a librarian. She had on a flared red three-quarter length skirt and a tight black jumper. She gave Jill a warm smile as she rose from her chair to give her a hug and a kiss. Jill was taken aback but had the presence of mind to reciprocate. Then, still holding her hand outstretched Sue gave her an appraising up-and-down look and declared: 'You look lovely, pet! I do like your…blouse.' And there was just enough of a pause – accompanied by the swiftest of glances – to suggest that it wasn't just the blouse she liked! Jill blushed and to cover her embarrassment asked what she'd like to drink.

'No way, hinny! This is our treat! But you're the regular – what do you recommend?'

'Well I usually drink the Amber. Unless it's a special occasion!' she added.

'Amber it is then – to start with. And you can tell me your celebratory poison later!' She strode over to the bar and Jill noted she got the full treatment from Trev, which appeared not to faze her in the least. 'There, two pints of Amber,' she announced putting the clear-glass bottles and two schooners on the table. 'Bottoms up, pet!' she teased. 'Congratulations!'

At which point Joyce arrived. She was dressed just as Jill had anticipated: in smart brown trousers and a modest fawn jersey-top. She seemed equally pleased to see Jill and there were more hugs, though no kisses, before she asked for a glass of wine. This seemed to stump Trev for a moment – there wasn't much call for wine in the Engine. However, after rummaging around in the cellar he produced a bottle of Chablis which Joyce pronounced 'very drinkable' and they settled down to talk books and bright-futures; but not boys Jill noted, thankfully.

A while and two pints of Amber later Jill had succumbed to Sue's friendly pressure and was on brandy and Babycham. It always went straight to her head but unless she was being treated by some hopeful, hopeless suitor she didn't normally have more than two. By now, however, she was on her third and really enjoying herself. She needn't have worried about anything – the lit twins were wonderful company and any age difference seemed irrelevant: except when it came to prospects, of course, when they became understandably but not in the least condescendingly solicitous.

'Whatever you do, pet, you must keep up your reading,' advised Joyce. 'It'll stand you in good stead for the rest of your life.'

'And you'll never be bored on holiday,' laughed Sue.

When Jill explained she was waiting to hear whether she'd been accepted on a pre-nursing placement at the Royal Victoria Infirmary they were delighted. 'My sister trained at the RVI' said Sue. 'She reckoned not only was it the best teaching hospital in the country but you have the best time there! When will you hear if you've got in?'

'Next Monday, I hope.'

'Fantastic! We can have another outing to celebrate your success. If you'd like to, of course,' added Sue diplomatically.

'Ooh yes please; but if I've got in the first round's on me!'

The following Tuesday the letter dropped through the letter-box of 124, St Peter's Road: Jill had been accepted as a Nursing Cadet at the RVI and was to start next month. They didn't have a 'phone at home and the box on the corner by the newsagents had been vandalised months ago so Jill dashed down to Ferndale Avenue to give Sue the news in person. To her acute disappointment she was away on a course but if Jill 'would like to leave a note' she would get it the following day.

The day after that a buff envelope lay on the mat, addressed to Jill. The note inside was written on council library-service paper and read: 'That's

wonderful, pet! Well done! I'll do some research for you. See you Sat.
Love S. x'

Jill's surprise at receiving a letter was rapidly overtaken by the thrill
of seeing the 'x' at the end of Sue's note. It didn't mean anything, she
counselled herself, but then again Sue needn't've added it so perhaps it
did...once again Jill couldn't wait for Saturday.

They met in the lounge of the Engine once more, but the evening was
a bit of a let-down. To start with, Joyce was on her own when Jill arrived
and although she was pleasant company and as friendly and supportive as
ever, it was Sue that Jill had really been looking forward to seeing. Then
when the latter arrived she seemed a bit distant. There were hugs and
kisses for Joyce but only a perfunctory peck for Jill who was a bit hurt.
As promised she bought the first round (for which she'd had to raid her
savings) and felt more relaxed after it. Then when Joyce went to replenish
their glasses and she shot Sue a glance which she hoped was both puzzled
and distressed she was relieved when the older girl smiled reassuringly and
blew her a surreptitious kiss.

But when Joyce returned Sue was very business-like: 'I've brought
you a folder of notes, pet. The research was actually really interesting.
Turns out the hospital was founded way back in 1751. It was first based in
a house in Gallowgate. It had no water supply – though apparently they did
have a silver chalice for communion! And there were just seven patients.
Imagine! By Florence Nightingale's time they had eleven nurses looking
after about 180 patients around the clock. Then in 1887 the powers-that-
be asked to be allowed to call the hospital "Royal" and when Queen
Victoria agreed it became' (she glanced at her notes) – 'wait for it: "The
Royal Victoria Infirmary of the Counties of Newcastle, Northumberland
and Durham". What a mouthful, eh! There's loads more stuff in the file
but there's one other thing I wanted to tell you about. The hospital kept
expanding and running out of room. So by the time of the Diamond
Jubilee in 1897 they needed completely new premises. Newcastle's Mayor
and other local worthies raised over £200,000 – that'd be millions today
– and built on a brand new site at the Leazes. And that's where the main
buildings are now. It'll be handy for supporting the Magpies, eh?' She
handed over the library folder and, glancing dutifully inside Jill could see
pages of typewritten notes and a few photographs, some of them old sepia
plates like the ones of your grandparents.

She expressed her gratitude and the talk turned to books and the
literary circle. Joyce urged her once more not to neglect her reading:

'You'll be doing more study in your nursing course so ask them if you can take 'A-Level Literature.' If there's any problem let me know and I'll speak to them myself. One of the senior administrators is a family friend,' she added, reminding Jill that Miss Charlton had always been a bit posh and remained well-connected. Then the evening had sort of petered out, though not before they'd all promised to keep in touch via the circle. And at least there were kisses and hugs to end, including Jill noted with relief, a discreet but very affectionate squeeze from Sue.

Thirty-Two

The new school year had begun with autumn term as it was now to be called, much to the collective disgust of the Upper Fifth, who suddenly discovered a preference for the university-style nomenclature previously endured. School mores were to be less traditional – a decision by the new head, one GWJ Funchard. He was instantly unpopular and traditionalists like Jay who had received numerous beatings at the hands of Scruff Hevitt found themselves nostalgic overnight: corporal punishment was consigned to history. Funchard exhibited other failings. He was plain 'Mr' for one thing and not only had he been at Oxford (Wyndhams had a Cambridge tradition) but at a most unfashionable, new college to boot. Moreover, according to a deliciously indiscreet aside by their revered English master, SE ('Duke') Bartleby, their new head had a positively mediocre degree. And even though they knew that Duke – who'd received a starred First and been offered a Fellowship – regarded any academic achievement inferior to his own as distinctly shabby, the news was taken as further evidence of a second-rate successor.

All these shortcomings paled into insignificance, however, by comparison with his principal sin: he was presiding over the admission of two year-groups of girls. Yuk!

Moreover, the girls brought with them a number of new mistresses. The bountiful Mrs Hunt had left – some said under a cloud – and her replacements were both seriously academic and unattractive. Jay had long since dropped art and woodwork in favour of classics. You had to choose after the third form, and whilst he'd been sorry to part company with Knockers, he'd had no such regrets at escaping the bucolic attentions of 'Vlad' Vickers. The woodwork master was one of those who'd had it in for Fincher since he'd first arrived as an underage transfer and he was fond of pillorying Jay's efforts. True, he'd never be a carpenter but he'd been singled out for criticism at every opportunity.

The most traumatic occasion had featured a coffee table he'd been making for his mother. Admittedly, the legs didn't fit very well, the varnishing was patchy and it had a slight wobble but there was still no call for Vlad's reaction: 'Fincher, bring your…er…*table* out here so everyone can see it properly. Thank you.' A few snickers began from those who knew what was coming and didn't like Fincher anyway. 'Now, Third Form, I want you to take a good look at this remarkable specimen.' More giggles as the sneer rose to a snarl: 'It is undoubtedly the most inept and pathetic table it's ever been my misfortune to see!' This time the sporadic laughter was cut short as Vickers tore one of the legs off the table and smashed Jay round the head with it. He flinched but was determined not to cry and a deathly hush underlined the fact that the teacher had gone too far. Jay picked up the leg in silence and retired to the back of the workshop. No one said a word until afterwards when it emerged that he had gained considerable face. Later he mended the table and took it home to his mum. She was delighted and treasured it ever after; Jay never went to another woodwork class and Vlad never enquired after him.

Most of the new teachers were for girlie subjects like needlework and home economics and didn't affect Jay and his mates. But the biology mistress was another matter. First, it was a shock to have to do Biology at all – *and* Chemistry, *and* Physics – when most of them had received no science teaching whatsoever for some years. Secondly, the subject matter was nauseating enough without the added embarrassment of it being taught by a woman. Finally, there was Miss Boden herself. She was as plain as a pikestaff but had a curvaceous figure and seemed to select outfits to demonstrate it even though like all the academic teachers she wore a gown. (At least Funchard hadn't dispensed with those – yet!) Unlike Tom Pearse's gown whose colour had gradually developed a hue of blue-black ink from the countless flickings of fountain pens during his interminably boring French lessons; or Plug's which had somehow assumed a mathematical angularity, Miss Boden's affair was short. As short as the skirts she espoused which, by the time Bobby Vee was imploring them to take good care of his baby and Dion was flirting with Runaround Sue, was very short indeed.

In the biology lab the pleas for help with dissections were constant and whilst those on the bench behind savoured the lissom legs, those in front turned round to ogle the shapely boobs which they swore threatened to break out for freedom altogether. The consensus was that Miss Boden was well aware of the effect she was having and there was some speculation about whether Oak-Tree and Beechen would resume their back-of-the-class activity. Of course, it might never have been abandoned. Jay didn't know as he no longer had the pleasure or lucrative side-line of marshalling the queue outside Mrs Hunt's art-room. However, as Miss Boden's discipline was strict, apart from in matters sartorial, nothing ever came of the possibility. All Jay knew was that the subject was tricky enough without the periodic erection he had to contend with.

Arousal apart, his studies were proceeding satisfactorily. The arts subjects were his forte – especially English – whilst Mathematics was proving a disappointment. The mystery was how a seven-year-old who could get to a million in twenty goes in his head could now be a candidate for mathematical failure: 'You'll get a Grade Nine, Fincher,' Plug assured him. So, boring as he now found maths, Jay was determined to pass it just to prove Jeremiah wrong.

Beyond class things were looking up. The poker school had taken a while to re-establish but was now providing a regular income and financing his continued popularity at the caff. As the autumn wore on he walked back to happiness with Helen Shapiro and with Elvis in support, sought to light upon his latest flame. The caff favourite was Anita, the waitress whose beehive gave her a distinct resemblance to the beloved Helen, whose poster Jay had above his bed. But the girl Jay really fancied was Valerie Heighway. Her father owned the largest department store in town, a Drapers and Furnishers on the corner of Market Place and Trinity Street; not that Jay had ever been in it, or intended to. He wouldn't be seen dead in any shop that didn't sell either books or climbing gear, preferably both. Valerie was part of Freddie Maidstone's crowd, and Jay was set on inviting her to his fifteenth-birthday party. It fell on a Thursday that December but they'd nearly always broken up by the time it came around so attendance shouldn't pose a problem. Besides, Valerie was at a girls' independent school and they always finished a good week before Wyndhams.

Engineering the invitation was easy enough – once she knew Freddie and Tom were coming she would know it was kosher. And her parents weren't a problem: Mr Heighway played golf with Jay's father whilst Mrs Heighway was a member of his mother's bridge club. As far as Jay knew she wasn't going out with anyone so it was just a case of ensuring she was receptive to the elaborate invitation card he designed with its distinctive *RSVP* in gold letters. She was and she did: Valerie was coming!

The party was conventional enough. Muriel Fincher put on a wonderful spread; Raymond set up a sophisticated stereo system which meant you could play different records in different rooms. Actually, a lot of the music was on tape, mostly recorded from 'Pick of the Pops,' David Jacobs' Saturday night slot which Alan Freeman had taken over three months previously. Guests brought their own 45s as well and Raymond ensured that everyone got their choices at some stage during the evening. Most popular was naturally Frankie Vaughn's *Tower of Strength* which was currently No. 1 but Jay's favourite was the much more romantic *Moon River* just released by Danny Williams, although originally part of the sound-track to *Breakfast at Tiffanys*. Jay preferred dark-haired women like Audrey Hepburn – and Valerie!

Sardines was the key. Only Jay's version was rather more exciting than the traditional variation on hide-and-seek, the crucial element being the requirement to hide lying down next to someone. Preferably someone half-pissed!

In addition to the soft drinks his parents were serving most of the boys had smuggled in bottles of pale ale and a couple of the more enterprising girls had procured wine and cider. Jay had also paid a visit to Smedleys, the wine merchant on Broad Street where his brother's best mate Smir who was now reading maths at Magdalen worked part-time during the holidays. He'd been accommodating enough to sell him three bottles of Sauternes, on condition that 'Young Finch' didn't tell anyone where he'd got them. These Jay had secreted: one behind the shutters which concealed the bow-window in the guest bedroom, one in a 'secret' cupboard (which was really a well-disguised walk-in wardrobe) in his brother's crow's nest and the third in the chemistry cabinet in his study. Tom and Freddie were briefed where to hide and had, in turn, let on to their respective quarries where they could be found. That would leave the rest of the guests wandering around for quite a while; and even those who found the other two and got to share their wine would not discover Jay. Nor, of course, Valerie.

Strictly speaking you weren't supposed to move once you'd selected your hiding place but rules were for conformists. Accordingly, once his father had signalled the off Jay, with Valerie in pre-arranged close but discreet pursuit, hid on the old servants' staircase which led from the kitchen to his bedroom. No one outside the family knew of its existence; so when they'd counted successive searchers rifling unsuccessfully through his room – including the curtained-off wardrobe which had looked a promising hideout – they shimmied up the steep stairs in the pitch black. Jay made the most of that bit, of course, ensuring Valerie didn't slip with a guiding hand. Then they were into his room, necking the illicit Sauternes and lying side by side – as good sardines were required to – on his bed.

With consummate timing the speaker on the landing was piping forth *Moon River* and his luck held when it transpired it was Valerie's favourite, too. He'd got it on a loop so after three other tracks and half the wine it came on again. They'd already kissed, at first shyly, and then a little more passionately when she whispered, 'you can feel if you want to!' She guided his hand down between them where, to his amazement and delight, Jay found she'd unbuttoned her blouse. Trembling with anticipation he slid his fingers inside the silky material and onto her bra. He hoped desperately that she wouldn't brush against his by-now-awkward erection, assuming that the embarrassment would ruin everything. But when she did she just giggled, 'Ooh, let me help.' Jay knew if she touched him it would spell instant disaster but fortunately Valerie had meant help with his ineptness in mastering the intricacies of her bra, which she promptly unclipped in a mightily-impressive contortion. Jay's instinct advised him to be gentle but even the tentative stroking he was applying to her beautifully smooth breasts seemed to be making her nipples stick out painfully. She moaned softly and he was afraid he'd hurt her. But when she didn't object he resumed, growing more adventurous. She sighed, 'Oh, Jay' and not knowing how to respond he began kissing her again.

By now Danny was rounding the bend for a third time and Jay panicked that however he was supposed to tackle the next bit there wouldn't be time. He was right. The music stopped abruptly as a signal for all sardines to return to the communal tin; but not before Valerie had squeezed both his hands against her breasts and murmured, 'That was lovely, Jay.' It was the nicest thing anyone had ever said to him. He rated the evening, subsequently, right up there with Sgurr Nan Gillean!

Thirty-Three

Jill loved the RVI. From the imposing statue of Queen Victoria which announced the hospital to the world to the most mundane out-patient clinic and autoclave unit it was everything she'd dreamt of. Even as a student nurse she felt part of a venerable institution. The pale-yellow dress that constituted a cadet's uniform might betray her as the most junior professional in the building but when she put it on in the changing room she was a nurse: a Geordie Nightingale. It was all Jill had ever wanted to be. If only she could wear it outside the hospital she would yearn, as she changed back into her civvies at the end of the day and walked down to the terminus to get the bus back to Holy Cross.

As a major teaching hospital it was home also to trainee doctors – not as young as her, of course, but bearing in mind how much less mature most men were many of them looked no older. And the white coats helped! Not that she was interested in dates, but admiration was free.

The regimen that thrilled Jill on the wards bored her in the classroom. Or at least that's how it felt. She'd expected the lectures to be different from college: more professional, more…well…medical. But all they were was more academic. Additionally, they covered much the same syllabus that her pre-nursing course at Ashington had and were nowhere near demanding enough for her. The only element that stretched her intellectually was the English course. But that had been difficult to arrange (impossible, she imagined without Joyce Charlton's influence) and was a source of contention. Not only did she have to leave the site and walk across to a lecture theatre that was part of the newly-constituted university (it'd been King's College, Durham until very recently) but her regular English tutor resented her doing so. It was almost like being back at Marsden's: 'I think you'll find this interesting, group, though doubtless Cadet Walker has already covered this topic. Perhaps she'd indulge us,' he would add snidely. Jill hated it.

Holy Cross was little better. At 'work' she was an adult, a trainee maybe but in a distinguished vocation. Back home she was resented: partly for having thoughts above her station (which was unfair) but mainly as a drain on the household who contributed nothing financially (which was true). It was an unpleasant combination, and one she could see no end to in what proved to be an interminable first year.

Still, there were pluses. Although most of her year came from Newcastle itself, or from the two counties, some lived closer at hand so she began to broaden her circle of friends. And she didn't always catch the 5.30 bus home. Sometimes she'd stop off at the coffee bar with three of the girls who shared a flat in Jesmond (now there was an aspiration) and, on Fridays, they'd call in for a few drinks at the Collingwood Arms.

Mostly, she'd get the last bus and stagger up St Peter's Road, letting herself into the usually deserted semi before subsiding in her den in a state of mellow exhaustion. But occasionally, she'd stay over in Jesmond at the flat in Eskdale Terrace. It was entertaining when it was just the four nurses; although anxiety lurked at the back of Jill's mind over where she'd sleep. Two of the girls, Jean and Vicki, shared but had only single beds; the eldest, Sally, had a double. She was charming when sober but mischievous if she'd had too much to drink. Jill had called in a few times but it was only after the Christmas party that Sally, who was in her second and final year of an SEN course, had invited her to stay. What with drinks on the ward and a session at the Collingwood everyone was feeling festive by the time they got back to the flat.

There were copious supplies of wine, sherry and vodka and by midnight everyone was plastered. What had started as energetic jiving to the Beatles and the Stones had deteriorated into mutually-supportive smooching to Cilla, and Roy Orbison bemoaning the fact that it was 'over.' Various strangers had appeared and disappeared and the sickly smell of cannabis permeated the already-smoky living room. The party was disintegrating. Jean had gone off with one of the doctors, leaving Vicki their room to entertain a scruffy-looking law student whose name Jill hadn't caught. 'Enjoy the resht of your night, hinny,' slurred Vicky, 'and doan worry about Sally,' she winked. 'She can get a bit frisky like, but she divn't mean any harm. 'sides yer not a prude are you?'

Jill was apprehensive, but half-canned, she retired to bed as soon as she saw the opportunity. She didn't want to crease her party clothes but was reluctant to go to bed naked lest it seem like an invitation to her allegedly-libidinous hostess. So she compromised, stripping off to her bra and knicks and thinking that Sally might very well go on somewhere else anyway. Vodka-laced Morpheus embraced her as she'd slipped under the quilt and she was aware of nothing else until she awoke needing the toilet and had to liberate herself from the embrace of a naked, snoring Sally.

Having washed her face and cleaned her teeth Jill was feeling refreshed by the time she returned to bed. She tried to slide back in without disturbing Sally but her bedfellow rolled over as she did so and once more entwined Jill in her arms. Not wanting to seem like the prude Vicky had hinted at but even more anxious not to wake her friend, Jill thought it best just to lie still. It wasn't so simple. She'd been fairly sure Sally was asleep and was surprised but not unpleasantly so when her embrace slackened only for questing hands to wander up and down Jill's back. Sally's naked breasts jiggled against Jill who – more out of curiosity than desire – trailed her free fingers up and down Sally's side. They came to rest between her boobs and Jill couldn't resist ever so gently stroking her friend's nipples. The feel of her body was stimulating and Jill, by no means as sober as she'd thought and always randy when she woke up after drink, decided it might be nice to show that she wasn't sex-shy after all. Experimentally, she allowed her other hand to sneak in between Sally's thighs but before it could get up to any mischief her friend sighed deeply and, turning over on her back began to snore rhythmically. Nuts! Smiled Jill silently; just when it was getting interesting…

Come morning she was both relieved, and a tad disappointed, when she found her underwear still on, albeit with one boob hanging indelicately out of her bra. She extricated herself gently, took a last – admittedly lingering – look at her naked bedfellow and sweeping her clothes off the armchair got dressed in the living room. It was nearly nine o'clock. She made herself a cup of Nescafé and leafed through the previous evening's *Chronicle* for a few minutes. Then she closed the flat door softly and walked wearily down the terrace before cutting through to Jesmond Road and catching the next bus to Holy Cross. Her mam had already left for work and her dad was snoring off Friday night's McEwan's Export. Neither enquired subsequently where she'd been.

Jill never knew whether Sally had 'taken advantage' that night although she received a warm and knowing smile when they met and an opportunist hug if no one else was there plus a 'how's my favourite cadet? When are you coming to stay again?' Jill made a couple of visits but managed to end up sleeping on the sofa, although not without the odd wistful speculation. They all seemed to drift apart, and after the Easter break no further invitations were forthcoming. Then it was the May ball. As a cadet, Jill wasn't eligible. She'd been working an evening shift though and got caught up on the fringes of a doctors' party that Sally had been helping organise. After a few drinks they fell in to talking just like they used to and it seemed perfectly natural to take up her friend's invitation to join them back at the flat. Once there, she found the routine hadn't changed: drink, illicit – albeit discreet – drugs, and sex. She wasn't in the market for the last two but was up for a few vodkas on top of the white wine they'd been drinking earlier. By midnight she was easy prey. She wasn't very clear who Charlie was but he seemed like a nice young man and, after a spliff or two, equally attractive. She remembered seeing midnight; then passed out.

She came round and tried to focus on her watch: two o'clock. She was slumped in an armchair, fully clothed, next to a small side table on which stood the remnants of her vodka. Surmising hazily that it might bring her round she picked up the glass and drank it down greedily. Hair of the bitch, and that… The glowing feeling hit her stomach a short while later and she felt somewhat refreshed: at least for the moment. She glanced around her. At her feet lay a comatose Charlie, also fully dressed she noted with relief. She thought she might get to like him, in an asexual sort of way. On the sofa opposite were slumped the near-naked bodies of two doctors; whilst through the open door she could see Sally writhing on the bed with a partially dressed cadet nurse. Maureen, she was called, thought Jill vaguely. It was difficult not to look and after watching their energetic antics for a couple of minutes she found herself getting aroused. She looted another vodka, and without considering whose it was, took a large slug from that, too. She felt delightfully light-headed and unusually horny: maybe she'd join Sally and Maureen: she was pretty sure neither would object and it looked like it might be fun. Alternatively, maybe she'd just observe and relieve her rising libido herself. She slid her fingers tentatively inside her blouse.

Then she changed her mind. If she started playing with herself, there was no telling where it would end – most probably in a threesome with Sally and Maureen. A prospect, she figured hazily, she might enjoy but regret in the morning. She decided to go home whilst she still knew how to get there.

It was a warm night and five minutes later she found herself, none too steady, struggling up Jesmond Dene towards the Coast Road. With some difficulty she worked out that the first buses wouldn't be running for another two hours. She'd have to walk the five miles home or hitch a lift; though the likelihood of anyone stopping at this time of the morning was remote. It didn't occur to her that it might also be hazardous.

She knew there was no chance of any motorist pulling up once she got onto the dual carriageway so she waited just past the last set of lights.

She was visible to anyone having to halt and it would be easy for them to pick her up before they gathered too much speed. Good theory, but after four or five cars had driven straight past it seemed less effective in practice. Then, just as she was becoming resigned to walking – well staggering – home a car stopped opposite. It was quite sporty – green and white, with two doors only. It looked vaguely familiar and when the driver wound down the window she realised it belonged to her Uncle Rex. What a stroke of luck, even if he was going the wrong way.

Rex was her mam's stepbrother, ten years younger than her mam and with a reputation as a bit of a wide boy. He was good-looking and knew it. He was also divorced so Jill was surprised to see a woman sitting alongside him as she made her way unsteadily across the road.

'Why our Jill, what you doin oot this time o' night? Get yersel in.'

Then as Jill scrabbled open the door and collapsed onto the bench seat he explained, 'ahm just takin Lucy back to Cramlington then aa'll run yer home. It's a bit oot the way like but it's betta than walkin!'

Jill thanked him, muttering that she'd got chilled standing at the lights. Then she felt Lucy lean over and retrieve a jacket from the back. She draped it round Jill's shoulders whereupon she fell asleep, slumped against her.

Jill had no idea how long she'd slept. When she stirred Lucy was no longer there. It was still not light and she assumed they were on their way back to Holy Cross although she didn't recognise the road. Her head was now resting partly on the backrest but mainly on her uncle. The latter's left arm was around her shoulders. Unthinkingly, she snuggled up closer to him and dozed. Waking periodically she registered a hand gradually sliding down until it rested gently on her left breast. In her drunken stupor she imagined it was Sally and mumbled incomprehensibly before drifting off again. The next time she surfaced they'd come to a halt; that was probably what woke her she thought glancing out at the now-lightening tree-scape. They were at the top of Engine Inn Road, past where the houses ended and the fields began. Her uncle had slid along the bench seat and was now tight up against her. His fingers seemed to be inside her blouse and he was endeavouring clumsily to unclip her bra. Bemused, Jill wondered fleetingly whether she should help him: she didn't want to upset him. After all he'd sort of rescued her and, besides, he was her mam's favourite brother. Well, stepbrother. Still befuddled she was trying to work out what to do when, suddenly, his mouth was over hers and his tongue was intruding between her lips.

That was what brought her to her senses. Bracing herself against the well-carpet she pushed him away vigorously and when he started to object scrambled hurriedly across the bench seat and half-fell, half propelled herself out of the passenger door. She didn't think he'd pursue her – not that close to home in near-daylight – but she ran nevertheless: the full-length of Engine Inn Road and left onto St Peter's. Within a couple of minutes she was home: badly shaken, greatly relieved and astonishingly sober.

Thirty-Four

It was Spring Term. How Jay and his fellow parvenu traditionalists pined for Epiphany! He ticked off three pluses. One, when Valerie had gone back to St Mary's he'd received a letter. Two, it was the cross-country season and Power kept his promise. Three, his musical talent was blossoming.

He couldn't understand why Valerie had waited until she was back at school before writing. Hearing nothing from her sooner Jay feared the worst and had already written off his chances not only with her but, as was his wont, all future female intercourse. His reaction was to scrawl on the inside cover of his maths book: 'All girls are fucking bitches.' Plug saw it and he was summoned to Funchard's office (he didn't even have a study). With Scruff the punishment would have certainly been severe: most probably three, or if he was feeling vindictive, four strokes of the cane. But it would have been over there and then with no further recrimination or bad feeling. Funchard lectured him at length on the sensitivity of the feminine psyche; set him a six-page essay on 'Respect' and required him to attend his detention for the next two Saturdays. 'What a wassock!' complained Jay, to a sympathetic Upper Fifth coterie. He was still serving his sentence when her missive arrived; which gave him both relief and an ironic laugh. Not that he shared either with anyone else (Autolycus treasured secrets, he recalled).

The sentiments were wonderful. He'd never received what he'd decided to classify as a 'love-letter' before. In an elegant script it thanked him again for the party which she'd enjoyed very much, 'especially the inebriate sardines,' and went on to invite him round to their place on the other side of town when she came home for half-term. Easter was late that year so it would be the beginning of March before they could meet: nearly two whole months. Still, he wouldn't need to fret that she'd meet someone else as she boarded at St Mary's and boys were strictly forbidden. For once, Jay silently applauded conformity.

Cross-country practice got you out of games. The short route skirted the playing fields at the back of the school and out across the heath. It picked up a C-road which climbed steadily between high banks and then descended though a muddy wood to loop back to the playing fields. It was only two-and-a-half miles but it took them about twenty-five minutes. As it was a new route there was no school record, although unofficially it was held by Thompson one of the Upper Sixth runners who'd been round in eighteen minutes. The long route simply went round twice. It looked like taking maybe three-quarters of an hour. After their first outing on a cold, drizzly January afternoon Power reckoned that in frost-hard or spring-dry conditions they could easily crack twenty minutes, and a fortnight later he had. Then the February freeze set in. A hardy band of a dozen boys set out but Power was absent. Jay completed the course in nineteen minutes dead. It was on his own watch though, so didn't count.

Power was now school athletics captain and persuaded their sports master, 'Buddy' Hawkins (the senior boys thought his use of Christian names over-familiar) to take the cross-country a little more seriously than it had been when Dr Hunt oversaw proceedings from a smoke-filled Zephyr. There was an inter-schools festival in March and teams of five could be entered provided all members had met a qualifying time of sub-twenty minutes for a school-certified 2.5 mile course. Their geography teacher 'Java' (he'd been in a Japanese POW camp during the Second World War) was persuaded to root out a six-inch map of the vicinity and Buddy went round the course with a pedometer. Both were agreed on the distance. Every other Saturday Power cajoled a dozen or so volunteers from the fifth and sixth forms to turn out and Buddy Hawkins accompanied them, stopwatch in tracksuit pocket. As they reached the playing fields on the return loop he sprinted off ahead of the pack and was there to record the leading three times. Thompson finished in 18.20 with Power running him a close second in 18.25. Jay was third with a time of 18.50, confirming his unofficial exploits of a month earlier. Power seemed as proud of him as he was of his own second place: 'That's ace, Finch. I've been running for two years and Tommo for three. What was that: your fourth circuit?'

'Fifth' admitted Jay, breathlessly. He knew he could go faster and was set on a school record that spring.

Meanwhile, his musical progress had accelerated equally rapidly under the stern tutelage of Miss Byron. He'd started with her shortly after they'd moved to The Lodge and she'd put him in for the Associated Board's Grade Two piano exam when he was nine. A year later he'd got a Merit at Grade Three; but then the lessons had taken a back seat whilst he got into grammar school. Nobody thought to start them again until he was in Year Two but when, six months later, he received a Distinction at Grade Four

Miss Byron advised his parents that Jay might have some talent.

There was music in the family on both sides. His mother's uncle was first violin with the Liverpool Philharmonic whilst his father, although self-taught, played the fiddle to an acceptable standard. He and Freddie Maidstone's dad, a local GP who played the cello, got together with James McDonald and formed a piano trio. Jay was rather hoping *Mrs* McDonald might prove to be musical. He'd definitely attend a performance if *her* embonpoint featured!

Raymond Fincher's work took him into most of the secondary schools in East Anglia and although music was no part of his remit he made a lot of contacts. Once every few months he would take Jay to a piano recital on a Thursday evening. They were usually held in Great Yarmouth or Lowestoft so Jay had the additional thrill of the journeys during which his father drove considerably faster than when his mum was with them. Once they heard William Fellowes, another time Arnold Baxter and, the highlight of that period, Joseph Cooper, who by then was a regular with the BBC where he performed on *Call the Tune*. What intrigued and delighted Jay most was that he was always introduced to the pianist at the end of the performance (his father seemed to know them already). When they met Mr Cooper, Jay had just received a Distinction at Grade Six. He'd been thirteen then and mightily encouraged when the virtuoso told him he should persevere as he was young enough to make a career for himself.

Now he'd recently completed Grade Eight and, though disappointingly without either Distinction or Merit, even the undemonstrative Miss Byron expressed herself pleased with his application. An RCM qualification beckoned.

Progress in the two other directions, however, was stymied by Jay's contracting measles just before half-term. The inter-schools cross-country came and went; Wyndham's best performance was from Power who came sixth. And some kind soul (Jay deeply suspected Freddie who intimated he didn't think Jay was 'good enough' for her) told Valerie that Jay was seeing someone else. Meanwhile, it transpired that Chris whom they'd all expected home for Easter was being sent 'on manoeuvres' and would get no home leave until August. He'd never been away for that long before and although they'd frequently fallen out it had never been seriously. Now Jay was missing him; although naturally he didn't confess as much to anyone – even his dad, to whom he seemed to be much closer than most of his friends were to theirs.

The rest of term would've proved an irrevocable anti-climax but for an ironic upside of his illness. Dr Maidstone had prescribed a break from physical exercise. So, instead of languishing on the hockey field in lieu of cross-country he spent their PE ('exercise' having superseded 'training' – typical!) and games periods in the library.

Apart from the swimming pool which Jay looked forward to using in Trinity – sorry, Summer – Term the library was by far the most prestigious of the new facilities. It was on the first floor and had a splendid view of the town below, over Oulton Common and across the valley to their old house. It had at least four times the number of volumes their previous library possessed, proper chairs and reading tables, newspapers and an easy-to-use filing system which Jay, as an assistant librarian, had helped to devise.

In the splendid isolation he so relished, Jay was free to roam. Early on he discovered a three-volume set of *Lord of the Rings* which he vaguely recalled his father starting to read to him when they were first at The Lodge. They hadn't finished it which was a puzzle. He knew they didn't have a set themselves so perhaps it had gone back to the town library and never been recovered. Or maybe he was too young. Now he devoured it – first in his solitary convalescence and then at home since he immediately signed out *The Fellowship of the Ring* to himself. Good word that: 'fellowship.' He made for the reference section and pulled out The Oxford Dictionary of Etymology. There it was on page 350: 'Fellow – mate, good fellow, agreeable companion, one of a company... Hence fellowship XII; after ON, *felagskapr.*' Difficult to work into a casual conversation! Maybe rechristen the Pokists? And he was never one of a company anyway. But he did have mates. He and Malc had kept in touch, and actually wrote on an occasional basis. They'd started addressing each other as 'Mate' in the correspondence they were currently exchanging about their forthcoming Lake District trip. So that was it: A Fellowship for the Fells – appropriate if not especially original.

The following Thursday he rifled through the card index to 'Shakespeare' having had a sudden urge to revisit his old friend Autolycus. He located a copy of *The Winter's Tale* and flicked swiftly on to Act IV, Scene III. There it was again: 'My father nam'd me Autolycus; who being, as I am, littered under Mercury, was likewise a snapper up of unconsidered trifles.' Ah dear old Autolycus, such constant fellowship!

When he returned to the index a couple of cards had slipped over and he was intrigued to read 'Sillitoe, Alan: *The Loneliness of the Long-Distance Runner.* Pub W H Allen Ltd., 1959.' He zipped over to the 'Q-R-S' island and searched it eagerly. There it was: a handsome yellow and black hardback. He'd already got the maximum two books out (it would be four next year, in the Lower Sixth) but he wanted to read it that weekend, not risk someone else taking it out and perhaps not obtaining it again that term. Tailor-made trifle, he grinned, and slipped it down his trouser-fronts, as an Upper Sixth tutorial trouped in. It wasn't stealing: he'd return it as soon as he'd read it. But he did take the precaution of removing the reference card: otherwise he'd've had to fill out an exit slip.

He read *Runner* that weekend. Somehow it seemed even more appropriate to have snapped it up when he discovered the hero, Colin Smith, had ended up in Borstal for robbery. Jay identified strongly with Colin: he too was a loner, a bit of an outcast, a talented runner and, best of all, a non-conformist. What a brilliant repudiation of authority: having the race won for the bastards and then throwing it away on the finish line! There was a sort of asymmetry attached, too: he'd done just the opposite in the 880 that had set him off on cross-country. And even though the season was petering out he decided he was going to devise his own route and then, next year, challenge the best. And of course, Authority...

Thirty-Five

Jill was frustrated: bored with the hospital lectures and impatient to become a 'real nurse.' September seemed an age away. She still relished her A-Level work and found the Shakespeare particularly absorbing. Their texts were *A Midsummer Night's Dream* and *King Lear* and the contrast between the burlesque antics of the Mechanicals and the tragedy of Lear's decline and madness greatly impressed Jill. She was incensed by Lear's treatment of Cordelia and said so, which both provoked lively discussion and led to her being labelled a feminist by the less enlightened male students in the group.

She was feeling reet brassed off when she recounted this to the lit twins at the June circle but was reassured by their habitual support and sympathy. Then, out of the blue, prospects really took a turn for the better: Sue broached the possibility of Jill's accompanying them to Lindisfarne that summer. They were due to attend a literary seminar (which sounded like a posh name for a study group) just outside the priory and were to rent a cottage for the week. It wouldn't cost Jill anything but her food as they could all go up in Sue's Mini and the cottage was already paid for. Apparently, they'd stopped in it several times before. She jumped at the chance, and when her parents raised no great objection Jill was ecstatic. Her mam even promised her supplies from Watson's, the butcher's she now managed, although she couldn't resist a dig: 'Watch those two don't corrupt you, mind. With their fancy ideas!'

Jill bridled, but decided to let it go. 'Divn't worry, Mam, I'll make sure they don't.'

And since her mam expressed no further reservation Jill concluded she was probably just glad to get rid of her for a week.

The summer term dragged a bit thereafter and the first two weeks of the holiday were consumed by hopes (she knew she'd learn loads) fears (what would she wear?) and planning. The last was slightly complicated by her birthday falling during their week away, but Jill had nothing in prospect. When she let slip to Joyce that she'd be eighteen whilst they were in Lindisfarne her one-time teacher promptly announced that she and Sue

170

would throw a party for her: 'One to remember, young lady!' No one had ever called her *that*.

As far as the days were concerned Jill had no qualms. She knew that Lindisfarne – or Holy Island as they called it in the Walker family, even though no one had actually visited – had beaches, and dunes and headlands. Surely it would, like the Farnes, have loads of birdlife; and there'd be interesting places to explore. And swim. And naturally, there'd be books to read. Sue had promised to 'bring a stock' and to introduce her to 'someone new.'

The evenings were another matter. Jill didn't imagine there'd be a cinema or a night club, a fear confirmed when she discovered in a dog-eared one-and-sixpenny guide that only 'two or three hundred people live there permanently.' Although during the tourist season there'd be a lot more than that. There were a couple of pubs apparently and if she could get served down Wallsend she was confident there'd be no difficulty on the island. If anything she encountered the opposite problem: since she looked and acted as if she were much older than seventeen she was frequently propositioned by men who turned out to be in their early twenties. It was quite flattering but when she didn't disabuse them of their assumptions they tended to expect more physically than she was interested in. What about Sue and Joyce though? She knew they went to pubs and liked a drink. But beyond Ferndale's literary cloisters she didn't really know much about the lit twins at all. And here she was: about to go away for a whole week with them...jeepers!

Finally there were the journeys. The Walkers didn't have a car and nor did any of her friends' parents. She'd got used to the daily commute to Ashington, and subsequently the shorter haul to the RVI, but she could count on her fingers the number of times she'd actually been driven anywhere. And Minis were small. She didn't anticipate claustrophobia – more likely travel-sickness – but you had to consider these things. On a positive note Jill knew that Holy Island was north of Bamburgh and, if you made a slight detour, you could take in Seahouses. Whilst recalling their rather snobby attitude to the village, Jill wondered whether she might nevertheless persuade them to stop off on the way – or the way back – so she could call on the Hortons. She'd exchanged Christmas cards with Morag ever since their trip and assuming she had fulfilled her academic aspirations she might still be at Durham University. Jill would love to hear about 'real' college life (i.e. when you didn't have to live at home) plus she speculated vaguely about how Jamie might've turned out. Yeah, the journeys were fraught with possibilities...

August shuffled along frustratingly. Recognising her impatience, Jill smiled: it was like when she was a kid and she couldn't wait for her birthday! All that expectation and then…nothing: no cards, no presents, no party, just temporary superiority over mates who were now playing catch-up. This would be different, though – she'd make certain of that. And sure enough when their departure date came there was no deflation, rather a burgeoning sense of anticipation. She'd borrowed a smart new grip off Aunt Louisa and packed and re-packed it three times the day before. Even then she was dissatisfied. She hadn't the slightest idea what you wore on an island. In fact, since it was a particularly hot August her sole certainty was her bikini, of which she was justly proud. She wasn't vain but her cousin Robert, who was a professional photographer, had told her she looked great in it one day down at Longsands. He'd promised to do a photomontage next time he was up from London, declaring she was 'photogenic – well for a Walker anyway, cos!'

Still, at least the grip fitted in the miniscule boot! Just as well considering the amount of luggage the lit twins were taking: the overflow was stacked up on the rear seat crushing Jill into a corner. But at least she had something to rest against and wouldn't be flung about. So the possibility of travel-sickness seemed remote; in fact it didn't cross Jill's mind again and they arrived at the causeway across to Lindisfarne in good fettle. There had been no way of checking the tides in advance but they were in luck; although since the sea was already lapping the road and they didn't know whether the tide was ebbing or flowing the crossing could've proved perilous.

Only after they were safely over did Joyce explain. Twice a day, for several hours at a time, the island was cut off by the sea. 'Even everyday stuff like bus times and postal deliveries are determined by the tides. And until recently there's been no metalled road: just a track across the sands. You had to follow it whether you were a visitor or you lived there. Like the medieval pilgrims,' she concluded. 'There's a jingle about it but I can only recall the first couple of lines:

> 'For with the flow and ebb, its style
> Varies from continent to isle'

Then there's something about the pilgrims keeping dry shod but I can't remember the rest.'

After the crossing they followed the road to Chare Ends and then swung south into the centre of the village. 'Sheldrake Cottage' was only a long stone's throw from The Ship Inn and when Joyce announced they'd get a bar snack there later and worry about cooking tomorrow Jill dared believe this holiday was going to be okay.

Thirty-Six

His father's desk was in the study overlooking the orchard-lawn. It was quiet, though not when the stereo was blaring out Ray's latest recording from the Third Programme of Beethoven's Seventh. His dad seemed to have to do more writing than ever now: not just school reports but all the correspondence the Ministry held on any subject even remotely connected with his role as Chairman of the National Camping Panel. So Jay was used to an array of buff files and papers bestrewing its surface. He had his own study upstairs but had permission to use his dad's if it were free and he needed more space or wanted music whilst he worked.

It was a Saturday in late June. His parents had gone to Norwich and he was revising for his final exams. He pushed aside three or four files to clear some space and there it was: an official HMSO envelope with Thursday's date-stamp on the front and a gold crest on the back. It had been slit carefully open by his father's brass paper-knife so Jay extracted the contents: a white, gilt-edged invitation card with the seal of Britannia on top. In royal blue italic script it read: '*The Commanding Officer, Members of the Staff & Officers under Training of the Britannia Royal Naval College...*' And then in smaller writing, '*request the pleasure of the Company of Mr and Mrs Raymond Fincher*' (that in Chris's hand) '*on Friday 27th July 1962 at 11 o'clock when Her Majesty the Queen will review the Passing out Parade.*'

Buggeration! When were they going to tell me wondered Jay bitterly. He was intensely proud of his big brother, RN, and had been looking forward all year to seeing him at his parade. And the Queen was to review it! Then he paused...and thought again. The invitees were in his brother's handwriting so it was *Chris* who'd excluded him. That couldn't be right. He just wouldn't do that. There must be some other explanation.

They'd been getting on great since he left. They exchanged letters at least once a fortnight and there'd been the occasional 'phone call, too. Jay kept a diary and an entry for the previous September read: 'Chris joined the Navy: 1600 hrs. GMT: 17.9.61. Cadet Fincher RN.' Just one week later he'd received his brother's first impressions of Britannia Royal Naval College.

'Dear Jay' it began, 'As far as I can remember this is the first letter I have written to you, but it won't be the last I can assure you. We have just finished Sunday Divisions and Morning Service. The former consist of a parade of the entire college in its Sunday best which means loads of gold and swords and medals for the officers and loads of hard work for us.' He'd gone on to describe the accommodation ('very comfortable but it has to be kept spotless') and the routine ('up at 0530 and bags of jobs before going to the Parade Ground at 0640...lessons and practical classes all morning. Then lunch then back to work: seamanship and communications. The evening is our own apart from two hours sailing, evening parade and all my various jobs'). He'd then imparted what Jay could now see had been good advice '...don't deliberately quarrel with Funchard, Pearse or Dad or if you must quarrel with the first two don't with the third.' The letter had concluded with more details of the day's activities and a closing sentence which had set the tone for all their subsequent correspondence and had touched Jay deeply: 'So you see, kid, we don't have too much spare time to think about home but nevertheless I find time and I don't think about the squabbling and the fights which took place but about all the good times we've had...'

The explanation emerged next day: 'Thought you'd like to see this, son.' His father reserved that tone for when Jay had committed some particularly heinous felony or when there was bad family news. Jay knew this to be neither but appreciated the sympathetic handling. 'It's a real shame you can't come with us, old boy, but the invitation is limited to two persons only, with a presumption for their being parents. I'm sorry!'

Jay looked suitably downcast but was secretly relieved – of course his big brother wouldn't have excluded him! Later, it being Sunday, his parents were taking afternoon tea in the drawing room. He was padding noiselessly along the corridor towards the staircase which led ultimately to his brother's eyrie when he heard his mother's voice: 'Well I thought he took it very well. He must've been disappointed. Let's just hope the Navy Days compensate.'

Things were looking up. The Lake District trip was already arranged for mid-August and now it seemed like there might be a visit to Dartmouth as well. All he needed then would be some decent exam results and look out sixth form!

The visit however was not to Dartmouth, where Ray and Muriel had proudly watched their elder son's Passing out Parade in the presence of Her Majesty the Queen, but to Plymouth where the Navy Days were to take place over the first weekend in August. Chris would drive down with their parents; Jay would get the train. The prospect was both exciting and a little daunting: he'd never undertaken such an ambitious solo journey. Freddie's father, who had no surgery that Friday morning, had promised to drop him off at Norwich Thorpe from where he would take the 8.30 to Liverpool Street. Then he had to get himself across London. That sounded tricky but apparently entailed locating only the Circle Line underground and following it for nine stops to Paddington. Autolycus the Itinerant had memorised the main ones – Aldersgate/Farringdon Square/King's Cross/ Baker Street/Edgware Road. When he got there he needed to be ready as Paddington would be the next stop. From there he would take the old Great Western route direct to Plymouth. He should be alert once he reached Exeter: partly to enjoy the scenery – Dartmoor lay to the north of the line – and partly to ensure he got off at Plymouth and didn't finish up in Penzance! Once there they would spend Saturday and Sunday at the various events, escorted by newly-promoted Midshipman Fincher. Then they'd track south-east to Salcombe for a couple of days, drop Chris in Dartmouth and embark on the long drive back to Norfolk.

The solo journey was onerous. If it was an adventure it was a tiring one and a weary Jay was finally reunited with the rest of the family almost eleven hours after leaving The Gatehouse. The wait was worth it. As he strolled along the platform, glancing around anxiously for his parents, there was Chris, resplendent in full uniform. Jay knew he wasn't really supposed to wear it off duty so he swelled with both pride and gratitude for his brother's welcome. It got better still: his brother had been entrusted with picking him up in the Zodiac, and since they were staying in Ivybridge he suggested stopping for a quick one at The Lord Nelson. 'It's an old coaching house: all oak beams and horse brasses. Serves a mean pint of Bass as well; I came in with the old man last night.' They pulled into the car park and noticed that there were some seats and tables on the edge of a garden area. It was a lovely sunny evening and Jay could think of nothing better than sitting outside with a pint of bitter and listening to his big brother's Navy tales. Plus it would obviate the need for him to go into the bar; not that he was usually refused service these days but he was only fifteen, after all.

'So what was the parade like?' he quizzed as soon as Chris had brought out the Bass, served in heavy barrel glasses and foaming to the brim.

'Pretty inspiring actually, kid. Sorry you couldn't be there. All the ceremonial...just so impressive and what with Her Majesty reviewing in person it really was an occasion. Main thing I was worried about was fainting. We were standing to attention for ages and it was a bloody hot day. A bloke three places away from me keeled over and that didn't help!'

'You were okay, though?

'Yeah, but it was a bit of a blur after that. I was just relieved when it was over! Mum and Dad enjoyed it but it was all right for them, they were sitting down.'

'So what about these Navy Days? What gives?'

'Well basically they're a chance for the Service to show off. So we can interest young men like you in going to Dartmouth rather than Cambridge!'

Jay smiled. He knew the story. Chris had been for an interview at Peterhouse two years before. When asked what he'd do if he didn't get in he announced rather casually: 'Wouldn't matter too much, sir, I've already been accepted for Britannia Royal Naval College.' The panel had been less than impressed.

'Seriously though, kid, you've got a far better chance of a scholarship than I ever had. You could do really well.' It was the first time his brother had commented on Jay's academic potential and he swelled with silent pride. If he'd had any money left he'd've offered to buy the next round!

'Anyway enough speculation. Whilst I get 'em in you might like a butcher's at this,' and he handed Jay a programme. It was headed *Plymouth Navy Days* with the 'Plymouth' in royal blue across the top and the vertical letters of the 'Navy Days' each within its own yellow, blue or red pennant. In the background was a silver aircraft carrier and at the bottom it advised: 'All proceeds are devoted to naval charities.' It cost two shillings.

Inside the front and rear covers were adverts for Guinness ('for strength') and Senior Service ('the outstanding cigarette of the day'). 'See the ships! Meet the men!' it promised against a black and white double-page photograph of a cruiser somewhere in the Med. Straightaway Jay was immersed in the Foreword. It was by Admiral Sir Charles Madden Bt., KCB (Commander-in Chief, Plymouth Command) and it invited Jay's attention 'to the presence on board all ships and at the display stands of officers and men eager to show (you) round.' Actually it said 'them' but Jay knew the Admiral meant him.

By then Chris had returned from the bar: 'Reckon we'll sup these and then get off, kid. Mum and Dad'll be wondering where we've got to otherwise.'

The next morning they drove back through Plymouth to Devonport and located the car park next to the Church of St Nicholas. Given their ample time and her interest in matters ecclesiastical their mother insisted on rooting round. To be fair it was less boring than Jay expected. The church wasn't particularly old – fifty-odd years – but it had an intricate model of the Golden Hind hanging above the nave and a silver replica of Drake's Drum standing near the lectern.

'Oh no!' whispered Jay to his older brother, 'bet that sets her off!'

And sure enough, their mother promptly started quoting her beloved Newbolt. At least it wouldn't be the one about the 'breathless hush'…

'Drake he's in his hammock an' a thousand mile away,
(Capten, art tha sleepin' there below?)
Slung atween the round shot in Nombre Dios Bay,
An dreamin' arl the time o' Plymouth Hoe…'

'Oh, no Mum, not the whole thing!'

Their mother smiled and skipped to her favourite bit:

'Take my drum to England, hang et by the shore,
Strike et when your powder's runnin' low;
If the Dons sight Devon, I'll quit the port o' Heaven,
An drum them up the Channel as we drummed them long ago.'

Well at least you've seen the real Drum now; well sort of anyway. And it was supposed to have been heard on Plymouth Hoe at the time of Dunkirk!'

Fortunately, they were able to escape to what Jay considered the visit proper after that, taking a boat trip around the outside of the port so they could get an idea of the whole dockyard. Chris acted as guide pointing out the Depot ships on the north side of the basin before they swung south-east and the main flotilla came into view. 'Those three are anti-submarine frigates and this one in the centre as well. So are those two, the far one's HMS *Venus*. I've bin on that, we came through the Kiel Canal in it a couple of months ago. And inside it moored to the main harbour is HMS *Lion*.'

Jay realised with a thrill of recognition it was the cruiser featured in the programme: 'C 34.' 'Any chance we can go on board?'

'Yeah defers. A mate of mine's a sub-lieutenant on her. He'll give us a tour. We'll go as soon as we've finished this trip. If that's ok with Mum and Dad?' he added accommodatingly.

They toured the cruiser for the next hour and a half. She was massive: almost 12,000 tons fully laden, their guide informed them, with four 6-inch guns and six 3-inch. 'Capable of almost 32 knots,' said S/Lt Gooch proudly.

'Huh! Slowcoach,' remarked Chris dismissively '*Venus*'ll do 36!'

'Yeah, but she only weighs about 2,500 tons, doesn't she?'

'Well, 2,700,' conceded Chris…and so the tour continued with the two young officers scoring points in a good-natured manner until the three landlubbers were overwhelmed both by all the information, and the number of steps they'd been up and down.

Later they were just in time for 'Action Stations.' The harbour-side had been transformed, and banks of temporary seating had been erected. On a quick rows-x-seats computation Jay reckoned the stands held 350 people, through whom an excited buzz of anticipation now rippled. 'Action Stations' was the highlight of the Navy Days. It featured a Commando-raid on an enemy strongpoint with submarine opposition. The target was a coastal battery, heavily protected by underwater obstacles and mines. First, clearance divers were sent in by helicopter ('that's what I want to do next – fly!' announced Chris, much to the admiration of Jay and the consternation of their mother). Explosions near the jetty represented the demolition of the defences. Meanwhile, the main assault force was being disembarked in Gemini dinghies. Suddenly, an enemy submarine was detected off-shore and attacked by mortar bombs from a destroyer. The crippled vessel surfaced, but was met with heavy gunfire and sunk. Ashore, the Commandos had successfully destroyed the strongpoint. They took to their dinghies once more and awaited the arrival of the destroyer. When Chris explained that the Commandos were all intensively trained Royal Marines who specialised in parachuting, snow warfare and cliff climbing, Jay's career path was adumbrated: 'Bloody brilliant,' he muttered.

The final day they moved hotels in the morning, settling into a beautiful spot above the steeply-indented coastline of Salcombe. But they still had time to get back to Devonport to witness 'Beat Retreat.' Over smoked salmon and scrambled eggs in the elegant dining room Chris explained, 'It goes back to olden days when darkness meant battle-over for the day. The idea of the Retreat was to get all the guards in place for the night. And to warn anyone outside the camp that the gates were going to be locked. Then when everyone was in they'd all get together and sing the Evening Hymn. That's what led to the present ceremony. At first it was just drums (please no, Mum!). Then fifes as well. Now it's the lot – including our own band from BRNC.' It was a stirring finale. Jay re-read the end piece from the programme: 'The Royal Navy, whereon under the good providence of God, the wealth, safety and strength of the Kingdom chiefly depend.' Stuff Cambridge: it would be a life on the ocean wave for him, too!

On the final evening the boys were invited to what proved to be a well-provisioned but very snobby cocktail party at the Yacht Club. The food and drink were excellent but the conversation revolved around how expensive the guests' boats were. Towards the end of the proceedings a particularly insufferable toff enquired of Chris patronisingly, 'Oh, and what do *you* sail?'

Chris paused until the silence was deep enough for the answer to be conclusive and pointed over the supercilious shoulder to the estuary: 'A Destroyer!'

Thirty-Seven

Jill opened her curtains. The orange orb of the sun hung over the North Sea silhouetting Lindisfarne Castle. She padded downstairs and out into cool, crisp air. After a brief stroll past the picturesque cottages of Broad Street she returned to find breakfast ready and the lit twins keen to set the scene.

They'd attended this seminar a couple of times before: once in York and once in Lancaster. This year's was special. A facsimile of *The Lindisfarne Gospels* was on loan from the British Library and was the subject of their study group. They would work in one of the outlying buildings of the priory. It had been founded around AD 635, Joyce explained, and the Gospel had been written and illustrated here on the island in honour of St Cuthbert.

'You've heard of him, pet, if I remember rightly. He was the successor to St Aidan, the missionary bishop sent from Iona. Aidan had been given the island by King Oswald after he'd conquered Bernicia. The story goes that Cuthbert was tending sheep in the Lammermuir hills (near where I was born) when he saw lights shimmering in the sky. It was a dark night but when he woke the other shepherds to show them, the stars had already faded away. So they didn't believe him and claimed all he'd seen were the Northern Lights. But Cuthbert knew they were wrong. The lights he'd seen were to the *south-east* and it was only later that the news came that St Aidan had died on Lindisfarne. It sort of started Cuthbert's reputation as a seer. Then soon after, he entered the monastery at Melrose. We're going to be studying the text itself so we'll tell you more about it as we go.

Now, what are you gonna do with yourself?'

'Explore the island, and go swimming,' declared Jill decisively.

'Sounds good,' remarked Sue, 'there's a map above the hall table if you want to check it out before you go. And a couple of guide books as well. We'll see you about teatime, pet.'

Jill studied the map for some time. Then she grabbed one of the guide books and repaired to the living room. She'd been right to assume she could explore the island that first day. Turned out it measured only a mile-and-a-half from north to south and just a mile from east to west with a long narrow peninsular of sand dunes stretching back towards the mainland. Well, she could skip that bit cause that was the way they'd mini-ed in. There was confirmation that only around 200 people lived here and that they mostly relied on fishing and farming and latterly the tourist trade – although from what she'd seen so far it wasn't especially busy that August. Hopefully the beaches would be a lot quieter than Cullercoats.

Then there was some stuff about geology which Morag would've liked but Jill found boring. Except for the bit about a basalt dyke (not the sense she'd heard it used in before, she smiled) forming the rock of Beblowe on which the castle was perched. There was a lot of detail about how the castle was used as a garrison against the Scots and what had happened to it more recently. Apparently a family called de Steyn had given it to the National Trust in 1944. It was still open to visitors from April until September but she decided she'd save herself the two bob. She could walk underneath it for nothing and then head north past Broad Stones and Bride's Hole until she came to Emmanuel Head. In between there was an inlet called Sheldrake Pool. Could be where the cottage got its name, she mused, logging it as a potential swimming spot. The north coast had a few bays whose names she memorised and an extensive area behind them called The Links. That seemed to be the highest part of the island.

Time to get ready! Jill rolled out of the armchair in which she'd been lolling and padded back barefoot through the hall to the stairs. At the top there were a separate loo and bathroom and along a short landing two bedrooms. The smaller of the two which Jill occupied was on the right, the other, much larger bedroom on the left. It hadn't registered with her the previous evening that the lit twins were sharing this room but now she reflected: of course, there were only two rooms so, naturally, they'd share. The door was slightly ajar and she couldn't resist poking her head round it. The furniture was sparse: a wardrobe, a dressing table on which lay two hairbrushes, combs and vanity bags and a large double bed covered in a brightly-flowered counterpane. It was neatly made; on one pillow was a blue silk baby-doll nightie and on the other a pair of dark green pyjamas. Jill caught herself wondering whose was which, hoping that the nightie was Sue's and feeling a distinct temptation to try it on. Instead she held it against herself and glanced in the dressing table mirror. Then feeling guilty that she'd intruded she folded it up and replaced it. She didn't notice an embroidered handkerchief fall to the floor and withdrawing swiftly, she shut the door and retreated to her own room.

She selected her exploring gear. It was going to get hot so shorts and a T-shirt would suffice with a pair of comfortable, rope-soled loafers. She might not find anywhere to change, so she put her bikini on and stuck a spare bra and knickers in her trusty duffel bag along with a large red and orange bath towel. Then, suddenly all-in-a-rush, she hurtled down to the kitchen and assembled some provisions. Her mother had been surprisingly generous. In addition to half a dozen steaks ('you'll need to eat 'em by Tuesday, mind') which had gone straight into the larder, she'd packed two brown-paper bags of apples and oranges, some dates and peanuts and a big slab of cheddar. Jill emptied the apples into the oranges-bag and then cutting a chunk of cheese off she put it, plus an apple and an orange and a handful of peanuts into the spare bag. Then she rifled through the cardboard library-box the lit twins had brought, selecting a dog-eared paperback of *Sons and Lovers*. She thrust that and the food into the duffel bag, arranged the strings so that she could carry it like a rucksack and strode off down Broad Street towards the castle.

Hugging the coastline as far as Sheldrake Pool, Jill thought about a swim but was put off by the rather forbidding prospect of the heaving waves and steep entry which meant diving in. She'd no problem with that but wasn't so sure about scaling the vertical rocks to get out again; besides it was only about fifteen minutes' walk from the castle and she might get company. She pressed on past what looked like a broadcasting mast at Emmanuel Head and then struck west towards what she hoped would be a secluded cove behind The Links. It was empty and she'd seen no one since leaving Castle Point. By the side of a sandy inlet the rocks ran out to a small skerry and she spied a smooth flat slab just above the sea. Even if someone came into the main cove she wouldn't be visible. She took off her T-shirt and shorts and, spreading out her bath towel, lay down to sunbathe.

She must have fallen asleep and when she shook herself awake she was roasting. She'd swum naked before – years ago when she and Liz had been just kids – and then more recently one night when she and a gang of students had taken several bottles of Spanish white wine down to the Yacht Club at Tynemouth and someone had suggested it as a dare. Safety in numbers and alcohol had combined to make it a romp but she recalled how sensuous the feel of the cool water on bare skin had been and was keen to relive the sensation. She took a last, superfluous glance around then unclasped her red and yellow striped bikini top, yanked off her bottoms and slid smoothly into the water. It was cold and deep but wonderfully invigorating and she struck out strongly for the far side of the inlet, maybe fifty yards away. Pausing only to have another recce she swam more slowly back, luxuriating in the foamy current. She reached her spot and hauled herself carefully out. Then she lay back down, closed her eyes and let the sun dry her...

They were well known at The Ship and had the steaks grilled there that night; Joyce regaling her with their day's scholarship and embellishing her knowledge of St Cuthbert: 'After Melrose he helped found a new monastery in Ripon. Later on he came back to Melrose and succeeded Boisil as prior. Then, when word came that discipline amongst the monks on Lindisfarne had deteriorated, he returned here. He wasn't really cut out for management though! He got more and more solitary and started withdrawing to a little islet just off the main shore, which could only be reached at low tide. Then he moved down to the Farnes – where you saw his chapel.'

Joyce was in full flow and Jill's attention began to wander after successive monks, bishops, saints – and halves of Belhaven. She didn't recall asking for a refill but Sue seemed to just keep them coming.

Later, when they were quizzing her about her own day over several glasses of Chianti she thought she detected a knowing look and a quickening of interest – particularly from Sue, or was that just wishful thinking – when she recounted the pleasures of her nude swim. 'Jill's curriculum sounds a trifle more risqué than ours, hin,' Sue remarked suggestively to her friend, 'maybe we should play hookey and join her one day...' Jill hoped the conversation would lead somewhere exciting but Joyce seemed to grow a bit distant. Not wanting to offend her, Jill finished her wine and said goodnight. Back in her room and more than a little tipsy, she stripped off and subsided into bed with the door ajar and the landing light still on.

Early next morning, still half-asleep and garnering the mournful cries of the herring gulls, she couldn't be sure whether Sue had come in to kiss her goodnight or whether she'd dreamt it. Rather than spoil the fantasy she decided to lie in bed until they'd gone off to their seminar: they'd probably just think she was hung-over!

She heard the front door close and waited a long five minutes. Then, naked and cautious, she opened her door – surely she hadn't closed it last night – and peered across the landing. The coast was clear so she sneaked into the other bedroom. The pyjamas and the negligee were neatly folded as before so she scooped the latter up and slid it over her head. It felt dead sexy; she was determined it was Sue's and she ran her hands up over her boobs so the silk ruffled her nipples. Christ! she felt hangover-horny!

She was about to relieve herself when the front door snapped open. Jeepers! Jill whipped the negligee over her head, folded it as neatly as her haste allowed and was just about to lay it back on the pillow when she noticed a small, square card previously covered by the nightie. Unthinkingly, she grabbed it. Then reckoning she couldn't get back to her room without it being obvious to whoever was below that she was trespassing, she zoomed into the loo, waited a few moments and pulled the chain. She emerged just ahead of whoever was coming upstairs and dived back into her room, unsure whether she'd been spotted. Minutes later, the steps retreated and silence reigned once more. Her heart still thumping, she pulled the covers back down from their face-over protection and gazed at the paper: it was a blank postcard cut in half. Jill flipped it over and on the obverse was drawn a large 'X' in scarlet lipstick. Oh, boy, she sighed…

Thirty-Eight

That summer the Finchers entertained an exchange student – Pierre Marceaux from Juan-les-Pin. Jay would make the return visit the following year. Not a bad swap: deepest Norfolk for the French Riviera!

They'd spent the first fortnight around The Gatehouse shooting pigeons and the occasional illegal pheasant with the Webley Mark III .22, and fishing for pike in the Waveney. There were daytrips to Great Yarmouth, Southwold where they sampled the freebies from the Adnams Brewery, and Norwich. It was on the last of these excursions, chauffeured by his dad who contrived to combine them with official visits to Ministry of Education offices, and schools, that Jay encountered his French friend's kleptomania. They would venture into a confectioner's and, as a dare, Jay would filch a couple of Mars Bars; Pierre would emerge with a two-pound box of Black Magic which he subsequently presented to a delighted Muriel. Strewth! thought Jay: she wouldn't be so *enchantée* if she knew. Later they hit WH Smiths – Jay feeling honour-bound to purloin some postcards: Pierre strolling out with a 1,500-page, Fourth Edition Concise Oxford English Dictionary stuffed down the front of his maroon cords! A similar tendency prevailed throughout his month-long stay; additionally their language skills both improved – particularly in the area of slang and unconventional English/French (good ole Partridge, conceded Autolycus).

The Elterwater trip had been planned months back. Neville Armstrong, in whose rented chalet they'd stayed three years previously, now owned a large static caravan on a wooded promontory overlooking Harrison's Tarn. The tacit understanding was that, provided his exchange student turned out okay, he could come as well: the van comfortably sleeping four. Jay had no qualms. His mate Malc was the easiest-going bloke he knew and Pierre was a good laugh. They'd be fine.

Muriel's parents were getting on a bit and she hadn't seen them in over a year so they'd combine the trips: dropping the boys off at the Croft and then carrying onto Southport. This time Malc's father would do the honours and doubtless, remembering that Ray had covered the sixty-four miles in a new record, would aim to lower his time. Sure enough he revved up the Jag to such an extent they reached the estate in an hour and twenty minutes. 'Be sure to tell your dad, young Jay,' he said laughing. 'And look after things here, Malcolm. Don't do anything I wouldn't do!'

Malc grinned and returned the standard response: 'That should give us plenty of scope, Dad!' A guffaw from Neville and he was gone in a scattering of slate-flakes and a throaty farewell from the Jag's twin exhaust pipes.

The caravan was luxurious and the two 'regulars' soon showed their visitor around the grounds. Jay was a tad piqued. He was used to running the show and resented Malc's greater familiarity with their immediate surroundings and Pierre's inclination to defer to his authority rather than Jay's. He'd show 'em once they got on the hills!

He didn't have long to wait. They dropped lucky with the weather and the next day was gorgeous: warm and sunny with just a few streaky clouds white against an azure sky. 'Cirro-stratus,' he explained loftily, 'gonna be a good spell of weather. We should make the most of it. We'll go for Bowfell I think: 2,960 feet – apart from Great End it's the highest peak under 3,000 feet.'

They caught the dull-green single decker bus just outside the estate gates and took it to the terminus, walking expectantly the rest of the way up Great Langdale to where it divided. To the north lay the U-shaped valley which he and Chris had trundled down when their dad had taken the Armstrong boys down the easy route on their Pikes outing. To the south, a less well-defined rougher trough. Keen to reclaim some credence, Malc enquired: 'So which route: Mickleden or Oxendale?'

Pierre looked impressed by this local knowledge, so Jay capped it crushingly: 'Huh, neither mate, we're going up the Band. See: that ridge that goes straight up the middle. Then we'll take the Climbers' Traverse off to the right and go up over the Great Slab. If you're up to it?' he concluded challengingly. They were; and after a strenuous and, beyond Cambridge Crags, exposed ascent they reached the top which, disappointingly, seemed to have attracted the only clouds in the vicinity. The promised view was shrouded in thick, dank mist. Slightly dispirited they made their way back via Three Tarns. The variation above the rocky defile of Hell Gill partly compensated for the lack of views from the summit as they dropped down to track alongside Oxendale Beck. It had been a good outing so far and there was no doubt who was in charge.

Then it started. At first it was just a bit of stone skimming across some of the shallows in the beck, and a search for larger blocks to plummet down into the deeper, rock-encircled pools. By the time they reached the point where the two streams merged to form Great Langdale Beck it had developed into a somewhat puerile but nevertheless enjoyable competition of who could soak the other two with the most strategically-directed boulders. Jay prided himself on his stone-throwing ability and whilst he was in the ascendancy he found the pastime amusing. Perhaps stung by his superior attitude during the climb, however, Malc and Pierre now joined forces. Jay held his own until the beck crossing. The bridge had been torn down in the winter floods and presently you had to use stepping stones when it was understood without saying that all hostilities were suspended. Except, it seemed, in French: two-thirds of the way across Jay turned to draw attention to a buzzard perched on the gatepost ahead of them when he was caught by an enormous slab that Pierre contrived to smack against the surface right next to him. He was absolutely drenched, and furious; the laughter of the other two merely exacerbating matters. On reaching the bank he stomped off, dripping, and didn't speak to either of them for the rest of the afternoon.

'*C'était trés drôle, mon ami, n'est-ce pas?*' offered Pierre back at the caravan when he judged Jay to have calmed down a bit.

'*Sal pedal à la chat vérole!!*' spat back Jay employing his best Riviera argot in the rudest phrase Pierre had so far taught him. Then he stalked out pretending to be still annoyed, but actually rather pleased with his bon mots.

A little later the three musketeers were reconciled. They couldn't normally get served at The Britannia, Elterwater's sole and somewhat strict public house; but fortunately they'd bumped into one of the gardeners from the estate and he'd agreed to help. Jimmy was from Oban. Jay didn't normally fraternise with the staff but when he discovered that Jimmy was a climber he made an exception and they hit it off. And when Jimmy established that Jay had climbed in the Cuillin (he didn't admit he'd only done the one peak, even if it was Sgurr Nan Gillean) they soon became cronies. The pub was always packed which meant that drinkers often stood outside or sat on the white metal bench which encircled the gnarled oak, bursting through the centre of what passed for the village green. In the last hour and a half Jimmy had had no difficulty in smuggling out five rounds of Jennings' Cumberland on condition that they paid for his as well. For a while they all talked together but when his mates arrived Jimmy procured one last round and left them to it: they weren't *that* friendly.

Deprived of their gopher and slightly merry anyway they decided to head for the van. The path led round the back of the pub and through a narrow slate-posted gate. There was a crash of glass to their right as a barman jettisoned a container of empties. They decided to investigate and found the lean-to doubled as a store. 'Let's borrow some,' suggested Jay and he and Malc grabbed a couple of indiscriminate bottles each from the darkness of the shed and ran for the gate. They crouched down behind the wall to make sure they weren't being followed.

'Where the hell's Pierre?' hissed Malc, 'hope he hasn't got himself caught. Reckon we should go back for him?'

Jay was torn between 'Yes, let's' and 'Sod 'im,' but before he'd committed to either there was a scraunching noise from the gate as Pierre squeezed through clutching a bulky box. The bugger had only half-inched a double crate of Guinness!

'*Vite! Vite alors*!' he advised and they rushed along the narrow paths in complete darkness – but with no sounds of pursuit – until they reached the caravan.

Malc unlocked the door and they tumbled over each other into the carpeted living area. 'Good evening, gentleman,' drawled a familiar voice from the Stygian depths of the compartment.

'Jesus Christ!' shrieked Malc 'what the fuck...'

'Don't worry, it's not the law,' came the reassuringly languid tones of Chris. He lit the central gas-lamp with his HMS *Venus* Zippo and chuckled at the inelegant heap of bodies and bottles.

'How the hell did you get in?' demanded Malc.

'Easy. You locked the door and screwed up all the windows but forgot the skylight! Glad to see you've brought supplies. Oh, and aren't you going to introduce me?'

Pierre, having worked out who the stranger was, regarded him with deferential awe but summoned the presence of mind to offer him a Guinness. The rest of the night passed in a blur of stout and reminiscence...

Next morning, the hangover and restorative fry-up were accompanied by the explanation. Chris was simply dropping in on them for the night en route to Rosyth on the Firth of Forth, where he would take up a posting on the frigate HMS *Whitby*.

Thirty-Nine

The next three days passed in a similarly halcyon fashion. Jill found other coves beyond The Links but the first inlet, which she'd christened Fulmar Bay (fortunately the breeding season was long past so she could avoid being either dive-bombed or covered in puke) remained her favourite. She established a routine of reading and swimming naked which was both sensuous in the water and invariably left her feeling slightly aroused as she subsequently lay out to dry. She hoped Sue would enquire and didn't want to disappoint, though she soon sussed it was a conversation topic for two, not three.

The new author they'd promised Jill had been D H Lawrence and after *Sons and Lovers* she'd devoured *The Rainbow* and was now embarking on *Women in Love*. Sue was a stickler for acquainting oneself with a new author in chronological order. She'd also promised her *Lady Chatterley's Lover*. It'd been banned until 1960 so had naturally become the only novel by Lawrence or any other writer most of her college friends had heard of, or wanted to read. (Even her mother had a copy, surreptitiously enclosed in a brown-paper bag and hidden − so she imagined − on top of her wardrobe.) Even so, Jill was intrigued at the prospect, not so much for the illicit sex and infamous language, as by Sue's choice and timing. Voracious reader as she was Jill would not get to it until Tuesday − her eighteenth birthday: was it going to be a present?

Three serene days were capped by three wonderful evenings. They ate in, drank a little wine, and discussed the seminar and Lawrence and the island and the future. Jill was treated as the adult she aspired to be. However, she was kidding herself if she didn't admit that the highlight of each day was when she heard the front door close. She'd convinced herself that the 'signs' were from Sue and that the latter had indeed both kissed her goodnight and seen her retreating hastily to her bedroom the morning after. In which case, she'd probably seen her naked. Twice. Hope she liked what she saw, fretted Jill. On the Saturday she had breakfast then excused herself to go upstairs and read. As soon as the coast was clear she was removing the negligee to discover another postcard which read, this time in black biro: 'Like the negligee? Enjoy your day: Love, Sue. X.' Jill was delighted to have her hopes confirmed. She was eager to reciprocate but anxious not to cause any friction between Sue and Joyce. Relying on Joyce not being party to the messages, however, she felt bold enough to scribble on the other side: 'Thanks! I LOVE the negligee. Jill X.'

On Sunday, the message had been even clearer: 'Have a lovely swim. Glad you liked Miss Swish! Lots of love. Sue XX,' to which Jill daringly replied: 'Would love to see you in it!! Will be thinking of you. Loadsaluv J. XX.'

By Monday, Sue's missive was both explicit and tantalising: 'Can be arranged! Wish I was swimming with you, pet! Birthday treat tomorrow. S. XX.' Without completely giving herself away Jill couldn't think what to say in return so she just scribbled ambiguously: 'Can't wait!!' and then, feeling that was insufficient, added: 'Love U. J. XX.' There! That'd torn it, she thought recklessly, but it didn't occur to her not to leave it.

The morning of her birthday dawned flawlessly clear. Jill was contemplating a swim before breakfast and had donned her bikini. But then – just like when she was a kid – she didn't want to risk missing anything. So, deciding that she had a bit of licence this day of all days, she merely slipped on her shorts and a pair of low heels to set off her legs and strode a tad self-consciously downstairs. To set a tone of altruism as well as expectation she decided to make them all scrambled eggs, and opened a carton of orange which she poured into large cut-glass tumblers they'd borrowed from the pub. Then she called to them to come down and was relieved to note approval rather than censure (even from Joyce) in their reaction to her ensemble! The breakfast gesture seemed to go down well and both women wished her Happy Birthday and kissed and hugged her warmly before departing for the last session of their study group, which was due to finish at one. There was no need for her to take provisions today: Sue and Joyce were going to make a picnic and bring it up to 'Fulmar Bay.'

In her haste to run upstairs as soon as the front door closed Jill stubbed her toe on the bare wood of the top step, tumbling across the landing into the bedroom. She brushed the nightie off the bed and snatched up the expected note: 'Happy Birthday, pet!!' it read, 'Bedside cabinet! Lots of love. Sue. XX.'

Her toe throbbing unheeded, Jill scrambled into her own room and unfastened the little metal clasp. On the half-shelf were two parcels. She pulled out the one wrapped in birthday-greetings paper which she demolished to find something soft in blue tissue paper. More carefully she peeled the tissue to reveal a black silk negligee of similar design to Sue's. As she shook it down a gold greetings card fell out. Inside was written: 'Can't wait to see U in it!! Big kisses Sue XX.'

Trembling, Jill slipped out of her shorts and bikini bottoms and unclasped her top. She pulled the negligee over her head and revelled in the feel of the silk on her bare skin. She adopted what she felt was a suitably cat-walkish gait and strolled next door. She didn't *admire* herself in the mirror but was duly conscious of the effect she might have on an observer: hopefully Sue! It did suit her, after all; and it certainly left just the right amount to the imagination, although it wouldn't do to bend over too far, she giggled! Strangely, although she felt pampered, she felt nothing like as febrile as when she'd first tried on Sue's negligee. So she slipped out of it and back into her former garb. Then she remembered the other package and pulled it out of the cabinet. It was obviously a book and she hoped she knew which one. Sure enough there it lay, in its bright green and gold cover: a sumptuous hardback edition, published by Heinemann which Sue had clearly bought. It was far too lavish for a library copy!

Then free of all burdens other than the spanking new volume of *Lady Chatterley's Lover* wrapped inside her bathing towel, Jill set off for Fulmar Bay. This was going to be her best birthday ever...

She skipped the 'Apropos...' section, keen to get into the story itself and although, as with all the novels she'd read so far, she enjoyed Lawrence's writing she acknowledged that she was only skimming the early chapters to get to 'the good bits,' as her college mates termed them. Even so she read carefully enough to get the gist of the story. Before she even encountered Mellors she sympathised with his character because of the execrable Clifford's treatment of him (and anyone 'in service' – though not, of course, the odious Mrs Bolton). What she didn't like was Mellors' dialect; but she recognised that was her not him: she knew she still had a Geordie accent and wished she could get rid of it. This week had both helped and hindered. She was especially conscious of her brogue when she was with the lit twins; on the other hand daily exposure to their more 'refined' vowels was beginning to rub off on her. No doubt she'd get ribbed back at St Peter's Road.

Jill had enjoyed the scene with the chickens but not the first time Connie and Mellors had made love. Had sex, more like it, she thought, and then it was only really Mellors who'd been fulfilled. 'The activity, the orgasm, was his, all his...' Exactly! It confirmed what she'd long since decided: women were much more sensitive and less selfish than men and if you wanted affection and consideration then you were far better off with someone like Sue. Admittedly, Lady C did seem to warm to it in time but Jill was unconvinced. And as far as the infamous four-letter words were concerned the only shock was seeing them in print: you heard worse than that in the Engine!

She'd swum – in the buff as usual – earlier; but once dry decided to put her bikini back on. Whilst her nudity might appeal to Sue (or, at least, she hoped it would) she sensed that Joyce might disapprove. If they all stripped off to go swimming, of course, that would be different. Scanning Lady C in a somewhat desultory fashion she was surprised to hear voices – a first at the bay, unless you counted the fulmars, black-headed gulls and oystercatchers. She was about to reach for her towel when she realised with relief and pleasure that it was the lit twins; and as they made their way gingerly along the promontory she joked: 'Ooh you're nice and early: did you get time off for good behaviour?'

They both laughed and Sue teased: 'And you're looking very... respectable! Have you been telling us porkies about nude bathing?' She leant over and planted a kiss on Jill's hastily-moistened lips: 'Happy Birthday again, hinny.' Then when she stepped out of the sun Jill saw that – like Joyce and herself – she was dressed only in shorts and a bikini top. Never having seen her in anything other than formal dress at the library and casuals in the Engine and on the island Jill gazed admiringly at her slim legs and flat tummy. Her thick, flaxen hair fell over her shoulders and neck perfectly framing boobs which were much more voluptuous than Jill had previously realised. She felt herself starting to respond and wondered whether Sue could tell; she couldn't wait to go swimming.

Fortunately both women were sweltering from their walk and Joyce took the initiative announcing, 'Come on then, you've been raving about the swimming all week: let's get in there!' Peeling off her clothes so rapidly that Jill was left staring in astonishment whilst Sue followed suit. She slipped out of her own bikini in as alluring a fashion as possible. Whether or not Sue *had* seen her naked before her warm smile indicated she liked what she saw now! However, before admiration risked turning to embarrassment all three women were splashing through the shallows to brave the bracing seawater. They struck out for the far side of the bay and Jill was relieved to find that not only could she keep up but she was actually the strongest swimmer by far. The only fraught moment came when Joyce, struggling to stay afloat, flung her arms around Sue's neck and for a jealous moment Jill feared they were going to kiss. But Sue was content merely to support her whilst she got her breath back for the return swim and then all three hauled themselves onto the rocks. Jill tried in vain not to ogle Sue's cold-taut nipples too obviously but since she and Joyce were similarly affected the moment again passed without any awkwardness. Then all three were stretched out drying luxuriously in the hot sun.

This is brill, sighed Jill inwardly, wondering whether she dare accidentally brush Sue's thigh (they *were* lying pretty close together, after all). Just as she'd plucked up the courage, however, her fingers were intercepted by Sue's and given a friendly but warning squeeze. She desisted thereafter and pondered whether they'd remain naked. A nude picnic? She thought not; they weren't naturists after all, they just enjoyed *swimming* as nature intended. Jill was sure there was a difference and needn't have worried anyway – when Joyce announced, 'Picnic time!' the bikinis went on as naturally as they'd come off. The spread put Jill's previous snacks to shame. There were egg and cress, and tongue sandwiches; chicken drumsticks; sausage rolls; miniature pork pies and crisps. And to cap it all, Joyce produced a cold box with two bottles of chilled Sancerre. 'Mustn't overdo it, mind: we're dining at The Ship tonight and Bob's promised a special birthday menu. We want to do it justice.'

So they'd been quite abstemious and not opened the second bottle. Even so, Jill wasn't used to drinking at all through the day and whilst she made a valiant effort to champion the superiority of *The Rainbow* over *Lady C*, doing so lying on her back in the hot sunshine with two glasses of Sancerre inside her proved too much. It wasn't long before she was snoozing happily; as were the lit twins, who were similarly unused to indulging at lunchtime. They awoke – variously and refreshed – around teatime and after a last, modest swim in the now-chilly bay, returned to Sheldrake Cottage.

Forty

A couple of months later came the news that Jay was both anticipating and was hugely proud of: his brother was a fully-fledged Midshipman sailing the seven seas. Or, more precisely, the Atlantic waters off Senegal. The six-page letter was embossed with a proud red seal atop which billowed the sails of an earlier warship encircling a crimson arch, presumably symbolising Whitby Abbey. It was dated 4th December 1962:

'Dakar, I thought, was good fun. I'm afraid I didn't get any postcards a) because I didn't see any and b) because those who did said they cost three or four bob each.

'You can tell Java that so far his complicated systems of pressure belts and winds are a load of balls. We haven't had a breath since leaving the Channel and the barometer has read 1020 for a week.

'Freetown's next but I don't think I'll bother going ashore. The First Lieutenant's just issued a tourist guide to this heaven-on-earth which promises: "If the sharks don't get you the current does; if both fail then the insects will have you; if you bear a charmed life the rebels will kill you and if everything else fails, you just die of boredom!" Sounds like one to give a miss, eh!

'Can you do me a favour, kid? If Dad is very busy would you give him a hand with getting Mum's present? He'll tell you what I want. A lot of the blokes buy "rabbits" (souvenirs) of every place but I think I'll bring back something worthwhile like diamonds, or an elephant instead of the local rubbish which is all made in Birmingham anyway.

'Well I'll turn this in now. Give my love to Mum and Dad and my regards to any of the boys you run into. Yours Chris.'

Chris-tmas brought a tan-leather briefcase with the initials 'J.F.' in gold (Jay had only sent cufflinks) and the New Year found his big brother in Cape Town.

'This apartheid business is a bastard. One is liable to five years in jug for sleeping with a coloured or any non-European girl. All public buildings from railway stations and trains to Gents are segregated. The whites aren't particularly worried and would have one believe the problem did not exist. However, it very definitely does in practice, quite apart from the intolerable constraint of not being allowed to talk to a coloured person. The beach, too, is partitioned off rigidly in some cases not only between colours but between religions.

'I must impart my cunning engineering dodge. I walk around in my filthy dirty overalls studiously wiping my hands on a filthy dirty rag. This is very crafty and designed to give senior officers the impression that I'm wiping off the muck obtained from the job I was doing the moment before. It's not that I'm skiving. I'm just not partial to engineering!

'I've got to tell you about my latest night out in Cape Town. I'd been to the flics and after that to a nite club 'til about 0200 when I was walking the streets. I often wander through cities at night as I enjoy the complete anonymity. However, I was standing outside the train station wondering what I was going to do with the three and a half hours before the train back to Simonstown when a coloured girl came up to me and asked me if I was English. Instead of pushing her on her back (in true South African fashion) I started chatting to her. We were having a right good chinwag when a car screeched to a halt. Out leapt the Gestapo, clipped the girl around the ear and shoved me in the back of the car (*Heil Hitler!*). I inquired about the reason for this uncouth behaviour and was sworn at in Afrikaans. When I said I didn't understand I was abused in English for some minutes. After a while I said I'd like to see a senior officer and they retorted that they were all senior.

'By this stage it was obvious they'd no intention of charging me despite their threats of prison, detention, magistrates etc. Anyway they proceeded to drive me round Cape Town telling me more and more frightening and ever more fatuous fates they had in store for me until they finally got to the point where they were going to take me out of town and shoot me. My roaring with laughter didn't go down too well and they drove me about four miles in the wrong direction before dumping me. They were going to give me a thick ear but I decamped in a rush and, after a few minutes, got a lift back into town with a courting couple. So ended my entertainment at the hands of the South African police!

'This bunch who are wholly recruited from the low-intelligence ranks of the Afrikaans country people, now have complete powers in SA – any one of them may detain anyone for any reason they like to make up and hold them indefinitely. There's absolutely no point in appealing if you're beaten up – hard luck! As far as I can see there's virtually no hope for white rule in South Africa. As the couple who picked me up said there are lots of people who hate the police state and abhor the colour-bar but will they do owt about it? Will they hell!

'Still one shouldn't go to SA without being arrested: it would be like going to Paris without visiting Montmartre – you wouldn't be making full use of the facilities.

'Don't say anything to the Administration though, will you. Mum'll only worry! I know it turned out OK but if I'd finished up in an SA jug I'd likely have been thrown out of the Navy. Any case I don't intend going into town again if I'm going to get treated like a criminal merely for talking to anyone I want.

'By the way, kid, when you've got a moment could you find my copy of Alan Paton's *Cry the Beloved Country* and post it to me? It's banned here so don't say what it is: just mark it 'Books.' I don't suppose they'll open it and if they do they'll only confiscate it.

'Well that's all for now, kid. Your loving brother, Chris.'

Thus letters continued to chart his big brother's progress around the Atlantic and Indian oceans: infinitely more entertaining than the drudgery of Jay's sixth-form studies.

He was in a rut. The academic side was okay. French was a bit of a bind, although given more focus by his up-coming visit to Antibes to renew his acquaintance with the notorious kleptomaniac Pierre. Geography was better. Java seemed genuinely interested to hear of Chris's latest adventures (suitably expurgated, of course) whilst parental support by way of additional text books and professional insights facilitated learning. English was best. 'Duke' Bartelby was brilliant once you were doing 'A' Level. If you demonstrated the right sort of attitude and application he treated you more like the undergraduate he was confident of turning you into. His eccentricities included daily lunch in the 'Golden Lion' where his appetite for Greene King enlivened many an afternoon session with Shakespeare. Predictably, it also earned him the soubriquet of 'Belch,' in honour of Sir Toby. Only if confronted with a particularly ill-advised challenge would he roar: 'I got a First at Cambridge, boy, d'you think you know better than me?' And even then, it was darkly assumed that his boast was merely to live up to his stereotype. His twelve English disciples admired him unreservedly.

Jay's social life was the problem. The move to the new school, compounded by the burden of considerable additional study, had exiled him from both the village and the nobs. He still knocked around with the latter occasionally in the holidays but had already resolved to find his own entertainment at the weekend (weeknights were for study, of course). Fired by his father's stories of 'reading Geography and billiards' at Birmingham he resolved to forsake girls (actually, they seemed to have already forsaken him) and take up snooker. Accordingly, he joined the 'Tute' as the Working Men's Institute attached to the town's print works was affectionately known. He was underage, of course, but presenting his brother's driving licence to the doorman on his first visit, he gained entrance subsequently by a confident, not to say dismissive air. And once in the snooker lounge there was never any question about your age: you had to be eighteen otherwise you wouldn't have been admitted in the first place.

Jock was his mentor. You attracted less unwanted attention and gained credence as a junior member (i.e. under twenty-one) if you acquitted yourself convincingly on the table. Jock was old, maybe even in his thirties, but had a reputation for looking after the youngsters and ensuring they kept out of trouble. That meant not hogging any table with another junior and most certainly not getting pissed and showing yourself up. Jay followed Jock's advice on both scores and whilst his snooker improved rapidly he managed not to fall foul of the 'Administration' at home. The three-mile bike ride was sufficient to eliminate the smell of Draught Bass. His mother thought he was at the Maidstones or the golf club – where for reasons he recognised it would've been okay to have a beer, bloody snobs! – whilst his father kept his suspicions to himself. On Saturdays when his parents were out to dinner he would have his regulation two pints in the Tute and then cycle down to The Morgue. He ranked as a regular now and Francis welcomed him cheerily enough: 'Usual, young Jay?' before disappearing into the back room and re-emerging with a flat, black pint of mild. Jay would have another, sometimes two, after that and consume twopenny packets of salted peanuts. Then he'd settle his tab with Francis, leap aboard his trusty Raleigh and cycle home. These days he could negotiate the return journey without falling off.

Life was simpler without girls.

On the day the summer holidays started the latest epistle from Chris dropped onto the stiff amber bristles of the porch mat. It was written from the Birkenhead Hotel, Hermanus in Cape Province.

'Very many thanks for your excellent and long letter,' it began. 'I don't know why you try and make out you wont' (spelling was not Chris's strong point) 'be having an idle three weeks in France. You're there to enjoy yourself. Make sure you do!

'Sounds like your love life is blossoming, though I use the present tense with a little circumspection in view of your recent preference for snooker over women! Sound judgment generally and akin to Kipling's preference for "a good cigar"! I still know very little about this dame as although you claim you told me in a previous letter I must've lost it. What's more, as the info was classified I've had only a few dark hints from Mum.

'Of the lineage, chattels, intellect or particular charms of this damsel I wist naught. *Quelle école etc. mon frère? Les inhabitants des Seychelles, les Seychelloises, parlant Francais par temps de temps, quand leur Anglais ne sont pas bon assez...* My duty as a citizen was to assist their English which I did in very gallant fashion – but that's another story.'

'*Quelle école?*' eh! Well that was a corker! Having studiously ignored the former female imports Jay had discovered – under the tutorship of Lothario 'Dream' Foster – that they had grown up behind his back. Well not all of them, maybe, but one in particular – Caroline Tillotson – a fourth-year girl only eighteen months younger than him. An only child, she lived in The Old Manse with her parents: a former Army officer and the beautiful Indian woman he'd married controversially some twenty years earlier when stationed in Simla. Colonel Tillotson was strict and upstanding and Jay foresaw some friction in that direction. Ranji – as she invited Jay to call her on his third visit – was, however, warm and generous-hearted. Caroline was dark-haired, olive skinned and not-half attractive, now he came to think about it. The snooker might have to take a back seat – temporarily, of course whilst he saw how the land lay.

'I shouldn't be inclined to get a more powerful bike as you will have far more opportunity car-wise than I did, Mum now being attuned to the idea that young sons need loan of mother's car! Anyway as soon as I'm back the first item on the agenda is a sports car: possibly a TR 2, or, if I can run to it, an MGA. The 1600 Twin Cam is a scorcher. So stick with the Triumph T20, kid, and look forward to sharing a proper car in a few months' time.

'At the moment I'm relaxing in Hermanus. Hotels here are very good and cheap and it's better than travelling back and forth which is either expensive or risky. Hitch-hiking is definitely not the done thing in the Fourth Reich! However, perhaps I'd better not get started on that subject right now as I've been feeling more and more steamed up about it since my visits first to Mombasa and then to the Seychelles. Both trips were the best education of my life and for sheer unaffected enjoyment there's no better company than the black, half-caste or Indian girls. They are intelligent, amusing and completely at ease and if, as in the Seychelles, they're fifty years behind the times, they find it as funny, or funnier, than you do. I'm told it isn't done for officers to mix with such girls but when I go somewhere I want to meet the people that make the place what it is, not the relics of the British/French/German/Dutch colonial systems which I can meet by walking fifty yards up the drive at home.

'All the best, kid, don't work through to the bone above the elbow. I'm looking forward to seeing a photo of Caroline and the original when I return. Your loving brother, Christopher.

P.S. I'd be grateful if I could borrow your Fascist belt – such apparel will soon be all the rage with the direction the SA Government is going in at the moment!'

Forty-One

Back in the living room Joyce announced that they were 'going to do this properly' and would be 'dressing for dinner.' Jill was familiar with the expression but worried that she didn't have anything remotely suitable to wear. Joyce, in charge, smiled knowingly: 'We'd like you to have your birthday present before we go out. You might want to wear it,' and she handed Jill a shiny, black and silver dress box. 'Sue and I have some business to attend to before we change. Then we'll meet here at 6.30 for pre-dinner drinks,' she instructed portentously, but with a grin that exploded the sham pomposity.

The dress was beautiful. It was dark blue, sheer silk with a plunging neckline, nipped in at the waist and flared in the skirt. The latter hung fashionably just above the knee. The twins were still out so she slipped into the main bedroom to hold it against herself and check in the mirror. Hmm, not bad, Jill Walker, even if you do say so yourself as shouldn't! She turned to go back to her own room and spotted the corner of a card peeping out from Sue's carefully-folded negligee. Delicately, she drew it out between her thumb and forefinger and glanced at the message: 'Cabinet! Hope you like them! Love & kisses. S.'

The little package must've been hidden whilst she was at the bay. She definitely wouldn't've missed it earlier. Inside was a pair of skimpy knickers, an uplift bra and a suspender belt. All were the same silky-blue as the dress. In a separate packet was a pair of seam-stretched black stockings. The note which fell out stated suggestively: 'Can't wait to see you in them!! XXX. S.'

Nervous was an understatement! The dress was shorter than Jill was used to and she was relieved the staircase didn't descend directly into the living room. She didn't normally flash her knickers; well not stone-cold sober anyway. She wasn't used to high-heels either. Her mam – a constant surprise these days – had lent her them: 'You never know, hinny, you might need them on your birthday' and she teetered precariously down the stairs. Feeling extremely self-conscious she made as graceful an entrance as she could to be greeted by cat-calls and applause from her mentors. She blushed as they sang Happy Birthday and gladly accepted the fluted-glass of bubbly that Joyce thrust into her shaking hand. 'It's only Asti Spumante, pet: poor girls' champagne! But it has the same effect. Cheers!! By the way, you look lovely: do you like the dress?'

'It's brilliant, thanks. It's dead kind of you both. I can't get over it. Cheers yourselves.' She embraced them in the dazzling smile that summed up how she felt and appraised her companions. They'd gone to so much trouble. Joyce looked prettier than she'd ever seen her with her hair curled fetchingly under her chin in that year's Jean Shrimpton look which she was slender enough to espouse. Sue was a knockout: a rich cream see-through blouse tucked into a dark brown miniskirt which almost revealed her stocking tops even when she was standing up! God knows what the regulars at The Ship would think!

She needn't have worried. The lit twins had been welcome summer – and occasionally Christmas – visitors for years and were popular and well-liked by those islanders who frequented the pub. Bob and his landlady-wife Norma were joining them in a private room above the bar. And by the time they had to make their way through the packed snug the bubbly had relaxed Jill enough to appreciate, not be embarrassed by, the whistles of approval. Joyce, who Jill noticed had consumed her bubbly rapidly (perhaps she was nervous?), and Sue seemed to enjoy the reception, too.

The meal was birthday perfect: prawn cocktail, sirloin steak (as good as her mam's) and black-forest gateaux. They'd had a different wine with each course: more bubbly, a rich burgundy ('*Châteauneuf du Pape*,' Bob had announced grandly) and, now, a strong sweet Barsac. Jill had been careful not to drink too much, but had only partially succeeded and was now feeling delightfully and wine-fully relaxed. She had begun to cast the odd longing glance at Sue whenever she thought no one would notice.

Joyce was tipsy; but was nevertheless making a good fist of describing to their bemused hosts how the Lindisfarne Gospels had come to be written. Currently, she was clarifying what a colophon was. 'Originally, it meant a finishing stroke. But it's also an inscription at the end of a book. It records stuff like the printer's name, the title and when and where it was printed. In this case it starts: "Eadfrith, Bishop of the Lindisfarne Church, originally wrote this book, for God and for Saint Cuthbert"' Oh, Cuthbert again, thought Jill: he seems to crop up all over the place, as Joyce continued her explanation which was erudite but starting to confuse her Aldreds with her Ethelwalds. Jill was impressed, though, when asked what an 'anchorite' was she not only explained it succinctly but advised that

Shakespeare used the term too: 'In *Hamlet*,' she slurred slightly, 'the Player Queen swears "An anchor's cheer in prison be my scope!" if she were to remarry.' Bob and Norma looked nonplussed; but Sue smiled indulgently as if showing off a prodigious but slightly muddled child. Jill hoped it had occurred to her, too, that Joyce's increasingly tiddly state might present opportunities later. Jill shot her what she hoped was a glance of lambent lust and was rewarded by a loving gaze in return. She wished she were close enough to touch her, but maybe it was just as well she wasn't. Joyce was now droning on about Billfrith – the anchorite in question – but fortunately the gateau arrived and chocolate stemmed the flow.

Dinner was adjudged a great success by Joyce and concluded with a final rendition of Happy Birthday to which Jill was apparently expected to respond. 'Speech Speech!' commanded Joyce. 'Up on your chair, pet,' and Jill, forgetting how short her skirt was, did as she was bid.

If she'd had time to think about it she'd have been petrified. She'd never made a speech, even to just four people. In the few seconds she had to marshal her thoughts she heard a sharp 'Phwoar!' from Bob and a hiss from Norma, neither of which she related to herself. Then, mustering all the confidence she could, she proclaimed, 'I just want to say thank you to everyone. This is most enjoyable birthday I've ever had, and the best dinner with the best company. Thank you all so, so much.'

Joyce led the applause, crying raucously, 'More! More!' And then betraying her real interest with, 'show us more knickers, pet: you look dead sexy!' Norma was still berating Bob whilst Sue just sat back enjoying the show. Jill blushed furiously as she realised what a view her audience must've been getting and hoped, fleetingly, that Joyce was too befuddled to wonder how she came to possess underwear like that! She really ought to get down from the chair straightaway, but couldn't resist performing a couple of rapid pirouettes which naturally caused her skirt to flare out even higher and not only gave her admirers a perfect view of her stockings and suspenders but also revealed just how skimpy her briefs were. Then she stepped down circumspectly feeling embarrassed, triumphant and excited in equal measure.

Nothing could follow that and the party gradually disintegrated; although the trip back through the snug seemed to take a while involving a lot of good wishes, most of which included unlicensed hands roaming over all three girls' bottoms. The cottage was only a couple of hundred yards away but their Gospeller was clearly going to need some help. Sue draped one of Joyce's arms around her neck and they set off. 'And you, pet,' Joyce muttered thickly, winding her free arm round Jill's waist.

The darkness of the unlit street engulfed them and Jill discovered that Joyce was not just drunk but randy-drunk. The hand that was clasped around her waist rapidly slid down her hip and over her left buttock. Then, flicking her skirt up, it began to caress her bum. Jill glanced across at Sue's silhouette and decided she couldn't possibly see anything in the murk. She wondered whether she should move Joyce's hand but it seemed ungracious and besides, mellow herself, she was curious as to what might happen next.

Joyce was most certainly feeling horny. Unbeknown to Jill the hand that was curled round Sue's neck had already fumbled open her top buttons, snaked down her blouse and was trying to scoop her boobs out of her bra. When it succeeded there was a loud sigh from Sue but Jill just attributed it to her bearing Joyce's weight. Besides she was preoccupied with what was happening to *her*. Joyce's fingers were all over her cheeks and as they walked the motion caused them to creep further and further between her legs. Jill wondered how long it would take them to reach the cottage. At this rate she'd be hot for it before they got home, never mind what lay in store for her then.

Perhaps Joyce was more burdensome than she looked cause Sue seemed to be breathing heavily and slowing down at the same time. That was fine by her, thought Jill excitedly (little realising that Sue's breasts were now enjoying both Joyce's teasing fingers and the cool night air). The longer the walk took the more aroused she was becoming. There was a deep sigh from Sue as they'd started walking again; but before anything further occurred they arrived back.

They stepped through the unlocked porch door and into the living room. Someone had earlier drawn the curtains and switched on two table lamps; the subdued lighting seemed just right. Joyce relinquished her grasp on Jill and Sue deposited her carefully on the sofa. As she did so she couldn't avoid her breasts swinging gloriously free above her bra and Jill realised why it had taken them so long to walk back! Not that she was complaining, although she was a bit piqued when Joyce took the opportunity to reach up and massage her boobs briefly before Sue stood and, without undue haste cupped her bra back over them, holding Jill's gaze as she did so. She didn't bother to fasten up her buttons though. 'Special coffee anyone?' she enquired brightly, disappearing into the kitchen.

Uh oh, thought Jill. It's a good job I've managed to stay reasonably sober cause if we're going on the 'special coffees' anything could happen.

It was a Hogmanay tradition normally. The men went out on the Eve until three or four in the morning and then, to bring them round before they went for the all-important New Year's Day pre-dinner session at the Club, Mam would make the coffees – two-thirds of a mug of very strong Nescafé topped up with 100% dark rum. And a McEwans Export to wash it down. The challenge was then to stay sober enough to do justice to dinner at about three o'clock, after which you were allowed a snooze before the evening session in the Club to round things off. Not the sort of challenge Jill really fancied right now.

Sue emerged from the kitchen: 'Looks like just the two cups, hinny! I think our hostess is ready for bed,' motioning to the recumbent figure who had subsided on the sofa and was snuffling like a sleepy piglet. 'Can you keep an eye on the kettle, pet, whilst I take her up?' Jill smiled with what she hoped was the correct mixture of concern and conspiracy and hoped Sue wouldn't be too long. She wondered if she should offer to help but concluded it could prove awkward; presumably getting Joyce to bed also entailed undressing her. Besides Sue swept up their friend with such aplomb that it occurred to Jill she'd done it before and didn't require any assistance. As they climbed the stairs unsteadily Joyce could be heard muttering incoherently and Jill wandered through to oversee coffee production.

As Sue seemed to be by far the most sober Jill decided it would not go amiss to strengthen her 'special' a bit. She smelt the cups first just to check that they'd already got rum in and then cast about for the bottle. She found it in a teak corner cupboard along with several other bottles of gin and whisky she hadn't known were in Sheldrake Cottage: why, you drunken old ducks you, she sniggered, extracting a squarish flask for inspection. Jill liked labels – she recalled Captain Morgan's nostalgically – but she hadn't seen this one before: 'Myers's' it pronounced, '100% Fine Jamaican Rum.' The oblong label was bordered in russet with a sash across at an angle proclaiming it to be 'Original Dark,' and in the background were sugar cane plants, a distillery and three barrels in a triangular pile. Disappointingly the 100% must have referred to its Jamaican extract as the actual strength was only 40%. Still, powerful enough, Jill mused, uncorking the red top and ladling a generous additional measure into the china mug on the right. She took the now-simmering kettle off the hob until she heard footsteps on the landing. Then, as she heard them disappear into the loo she poured the two coffees and carried them through to the living room. She found a couple of coasters and placed the cups at opposite ends of the low sofa-table before striking what she hoped was the pose propos.

'Sleeping like a baby!' chuckled Sue, as she subsided onto the not-so-far end of the sofa. 'Hmm, that coffee smells good – and strong!' she smiled sniffing it appreciatively. 'Well, hinny, how have you enjoyed your birthday – *so far?*' she enquired archly and before Jill could respond took a large gulp of the 'special.' 'Goodness, don't remember it tasting that potent,' she offered knowingly, 'hope you're not trying to get me stoned! So, what were the best bits?'

Jill shut her eyes momentarily and sighed with pleasure: 'Well everything really. The swimming was great, and the picnic – that Sancerre was delicious. I loved the meal. And I can't thank you enough for the dress. Oh, and especially the lingerie – it makes me feel dead sexy!'

'It makes you *look* dead sexy, too, pet. Very...what shall we say... desirable: in fact positively gorgeous. I could eat you up,' and she leaned across slowly and gave Jill an affectionate peck on the cheek. Then, when she was sure the girl was not alarmed she whispered, 'Happy Birthday, sweetheart,' and kissed her softly but full on the lips. Jill had been anticipating this moment ever since the promise of the lipstick 'X' and although she had no idea how to proceed thereafter, she'd decided her response days ago. She shuffled swiftly towards the older girl and wrapped her arms around her, hugging her close. Sue returned the gesture warmly and they remained glued together for what seemed like ages. Then just as Sue drew her head back and subjected Jill to a blatantly yearning gaze there was a loud bang over their heads: Joyce had fallen out of bed! 'Shit!' grimaced Sue, 'I'd better go and see she's okay. Don't run away!'

Frustrated and happy simultaneously, Jill sipped the rest of her coffee as she registered the clumsy manoeuvrings and muffled exchanges from above. The sounds went on for some time and Jill snuggled back in the sofa and closed her eyes for a moment.

When Sue emerged from settling Joyce, Jill was fast asleep.

Forty-Two

Pierre seemed much older. And much less friendly than he had the previous summer in England. When they knocked around with his French chums he barely acknowledged Jay and when he did, spoke in such staccato tones that the young Englishman struggled to understand him. It was a little better when they were off on a solo jaunt – shoplifting in the smart boutiques or swimming round from the public *plage* to one of the exclusive private beaches which ran down from the expensive hotels in Juan-les-Pins. The tactic was to get there early and invade the loungers before the security men came on duty: if you were already in residence they assumed you were stopping at the hotel. It also helped if you could adopt a dismissively haughty expression: both boys were good at that.

Even so, Jay was not really enjoying himself and confided as much to his big brother. The response was as swift as Air Mail allowed: 'I was unhappy though not surprised to hear that you were missing home more than you'd expected to. The phycological' (nice spelling, Chris!) 'effect of the removal of ones surroundings is considerable and I recall I loathed the first few weeks at Dartmouth with a steady and quite illogical hatred. Fortunately the feeling soon diminishes and after two or three twinges, the last being the first day in *Venus*, I am now perfectly able to go anywhere and be phycologically self-sufficient.

'All this is fairly general and I'm telling you so you know I sympathise. Anyway kid, you'll stick it out as I stuck out Dartmouth. There is nothing heroic or English schoolboy-paperish about the business: it's purely and simply the reaction of one's mind to the sudden dismantling of its foundations. I just wanted you to know it isn't peculiar to you nor is it in any way a defect.

'I'm surprised you mind the heat, though: I rather like it – and the eighties, my boy, are a luxury. Now I remember when I was in Aden back in '63, it was 110 degrees in the shade and there wasn't any shade, harrumph! harrumph!

'The money side of things is bound to be a bit more of a bore, kid.

I don't want to sound like a Dutch uncle but it shook me when three whiskies came to 453 pesetas – £3. 10. 0 – in the Canary Islands. You just have to accept that you're gonna get ripped off a bit. Night clubs are run on that principle in most parts of the world and being designed originally to trap tourists on the Riviera they are especially expensive.

'In some ways your experience is very valuable as it'll make you even more self-reliant than does my vastly wider travels in the insulated cocoon of Whitby. Anyway I think you can overcome your problems, particularly with your ability to speak the language. To hell with walking the streets, park yourself on the beach or the coffee bar, spark up a Gauloises and in the elegant words of the Bessarabian prophetess, "stuff 'em!"'

There was more in the same vein concluding with an apology for sounding 'like an epistle to the Corinthians' before reverting to their favourite shared subject – cars. Chris still had his heart set on a Triumph or an MG when he returned that autumn. His savings would not run to either but he figured that a combination of parental largesse in recognition of his twenty-first and wheedling a loan out of his nan might fund the shortfall.

'There's only one snag: if things go according to plan I won't be back to use it! This is because I've volunteered for Submarines and the course is five months based at HMS *Dolphin* in Pompey. After that most subs are home-based but you're at sea a fair bit. Still, I'll be at home as well and could soon teach you to drive it. The submarine decision was taken as a result of a thoroughly enjoyable spell in HM S/M *Alliance* and although there are drawbacks (much riskier than conventional boats) there are some tremendous advantages particularly suitable to my temperament – lack of formal discipline, abolition of uniformity, more pay etc.'

Strewth! thought Jay, wonder how Mum'll react to that: sounds dangerous! But it also sounded pretty glamorous and, for the first time, it dawned on Jay how much alike they were. Until now he'd always regarded his big brother as slightly remote and a pillar of the community. But his earlier revelations about the Fourth Reich and his admission that basically he was as ill-disciplined and unconventional as Jay himself struck a chord. He couldn't wait for him to come home! Fraternal affection was rewarded not by reciprocity, however, but by a long silence; explained subsequently by their having been on manoeuvres in something called 'CAPEX.'

'We've just spent upwards of a month off and on at sea: quite interesting and diverting if somewhat antediluvian. We were pretending we were fighting the last war again and were accordingly convoying each other up and down across False Bay waiting for the Brass in ALLIANCE to sink the convoy for the ninety-third time! If you take a butcher's at Dad's

Reader's Digest Atlas you'll see where I mean: False Bay is between Cape of Good Hope in the west and Cape Hangklip maybe fifteen miles east. Imagine a line connecting them, only further out to sea and you'll have a pretty good idea of where the exercise was, although I'm not supposed to reveal that, of course!

'Anyway, Frazer and I were allowed to be ORO, which is Ops Room Officer in charge of all the radar, asdic and display gear whilst not actually fighting the submarines. As the whole outfit must have cost in the region of two million quid you'll appreciate you can have quite a lot of fun. I don't suppose it'll make the English papers but LEOPARD and PIETER MARITZBURG contrived to write each other off. One never knows whose fault these things are until the subsequent Courts Martial but the main tragedy was one killed in Leopard and thirteen on the Maritz. The whole thing has been pretty nauseating; I can't wait to head for South America and the final leg of our tour.'

And that was the last Jay heard for a while. Six weeks later he got a tape from Rio and relished the sound of his big brother's excited tones describing the nightlife there with Conchita, and in Buenos Aires where it transpired he had a girl too, Rosa, and was commuting the 1,200 miles between them by RNVR flying boats! There wasn't a lot of detail – lest it fell into the inquisitive hands of the Administration – but there was enough to show off with in the prefects' room, which Jay now inhabited in his final 'A' Level year.

Things were looking up. He gained a fair amount of kudos for having a brother who was a Naval Officer and just as much for having a girlfriend like Caroline. Well, that's how he thought of her now: as a girlfriend. They'd been going steady (if you could describe their somewhat turbulent relationship thus) for a couple of months. She'd made the first move.

'Are you allowed to park that thing there?' she'd enquired in less-than-friendly tones.

'Yeah, prefect's prerogative,' he responded, trying to adopt a compromise between dismissiveness and nonchalance.

'What is it anyway?' she persevered as he took off his helmet and shook loose his tawny mane.

'Tiger Cub Sports,' he rejoined more emolliently, impressed that she even bothered to ask.

'You're Jay Fincher, aren't you. The one whose brother's in the Navy.'

Jay softened further. How did she know? 'Yeah, I am. He's a navigation officer on a frigate.' He didn't know what else to say and sensed the conversation was about to fizzle out. Vaguely conscious that he didn't want that, he floundered through the emotional swamp when he suddenly remembered what Dream had told him. 'And you're Caroline, aren't you? Caroline Tillotson.'

They'd arranged to meet for coffee, but not at his usual haunt. Too public. Jay certainly didn't want to risk running into Denham and the gang on their first 'date.' So they settled for the tea shop on Trinity Street which turned out to be full of old biddies.

'Strewth! We're the only people here under fifty!' Jay was nervous and worried about his faux pas. But he needn't've been. She just laughed and hoped their respective mothers wouldn't walk in. It broke the ice!

After that they went to the Mayfair where Jay began to appreciate the potential of the 'three-and-sixpenny-doubles,' although he was on his best behaviour. They held hands walking back and that would probably have been it if Caroline hadn't taken the initiative. Their conversation had dried up in waiting-for-bus awkwardness but just before she boarded the single decker to Wortwell, Caroline grabbed both his hands and assured him, 'I've had a lovely time, Jay,' and before he could respond, planted a smacker full on his lips. Then she was blowing kisses from the bus and he was hoping he really had heard the words 'next time.'

They were constantly falling out, principally because Caroline had a mind of her own! She didn't seem prepared to accept the subservient role which her age and sex predetermined, as far as Jay was concerned. Then, when he briefly realised the error of his ways, they'd get back together again before Power or Vincent could move in. He remained pally with Power through their cross-country prowess and great things were expected of both of them in the forthcoming season. They were certainly training hard. Although Power lived eight miles the other side of town he'd cycled round to The Gatehouse a couple of times after Jay had told him about his 'circuit.'

He'd devised the route himself, using his knowledge of and access to the countryside around the Kirkstead estate. You could run up the lane at the back of their house and break out over headlands to where the Hoods farmed. Then, with Mr Hood's permission, you could cut right across his arable fields – well round their headlands anyway – and down to the valley where Bombadil once ruled. Jay smiled to himself. With his penchant for trifles he felt obliged to christen his course and was almost tempted to call it 'Withywindle' but then he'd have to explain why and being disinclined to he went for 'Target.' It sounded vaguely competitive but actually reflected the toughest, climactic stretch of the route: after you'd run alongside the Waveney for a spell you came to Target Hill, the old wartime firing-range. It wasn't much of a hill by Jay's standards but it was the steepest incline around. It would toughen them up for the rigours of the inter-schools festival where most of the competitors were quicker than Power or Fincher but might not match them for the stamina Jay figured they'd build up on Target Hill. (The route continued towards their old house but then dropped down the bank and doubled back through the alder-brush so that you actually climbed the Hill twice.) Moreover, 'Target' was quite a bit longer than the competition route. He'd borrowed one of his dad's six-inch OS maps and carefully marked off the twists and turns of his course with a pencil and postcard. It was a tad under six miles. Power was impressed; the more so after they'd run it together and he'd been unable to keep up with Jay on the Hill, although he'd overhauled him on the flat-track last-half-mile. Much to Jay's ill-concealed disgust.

Maybe Power wouldn't have made a move on Caroline (although he had confessed a certain warmth before Jay had even noticed her), but Vincent certainly would. With the illicit manipulation of the Beechen appendage long forgotten (except by Jay), Vincent now had a reputation as a real ladies' man. There were rumours that he'd already nearly put Caroline's friend, Jenny, in the family way and Jay wouldn't've trusted him in the same county with his girlfriend. So a malicious comment that 'he wouldn't mind a look there myself' immediately had Jay on his mettle; and apologising to Caroline for his latest misdemeanour. Not that he need've worried. Caroline was far shrewder than him in such matters and when she announced she 'wouldn't touch Vincent with a disinfected bargepole' she meant it. Although she added mischievously that she might entertain an overture from Power or – especially – Denham.

Denham was Head Boy. He'd always been top of their class until the sixth-form when such judgements no longer applied. But Jay knew he wasn't anything like as bright as him at English which, given the awe in which Belch Bartleby was held, was everyone's favourite subject. Neither he nor anyone else in the group had Jay's facility for memorising huge chunks of Shakespeare (he currently knew all five of Hamlet's soliloquies by heart, plus another thousand lines of the play), nor was he as astute when it came to textual analysis. But he was an all-round good egg: handsome, skilled in team sports and, crucially, popular with the teachers, especially Funchard. It was a surprise to no one but Jay (and Chris who'd confidently forecast the elevation of his little brother) when Denham was appointed. Apart from the prestige foregone, Jay wasn't too upset. He preferred a lower-profile and he certainly wouldn't've relished the representative duties the post entailed or the toadying up to Funchard that was allegedly *de rigeur*.

No! Room for manoeuvre was what suited Jay: that and the chair by the window. There were only two and obviously one belonged to the Head Boy. No one was ever quite sure how Jay claimed the other. He wasn't deputy or head of games or even speaker (an arcane position linked to debating expertise); he'd just decided it was his and tacitly challenged anyone to oust him. No one did. The prefects' room was at the head of the stairs, opposite the library, so the window chairs commanded the best view of the playground. They also encompassed the low table on which the prefectorial record player resided. That meant that either Denham or Fincher effectively controlled the choice of lunchtime music. Not that there was much by way of either choice, or disagreement. The Beatles reigned; they'd been top of the charts for eighteen weeks since early summer: first, with *From Me to You* then with *She Loves You* and now, as the end of term approached, with *I Wanna Hold Your Hand*. The Mersey Beat trailed a distant second with Gerry and The Pacemakers, and almost out of sight were Billy J Kramer and the Dakotas, who sounded to Jay as if they came from the American plains but in fact hailed from rather-less-glamorous Bootle.

So he might not be Head Boy but dogged cross-countryman, chief wordsmith and controller of music was not a bad combination. That, together with the cachet provided by Chris and Caroline, meant Jay was pretty pleased with life as his seventeenth birthday passed. The only cloud on the horizon came in the shape of the glasses he needed to see it.

The first he knew of it was in the New Year. Since his sixteenth birthday he had squandered his grandpa's bequest (the source of family dissension since, inexplicably, he'd left nothing to any other grandchild) on successively more powerful motorbikes. This despite the fact his parents had promised a share in his mum's car if he didn't succumb to a motorbike. Now, however, Jay was keen to progress to four wheels. He'd applied for his test at the beginning of December and it had come through on January 3rd. That was good – a Friday and before term started so he wouldn't have to ask for time off and, in the unlikely event that he failed it, no one need know.

His dad identified a meeting he needed to attend in Norwich and gave Jay a lift. They arranged to meet for lunch as his test was at 10.30. All went swimmingly and his somewhat elderly examiner professed himself pleased with Jay's performance: 'Very good, Mr Fincher. You coped with all aspects well. There's just the formality of the eye test. Strictly speaking, I should have requested that at the outset if we hadn't been distracted by that accident. Just read me the registration of that blue car over there, please.' Jay stared in the direction of the examiner's outstretched finger. He could see the car, some thirty yards away, but the number plate was a blur. 'Well, perhaps it is slightly over twenty-five yards,' said his scrutator considerately and they walked a little closer; but to no effect. They walked closer still, and it was only when they were within fifteen yards off the turquoise Anglia that Jay could actually make out its registration. 'I'm awfully sorry, Mr Fincher, but I'll have to fail you. It's a shame; you'd done really well until then. You need to invest in some spectacles.'

Jay was devastated; not so much at failing the test but at the prospect of having to wear specs. It never occurred to him that he might easily have crimped his bike any time in the previous twelve months, only that he'd look a right burke in glasses and Caroline would probably stop going out with him.

Within the month he'd got a smart if slightly scholarly pair of brown horn-rims; Caroline had not deserted him and he'd applied for a second test.

A fortnight later he fell lucky again. It was half-term and once again he'd cadged a lift off his dad. It was market day and Norwich was busy. His examiner this time was a pedantic young man who gave him instructions in a very precise, rather superior fashion. Jay took an instant dislike to him, but was determined not to let it affect his driving. All seemed to go well: reversing round the corner was a piece of cake; the three-point turn executed neatly without touching the kerb; and the emergency stop performed with sufficient urgency to cause the pedant to drop his clipboard. The test over, Jay waited confidently.

'I'm afraid you've failed, Mr Fincher: dangerous driving occasioned by giving confusing signals to a pedestrian.'

Jay wracked his brains and, although he sensed it was useless to argue, bristled with defiance: 'When?' he enquired.

'As we came down Mountergate, you quite rightly stopped at the pedestrian crossing but when that young woman hesitated you shouldn't have waved her across.'

'What the hell was confusing about that?' Jay was starting to lose his temper but he couldn't help himself: the bloke was an idiot. 'She knew exactly what I meant. She crossed safely enough, didn't she?'

The examiner sneered condescendingly: 'And if something had been coming the other way?'

Out-of-control, Jay snorted furiously: 'It was a fucking one-way street you dick!'

The examiner flushed with embarrassed indignation but his clipboard waved away Jay's objections decisively. He'd failed for a second time. Right yer bastards! he resolved, as he stomped down Elm Hill to his father's office. You can stuff your cars, I'm getting a Bonneville!

Forty-Three

The following morning Jill awoke early. She was fully clothed under a light blanket that Sue must've draped over her. She padded softly upstairs, got out of her finery, feeling somewhat foolish, and arranged it carefully over a hanger in the wardrobe. Then she donned shorts and a T-shirt before heading out for a coastal stroll. She didn't feel like swimming but the cool air cleared her head. She was fairly sure she hadn't done anything embarrassing – apart from her antics on the chair which could be put down to party spirits – and wondered how the others were feeling. Especially Sue. They were due to set off home today, hopefully via Seahouses, the lit twins having agreed to set aside their aversion to 'Northumberland's Blackpool' and call on the Hortons.

She glanced at her watch. She'd been out for nearly an hour and although it was still early she figured she'd better be getting back. If they were going to return via Seahouses and they'd still to pack and close up Sheldrake Cottage there was a lot to do. She still felt a bit nervous about what sort of atmosphere awaited her but needn't have worried. As she opened the door there was a sound of sizzling bacon and a wonderful smell wafting out of the kitchen from which Joyce emerged looking perky and business-like. 'Bacon butties, pet: thought we could all do with a lining to our stomachs after last night's revelries!' As that was the only reference she made to the birthday shenanigans Jill figured she'd either forgotten how drunk and frisky she'd got or chosen to ignore it. Either way Jill was relieved: there was to be no inquest, no recriminations, at least as far as Joyce was concerned. And she couldn't imagine Sue would have any cross words.

She hadn't; although she seemed a little brisker than usual, announcing that they couldn't linger too long over breakfast as there was tons to do and they wanted to, 'Leave plenty of time to catch up with your friends in the delectable Seahouses!' At which she gave Jill a conspiratorial wink, much relieving the latter's incipient anxiety. The butties were accompanied by mugs of steaming tea and suitably fortified they set about cleaning and tidying the cottage throughout. When all was to Joyce's satisfaction they locked up and formed a three-girl delegation to take the large iron key back to the pub and thank Bob and Norma for their wonderful hospitality. Bob managed to flash her a broad, knowing smile when Norma wasn't looking but Jill didn't mind. After all it was based only on what he'd enjoyed at the dinner table and she *had* made a bit of an exhibition of herself! 'Aa'll look forward to seein the two of you at Christmas; and yer welcome any time too, pet.'

Then after suitably restrained hugs it was into a packed Mini and back across the causeway to terra firma. They soon picked up the A1 and then the inquisition began. 'You're sure your friend will be there?'

'Yeah, once you said it was okay in principle I rang her from the island.'

'So what's she like? When did you meet and how? Tell us all about her!'

It was all very friendly – bantering even – but Jill felt like Father Dominic was putting her through her catechism in preparation for confirmation. She said so and Joyce laughed sympathetically but ever-inquisitive added, 'So, just as a matter of interest, who *were* you confirmed by?'

'The Bishop of Hexham and Newcastle I think: but it's ages ago.'

'Ha!' exclaimed Joyce as if she'd just emerged victorious from an abstruse ecclesiastical dispute, 'I thought so. That's another connexion with St Cuthbert you know. He was joint patron of the Diocese, along with Our Blessed Lady Immaculate.' As usual Joyce spoke with authority. It had never occurred to Jill that she was Catholic but, thinking back, since her first teaching post had been at St Kits it figured. Anyway it was only a brief respite: she knew she'd have to spill the beans on Morag.

They sped along the A1, past the hamlets of Fenwick and Buckton, so those must be the Kyloe Hills on the right, mused Jill. Sue had pointed them out on the way up.

'So which college did she choose?' enquired Joyce, ever the one for detail.

'St Aidan's. But when I visited she was sharing a flat with a couple of other girls just off Darlington Road. Apparently she'll be moving into college for her final year. Brand spanking new an all, designed by Spencer somebody, Morag said.'

'Spence. Sir Basil Spence,' chipped in Sue, chuckling, 'fascinating bloke. Must be nearly sixty now. He won the competition to design the rebuilding of Coventry Cathedral. You know, the one the Nazis bombed.' Jill didn't but she nodded politely anyway and Sue continued: 'Yeah, he's done loads of public buildings. He did the new library at Edinburgh

University too. The one on George Square: I went there for a summer school a few years back. It's one of the biggest library buildings in Europe. Most impressive. St Aidan's is supposed to be really picturesque, spread out in a semicircle round a lawn. Make sure you visit her if you get the chance.'

'Yeah, I will thanks. She's really enjoying it there. Studying Geography – she always liked that.'

'*Reading*, pet,' corrected Joyce, 'she's *reading* Geography'; but she didn't explain why and Jill, smarting from the mistake, didn't feel like asking. What on earth difference did it make?

'Well anyway her flatmates were out when I visited so she told me all about Durham and her year in London. I don't remember much of it cause it didn't make a lot of sense. Too many names I'd never heard of!'

'How come London? What did she do there?'

'I think it was her aunt – Mrs Horton's sister – lived there. Is there somewhere called Camden?' and receiving a nod from Sue she ploughed on: 'Right, she lived there near one of the stations – Euston? – but she worked in a bookshop in Bloomsbury. I know that's right cause I recall thinking what a funny name it was!'

Sue's turn to interrupt: 'Might sound funny but it's a fascinating part of London. Heaps of literary connections. There was a "Bloomsbury Set" in the early part of the century. Included Virginia Woolf. Bit unfashionable these days but if you wanted to sample her you could try *To the Lighthouse*. I've got a copy you could borrow. Not sure if you'd like her though. Rather precious!'

'Well that was where Morag went – her aunt's shop. Then later she helped out as a classroom assistant at an infant school in Islington. And as a barmaid at a pub called "The Lamb", all green leather seats and smoky glass apparently. I definitely remember that, cause she said it was the best bit of all – until they found out she was only sixteen – and she'd take me there if we were ever in London together. Not that there's much chance of that,' she concluded pensively.

After that the conversation tailed off a little as the A1 swept inland to avoid Fenham Flats. Once in Belford they turned left towards the sea again. The landscape was dull for now: smooth and treeless. But they soon re-crossed the railway and suddenly came upon Bamburgh. 'Now this is a place we should visit,' promised Sue brightly. 'Maybe not today but certainly next time you're up with us. The castle is stunning and there's a wonderful library owned by the Crewe Trustees. You have to get special permission but I reckon we could swing it.' Jill cheered up again – so the Seahouses diversion wouldn't prove to be just for her benefit, after all!

The Hortons were out to greet them as soon as they turned into the farm which lay a little back from the outskirts of the town, above the caravan site where the Walkers had once stayed. It was weird: Jill recalled the place instantly but it all seemed much smaller than she'd remembered. She looked round for Jamie but he wouldn't be meeting them; he was in Australia! Jill was disappointed and intrigued. She'd been speculating about how the shy but canny little lad of eleven might have turned out, but then – Australia? What the hell was he doing there? No big deal it transpired. Like the Walkers, and plenty of other Geordies who'd taken advantage of Australia's 'populate or perish' immigration policy of the fifties, and the sweetener of a £10 fare, Mr Horton's younger brother had ended up in Victoria. Married now and settled in Geelong, he'd invited his favourite nephew to come for an extended stay. Jill wondered whether Geelong was anywhere near Bendigo where her cousin Billy had recently emigrated. She was about to risk showing her ignorance – though maybe the lit twins all-encompassing knowledge didn't extend to Antipodean geography – when Morag burst out of the barn and, running across to the assembled party, greeted Jill with warm and protracted hugs.

That was nice, thought Jill, realising she'd been a bit apprehensive about her reception; and then immediately fretting about what Sue would think. She covered any potential embarrassment by effecting the introductions and soon everyone was seated round the oak trestle table in the Horton kitchen for elevenses, sipping ordinary, instant coffee and savouring the oven-fresh rock buns that Mrs Horton had baked specially. However, once pleasantries and enquiries had been exchanged it soon became obvious that, as a group, they had little in common. Jill realised she was the nexus: with the Hortons, with Morag and, of course, with the lit twins. Each component was comfortable with her but not the others. However, it was one thing recognising it and another having the skill and experience to do something about it. And Jill had neither. She racked her brains for a solution: a suggestion that would get them out of the hospitable but claustrophobic kitchen.

It was Morag who came to the rescue. 'Anyone fancy a walk along the coast? If you've got time we could drive down as far as Craster and stroll back north to Dunstanburgh Castle. That way you'd be headed in the right direction afterwards.'

Joyce was decisive: 'That'd be lovely, pet; all the years I've been coming up this way I've never actually been to the castle. We can save Bamburgh for next time, eh?' she submitted, glancing towards Sue for endorsement, and then when it was forthcoming continuing, 'Can we all go?'

Mr and Mrs Horton having pleaded chores and caravan changeover duties, Joyce invited Morag to come in the Mini, offering to drive her back afterwards whilst Jill and Sue got provisions in Craster. That sounded promising and Jill could've kicked Morag when she announced, 'Thanks but it'll only take you back on yourself. I'm quite happy to walk back. It'll only take a couple of hours, scouts' pace.' Bang went her chance of some time alone with Sue!

Goodbyes over as swiftly as hellos, the explorers motored the ten miles or so down to Craster and parked up close to the smokehouses. They could see the castle etched majestically against the deep-blue August noon and were soon relishing the short springy turf of the coastal path. Morag assumed tour-guide duties just as she had on the Farnes. Her knowledge of the local geology was now much expanded and although never as interested in the birdlife as Jamie had been she was well-informed by comparison with the other three. Ornithology, it seemed, was not the lit twins' forte either, concluded Jill a little mischievously.

'The castle's here because of the whinstone sill,' began Morag. 'It stretches right across Northumberland. Ages before the Barons of Embleton built it here on the sea, the Romans had completed most of what we call Hadrian's Wall. That takes advantage of the sill as well. And there's good climbing on it. Jamie and his mates go out to Crag Lough. The far side of the castle it drops vertically into the sea for a hundred feet or so.

'I've come across the Embletons before,' interjected Joyce, 'part of the Charlton family heritage – withstanding the rievers. Or, some say, in cahoots with them,' she conceded.

It was Jill's turn to interrupt the historical exchange, 'Look! What are those birds, the ones flying really close to the water? They're too small for fulmars and too dark. What are they?'

'Oh well-spotted,' cried Morag admiringly, 'they're Manx Shearwaters. Their flight's very like a fulmar but you're right, they're a lot smaller. And they don't have that disgusting puking habit either!'

'Are they the ones that fly fantastic distances to get food for their young?'

'Yeah, anything up to 600 miles, they reckon. And at night too. It's amazing. 'Specially how they find their way back to their burrows.'

They drifted north over The Heughs and the talk continued to alternate between birds and rocks, dominated by Morag. As they got closer to the castle and the rocky spur of Scrogg Hill they split naturally into two pairs. Jill was listening to Morag but watching the lit twins in the distance as they enjoyed their stroll. Whatever they were discussing

(Gospels or her? wondered Jill), the two younger girls' focus switched to their respective studies and when reciprocal visits might be arranged to St Aidan's and the RVI. Morag was incredulous that Jill hadn't been able to go to grammar school ('You'd've walked it at Alnwick!') but complimentary about her 'A' Level studies and offered to help any way she could as she'd still got her own English Literature texts.

They coalesced on the clambering Dunstanburgh dolerite and spent a while marvelling at the imposing architectural mix of towers, keeps and wards perched precariously high above Embleton Bay. Then Joyce announced it was time they were heading back south whilst Morag began to jog off north. But not before they'd sorted out Jill's visit to Durham the following term.

Forty-Four

Jay never bought the Bonneville. He didn't need to.

On Chris's return from the 'SA & SA' tour of duty (commemorated by a pewter pint-mug) he had achieved his ambition and entered HMS *Dolphin* for his submariner's training. And with the help of his nana he'd bought a second-hand MGA. (The funding was mysterious. It was supposedly 'a loan,' but his nan had told him confidentially she wouldn't be asking for it back. Chris wondered whether it was her way of correcting the injustice of his grandpa's will which had left money to Jay but nothing to him or his cousins.) The additional cash enabled him to acquire a much smarter model, too. Originally, having abandoned the idea of a TR 2, he'd been looking around for a 1500; now he was the exceedingly proud owner of a bright red, convertible Twin Cam 1600. It wasn't the most reliable car on the road but, boy, was it smooth!

He hadn't said anything about his purchase. He'd a long weekend's leave and drove up from Portsmouth early on the Friday morning. It was the Easter holidays and a lovely sunny day so he'd got the hood down. When he rolled into the gravel drive leading up to The Gatehouse there was a whoop of jubilation from his little brother who was washing their father's Wolseley 110.

'Hiya, kid, fancy a spin?'

'You bet! When did you get this? Must've cost a bomb! Do Mum and Dad know?'

'Whoa! Steady on: less of the third degree! But since you ask – last weekend, yeah not cheap, and not yet! In that order. C'mon let's burn into town. I can't wait to show it off to Smir and Humph if they're around. Quick, jump in before the Administration rumble us.'

They sped off down Hollow Hill and across the valley towards town, Jay bombarding his big brother with questions and comments. The MG was certainly fast; there was a smell of hot oil and the tyres squealed impressively on the sharper corners. 'Double overhead cam-shaft and disc brakes: nought to sixty in nine seconds! And what about the number plate?' In his excitement Jay had failed – probably for the first time in his life – to spot it, so Chris continued gleefully, 'MTB 620. Spot on, eh. Not that a submariner normally welcomes a motor-torpedo boat, but it's pretty naval, what!'

They garnered several appraising looks scorching round town but as neither Smir nor Humph was in Chris was persuaded to run out to Wortwell, mainly on account of it being a notoriously bendy drag. He'd never met Caroline, although approving comments had greeted the photies, and Jay was suddenly torn. He wanted her to see him in the MG and meet his illustrious elder brother; he was also seized with an irrational apprehension that she'd fall for him. He glanced across: yeah, it was worse than he feared. His brother had the dashing Fincher looks all right. Unlike himself. Chris's hair was thick and black, longer than a regular officer would've been allowed. He had deep brown eyes and the aquiline nose of their Grandpa Hughes. His light tan slacks were enhanced by a standard submariner-issue cream polo-neck. Shit! Big mistake, concluded Jay ruefully.

He needn't've worried. Chris was friendly but impeccably mannered and Caroline, if she were smitten, certainly betrayed no signs that were obvious to Jay. They'd swung into the semi-circular drive at a fair tilt, squirting pea-gravel over the stone steps to the front door. They didn't need to knock, Caroline was there already, with her father in close attendance. Jay trusted he wouldn't get all military, considering he'd reacted favourably when first told of the elder Fincher's occupation.

'So, Sub-Lieutenant Fincher, I presume,' smiled the Colonel extending his hand, 'welcome to The Manse.'

'Good to meet you, sir!' returned Chris leaping from the car, and almost to attention. 'And you, Caroline. Jay's told me lots about you: all good, it goes without saying.'

They were joined by Ranji who appeared far more agitated than her daughter but immediately invited them in for coffee. Jay was not too keen but was rescued by his brother's explaining that they really ought to be getting home since he'd missed his parents earlier, and had yet to say hello!

The visit set the pattern for the summer: twice more Chris managed to convert a shore-leave into a flying let's-impress-the-natives routine. The first time was at Whit. He'd got a long weekend and they decided to drive up to Lancashire. The intention was partly to go over to see their nan in Southport so Chris could show her the result of her generous loan; but mainly to catch up with the Armstrongs with whom they'd be staying. The bonus for Chris was that fellow-submariner, Nick Hunter, lived in Blackburn and would be on shore leave at the same time. Nick owned a Morgan Plus Four and the rivalry between the two marques had yet to be tested.

For once there'd been no one-upmanship with the Armstrong boys. Their father, Neville, had given the MG the seal of approval and since neither Hugh nor Malc owned a car they had no basis for competition. Conditions were perfect and the drive up from Norfolk had been fun, albeit still long, even in a sports car. They'd cut through the lanes past the Hoods' posh public school to pick up the A47 at East Dereham and then on to Swaffham and King's Lynn. There they switched to the A17, trailing through the tediously-flat, black-soiled Fens to Spalding. After that they picked up a short cut on back-roads through Bourne and Melton Mowbray ('where the pies come from,' advised Jay knowledgeably), skirting Loughborough to the north. Then it was onto the majesty of the A6 (Autolycus 'collected' important roads – trunked and in single figures) through Derby and Matlock and via the Peak District to Buxton ('where the Spas come from,' smiled Chris, returning the compliment). They took a wrong turn in Manchester, much to Jay's chagrin as navigator and temporary guardian of his dad's 1963 AA Handbook. Jay prized the Handbook not just for the excellent maps but for the information it included on all the major towns and cities. He particularly snapped up the populations – London top, of course, on 8 million followed by Birmingham then Glasgow each around a million. Manchester and Liverpool came next nudging three-quarters of a million, then Leeds and Sheffield both comfortably over half a million. Jay had memorised every centre over 100,000: a feat which didn't surprise but nevertheless impressed his family and those of his friends on whom he inflicted his superior knowledge.

Also on loan was their father's AA badge, removed from the Wolseley 110 and screwed firmly to the grill of the MG in a prominent position. Chris explained: 'You remember that stuff yonks ago about AA patrolmen saluting Dad cause he was important and the Armstrongs claiming that Neville got the same treatment?' Jay nodded vaguely, noting that Chris was apparently on Christian-name terms: privilege of rank, I s'pose. 'Well it turns out they were right, of course, but it's even more significant when they *don't* salute.' Jay looked puzzled and his brother elucidated. 'Thing is, the AA was founded back in the early part of the century, right. It was after they'd introduced speed limits. And penalties for breaking 'em. Initially, the patrolmen used to wave at drivers to warn them of a policeman. But that was deemed illegal. Then they decided that they couldn't be prosecuted for *not* signalling so if a driver with his AA badge didn't get a salute he knew summat was up. Pretty cunning, eh! Thought it might come in handy in this – being as there's just a chance we might break the odd speed limit!'

Soon after, they regained the arterial road before finally leaving it in Bolton to head over the Belmont Moors to Darwen and drop down through Blackburn to Wilpshire. From The Gatehouse to the Croft had taken them seven hours – a full hour shorter than their dad normally took. They were chuffed.

On the Sunday they nipped over to Southport. Their nan was delighted to see them and apparently impressed with the purchase her elder grandson had made with her largesse. She declined the offer of a test drive, however, contenting herself with a complimentary comment about the car's looks and how it was rather sportier than anything their granddad would've espoused.

Marjorie had no such qualms and when Chris took her for a run on the steep, twisty road which wound up above the golf club and came down the side of Whalley Nab she shrieked with delight as the brakes and tyres complained at the sharpness of the downhill bends. If she'd been in her husband's Jag he'd have received a right bollocking but Chris could do no wrong, it seemed.

Malc had a mate called Dave, though everyone called him Fritz. He played in a group and they were due to practise that afternoon in Darwen. Malc and Jay were invited if they could get themselves there. As luck would have it Chris's colleague, Nick, was in the vicinity and had rung the previous evening to see if he was up for a challenge. So Jay was seated alongside his big brother, whilst Malc made a beeline for the Morgan. The drive over was relatively sedate.

The practice session went well. The group had originally been the Lionel Morton Four but as they'd met in a room above Mary Reidy's music shop in Penny Street, Blackburn, the bloke who managed them had decided a catchier name would be, *The Four Pennies*. Jay had never heard of them but, as was his wont, didn't let on. They went through their full repertoire, promising to end with *Juliet*. It was a virtuoso performance and Jay took Malc's lead by nodding approvingly and tapping to the beat at all the right moments. It was only afterwards that he discovered *Juliet* was No. 1 in the hit parade that very week!

Even if he'd known, though, the drive back would still have been the highlight. It was starting to drizzle when they came out but Nick declared it didn't matter: he wasn't putting his hood up. Chris had to agree, remarking casually, 'Course not: you don't get wet as long as you go fast enough!' That would've been okay if they'd been on the Preston

By-Pass (as the cognoscenti still called the stretch of the M6 opened almost six years earlier, but still the place to race. 'We'll shoot this one at a 100, Jay boy,' Neville had promised – and they had, passing under the motorway bridge at 115 mph!). Unfortunately, they were in a built-up area and the rain was falling faster now. Mercifully there was no traffic – neither police cars nor AA men to not-salute them – which was fortunate as they accelerated away bumper to bumper. Without warning Chris shouted, 'Let's go continental!' and swerved across to the right-hand side of the empty road. Moments later they were side by side doing sixty-five down Darwen High Street. They held station for several hundred yards until the approaching bend forced the MG to drop back in behind the Morgan. 'Bollocks: I thought we'd got 'em,' roared Chris, 'don't worry I'll have him at the lights.' And sure enough as the traffic lights turned red he drew up, still on the wrong side of the road, alongside the Morgan. There followed a deafening squeal from eight suffering tyres and the superior acceleration of the twin cam (or Chris's skill, Jay liked to think) allowed them to cut back in front of the Morgan just before the next bridge. After that there was no further opportunity for overtaking as they arrived back at the Croft nose-to-tail. And no one was wet!

Later that summer Jay persuaded Chris to chauffeur him from Fielden Avenue. It was a hot July Friday, the last day of term and he'd arrived just at turn-out. The main drive was crowded with youngsters waiting for their buses so Chris had driven straight up to the front door where Funchard's uninspiringly-maroon Austin A55 Cambridge was parked. As Caro and Jay strolled round the corner hand-in-hand, Chris was just vaulting out of the MG to greet their headmaster. Jay feared the worst, what with Chris's encroaching on the head's space, and in front of a couple of hundred pupils to boot, but he'd forgotten the two had met before and were on good terms. (By some stratagem Jay had never fathomed, Funchard had been invited to visit Dartmouth and been shown round by the then Cadet Fincher. Subsequently, Chris had been asked back to give an old-boys' career talk. It had gone down very well and Funchard had said so, much to the satisfaction of Jay who thereafter cut him considerably more slack.) They waved their goodbyes to a smiling head: Caro snuggling down into the passenger seat whilst Jay, bursting with pride, perched on the boot-lid between them. Chris, long black hair billowing out behind him, looked like Graham Hill, without-the-moustache! What a send-off!

By August the MGA had given way to a light green Mini Pickup. It belonged to Tom, Jay's former best friend. Not that they'd ever had a row or anything, they just seemed to have drifted apart. Now an invitation came out of the blue: did Jay and Caroline want to come to a barbeque? The Maidstones and the Kirksteads were coming, and the Hamiltons; and Jay and Caroline could have a lift with Tom and his girlfriend Jane, so long as they didn't mind roughing it in the back of the pickup. They were going to California and wouldn't be back 'til morning.

Jay was dubious, but when he rang Caro she was elated: 'Course we should go: it'll be great. Don't worry about the crowd: you'll be with me! Oh, and assuming we're not due Stateside, where the hell is California?' Jay didn't know but promised to find out. His father's OS map Sheet 126 'Norwich' held the key but it took him a while to find it. It hadn't occurred to him that it would be on the coast; he just assumed a barbeque would be hosted on someone's farm. The map was an old 1945 Sixth Edition which appeared to belong to his mother (presumably for her geography teaching) and wasn't very clear, particularly as he spent some time searching in the wrong place. Then the blue sweep of the North Sea and the designation 'Yarmouth Roads' caught his eye and he followed the coastline up through Great Yarmouth and Caister-on-Sea until he found it – right at the end of a little 'B' road just south of Hemsby Hole. Suddenly, he was much keener: a party on the beach with plenty of space to be alone with Caro. That sounded more like it: 'California Girls,' eh!

They'd gone in convoy through Bungay and sought out a series of back lanes to Caister. Someone – Jane presumably, Tom wouldn't've had the gumption – had spread out a load of rugs and cushions on the boarding which covered the metal floor of the pickup. It was comfortable enough but difficult to stay upright whenever Tom showed off his rallying skills. Jay took due advantage, and after several horizontal lurches persuaded Caro to stay down. They kissed – gently at first, then more passionately as they writhed around on the mobile bed. Once he judged he could get away with it Jay risked caressing Caro's breasts through her tight sweater. She didn't object so he slid his hands up inside and toyed with her bra. She wouldn't let him take it off, but seemed to be enjoying their fumblings as much as him. She was only wearing shorts but when he tried to insinuate his way between her legs she stopped him.

'No Jay. Not here! And when he whinged his disappointment she added, 'Later, sweet, honest.' And she gave him a loving squeeze which only inflamed him further. Still, he consoled himself, he was definitely on a promise!

The fine sweep of California Bay was empty and they parked the van and other cars out on the sand, but well above the high-tidemark. Then it was all hands to searching for driftwood. Within the hour they had a good blaze just as the sun sank behind them shading the calm sea a deep-crimson glow. The drink was plentiful – mostly bottled beer and cider although Jane and one of Freddie Maidstone's entourage had managed to procure several litre-flasks of cheap Chardonnay. So everyone was quite mellow as the fire's embers reached peak grilling temperature and the bangers and bacon were being readied. There were baked beans, too, and spaghetti rings which they heated through in battered saucepans from Freddie's camping collection. (Jay being reluctant to borrow his father's set of lightweight billycans.) By the time they'd eaten Tom had rigged up a portable record player, powered by the van's battery and slightly tinny renditions of the Beatles, Manfred Mann and the Honeycombs were drifting across the beach.

Jay was hoping someone would have a 45 of *Juliet* so he could dine out on his Four Pennies story but no one did and he couldn't contrive a way of introducing it without obvious gamesmanship. Fractious at not being the centre of attention, he ended up arguing with Freddie about whether the Honeycombs really did have a girl drummer; Jay claiming they had and Freddie dismissing the prospect as ridiculous. Not for the first time Jay reflected that some of his public-school friends' attitudes were a mite chauvinist; although it didn't seem to extend to dancing. Freddie was a confident mover. Jay, knowing his own limitations, sat out dance after dance, much to Caro's irritation as she liked dancing and was good at it.

It should have come as no surprise when Caro, fed up with her boyfriend's surly immobility, acceded to Freddie's blandishments, but when they continued dancing number after number Jay, peevish, stalked off on his own. It wasn't exactly the stroll along the beach he'd planned. When he stumbled back to the dying glow of the fire the couples still sober enough to stand – including Freddie and Caro – were smooching to the big Roy Orbison hit of earlier that summer: *It's over.* Highly appropriate muttered Jay to himself, conscious of his tendency to sulk but unable to resist the temptation. He helped himself to another bottle of Worthington and headed off to the shallows, splashing through the low-rippling waves and ruining his sneakers. He and Caro didn't speak the rest of the evening and the drive back as the sun was rising was equally frosty. Ironically, the last tune he remembered before the record player packed up was from Gerry and the Pacemakers: *Don't Let the Sun Catch You Crying.* Well, bugger that, he thought bitterly, but it remained his enduring memory of the fiasco. That and bloody Orbison.

It *wasn't* over. After a lengthy exchange of billets-doux, Jay saw the error of his ways and fashioned a handsome, if verbose apology – once again. More was needed, he sensed; otherwise he risked losing her altogether. He'd have the house to himself that Saturday so he rounded off his latest epistle with an invite. Would Caro like to come over for the afternoon? He'd be happy to pick her up if she could elude the watchful gaze of the Colonel and didn't mind riding shotgun. She could have his crash-helmet, of course.

He cut the engine and cruised to a halt just short of The Manse. It was dead on one as Caro emerged from the drive with a buff satchel slung diagonally over her shoulder and a back-long, fleeting glance. It hadn't occurred to Jay that she'd need to wear something suitable and he was momentarily crestfallen to be denied a basinful of the Tillotson pins. But when he saw how tight her jeans were, not to mention the glimpse of snug cream sweater under her leather jacket, he soon perked up. 'Shame to crush your beautiful hair under a skid-lid, but I think you should put this on.'

'Very noble, Sir Galahad,' she chuckled, 'don't worry, it'll soon shake out again.'

Then he was kick-starting the Tiger Cub and accelerating briefly along the main drag before plunging into the back-roads which would hopefully conceal them from the eagle eye of the law. He'd carried a passenger just often enough to appreciate the effect it had on the handling and he wove circumspectly through the high-banked lanes, conscious of the tightness of Caro's grip around his waist. Lower, lower! he thought wishfully and was rewarded after a couple of particularly tight bends by more intimate squeezes. By the time they reached The Gatehouse Jay was 'hully steamed-up' and Caro looked distinctly flushed. 'Wow! You didn't say it'd be that good!' she grinned, swinging her leg over the saddle and shaking momentarily matted locks from the helmet. 'I feel quite shaky! Look!'

Even Jay recognised the invitation and capturing Caro's outstretched hands swiftly, he drew them round his neck, simultaneously encircling her and drawing her close. He hoped she was as excited as he was. The embrace was lengthy and the kisses enrapturing. Finally, Caro pushed him gently away: 'Phew!! That was nice! *What* did you say we were gonna do thisafter?'

'Er...um...yer know,' he laughed, 'play scrabble, watch an old flic, have a nice cup of tea!'

'Hmm...okaaay! How about a walk first?'

'Yeah, deffers! D'you wanna drop your bag off in the house? Or anything?'

'No, no: it's fine. Oh, well, maybe just my jacket. It's warm in the sun.'

The orchard was beautiful: the apples September-red, the pears succulent. The grass was lush but dry, as, hand-in-hand, they kicked through the first-fallen leaves. Lurking in the depths of Jay's intent was the abandoned barn on the edge of the ten-acre stubble. Caro had other ideas. 'Here's the perfect spot. Let's enjoy the sunshine.' To Jay's delight, she peeled off her sweater, revealing a brown bikini top and a flat, sun-tanned tummy. She extricated a large tartan rug from the satchel and spread it out; then subsided gracefully onto the woollen couch, pulling Jay down beside her. She kissed him forcefully, and he responded eagerly, but then before he could get his mitts on her breasts she pushed him away.

'Now, about all this nonsense...'

'I know,' shrugged Jay apologetically, 'I'm really sorry. I know I'm a right berk sometimes.'

'Frequently, darling! Frequently!'

'Yeah, guilty as charged. But I'm working on it, honest.'

'Well you need to. Cause I'm not promising never to go out with anyone else. It's not as if we're engaged or anything.'

Jay signalled what he hoped was the right mix of resignation and contrition. It was, after all, a beautiful afternoon; and Caro looked ravishing.

'Well, I'm glad we've got that straight. It's too nice a day to argue. Now...where were we up to?'

'What, before the nonsense?'

'Yes, darling, of course before the nonsense!'

Oh...right! You were just saying how hot it was?'

Forty-Five

There were thirty in Jill's 'set,' and for the next twelve weeks they lived in 'Block.' The nurses' home was Victorian, bleak and Spartan. Most of the set were housed in a large dormitory but Jill was lucky, she and three other girls occupied a side dorm with a bit more privacy. The hours were long and the regime strict throughout the week. If they did go out on a Friday or Saturday night they had to sign back in by ten, although they soon found a way round that. They simply signed as they went out leaving one of the ground-floor windows open to sneak through on the odd occasion that they found a party that lasted after midnight. Once in a while an over-officious orderly would make a point of locking all the windows, but the all-night café up Percy Street was very accommodating – particularly for nurses.

They weren't in uniform of course but once the owner, Reg Dobson, knew you were 'at the Royal' he was happy to let you make two cups of coffee last three or four hours whilst snoozling gently, head-resting-in-elbow on the brown-plastic table top. Reg's wife, whom no one had ever met but everyone felt they knew, had been gravely injured in a hit-and-run accident near the junction of Barrack Road and Holland Drive. The ambulance had got her to the RVI in minutes and she went straight to theatre. It was almost certainly the proximity of the hospital that saved her life but Reg swore it was the skill of the surgeons and the care of the nursing staff that pulled her through. No one could say a bad word about the RVI to Reg, and any nurse was welcome ever after.

The trickiest of the orderlies was a lean-featured, red-haired Scot in his early forties. No one knew his real name – he was dubbed Stirl for no better reason than it was rumoured he originated from Stirling. If he took to you he could be kind enough, if ingratiating, but mostly he didn't like nurses or doctors, resenting their superior status. Jill had been well-schooled in not rubbing people up the wrong way though, and was forewarned about Stirl by her mate Sally. 'Keep on the right side of him, pet, and you'll find Block's okay. Don't encourage him too much though and make sure you're never alone with him. I've heard he's not above undoing that long khaki coat and showing you something you'd rather not see. Vera – who's no better than she should be – did claim he was very well endowed. Said he didn't actually do her any harm. But she's a bit of a fantasist that one so you don't really know whether to believe her.'

'Why? What did she say?'

'Well according to her she was having a sly fag in the storeroom when he came in and locked the door behind him. Told her not to be alarmed, he wasn't gonna hurt her or owt. He'd just got summat to show her. Then, when he unbuttoned his coat there it was – already out and stiff as a poker, so she said.'

'Christ! What did she do?'

'Well she figured he wouldn't harm her if she didn't panic so she just gave him an appraising glance and tried to be dead casual about it.'

'What happened then?'

'Well, according to Vera – and this is the bit that's suspect – he grabbed her hand, wrapped it round his prick and ensured she gave him what he wanted.'

The story stirred a long-ago unpleasant memory in Jill and she resolved to treat Stirl cautiously.

Her first ward was female surgical. The staff nurse was quite old and very strict. Sister was God. Between them they ran an austere, disciplined regime but one that was fair and supportive provided you did exactly as you were told. Jill didn't mind that: she liked to know where she was with people. And she revelled in presenting herself as smart and tidy in her brand new uniform. It was blue-and-white striped and made her feel like a real nurse. The discipline didn't stop with Staff and Sister, though: first-years like Jill deferred to second-years and second-years to third-years. It was all surnames and as well as being at everybody's beck and call, the students were also the butt of usually-good-natured humour. Jill fell for it in her first week on ward. She administered an injection under Staff's watchful eye. The patient was elderly and when she died the next day Jill thought it was her fault. The seniors didn't disabuse her and she spent a thoroughly miserable few hours before Staff realised what had happened and quietly assured her that Mrs Hurst would've died whatever anyone had done and she was never to blame herself for what was a regular occurrence on what was virtually a geriatric ward.

The weeks flew by. Jill enjoyed herself and, without being conceited about it, felt like she was doing a modicum of good. Some of the patients were a bit crotchety – most were really old – but others were delightful and couldn't thank her enough for the slightest task she performed for them. That was the best bit; that and Friday nights.

Well, not every Friday, every other one – when funds allowed. Jill and her dorm-mate Christine would venture out around seven to the pubs on Percy Street, usually the Hotspur or the Three Bulls Heads, and just have a cider. Then as early as was decent – you couldn't appear too keen – they'd get installed in the 'Bun Room,' as the Newcastle University students called their Junior Common Room. There, cider and green ginger was the favoured bevy which at a shilling a glass was considerably cheaper than in the pubs. If you were lucky, especially later in the evening, you'd get bought a drink or two. Most of the students were as impecunious as the nurses but some weren't and the trick was to latch on to them without ending up with some posh prick thinking that buying you a couple of ciders meant you were going to sleep with him. It happened sometimes, of course, but not to Jill. She always made it back to Block, even if she was escorted by some amorous swain who was anticipating a suitably grateful embrace. A thank-you hug and a peck on the cheek was all they were likely to get, as far as Jill was concerned.

One evening they staggered back in the early hours to find the ground-floor windows all apparently locked. As they tipsily debated the alternatives, a shadowy figure flitted along the corridor inside and there was a sharp click as the catch on one of the windows further down was released. It was hard to tell, but Jill thought she discerned the outline of Stirl disappearing into the inner-court. Surely he wouldn't have done them such a favour? She said as much to Christine who grimaced: 'Yeek! I can't stand him. He's creepy. And he doesn't like me at all. He must have a soft spot for you, hinny. You wanna watch out!'

'Oh, I dunno. He's always been okay with me.'

Later the next morning, still hung-over, she was on laundry duty. It wasn't as bad as it sounded. The room was warm and secluded. Provided you folded your quota of sheets and pillowcases no one was likely to bother you and if you'd had a rough night it was a safe place for a kip. Her chores completed, Jill unlocked the storeroom and lay down on a bundle of blankets. Within a minute she had nodded off.

How much later she didn't know but a rustling awoke her. Instinctively, she opened her eyes just enough to glimpse what was going on. After all, she wasn't supposed to be in the store, nor sleeping on her shift. It was Stirl. Trying not to panic she decided it was better to play possum than get embroiled in some kind of exchange. Surely he wouldn't do anything untoward on duty. Peeping through the slits of her eyes and trying hard not to squint, Jill was faced with the very prospect she *didn't* want to see. Stirl was unbuttoning his long starched coat. She wondered why the sight of a fully clothed sleeping nurse would be a turn-on for him; then she realised the rustling that had awoken her had been Stirl undoing the bottom buttons of her uniform, which was now pushed up to her waist and presumably exposed her stay-up stockings and navy-blue uniform knickers. Bugger! That's what was getting him excited. Pervert!

She debated whether she could successfully make a dash for it but dismissed the idea rapidly. She probably wouldn't make it out of the store room before Stirl grabbed her or, even if she did, she'd have given the game away. It would've been obvious she was pretending to be asleep and God knows what kind of grudge he would hold if he felt he'd been duped. Safer to continue the deception and hope he wouldn't do her any harm. Besides, with the latent prurience that embellished her hangovers, Jill realised she had the ideal opportunity to find out whether Vera's allegations were true. She kept her eyes slit.

She didn't have long to wait. The orderly had pulled his coat tails round behind him and tucked them into the back of his trousers. He had already slid down his zip and was rummaging inside his flies. He pulled it out and Jill's astonishment nearly betrayed her. It really was long even though it seemed still to be fairly flaccid. She gasped inwardly and felt her fingers wrap themselves into tight fists. He began to ripple it up and down and it swiftly grew longer and more rigid. Aghast, but simultaneously fascinated, Jill nevertheless felt an irrational temptation to reach out and touch it. She stifled the urge with some difficulty sensing that any movement on her part would simply make a fraught situation even more hazardous. She risked a glance at his face and was not at all reassured: his expression was a mixture of concentration and lust. Again she weighed up the chances of flight: anything would be better than his relieving himself all over her knickers. Yuk!

Then, just as she'd steeled herself to run – and stuff the consequences – the outside door to the laundry opened and the shrill tones of Staff rang out: 'Nurse Walker, where are you? I hope you've not fallen asleep on the job. There'll be trouble if you have.'

Never had Jill been so glad to hear the promise of retribution!

Stirl, on the other hand, looked intensely frustrated, and with no time to re-arrange his clothes he dodged behind the screen where the metal lockers partially concealed him. Reckoning that his presence now held less threat than Staff's Jill called out: 'Just getting a drink, Staff.' Then she sprang up, smoothing down her uniform as she went and crossed quickly to the corner washbasin. She could see him in the mirror and briefly caught his eye. Saucer-eyed, he implored her silently not to give him away, raising a finger to his lips. The plea was slightly sullied by the fact that his prick still stuck out stiffly and she was unable to stop her gaze taking in his erection as well. He realised; and their conspiracy was sealed.

She half-grimaced, half-smiled at him as she passed, stifling an urge to reach down and give him a painful flick for his effrontery. 'It was hot and I was thirsty. I was just getting some water,' she explained emerging into the main room clasping a white plastic beaker.

'Good! Just as well. I see you've pretty well finished here anyway. Well done, Nurse. Now get yourself back on the ward.'

Forty-Six

Years later, Duke would speak with nostalgic pride about his 'Class of '64.' Out of the eleven he'd expertly coached through their 'A' level Literature, ten had got Grade As, the exception being a brainy scientist called Wrightly who had only been persuaded to add English to his portfolio of Physics, Pure Mathematics, Chemistry and Biology so he could establish a school record of five 'A' levels. He and some of the other scientists were stopping on to have a crack at Oxford Entrance (Funchard would be pleased) whilst Denham – who remained Head Boy, to Jay's envious resignation – and Henley would try for Cambridge along with Jay himself. Of the three, Henley had elected to go for the relatively easier option of a new (well, Victorian) college, Fitzwilliam, rather than the more prestigious Peterhouse which Jay was quick to point out was almost 600 years older. Jay had disliked Henley ever since he'd achieved notoriety with his dubbing of Cutters as 'Oak Tree' almost five years earlier. The general consensus that his own christening of Greene as 'Beechen' was neater didn't entirely compensate for Henley having stolen the initial thunder. The fact that he also harboured lecherous inclinations towards Caro compounded matters. Denham, habitually a most affable individual, didn't like him either so he and Jay rather meanly took every opportunity to take the owlish Henley down a peg or two.

What proved to be Jay's final term at Wyndhams passed uneventfully. It was odd being in such a small, if select, group. No one knew quite how to treat them bar Duke, who'd been in a similar situation many years before. There'd been no third-year-sixth in the interim and as the older members of the cadre were scarcely younger than the latest recruits to the teaching staff they felt they should have some standing over and above the other incumbents of the prefects' room. But no such recognition was forthcoming so they remained in a kind of categorical limbo.

The course, too, was weird since they were no longer following a syllabus nor reading set-books; rather they studied former scholarship papers and discussed possible lines of response before devising their own research programmes carried out unsupervised in the library. That suited Jay more than the others. He was confident he would fare better than Denham or Henley so was pretty shaken when the actual exams came around. He discovered, for the first time, that he was out of his intellectual depth. 'Opera – a bizarre and irrational entertainment. Discuss.' Other than vaguely recognising the comment as Dr Johnson's Jay was stumped: he knew nothing about opera. Since the closest he could come was Gilbert & Sullivan he proceeded to base his refutation of the good doctor's dismissive judgement on a robust defence of *The Yeoman of the Guard*, *Iolanthe* and *The Mikado*. His ability to quote large chunks of the texts would, he hoped, convince the examiners of his intellectual capacity if not his experience of opera.

It didn't. He failed, and was bitterly disappointed; the more so that whilst Denham did too, the odious Henley got an Exhibition to Fitz. His father, who by now had connexions in high educational places, offered to pull strings. He could secure him a place: but not as a Scholar and not at Peterhouse. Jay's pride would brook no such intervention. He declined and left Wyndhams forthwith.

At first he felt he'd wasted the term. He'd previously been accepted to read English at both Leeds and Birmingham but had turned them down for the chance of Cambridge. His parents would've loved him to follow in their footsteps at Birmingham and the interview panel, too, had made it clear that they welcomed the then-rarity of second-generation undergraduates. Jay had fancied Leeds. The clincher, however, had been age. He would lose no ground by staying on; whereas if he'd gone up that October he wouldn't even have been eighteen. Imagine an undergraduate unable to drink! (Well, not legally, anyway.)

In the interim his A-grade secured him a berth at either Nottingham or Durham. He leant towards the latter. Up for interview in a deep and dark December he'd liked the city, and its collegiate structure made it the next best thing after Oxbridge. What he didn't want to do was stooge around school for the next six months. He hadn't got the funds for extensive travel and it didn't seem fair to sponge on his parents when they'd be supporting him through university. What he needed was his own brass: so, a job.

Unbeknown to Jay his father intervened, though it didn't require any influence. He'd been chatting with Roger Hood and it transpired he was looking for a new 'boy.' The term was not literal but a job description – a 'boy' could be any age and was expected to be the farm's dogsbody, turning his hand to anything from slurry-clearing to milking. He would start at

Brooklands in the New Year on the princely sum of £6.10.0 for a full week – forty-eight hours. There would be no concessions for friendship. He'd work with the other men and pull his weight. Sounds good, thought Jay, just the way I like to be treated – as a man, with no favours. Not as a 'boy'!

New Year's Day fell on a Friday that year so he didn't have to start until Monday 4 January. He'd to be at the farm for seven o'clock even though it would still be dark. First though, breakfast. Before she went to bed his mother had left two rashers of bacon and a small chunk of lard in the frying pan by the side of the cooker. They were covered by an upturned white china plate, on which Jay noted meticulously was an emblem pronouncing: 'Dudson Duraline Finest Vitrified: Stoke-on-Trent, England.' Next to it were a slice of white bread and an egg. All he had to do was to lift one of the hob-covers on the lurid green Baby Belling and slide the frying pan across. Then, whilst the smell of the crisping bacon began to permeate the kitchen he placed the large steel kettle on the other hob so that it was boiling by the time the bacon was ready. In went the egg, and a couple of minutes later his labourer's breakfast was ready.

There were also sandwiches, which along with an apple, orange or banana went into the yellow, tin picnic-box he took for the thirty-minute break they had at lunchtime. He'd decided to pedal the mile-and-a-half to Brooklands, figuring that arriving on a shiny Triumph T20S when the older men all walked or arrived astride ancient black bicycles was unlikely to prove the most diplomatic of entrances. First impressions, his dad always said, were important; and his battered, mud-maroon, ten-year-old Raleigh Rudge ought to fit the bill. Not that it made him inconspicuous. Here was a slightly-built eighteen-year-old lad, friend of the gaffer's son, filling in his time before university amidst a workforce of gnarled old giants. Workforce was a bit strong: there were four of them, including Gorbel the foreman, but they *were* all big and strong and two of them looked at least forty. They were friendly enough and although he rapidly learned that being the 'boy' was also to be the butt of all humour and practical jokes, their ribbing of him was invariably good-natured. Moreover, once they saw that he was a worker – albeit not a very skilled one – they soon gave him the benefit. And Mick, the cowman, took him under his wing, satisfied that the lad had a natural way with animals, so that within a month he could milk both by hand and using the electric machinery.

It was tough though. Once away from the farm buildings it was bitterly cold; the dykes were frozen solid and the headlands January-hard. Chopping beet was back-breaking work the execution of which confused him. On the first few days Jay marvelled at how laboriously his fellow weeders approached the task by comparison with his energetic speed. And yet, by the end of the day, when he was knackered from thinning out a couple of 200-yard rows they seemed as fresh as when they'd started, having covered at least a dozen. Could it be a case of 'trop de zèle' suggested his mother kindly when he was describing this conundrum, explaining it was the phrase she'd come across in Haggard's *A Farmer's Year*, which in a show of maternal support she would read over the next few months. Jay was sceptical but put the point (not in French) to Gorbel.

'Ah, thass the pace, young Finch,' he smiled, shouldering a two hundred-weight sack of meal and swinging it effortlessly onto the trailer he was loading. 'The faster tha goes the slower tha'll be.' Jay wasn't sure whether he was serious or, as so frequently, was taking the piss. But he decided to follow the advice and within a fortnight, although not conscious of any marked variation of his rhythm, was chopping out four rows a day instead of two. It did not go unnoticed, particularly by Gorbel.

The best bit was Saturday lunchtime, although it also demanded a degree of diplomacy. They would all line up in the ante-room to the Brooklands kitchen where Farmer Hood Senior would hand them their wage-packets: Gorbel first, then Mick, followed by the two general labourers, Fred and Sloaney, and finally Jay. On the outside of the brown-paper envelope was scrawled his wage '£6=10.' It was the most he'd ever earned in one go and he was justly proud, especially as his aching back, shoulders and arms told him he *had* earned it.

It was the transition that was tricky. Immediately after receiving their wages the others dispersed: Gorbel would go off fishing, Mick home to his wife and kids and Fred and Sloaney would head for the village rec to play football for the local team. Jay, however, was invited into the kitchen where he must morph rapidly from labourer to friend of the family. Fliss Hood's famous shortbreads materialised, along with a steaming mug of thick, black coffee (Jay had started taking it without milk in the prefects' room, to seem more sophisticated). If Tom were around he would join them, otherwise Jay would chat happily to Fliss, as he was now invited to call her. She'd ask him about home and how Chris was getting on at sea; he'd reciprocate by enquiring about how farming prospects were looking and how she was finding her charity work. Mrs Hood had recently become a volunteer with the Norfolk branch of the Royal Agricultural Benevolent Institution; she explained the background to Jay.

'Well, if you're sure you're interested…it was founded about a century ago. A group of farmers down in Essex, I think. They were worried about the levels of poverty there. In the early days they organised grants for the needy. It was £40 a year for a married couple, along with one-and-a-half tons of coal. Both on a weekly basis. These days we're much more likely to be seeing who needs fridges and cookers.'

'So where do you come in Mrs...er...Fliss?' asked Jay tentatively. It was the first time he'd used her Christian name and he felt a slight thrill, as if indulging in excitingly illicit behaviour. He glanced surreptitiously at her. She was very pretty and her lustrous black hair had no suggestion of grey, unlike his mum's; but then she was, by Jay's reckoning, all of fifteen years younger. She also had big boobs. (Jay was a tit-man like most of his Wyndham buddies; only Henley had professed to be a leg-man and Jay suspected that was just so he could be different. He'd also claimed Caroline as the model for his preference which irritated Jay no end, not least because she had indeed got shapely legs.) Fliss also had a warm, embracing smile and, not for the first time, Jay wondered whether you could fancy a friend's mother. Her reply drew him back to reality.

'Well that's the tricky bit! A lot of country folk are poor, but they're also proud. So the last thing you want to do is get their backs up by implying they're inadequate in some way.'

'That *must* be tricky,' commented Jay admiringly.

'Yeah, it is. And it'd be impossible if they knew you. It'd be really intrusive. That's why we're given patches some way away. Mine's the villages south of Norwich. It's a good ten miles from here and country folk don't travel much, so no one's likely to know me. That's why we bought the Austin. Isn't that the same make as your mum's?'

'Yeah, just a newer model. Nice colour, too,' but the mention of his mum had rather burst the bubble his febrile imagination was inflating and the conversation went no further that Saturday.

Thereafter, he'd be invited in fortnightly and although he realised the other men must know, nothing was said. After all it was no big deal. He was a friend of the family and no matter how much he might strive to be 'one of them' at work he wasn't and never would be. Sensibly, he made no reference to the regular tête à tête, keeping his thoughts – and especially his nascent feelings for Fliss – to himself. Nevertheless, he found himself hoping Tom wouldn't be there and when, at their second encounter, Fliss was wearing a much more stylish and revealing jumper than she had previously Jay's fantasies soared; only to be brought back to earth when it transpired she was going out to lunch. Even so he was given what Denham used to call 'a right eyeful,' as Fliss bent obligingly low over the square wooden table to offer him a second, then a third shortbread.

'You like those, don't you, Jay,' she smiled into his eyes.

'They're...they're beautiful,' he stammered.

'I meant the shortbreads, you naughty boy!'

Jay was smitten; and the best bit was he could tell no one. He'd always liked secrets!

He also liked learning and resolved to find out as much as he could about farming before he departed for academe. Knowing Fliss was the custodian of the records he asked her in one of their more serious exchanges (by March, she was flirting gently with him whenever they were alone) about maps of the farm. She took him through to the living room and motioned to a large oak desk. Inside the drop-down frontage was a series of cubby-holes full of papers. She rifled through several, setting three or four aside, before handing him a rolled parchment which, when opened out, had a large-scale map on one page and a cadastre on the other. The map Jay recognised as twenty-five-inch-to-the-mile; it showed every field – pasture and arable – with numbers corresponding to the schedule. There were forty-six in all – far too many to memorise at a single sitting – so Jay asked if he could borrow the charts to study at home. Knowing they would be looked after in the Fincher household, Fliss readily agreed.

Back at The Gatehouse he concentrated first on the parchment, spreading it out on the map-table in his father's study and anchoring it with four brass, seventy-five mm-shell paperweights (a present from Chris). Then he took out one of the many buff HMSO notebooks from his dad's supply and proceeded to transcribe the details into four columns: the number of the field/whether it was pasture or arable/its acreage/its present crop. When he'd finished, the first thing he did was to total up the third column: 365 acres. That, he recalled from his geography, made it a small/medium sized farm in East Anglian terms.

He couldn't be expected to get all the constituents by heart, but Autolycus would be disappointed if he didn't at least master, say, the top ten by size and usage. His intention was immediately rewarded when he discovered he knew several of the fields, including the largest: the nineteen-acre Brough down by The Lodge. He noted other fields of kale, together with barley, wheat, vetches, beans and beet (he knew all about those!). Roughly, a third was under pasture currently and two-thirds arable. He was also intrigued to spot that the smallest field – well at just under an acre an enclosure really – bordered the woods near The Gatehouse. He spent the next few evenings and a lot of the weekend (Caro was singularly unimpressed) poring over the charts. By the time of his fortnightly meeting he was well prepared.

His suggestion was to spread out the parchment on the kitchen table and to invite Fliss, who was sporting a low-cut, tight pink jumper, to share his knowledge. If their last couple of sessions were anything to go by she'd take the hint and he'd get an ample helping, not just of shortbread but, hopefully, of the Denham-eyeful! Fliss had smiled knowingly at this ploy and, as she was now generously inclining to every detail Jay was pointing out, his strategy was working well. She almost seemed to be encouraging him (surely that top button hadn't been undone originally, he could see the pink of her bra) and he could feel himself getting excited. He wondered if she'd notice and whether she'd be annoyed or amused. He just hoped she wouldn't laugh at him. Then, as he was stealing himself to make God-knows-what move, the outer door opened and footsteps echoed across the stone flags of the ante-room. Fliss swiftly did up her button as in marched Farmer Hood and Gorbel demanding mugs of tea. Jay logged how nonchalantly Fliss rose in acquiescence to shift the kettle onto the hob and hoped he could be equally composed. He decided to put his newly-acquired knowledge to use and enquired casually:

'Given the acreage of Brooklands, would you say you were medium or small farmers, sir?'

'Now then, young Finch, small or medium, eh? What d'ye reckon Gorbel?'

'Well, being as yer well over six foot and I'm six-two I doan hardly think we're *small* farmers, d'you sir!'

Roger Hood roared with laughter; Fliss smiled sympathetically; Jay flushed bright red. Things had not exactly gone according to plan.

Forty-Seven

Their time on Block was almost over. In the New Year, the students would be free to come in to work from home or to find lodgings closer to the hospital. Plus Jill was due to transfer to the male orthopaedic ward in January and was looking forward to it. The majority of patients were healthy in themselves as many were recovering from motorbike accidents, so you tended to have a bit of a laugh. Christine and Belle, their remaining dorm-companion, were also due there, and the Sister on Ward Five was young, vivacious and apparently a real pleasure to work for.

Meanwhile, the Christmas Concert was looming, with the party afterwards. The concert was legendary. Doctors and senior nurses performed skits – many of them distinctly risqué – for the benefit of a mixed audience: a handful of more mobile, younger and healthier patients, the junior nurses and the auxiliary staff (including, presumably, Stirl). There'd be heaps of jokes at the expense of the consultants who were expected to take it in good heart regardless of whether they were amused or offended.

The assembly hall had been laid out cabaret-style with maybe a couple of dozen tables each with six chairs in a three-quarter circle so that no one had their back to the stage. Hit records from earlier in the year were being piped through hastily-erected loudspeakers at the side of the room: The Beatles asking for Help! whilst their Rolling Stone rivals complained of a lack of satisfaction. Jill knew just what they meant but had to smile when Ken Dodd's mellow tones lamented *Tears*. C'mon she thought: it's not *that* bad! There were two bars, one at the back of the room, one down the side. In theory they weren't due to open until after the show. In practice they were already doing a brisk trade, principally in bottles of Newcastle Brown, and Amber. Jill gratefully accepted a glass of cider from Belle. Christine was already on the Babycham. When she rummaged in her handbag to produce a flask of brandy Jill knew her friend was planning a good night. She declined the offer of a shot, deeming the combination fraught so early in the proceedings: she just hoped she wouldn't have to put her friend to bed later. Then the three young nurses settled down to the entertainment, toasting each other's success in getting through Block without any major mishap (she didn't count her recent Saturday experience as, on reflection, it hadn't really ranked as 'major,' and in any case nothing had come of it and she hadn't told anyone).

The first act was a comic turn set to the tune of 'I'm a little teapot...' but featuring Staff Jenkins from female orthopaedic as an ovum being pursued by a trio of housemen-sperm. 'I'm a little ovum...' resisted their advances for some time until she was overcome by weight of numbers and collapsed under an impregnating heap of white coats. It was in disgustingly bad taste – and hilarious!

This was followed by the first of three cameos from the hospital's very own answer to 'The Seekers' – two trainee doctors performing as Athol Guy (complete with Peter-Sellers glasses) and Bruce Woodley on double bass and guitar respectively, ably assisted by Staff Peel as Keith ('the-one-with-the-grin') Potger on banjo and Sister Watson playing both the piano and the tambourine (though not at the same time). All four had good singing voices and a following well beyond the Christmas Concert: they'd been invited as backing at the Cavendish Club recently (although the cynics alleged that was only because the manager there was having an affair with the hospital administrator). Their first offering was *I'll never find another you* which had been popular for months, having been released this time last year. The Seekers were one of Jill's favourite bands (although not in the same class as Elvis, of course) and she'd been delighted to receive the LP *A World of our Own* for her birthday. She'd been less-than-chuffed to discover that it was only the title track, the rest comprising a compilation which included two songs from Bob Dylan, whom she couldn't stand. The band were really accomplished and got a tremendous reception with Christine and other more demonstrative members of the audience banging the tables with their still-to-come-buffet forks. Staff Peel (whose real name was Keith) was a particular draw for the younger nurses being that rare commodity of a very good-looking senior male nurse. 'Shame he's gay!' seemed a particularly myopic reaction to Jill who, on the odd occasion when she'd been in his company, found him charming.

The highlight of this year's concert proved to be a spoof on the orthopaedic operating theatre with the consultant, Mr Karadik, being sent up by a personable young houseman, Wilf Gordon. The theatre staff led by Sister Watson all paraded around in low-cut blouses and immodestly short skirts with suspenders and stockings. It brought the house down: and Dr Gordon an inordinate number of offers!

Not that Jill had any aspirations in that direction. Housemen tended to hook up with senior nursing staff: it wasn't the done thing for them to get off with first-year students. Besides, if she had a choice, Sister Watson was much prettier! Not that she was under any illusion there either: Trish Watson was recently married and even given the licence of the Christmas party, would be up for a bit of fun with a handsome young doctor not a student nurse, however attractive the latter might be. And Jill Walker was certainly that. She was never short of offers: just not the ones she was looking for...

Maybe she was a lesbian like Sue and Joyce; or perhaps bi, like Sally, she mused. Her earlier sexual experiences seemed to suggest that to her; and even when she and Marge had got up to no good with Billy Turnbull it wasn't really the latter's dubious charms that stuck in her mind. And if she did take to a boy it was someone like Keith Peel; Sue had once said that gay men made the best boyfriends. On the other hand, she'd been fascinated rather than frightened by the laundry episode and could recall vividly a moment when she'd had a distinct urge to reach out and help Stirl's frenzied efforts. Her impulsiveness in helping him evade Staff had seemed complicit rather than culpable. It was all very confusing, she concluded, emerging from her reverie as Christine, now on her fifth B&B, slurred enthusiastically, 'Trish 'n' the boys are back.' As a finale their rendition of *The Carnival is Over* pricked Jill's eyes and made them water. It did that every time she heard the real version – which was pretty frequently: it had been No. 1 these last three weeks.

The buffet was magnificent. Not just the usual sausage rolls, sandwiches and crisps, though all those in abundance, but unusual-for-Jill delicacies like smoked salmon and individual prawn cocktails. And, out of the blue, housemen-waiters suddenly plonked down bottles of Chablis, Claret and Mateus Rosé on each table. Anyone who wanted to attend the concert party had been paying half-a-crown each week into the communal fund all term so the wine seemed free and was certainly consumed as if it were. As a table finished its supply you could buy additional bottles at a flat rate of five shillings which didn't seem too steep between three or four of you. By the time the refreshments were cleared away and the tables pushed to the side of the room, Jill had lost count of the number of 'refreshers' they'd purchased. She'd intended to stay sober but as both Belle and Christine constantly refilled her glass well before it was empty she was fighting a losing battle.

Several of their table, including Belle, had already drifted off when Christine returned after a brief sortie onto the dance floor with two trainee

243

doctors in tow. Both were third-year undergraduates and presentable enough. Jill had seen one of them on ward-experience not so long back: Ben someone? But before she could recall his surname he held out his hand: 'Benedict Stanton, Ben to my friends: nice to meet you. We bring replenishments.' He swayed slightly as he placed the two bottles of claret in the centre of the table with exaggerated care but parked himself neatly enough in the chair next to Jill. 'Refill, Nurse? Sorry don't know your name.'

'Jill. Jill Walker. Yeah, that'd be nice, thanks.' Fortunately, their disc jockey – a youngish surgeon who considered himself especially groovy to be playing an LP released within the last fortnight – chose that moment to pipe through *Rubber Soul*. Thank God, thought Jill, no need for small talk. The alternative, however, was equally unattractive: she was hauled up to dance. Christine and the other doctor were already on the floor and the four of them gyrated inelegantly to the blast of *Drive my Car*. Jill felt a bit dizzy but otherwise relatively sober considering the amount she'd had to drink already. She was not alert enough, however, to avoid being clutched around the waist and swirled slowly across the floor to the strains of *Norwegian Wood*. Ben behaved respectably, though, and didn't attempt to smooch her.

She managed to excuse herself and sat down, accepting another glass of wine and then half-listening through the next few tracks to how Ben was going to revolutionise medical training methods when he took over the RVI. It was almost a relief to be dragged up to revolve sort of gracefully to *The Word*, but the mournful beauty of *Michelle* seemed to awaken Ben's romantic inclinations and she was gradually drawn closer and closer to him during the song. Happily, it lasted only a couple of minutes but as the music, and the lights, temporarily died he sought to plant a kiss on her lips. Jill had to decide whether to let him (he was their vintner, after all) or push him away (how dare he press his attentions on her) but the lights came back on and she led him decisively back to their table.

The pattern continued – increasingly uncoordinated jiving to the quicker tracks, gradually more intimate smooching to the slower ones. Somehow, with each successive glass of claret Ben appeared less unattractive. Her downfall really began when, 'By special arrangement' as their DJ grandiosely announced, the evening was brought to an end by a very romantic finale: the 'RVI Seekers' reformed for *The Carnival is Over*. Once again Ben clutched her tightly, deliberately brushing himself against her breasts so that, in spite of herself, her nipples became aroused. Unsurprisingly that had the worst effect on her suitor and since he was only a little taller than Jill she could feel his erection gradually hardening as he ground it against her mound. Sober she would have pushed him away firmly: decidedly drunk she couldn't work out whether to or not, which only egged on the libidinous houseman more. Fortunately their smooch came to an end, rather than a climax, as the carnival died although before it *was* over Jill was starting to return Ben's overtures.

The night was cold and the short walk over to Block brought Jill to her senses. She anticipated Ben's request to 'come inside to say goodnight' and declined as charmingly as she knew how, explaining that she'd had a lovely evening but was really tired now.

'Well jusht a goodnight kish then,' he slurred, apparently acquiescing with what Jill thought surprising good grace. Unfortunately, once he'd got his arms round her it became more of a grapple than a kiss as he propelled her through the front door (why the hell was it open? she panicked) and onto the leather sofa in the hallway. She tried to push him away demurely but he seemed to interpret anything less than forcible rejection as acceptance.

'Stop it, Ben! I don't want to,' she complained, as he kissed her clumsily on the mouth and forced his tongue between her lips. She wrenched her head out of the way and tried to push him off but he was too heavy for her and sliding his hand under her tight jumper started to fondle her breasts. 'Give over yer sod,' she hissed as he succeeded in unclipping her bra and scooping one of her boobs out in his cupped grasp. Then as she struggled to get her bra back on she felt his fingers tugging at the zip in her trousers and before she could prevent him he'd pulled it down and was threatening to sneak his fingers inside her knickers. She was gasping 'No! No!' and almost sobbing with indignant, but impotent fury when suddenly a figure emerged from the shadows of the hallway and yanked him off her so violently that he ended up in a dishevelled heap against the corridor wall.

'The lady said no, you little creep! Now sod off before I call security!'

Jill wasn't aware the hospital had security; clearly nor was Benedict, who scrambled to his feet and legged it out of the door as if pursued by phantom proctors.

'Told you I'd look after you, Nurse Walker,' confirmed Stirl stepping out of the shadows with a reassuring smile rather than his habitual leer.

Oh, God! Out of the frying pan…thought Jill; but she allowed herself to be lifted gently to her feet, still trembling as Stirl sought, in his unaccustomed way, to comfort her. Sensing that he meant her no harm and properly grateful for his intervention, she let him put his arm around her shoulders and lead her along the dimly-lit corridor and up the stairs to her dormitory. Two of the girls had already gone home and Christine had probably succumbed to an invitation back to her doctor's place. She'd promised herself she'd never be alone with Stirl again but somehow she felt no misgivings. He deposited her gently on her bunk and sat down opposite her on Christine's.

'You okay now?' he enquired solicitously but with no insinuation.

Jill wondered whether she should just nod and ask him to go but that seemed a tad churlish given his quixotic intervention. Instead she admitted, 'Yeah, still a bit shaky though. You don't think he'll come back?' And when Stirl assured her that she was safe now she added, 'Thanks, but will you stay a bit longer just in case?'

Reflecting on the evening later she had no explanation for what happened next. It had been cold walking across from the party and she was certainly shaken by Ben's untoward behaviour. But she was still surprised to hear herself blurt out: 'Christ! It's cold in here. I'm frozen,' and tremble as she flashed Stirl an imploring, shivering glance.

He rose and sat down next to her, putting his arm around her shoulder once more and rubbing the top of her arm. They sat in silence. Jill gradually calmed down and Stirl made no unwanted advance. She was reassured; so much so that a bit of her wanted to clear the air over the laundry incident. But she couldn't think how to and was worried that if they started talking about what had and hadn't happened he might take it as a come-on. So reluctantly she decided it would have to remain her secret. Another time maybe. She was exhausted: it had been a long and eventful evening and it was time for bed. Conscious of how good he'd been to her, however, she didn't just want to turf Stirl out unceremoniously. So she murmured, 'I'm okay now, thanks. You've been very sweet.'

'Any time, hinny. I always said I'd look out for you. I'm glad I have.'

'Yeah, you have. Thanks again. G'night.' Jill kissed him gently on the cheek.

'G'night, pet,' he said quietly, giving her shoulder a final affectionate squeeze, 'Happy Christmas!'

Forty-Eight

The weather relented somewhat by Eastertime – it fell in mid-April that year. The week after, as he cycled home from Saturday work (but no shortbread) under a cold, sun-streaked sky, Jay was startled by an extraordinary meteorological phenomenon (as he verbosely described it later). Halfway down Free Lane his chain came off and he stopped by the verge to turn his trusty Raleigh over on its seat and handlebars so he could wind it back on again. Preoccupied, he didn't see it until it was whirring across the eight-acre field towards him. He knew from his research that the field had previously been under vetch but was lying fallow this year. The dry spell had left the shallow furrows desiccated and a miniature whirlwind was spiralling the dust, together with a load of small twigs and dead leaves high into the air where they twisted round and round maybe fifty feet above him. The road was open – no hedge or dyke – and it swept straight over within twenty or thirty yards of Jay, then careered across the pasture beyond. Lucky it wasn't a cornfield, thought Jay: wouldn't've done it much good.

'Never mind the cornfield!' exclaimed his mother when he told her later, 'You could've been seriously injured!' That possibility hadn't occurred to Jay: he was just pleased to have been the only one to witness it.

His mum, having calmed down, suddenly became more animated again: 'But I've read about one just recently! Rider Haggard, I'm sure. You know I've been reading his diary. As you were busy with all the Easter work I was catching up with his entries for April.' Muriel had decided this might be a way of getting closer to her younger son before she lost him to university and the glittering career she was convinced lay ahead of him. It was working and the two – although never as close as her and Chris, reflected Jay resentfully – were relishing the shared interest. He recounted events in the daily round he knew would be of interest to her; she mirrored with literary and geographical theory. It was the first time Jay had realised: it wasn't just his dad, his mother was pretty bright, too!

His father being on an extended FI in Jersey – lucky devil – and his big brother on submarine duties in the Far East, Jay was the man of the house. He and his mother had taken to having tea together in The Gatehouse's elegant but irregularly proportioned drawing room where the polished oak floor was as uneven as the angles: the low, rectangular glass table was shored up by two neat wooden wedges to counteract the incline. He could remember the table in the lounge at Ivy Bank. It had a neat pile of (up-to-date) *National Geographic* mags in one corner but in the other, beyond the afternoon-china and the remnants of one of his mother's chocolate sponges, resided a purpley-brown copy of *A Farmer's Year – being His Commonplace Book for 1898*. Muriel's version was a re-issue from 1906 and she scooped it up keenly to flick through the pages, checking a number of markers as she went.

'Here it is,' she announced triumphantly, 'page 159: "Today, Sunday, is also very cold, with east wind and occasional bursts of sunshine. On my way to church I saw a little whirlwind – Roger's Blast is the local name – tear across the field and strike the road in front of us..." On his way to church, see. The family lived way up beyond Free Lane: it could've been in the same place. And look at the date April 24! Extraordinary coincidence: it's the very same date! What are the odds against that? We should write to the *Eastern Daily Press*.' Her elation having carried her away a little his mother subsided and they smiled understandingly at each other: both knew they wouldn't be likely to write to the paper. It wasn't their style.

'Still,' she continued reflectively, 'they'd be interested at Brooklands, I'm sure. You should tell Mrs Hood.'

'Fliss,' corrected Jay, unthinkingly.

'Pardon?'

'Fliss, that's what I call her.' He explained guardedly: 'It's okay, she asked me to.'

'Well if that's what she said I suppose it's all right. It wouldn't do for me though,' she added sniffily. 'I hope young Tom doesn't think he can call me Muriel!'

Jay smothered a guffaw: 'I don't think that's very likely, Mum, somehow.' And it wasn't. His mother, the mildest mannered of women, neither exuded approachability nor gave the impression of suffering fools gladly. (It never occurred to Jay, hypersensitive in some ways and remarkably obtuse in others, that *that's* where he got it from: so desperate was he to emulate his *father's* attributes.)

'Anyway,' resumed his mother, anxious not to seem snobbish but unable totally to forget that she was an eminent headmaster's daughter and a university graduate whilst her friend was a farmer's wife. 'Anyway, you seem to be getting on very well with Mrs Hood. I mean Fliss,' she concluded reluctantly.

Jay's antennae twitched cautiously: 'Yeah, she's okay,' he offered in what he hoped was the right mixture of respect and insouciance. 'She's been telling me about her charity work. You know with that Benevolent thingy.'

'Oh yes,' rejoined his mother enthusiastically, keen to recover what she felt might be lost ground. She didn't want her younger son to think she considered herself superior and, besides, she genuinely admired Fliss's voluntary work. 'The Agricultural Benevolent Institution: that's a really good cause. I think she does magnificently to take it on as well as all the farm accounts and so on.'

'Yeah, it sounds quite interesting.' Jay strove hard to make it sound like mere politeness: 'She said I could go out with her on one of her trips. But I dunno...'

'Of course you should, darling. I'm sure you'd find it fascinating.'

'Well, maybe...' Jay trailed off artfully, calculating that his mother's inevitable intervention on his behalf might produce just the invitation he was after. So far Fliss had suggested no such thing.

Now that he was strong enough, Jay was expected to take his turn in sacking-up. The Hoods had recently invested in a series of grain-deliveries of God-knows how many tons (accountant-Autolycus had enquired but when nobody knew was sensible enough to desist). Bulk delivery was cheap but it needed storing and the silo into which the lorries disgorged their grain was only a holding measure. It had to be sacked and stored for winter feed. The coarse hemp sacks held twelve stones each and Jay could just about manhandle them onto the trolley and up the ramp to the low-roofed dusty barn where they were stacked up in rows. Although it was hard graft, he was pleased; when he first arrived on the farm he'd struggled to lift a hundredweight sack and although, naturally, no one said anything he felt like he'd achieved some rite of passage.

More significantly, and much more enjoyably, he was now entrusted with tractor driving. The farm had two Massey Fergusons and a Fordson Major. The Fordson was the most modern and Jay's favourite. It was bright blue with orange-red wheels and a rackety aluminium exhaust pipe which stuck up vertically from the left-hand side of the engine and produced belching black smoke and an agreeably raucous throbbing noise. It would've been great just to race around the farm tracks – like he and Tom had done when they were younger – but this was work, which meant transport, which meant trailers. Jay quickly learned how to attach the trailers and became adept at carrying round his cargo of sacks or bales to various destinations on the farm.

The problem was reversing. Two-wheeled trailers weren't so bad: he soon mastered the need to reverse your lock on the steering wheel for the trailer to go in the desired direction. But four-wheel trailers – although they should, in theory, have been easier – were a bugger. He was forever under- or over-estimating their length and ending up with numerous reversing and shunting manoeuvres which was frustrating even if no one was watching, and embarrassing if they were. One Friday afternoon he was attempting to reverse into an especially tight yard and forgot that the front of the Fordson was also equipped with high-lift baling-spikes which you had to lower when working in confined spaces. Too late Jay remembered and, panicking, hit the wrong control so that as he swung round the spikes rose swiftly to their maximum height and tore down a twenty-foot strip of iron guttering. There was a tremendous crash; whilst it luckily missed Jay and his tractor it demolished a row of cattle feeders in the corner of the yard. Fortunately, there appeared to be no witnesses so Jay beat a hasty retreat. Mick stepped out of the gloom of the cowshed smiling.

Later, before Farmer Hood's curiosity could develop into an inquest Mick intervened: 'Bin threatnin to come down ever since the storm, mester, 'twas only hangin on by a thread. Lucky no one got hurt, eh,' and as he turned away from the boss he winked at Jay who shot him a lop-sided grin in return. After that, Jay opted for two-wheel trailers.

'Listen to this, darling,' said his mother. It was mid-July and once again they were on their own. (Chris was in action off Indonesia and communication was non-existent; they were worried. Raymond was running the Ministry's annual camping course on the River Wye near Llanstephan.) 'It's Sir Rider's entry for July 15th: "St Swithun's, and a beautiful day, with a rising glass and a north to north-easterly wind. Clearly the Saint does not intend to 'christen the apples' this year; indeed, everybody thinks that he is going to give us a long spell of fine weather." Well, it was lovely on Thursday so here's hoping.'

'They really believe that stuff round here, don't they,' replied Jay. 'Completely unsolicited yesterday Gorbel reckoned it wouldn't rain before the end of August. Mind that's probably self-interest. If it didn't, we'd have the harvest in and they could take holidays early: it's the best chance of getting some September sun when they mooch off to Felixstowe.'

'Well there you are then! It must be true if they say it down on the farm! Oh, that reminds me: I finally got round to meeting up with Mrs Hoo...with...with Fliss – it's just been so hectic this last half-term.'

(Muriel was teaching part-time once again and, as was her wont, put in more preparation for her three-days-a-week than most of the staff did for five.) 'I mentioned that you'd like to help out on one of her trips. I think she'd forgotten but she seemed pleased anyway.'

It was always understood that – if he persevered that long – Jay would finish work at Brooklands when the harvest was in. That suited the Hoods; it suited Jay, too, as it meant he'd get some holiday before going up to Durham in October. Gorbel and St Swithun had been right: the weather held and the lumbering, lurid green Claas Matador harvested the last wheat fields on St Bartholomew's Day. The timing couldn't've been better: it meant that the traditional harvest party the following Saturday would coincide with the new August Bank Holiday so everyone would get a long weekend. And the tomfooleries of Saturday would be forgotten by the following Tuesday.

All the labourers would be there, of course, with their families. The Hood tribe would be out in force – the younger generation with their girlfriends – and Jay was invited to bring Caroline. He was dubious, fearing that she might not mix with the people he had got used to working with and, besides, he hoped to get a chance to chat up Fliss. He decided not to mention it but as ill luck would have it, Tom bumped into her at a church fete and couldn't help himself. Caroline was not best pleased she hadn't been asked but Jay convinced her it was just a misunderstanding and she agreed to attend.

It would be a riotous occasion, Jay was led to expect by Mick, who regaled him with stories of previous 'Barties' as they were called when they coincided with St Bartholomew's Fair. (So the early harvest was by no means uncommon and St Swithun clearly knew a thing or two!) There would be much eating and drinking (good) and dancing (oh, bugger!): Mick caught Jay's expression and assured him, 'Tha doan wanna worry bout the dancin, bor. Everyone'll be too pissed to care whether you can dance proper. Thass just a laff!'

The reality was even more Bacchanalian than Mick had forecast. The Hoods' hospitality was overwhelming, and, even before dusk fell, everyone was well and truly plastered. A brief, gymnastic sojourn in the Home Pasture with Caro ended not in passion but with their rolling about laughing and being unable to recall what they were doing in the field in the first place. And by the time they got back to the farmyard the sound of the dance music was only just audible above the cries of drunken revelry. For once Jay danced without inhibition – not only with Caro, but when she was being swept off by Tom's older brother James, with Fliss as well.

Gyrating clumsily to the blare of The Hollies was tricky enough; indeed just staying on his feet was a challenge. But when the tempo slowed as Elvis was crying in the chapel Jay would've fallen over if Fliss had not stepped forward decisively and clasped him in her arms. She was a little taller than Jay and a lot more sober; although Jay's head seemed to be clearing remarkably swiftly as his desires quickened to the possibilities. It didn't seem to matter that they were virtually smooching in public; after all everyone else was too including not only James and Caro (well, sod her, she's welcome!) but also Gorbel and Mick! He surrendered avidly to Fliss's embrace and she guided them unobtrusively through the mêlée until it seemed only natural to glide behind the nearest straw-stack. Jay didn't really register the fact that they were alone but as the music receded his head fell forward until it was resting on Fliss's inviting bosom. He vaguely recollected kissing her neck and chest but before he could make a real fool of himself the music began to fade and Fliss manoeuvred them gently back towards the throng. Just before they were visible, however, she raised his head and, lowering hers, kissed him gently but lingeringly on the lips. 'That's enough for now, Jaycy boy. But there's more where that came from. Next Wednesday, sweetie: come out on my visits with me…' Then they were absorbed into the crowd as the tempo of the music quickened once again and the Beatles promised him a ticket to ride… He wasn't aware of who he was dancing with: nor of the silly grin on his face.

Forty-Nine

'Well it's orthopaedics for me, thass for sure!'

'Getting a bit ahead of yersel, hinny. We've two years to go yet, like!' cautioned Belle.

'I meant when we qualify,' covered Jill.

'Don't yer mean *if*, pet? Let's not get too cocky.'

Jill blushed. She wasn't one to be boastful but they'd done okay so far, surely. That was mainly down to Sister Watson's leadership and encouragement. In fact she'd recently taken Jill to one side and said she'd keep an eye open for her when the time came as she was always on the lookout for good staff nurses – especially ones with the potential to progress to their own wards in due course. High praise indeed and Nurse Walker thrilled to it; although Miss Sharples had long ago taught her to keep such accolades to herself. So she said nothing to Christine or Belle.

Still, she *had* done okay! She'd managed the transition from home to Block to home again without any of the dramas that seemed to afflict some of her set-mates. Her academic achievements within the hospital had been adequate; whilst she'd maintained her 'A' Level studies, albeit with a complicated arrangement which necessitated her attaching herself to a university extra-mural class. The highlight had been *Macbeth*, to which she took with such enthusiasm she wondered whether all the blood and guts were a natural attraction for the medical profession! Both the lit twins and Morag had helped; the latter when Jill had managed to get down to St Aidan's before her friend graduated. They'd vowed to keep in touch, however, and unlike with most holiday attachments Jill anticipated they would.

She had grounds.

Some years previously she'd been on her one-and-only school trip. They'd boarded a coach in Newcastle and driven down the A1, through London and on to Dover. There they'd taken the ferry across to Calais and motored through Northern France into Belgium. Clammy mist enshrouded the forested uplands of the Ardennes and they hadn't really seen much until they were over the German border and heading down the Rhine to Koblenz. Their destination was Boppard where various activities had been arranged in conjunction with the local high school whose principal was a one-time university friend of the headmaster of Marsden's.

On the last-but-one night there had been a 'social' at the high school. There was music and dancing and everybody seemed to mix naturally: not like the Catholic Club where the boys sat around like stooges. A coffee bar served light refreshments, although some of the boys had smuggled in dark brown bottles of lager-bier. She was persuaded to try one but didn't think much of it: too bitter. Nevertheless, not wanting to seem rude to her host – a tall blonde youngster who introduced himself as Wolfgang – she drank it with such apparent relish that he immediately went in search of more and returned with two larger bottles: litres, he explained. Jill had never heard of litres but this bier was much darker and sweeter. It was also considerably stronger as she realised when Wolfgang asked her up to dance.

She felt a bit wobbly but was a natural mover and, if he noticed, her consort was far too polite to say anything. They'd jived energetically to several tunes she'd never heard before and then a slow waltz was played. Recalling her by no means unpleasant experience with Archie Dodd she'd expected to be embraced tightly and wondered whether Wolfgang would be afflicted by the same rigidity that had earned Archie his nickname. Not that she minded – he seemed nice and, relaxed by the alcohol, Jill was not about to upset him. It came as a surprise – no, a disappointment – when he held her very correctly and waltzed formally, and with military precision, around the parquet dance floor.

She'd agreed to meet him on the last day for a coffee and they'd got on okay. He'd suggested they exchange addresses and, even though Jill didn't have any intention of writing to him, she'd acceded. He'd turned out to be a bit older than her and seemed a lot more mature than most of the boys in her year or those who hung around the Club. They'd corresponded infrequently in the interim – he in perfect English and regularly, she in English and broken German, often several weeks later.

Now, falling from a Teutonic sky came the invitation to Boppard that July.

When they worked out the dates her dad was aghast, 'Why, man, yer'll miss the World Cup!' Jill hadn't the heart to tell him she wasn't that bothered since he still harboured fond memories of their visits to watch the Magpies and assumed she did too. Anyway, there was no guarantee England would still be in the competition by the time she was due in

Germany. She wrote back much more promptly than usual accepting the invitation. She would stay a week and be a guest of Die Familie Schinkler.

She'd already got a bit saved – partly from her nurse's pittance, mainly from the continued generosity of Uncle Bill who paid her way over the odds for holiday shifts behind the bar at Atlantic House. When he heard of the proposed trip he immediately offered to pay her fare which was even more generous than it sounded: she was going to fly!

She'd been out to the airport at Ponteland a few times. Now that her mam had got a dead smart second-hand Triumph Herald they would drive there on a Sunday afternoon just to have coffee and watch the planes taking off and landing. It wasn't much of a set-up: mostly converted post-war Nissan huts, with a single-storey brick terminal where the check-in desks and the restaurant were. This Sunday, though, Jill's focus would be on the former. They had to be there two hours before her flight which would then take another two hours to Dusseldorf. Both Mam and Dad came with her which was both highly unusual and reassuring as she expected to be nervous. When the time came to go through to departures she felt a bit forlorn but as soon as they were on the aircraft she was fine. Rob had told her to take some humbugs so as they taxied across the tarmac towards the runway she slipped one in her mouth. It helped her swallow as they were borne steeply up into the sky heading east above Newcastle. Craning her neck Jill could see the buildings tightly serried below and the Tyne wandering through the centre of the city and out towards Shields. Although her ears kept blocking up the swallowing seemed to do the trick and soon they were out over the North Sea. With nothing further to spot, Jill was soon absorbed in her paperback.

She'd thought about taking the lit twins' advice but decided it was high time she made her own choices. Well, certainly in books. She'd slipped into what was effectively the university-bookshop on King's Road the week before. Something lighter than Sue or Joyce would suggest, she mused, but not so trashy she'd be embarrassed to admit it when, inevitably, they enquired about her holiday reading.

The bookshop was heaving. Working her way along the rows, and successfully avoiding Jimmy Curtis, one of the sexist dinosaurs from her 'A' Level group, Jill reached the 'Gs.' Greene? Hmm, maybe: he met her criteria – respectable without being too high-brow. But she'd embarked on *Brighton Rock* the previous summer and, taking an instant dislike to Pinkie, had struggled to finish it. Huxley? Her eye was caught by *Brave New World* which she thought was a quote from Shakespeare but didn't know which play. She read the blurb on the back and, for some reason, was reminded of Sue's caution about the Bloomsbury set: too precious for her! G – H – nothing in J; L – Jack London: she'd heard of him, surely. Then she remembered she'd read *The Call of the Wild* way back in the second year. School texts would never do: well, not unless they were Shakespeare and he definitely wasn't Jill's holiday browsing.

She'd just reached the 'Ms' when she was forced to take evasive action again, ducking behind the stacks as the repugnant Curtis looked like heading down her aisle. Fortunately he was intercepted by their equally obnoxious tutor (who'd done nothing to support Jill's so-called feminist stance) and she was able to resume her search. Mann – too European. Masters – too Imperial. Hmm, Murdoch – not heard of him, thought Jill, instinctively feeling she might have found what she was looking for. He turned out to be a "her" – Iris. And the good news was, if she liked her, a whole string of novels lay ahead. At least half a dozen she counted, picking out the last because of its title *The Italian Girl*; bang up-to-date, too, only published last year. Then she remembered Sue's insistence on sampling any new author in chronological order and went back to the beginning: *Under the Net*. She read the intro on the back, noting it'd only been published by Penguin in 1960, and discovered it was narrated in the first person by a male character. This didn't so much put her off as puzzle her: why would a female novelist choose to speak through a male character called Jake Donaghue in her first novel? Then she saw it was set in London. That was better. She liked the idea of reading about London. Even though she'd only been through it a couple of times she sensed, from Morag's anecdotes, that she would like it there. She wouldn't finish the book on the flight out but she would before next Saturday, so nestling in her hold luggage for the return journey lay *The Flight from the Enchanter*, Murdoch's second novel. She hoped she'd enjoy them both and that the lit twins would be duly impressed. You never know: for once they might not've read them.

Wolfgang and his father were waiting for her on the far side of Customs. Herr Schinkler looked just as Jill remembered him: tall and upright like Uncle Bill and with a similarly sunny disposition. Wolfgang was more handsome than before and a lot bigger – at least six inches taller than Jill. Still just as punctilious though. He took her suitcase and escorted her to Herr Schinkler's smart white saloon. Jill recognised it as a BMW and knew they were very expensive in England; she'd never been in one before. Herr Schinkler explained that they would take the scenic route so Jill could see the countryside rather than tearing along the autobahn. It would take them around two hours and Wolfgang would be her guide. That didn't work too well to start with as the scenery outside Dusseldorf was little improvement on Tyneside and Wolfgang didn't know the area anyway. As they got closer to Koblenz, and then Boppard, however, both the views of the steep, wooded valleys and her guide's commentary improved.

By the time they arrived in Badsalgic it was almost eight hours since Jill had left home and she was understandably tired. They had a simple supper of cold meats and cheese, helped down by condensation-cold lager and she retired gratefully to her small but comfortably furnished bedroom. Waking early, Jill explored the house. It was much bigger than home, detached with its own driveway and garden. With a large island table the kitchen was massive. It smelt of ground coffee and fresh bread.

After escorting her around the village Wolfgang took her out for lunch. He was an attentive host and treated her with a faintly disturbing mixture of respect and desire. Not that he did anything untoward and Jill certainly didn't encourage him. He was nice enough but she didn't fancy him in the slightest. They spent the following days gradually taking in more of the local beauty spots. The highlight of the sightseeing was the fourth morning of her stay when they took a boat trip down the Rhine and spent most of the day at the Lorelei. Here Wolfgang came into his own, explaining that its name meant 'murmuring rock' because of the sound produced by the combination of strong currents and waterfalls. Legend had it that the beautiful maiden Lorelei, having been betrayed by her lover, lured river-boatmen to destruction on the rock. The local bishop was reluctant to sentence her to death and instead decreed that she should be sent to a nunnery. She was escorted by three knights but persuaded them to let her ascend the rock one last time. Then when she did so, she fell to her death, the rock echoing with her cries and being named after her accordingly.

'It's very romantic, don't you think? Very beautiful. Almost as beautiful as you, my Jill.' It was the first time he'd said anything so intimate and it took her by surprise.

She could hardly demur and just murmured lamely, 'Yes it's brill, Wolfgang. Thanks ever so much for bringing me.'

Their exchange set the tone for the rest of her stay: her would-be sweetheart expressing himself in ever more ardent phrases, Jill trying not to lead him on but not to give offence either. It wasn't easy. But it was even more fraught when she discovered how jealous he could be.

Fifty

It was a bit strange cycling to Brooklands but not to work. A relaxed start too as Fliss had said they wouldn't be leaving 'til ten. Still, that was fortuitous. It meant that the others would be out in the fields and his arrival might go unheralded. He parked his Raleigh round the back of the barn, not in the passageway where the men normally left the bikes, and made his way circumspectly to the kitchen. The door to the hallway and stairs was open and Fliss must already have seen him coming as she shouted down to make some coffee and help himself to biscuits. He did so and settled down with the *Eastern Daily Press* feeling awkward in his semi-formal outfit of smart slacks and open-neck shirt (Fliss had instructed him to 'look presentable' as she was going to pass him off as her trainee).

The *Press* was as uninspiring as usual ('the local rag' his parents dubbed it, though they still had it delivered each day). Two articles caught his eye, though. One was about a motorcycle death – always a source of morbid interest for him – on the Acle Straight; but there wasn't much detail and what there was didn't involve a Triumph so he skipped on to the other. The reference to 'Bungay' had naturally drawn his attention but it turned out to be a piece on the 'Friends of St Mary's.' One for his mum not him, he concluded dismissively.

He glanced around the empty kitchen. The sturdy oak chairs were arranged neatly under the big square table. He realised he was tapping out nervous scales on the white-bleached wood. Embarrassed, he reached for his coffee. It was still too hot.

He turned to the sports pages to read about the Canaries' latest tribulations. He didn't support them but, with the passing years and Blackburn so far away his devotion to Rovers (never especially strong) had faded too. He'd mocked his erstwhile buddies when they'd fondly imagined that as the Canaries had played *so* well in the '59–'60 season they'd be allowed to skip the Second Division and gain First Division status instead. What a load of wallies! But a nodding acquaintance with their fortunes had been handy when working at Brooklands. All but

Mick (an unmentionable Blues fan) were supporters and it helped foster the impression that he was a fellow fan. This was given credence by his settling an argument between Fred and Sloaney about how they got the name 'Canaries' (courtesy of his mother's reading of H V Morton and his celebration of 'Norwich Plain Heads').

His reverie was broken by the entry of Fliss who 'fair took his breath away.' She was dressed not in her farm uniform of jeans and jumper but in an elegant dark brown skirt and cream blouse. The latter was done up primly to the neck; the former hung unfashionably below the knee but had buttons all down the front. She looked gorgeous but as Jay hadn't the words (for once) or the confidence to tell her so, he just gave her what he hoped was a longing smile. Fliss smiled back but in a rather remote, almost polite, manner. She seemed preoccupied and very business-like. Jay was puzzled – and disappointed: he'd been fostering high, if somewhat vague aspirations for today's trip.

'Oh good, you look smart, Jay: just right for my assistant. We're headed for the villages south of Norwich. I don't suppose you know the area.'

Jay seized the initiative, 'No, Fliss, but I borrowed this: I thought it might come in handy,' he said, brandishing the OS map. 'Maybe I could be your navigator...as well...' He wasn't quite sure how to finish the sentence and was relieved when Fliss relented with an appreciative grin.

'Thanks, Jay. That'd be a help. I got lost last time!' She handed him her itinerary with the addresses of half a dozen farm cottages on it and whilst she took a short 'phone call in the living room Jay spread out the map and located the various villages. Then Fliss swirled back into the kitchen and they were off up the drive in the once smart blue, now farm-mud-flecked Austin A40.

At the bottom of the steep, wooded lane they turned left onto the A144. Fliss eased the A40 past the beautifully-manicured grounds of Heddenham Hall, by-passing Woodton and Brooke then turning off the main road just before they reached Poringland. Their first two visits were in Framlingham Earl and Framlingham Pigot respectively and Jay's navigational skills brought them accurately through the low but dense copses to both hamlets. He was a bit nervous about the first call and was relieved when Fliss announced, 'I think I'll do this one on my own; the Houghtons were a bit wary before. Y'know what they say about Norfolk – "most suspicious county in England"!'

Jay would've liked to stretch his legs but didn't want to draw attention to himself; it might make Fliss's task even trickier if she had to explain to the Houghtons why she had a young man in tow. So he stayed in the A40, grateful that he'd had the foresight to bring *A Man for All Seasons*. Duke Bartleby had recommended it grudgingly as 'by one of the few popular playwrights worth reading.' Seemed a bit harsh, reflected Jay who also enjoyed Arden and Pinter. He'd seen it performed at the Maddermarket in Norwich the previous year and it had become a favourite. He particularly admired the character of Sir Thomas More: his coruscating wit, his fortitude and his magnificent dismissal of his pathetic critics: especially Rich! For Wales, eh! Typically, he had large chunks by heart and fantasised about impressing the pants off Fliss by quoting them. He was puzzling how best to bring Sir Thomas into the conversation when Fliss appeared and subsided into the driver's seat looking flustered.

'What's up?' he enquired solicitously.

'Oh, some people!' she exclaimed. 'They just won't be helped. They're living in squalor but they won't have it any different. Grrrr! Anyway, where are we due next?'

Judging that she was hardly in the mood for *Seasons*, Jay contented himself with directions. Ten minutes later they reached the next farm. However, still upset by the reception she'd received at the Houghtons' Fliss decided that, once again, Jay should remain in the car. He was philosophical but couldn't help feeling that reality was failing to live up to fantasy. Story of my life, he reflected, ruefully. But then his prospects began to improve.

'That was more like it. They were actually grateful. And more to the point we can help. Tell you what: you can be my secretary as well as my navigator! Can you make a note on the schedule, please: "Adisons, Town Farm Bank: reconditioned cooker and fridge". I knew you'd be worth your weight!' Fliss beamed at him and although the roles weren't exactly what Jay had in mind, it was a start. They wound through the lanes and across the main road to Caistor St. Edmonds in much higher spirits, drawing up outside the last in a row of farm cottages. Jay scrutinised them with dismay. Unlike the fine flint faces of Brooklands these were timber-framed and wattle-and-daub affairs. They'd been concreted over but the dampness had cracked the lime and the wood laths, like the window frames, were all splintered. The doors were solid but, again, the oak looked seriously weathered. Jay dreaded what they might look like inside.

He was so nervous he never noticed as he was introduced as Fliss's assistant to a charming old couple. The Odihams had clearly been looking forward to the visit; a pot of tea and a plate of Jacobs cream crackers, thinly spread with Philly, were rapidly produced. They seemed to treat it more as a social occasion than a means-test. The only tricky moment was when they asked about Jay's training but Fliss had obviously anticipated the query and launched into a detailed description of modules and assessment criteria. Excellent! They were co-conspirators once more: prospects rosier still!

Three successful visits later and they turned for home. Fliss was now far more relaxed and much friendlier: 'So, my trusty navigator, are you going to find us a nice scenic route back? There's no hurry: I said we wouldn't be home 'til mid-afternoon. In fact we could stop for a spot of lunch at The Feathers.'

They had a round of sandwiches each; and Fliss drank a large glass of chilled white wine whilst Jay knocked back a couple of pints of Adnams. He made sure he went to the loo before they left and it was only once they were in the car that he realised the top button of Fliss's blouse and the bottom two of her skirt had become undone. Jay wondered whether he should pretend he hadn't noticed or make it obvious that he had. He veered towards the latter, but was deliberating what to say when Fliss helped him out: 'Phew! It's got a lot warmer, don't you think. I feel quite overdressed!'

Jay blurted out, 'You look lovely. Excuse me if I appear to leer!'

Fliss giggled and their exchange set the tone for the slow-road home. Initially, Jay's eyes were transfixed by the steady rise and fall of her breasts; then he twigged: when she changed gear and her left foot depressed the clutch Fliss's skirt rode progressively a little higher up her legs. First he took in her knees, then the soft-beige nylon of her lower thighs. She wriggled a little in her seat and as she released the clutch once more the skirt rose far enough for him to glimpse the cream suspenders and the bare flesh above her stocking tops. Jesus! He gulped: he was becoming aroused, and it showed.

Fliss glanced across and murmured: 'I see you're enjoying the view! Pretty round here, isn't it!'

'I'll say,' he breathed appreciatively, before realising: Shit! I need a pee. Embarrassed, he apologised profusely and Fliss, scanning the lane ahead, considerately found a narrow grass track which led off under some willows beside a mill-stream. He retreated a few yards out of sight. Knew I shouldn't've had that second pint, he thought, making sure that it was well and truly siphoned before returning to the car. Fliss looked a little flushed but, to Jay's relief she'd made no attempt to pull down her skirt which still gave him a most enticing view.

'That better? My, but it *is* hot this afternoon, isn't it. Don't *you* think so?' she smiled provocatively hooking her thumbs into the lapels of her blouse and blowing downwards. 'See how warm I am?' Her nipples were clearly discernible through the creamy sheen.

Apprehensive and excited simultaneously Jay shuffled awkwardly across towards her almost impaling himself on the thoughtlessly-situated gear lever as he did so. 'Whoops! Careful, Jaycy: let me help,' and purporting to shift the offending lever she briefly slipped her hand between his thighs. Accidentally, of course…

Jay gulped as he wound both arms around her neck and kissed her tentatively, on the lips. She responded enthusiastically and they were locked together for some moments before Fliss disengaged his left hand and slid it down over her shoulder, cupping it firmly under her breast. He mumbled incoherently before their kiss resumed, this time more intimately as her tongue furrowed softly between his inexperienced but receptive lips.

She was undoing the buttons on his shirt – an invitation to reciprocate? – and rubbing her fingertips gently over his nipples. He was surprised to feel how stiff they became. He tried to express his appreciation but was distracted by the circular motion of Fliss's tongue entwining itself around his own. He screwed up his eyes tightly, feeling as if he was about to explode.

Then, just as he was emboldened to venture inside her blouse Fliss moved her fingers steadily down his stomach into his lap. This time her aim was more precise and he gasped as they rested on where he was lying cumbersomely against her thigh. He was fumbling inside her bra; reflecting momentarily that his count would probably not even get to fifty when a brisk little rub by Fliss caught him unawares. She must've felt the trigger-movement as she immediately flashed her fingers intently back and forth and almost instantly he was wracked with pleasure, soon-to-be superseded by frustrated embarrassment.

'Don't worry, sweetie,' she murmured understandingly as he slumped onto her shoulder, 'there'll be other times…'

But there never were; three weeks later he headed north to the cloistered circumjacences of Durham University.

Fifty-One

On Thursday evening they visited friends at a farmhouse on the outskirts of the village. Fritz Spentolz had fought in the war with Wolfgang's father and had lost an arm for his pains. Both had been in the Lutwaffe and Herr Spentolz had taken a particular shine to Jill when she revealed that her brother was in the RAF. Fritz, as he insisted she call him, owned a vineyard and their meal was both long and bibulous. She noticed that Wolfgang drank very little but she was enjoying herself and wasn't about to let him spoil the fun. In any case Adrianna, the daughter of the house, was excellent company and was encouraging Jill to let her hair down.

Adrianna was what the lit twins would have teasingly termed 'a buxom blond.' She had straw-coloured plaits and, you couldn't help but notice, extremely generous boobs which were accentuated by the snugness of the flower-patterned rustic blouse she almost had on. Jill assumed it was for Wolfgang's benefit and certainly his keen window-dresser's eye led him to compliment her on her outfit fairly early in the proceedings. Jill wondered whether the remark was designed to test her affections but since she couldn't return Wolfgang's increasingly amorous pronouncements it had no effect. It did, however, allow her to add her own appraising comment which seemed to please Adrianna rather more. Jill was a little hazy subsequently but reckoned that was the point at which her newly-acquired friend began to ply her with the strawberry liqueur that Herr Spentolz – sorry, Fritz – produced from his own fruit.

They had retired to the parlour where, in spite of the season, a large pine log fire was burning hospitably, releasing a resinous aroma. Fritz and his wife were busy in the kitchen and the three youngsters settled onto the burgundy-leather sofa. Jill was content to loll back on the cushions and leave conversation to those coherent enough to string more than a few sentences together; but Wolfgang and Adrianna's exchanges became increasingly animated, then strident. He was sitting between the two girls so Jill couldn't really work out what was going on, particularly as their altercation was being pursued entirely in German and at a rapid pace.

Without warning Wolfgang turned to her and announced, 'Come, Jill, we are leaving,' and when she demurred, insisting on finishing her drink and accusing him playfully of being a killjoy, he stood up and stomped out of the house.

Jill couldn't've cared less; but was sufficiently curious to ask Adrianna languidly if she knew why Wolfgang had made such a dramatic exit. 'He jealous,' she replied smiling, 'he think ve having too good time.'

'Oh, for Chrissake!' dismissed Jill, 'good riddance then. And yes, I don't mind if I do,' she grinned as Adrianna poured her another schooner of strawberry-doom. She drained it in one gulp and slid languorously down the sofa.

Jill woke late the following morning. She was alone in an unfamiliar room and in a strangely-proportioned bed: not a single, but not quite a double either. She was naked and had no clear memory of how she got there, just a feeling that it had been intoxicating when she did; and that that didn't apply just to the drink. She had a vague recollection of having to be helped to get undressed and similarly uncertain flashbacks of being cuddled and kissed: not only on the lips but on the breasts which evidentially felt a little tender that morning. As did the rest of her; but she was pretty sure it *had* been an extremely enjoyable evening. It was just as well, given that she had a splitting headache and when she finally managed to make it back to the Schinkler's, Wolfgang wasn't speaking to her. The frostiness continued right through the day and into the Saturday which augured ill for the party that afternoon.

Originally, it had been planned as a farewell but now it was to be combined with a football celebration: England had apparently survived the earlier stages of the World Cup and were due to meet West Germany that afternoon in the final. There was to be quite a get-together: Wolfgang's elder brother was joining them, the Spentolz family were coming and some other neighbours whose names Jill didn't catch as they arrived hurriedly just a few minutes before kick-off. In total there were fifteen of them packed into the living room and huddled round the black and white TV: fourteen supporting West Germany, and Jill.

Frau Schinkler had provided trays of rye-bread sandwiches and there were potato-frits, frankfurters, sausage rolls, gherkins, bowls of thin-sliced tomatoes and diced-cucumber, bread-sticks, skewers of cheese-and-pineapple cubes and a huge, round cut-glass dish with different sauces and pickles. Herr Schinkler served litre bottles of lager and dark-bier; whilst Fritz had brought across a crate of various wines including several bottles of his infamous strawberry-doom. After the previous day's enforced abstinence Jill tucked in with gusto, although resolving to steer clear of the strawberries. Shades of Magpies v Fulham, she recalled nostalgically.

Wolfgang was still being a prick and declined to sit next to her but before she could feel too isolated Adrianna waved her over with a smile and they squashed themselves into a large cloth-covered armchair. Quite soon they looked so well set that Wolfgang's brother Tomaz undertook to keep them supplied with lager and sandwiches and they didn't have to move for the duration of normal time.

To Jill's well-concealed disgust and roars of triumph from everyone else, Germany scored first. Adrianna announced that their striker was Helmut Haller, playing in his third World Cup for them. 'And if England score you must tell me about their player.' Jill fervently hoped she'd have to – preferably several times. They clinked bottles in agreement and cordial rivalry.

Within five minutes there was a room-wide groan; and the soccer education she'd received from her dad came to Jill's aid as she gleefully informed Adrianna that the equaliser had been scored by Geoff Hurst. 'He's from West Ham, one of our London clubs. They've got a great supporters' anthem called *I'm forever blowing bubbles*,' explained Jill. 'You'd love it, Adie, it's a great drinking song. Cheers!' And they downed the rest of their lager; only to be rewarded with fresh bottles by the vigilant Tomaz. Jill was beginning to take a shine to him. He was better-looking than Wolfgang – who sat across the room glaring at them – and a lot more fun. Indeed, in spite of the obvious rivalry, she was being extremely well-looked after by her several hosts, particularly Adie who had one arm draped around Jill's neck and was administering friendly squeezes coincident with especially exciting passages of play.

The rest of the first half sped by to the accompaniment of 'Oohs' and 'Ahs' and the consumption of numerous bottles of lager and white wine. Adie's arm had gradually slipped off Jill's shoulder and the nips and squeezes were now directed to her thigh, a generous amount of which was revealed as Jill's miniskirt rode steadily higher. There was a lot of milling about at half-time but Jill and Adie were comfortable and stayed put. Wolfgang continued to sulk, Tomaz to be solicitous (which put his younger brother in an even worse temper). It was noisy and Jill was feeling relaxed so it took her a few moments to realise that Adie was talking to her, well whispering really with her lips pressed to Jill's ear: 'I hope you're not *wund, Liebling*,' and when Jill looked puzzled she added, '*Bruste...* I hope your breasts aren't *wund*...sore? I enjoy very much kissing your *Nippel*.'

Jill felt herself blushing slightly but since it was roasting in the living room by now she hoped no one, apart from Adie, would notice. She hissed back: 'Ooh, you little devil...so it *was* you! I wish I'd not been so drunk,' she confessed, warming to the thought. 'I'm sure I'd've liked it!'

'Next time you enjoy more,' promised Adie, 'and...how you say... return the Gefallen? Favour?' The pincers threatened a blissful invasion...

'Definitely!' swore Jill, wondering how on earth there could be a next time when she left the following day. If only. But Adie had other plans and clinked her bottle enthusiastically as the second half got under way.

Half an hour sped by, Jill's mind only partly on the football, given the revelations Adie had imparted and her increasingly intimate touches. Jill's eyes had momentarily closed to savour her rising desire when there was a heavy collective groan as England's second goal went it. She missed the shot but the on-pitch celebrations suggested it was Peters so she took a chance and explained, 'That was Martin Peters: he's another West Ham player. So is our captain. There, look – Bobby Moore. You'll see him up close when he collects the cup,' she grinned cheekily, and received a series of strategically-directed prods for her insolence!

Her confidence seemed justified, however, and although she had no watch Jill was sure the match must be nearly over. She was just about to teach Adie a new phrase – 'Done and dusted' – when there was a deafening roar all round her as Germany equalised.

'Weber!' shrieked Adie triumphantly, 'another Wolfgang – like your "boyfriend"' she shouted above the fray with an emphasis which expressed her disbelief. Judging by the daggers she was receiving from his direction, it could be a doomed relationship, especially as in her now-tipsy enthusiasm Adie was doing little to disguise her amorous inclinations. Not that Jill cared. She was going home tomorrow; besides which if Adie carried on touching her *just there* it wouldn't only be the football which came to a climax!

But there *was* still a match to be settled. This time she did need a break and there was a long queue for the toilet. When her turn arrived, she was still that fired up by Adie's attentions she longed for the relief of masturbation. But there wasn't time and, besides, she hoped that particular pleasure would be consummated by her dextrous German friend. So, daringly, she took off her knickers and slipped them into the tiny pocket of her skirt. By the time she got back extra time had begun; and Adie – looking flushed and excited – rapidly shuffled across in the armchair so Jill could resume her place. As she sat down she felt her friend's hand at the base of her back.

The flickering figures flashed back and forth over the screen. The atmosphere in the room was electric and later Jill told herself that was what emboldened her to whisper in Adie's ear: 'Summat for you, hinny' as she slipped the damp briefs into her friend's hand. *'Ach, oh flittchen!'* muttered her delighted friend swiftly wriggling her fingers under Jill's bum which she raised obligingly.

Ten minutes or so later an on-fire Jill watched, mesmerised, as a brilliant cross from Alan Ball (her dad would be proud of her commentary) found Geoff Hurst. He swivelled and crashed a shot off the cross-bar into the goal. 'YES!!' bellowed Jill, unable to contain herself: 'Goal! Goal!' Her shout was immediately drowned by a chorus of *'Neins'* and *'Nichts'* but to no avail: the ref consulted the linesman and the goal stood. The groans included angry comments that Jill couldn't understand but Tomaz, who was hovering near their snuggle-seat with refreshments explained, 'Some of zem are saying it's fixed. We beat USSR in ze semi-finals and ze linesman is Russian. They're claiming it's revenge. They're wrong. It vas a goal all right. More lagers, Damen?'

Jill was now on tenterhooks – both from the exquisite manipulation she was receiving from Adie; and from the tension of the football. Everyone around her was willing Germany to score again: she was just dying both for her orgasm, and for the final whistle to go. And suddenly it *was* all over. As some of the crowd began to spill onto the pitch Geoff Hurst completed his hat-trick: England had beaten the old enemy 4-2. We've just won the World Cup, thrilled Jill to herself as she finally came – surreptitiously, but mightily – on Adie's probing fingers!

Oohh…God…she sighed: I hope Dad was watching!

Fifty-Two

'DURHAM is a city and non-county borough in the administrative county of Durham. It has an area of 4,578 acres and an estimated population of 21,140... The Great North Road passes through Neville's Cross, its western suburb. On this road Darlington lies eighteen miles south of the city and Newcastle fifteen miles north.' Jay fancied he might visit the latter more frequently than the former. 'Other main roads radiate to Sunderland, Hartlepool, Stockton, Bishop Auckland and Barnard Castle. These and many other places are covered by omnibus services. The railway passenger station is on the main line from King's Cross and many fast trains stop at Durham.'

Jay was studying his *Durham University Students' Representative Council (DUSRC) Diary* on just such a fast train. He was travelling light, his trunk having preceded him. The diary was one of the first, and most useful, volumes of university information he received. In addition to boring trivia there was a handy double-page map on the inside front cover which showed all the colleges and churches. (Jay's copy soon indicated the best pubs, too.) Two of the parish churches in particular caught his attention: St Cuthbert's on North Road, closest to his digs and St Oswald's on Church Street. But it was the cathedral in the centre of both the map and an incised meander of the River Wear that dominated the landscape and the city. He recalled it vividly from his interview. He'd admired it initially as the train slowed over the viaduct before pulling into the station. Then he'd been hugely impressed with its vastness as he'd traipsed around on that bitter December afternoon. He felt he might spend some time there.

The first days sped by in the confused, coruscating whirl of Freshers' Week. There were parties, a dance (which Jay sat out) and a coach tour to the Bowes Museum and on up Teesdale to High Force where tumbling, spray-blown, peat-brown waterfalls impressed him the more. Towards the end of the week they all trooped off to Aidan's where the Societies' Day was being held. The atmosphere was so boisterous that Jay (in Autolyclean anti-social mode) almost walked out. Only the desire to locate the Mountaineering Society detained him. He spotted a climbing set-up on the far side of the hall, but had to run the gauntlet of numerous undergraduate salesmen on the way. Most he just ignored. The siren sounds of the Musical Society intrigued him though; not least because a string trio, comprising an anonymous male cellist and two pulchritudinous female violinists, was giving a haunting rendition of *Salut d'Amour*. It was one of his favourite pieces of Elgar and when he paused in admiration the appreciative smile he received almost led him to succumb.

Tearing himself away he blundered straight into a bunch of Mexicans. 'Sail in the wake of Magellan and Drake,' they chanted, 'gaze with us on the Pacific!'

'What? *Silent upon a peak in Darien?*' he quipped. But receiving only stares of incomprehension, he rejected their invitation, albeit with reluctance knowing how chuffed his mum and dad would've been to learn he'd joined the Geographical Society.

He eschewed the temptations of the Literary Society – two blokes dressed as Dickens and Tennyson outweighing the rather tasty redhead who was presumably Rossetti.

When he finally made it to the farthest reaches of the caravanserai, the Mountaineering Club desk was deserted. On the bare ash of the trestle table stood a large white card: '*Big Jug* next Thursday, 8 p.m. Come and get roped in!' Jay smiled, partly at the weak humour but mainly cause he didn't have to engage in conversation with yet another solicitous stranger. Still, a society that met in a pub sounded more like it!

The term proper started with 'Matriculation & Registration' at their chosen colleges – in Jay's case St Cuthbert's at the far end of the Bailey just before the road dropped down to Prebend's Bridge over the Wear. It was the area which had so impressed him when he'd come up for interview originally. Late in the afternoon, viva voce successfully negotiated, he marched confidently over the bridge on his way up to the hotel in Neville's Cross; it began to snow. He cut through the woods above Quarryhead Lane and by the time he reached the top the trees were laden with dusk-defying shiny-hopeful flakes. Jay had always liked snow.

Memory-deep, Jay found himself in Palace Green. He was supposed to be at Cuthbert's but was drawn to the cathedral. Resisting the temptation to swing on the sanctuary knocker he stepped into the chilly gloom of the nave. The Norman pillars rose majestically to the embossed ceiling, but he squandered no time in the main body of the church. He strode across to the studded door into the cloisters.

He dredged up some Hardy that seemed appropriate…something

about 'a lone cave's stillicide.' He didn't know which poem it came from but he liked that word. 'Stillicide': kind of sepulchral and exclusive at the same time; just the atmosphere for a dusky cloister. A distant murmur of voices impinged. He thought about turning round to avoid them then decided: sod 'em, I was here first!

It soon became apparent they were female, two by the sound of it, and young. By now they were quite close and although he didn't plan to eavesdrop he couldn't avoid hearing a slightly posh, but still local tone advising: 'There! Said you'd find the tomb fascinating.'

'Yeah, it were brilliant, thanks,' returned the other voice whose accent was more markedly Geordie.

'Especially with you being so into Cuthbert an all. Ever since Seahouses, eh!'

'Howay! Fancy you remembering that! Yeah, it were me birthday.'

'And that other time,' added the first voice casually. 'At Dunstanburgh. You know, with your two mentors – that blond and her mate. What was she called?'

'Er…Joyce?'

'Yeah, she was dead smart!'

The laugh in response seemed relieved. But it also reminded Jay of someone he'd talked to before. It seemed a long time ago though; he couldn't place it. Maybe if he said hello…?

But before he could summon up the courage to break in on their conversation the two girls were heading through the door into the chancel. Jay's fleeting impression of the owner of the laugh was of someone small. And dark. And very pretty.

Then they were gone. He was alone once more, and remembered he was supposed to be on his way to college.

St Cuthbert's was not a college however, it was a Society. This was a source of some dissension. Others from supposedly more prestigious institutions – University, Hatfield and St John's (for God-men) – tended to be sniffy. Theirs were true Cambridge-type colleges with Masters and long-established traditions. Cuthbert's was new and unfashionable and boasted merely a principal. That suited Jay perfectly, of course: it was different.

The Society was housed in a shallow Georgian crescent. Four-storey converted houses preceded a white-walled, rectangular monstrosity which comprised the Junior Common Room on the ground floor with undergraduate accommodation above it. This was apparently much sought after for its modern facilities; Jay demurred, promising himself that, when his turn came to live in college he would opt for more austere Georgian elegance. Between the buildings lay the admin centre, the Senior Common Room and the assembly hall where formal dinners took place. Jay was only compelled to attend these periodically and did so under protest: they were the most traditional – white tie and tails – element of college life and the one that was least to his liking. It was partly the formality, partly the compulsion. Thank God he hadn't ended up at Peterhouse!

There was another bit of tradition that couldn't be avoided. Gowns were mandatory both for dinner and for lectures, seminars and, in theory, tutorials (though that depended largely on your tutor). Undergraduates were directed to Gray & Son Ltd on Saddler Street: 'ROBE MAKERS. By appointment to THE UNIVERSITIES OF DURHAM AND NEWCASTLE. The recognised authority since 1896.' They also stocked hoods and scarves, ties, cufflinks, blazers and badges. Jay smiled at Gray's direction: he wouldn't be sporting one of *their* products to announce to an unimpressed City 'I'm a new student.' He'd had a choice of familial hand-me-downs and had opted for his Auntie Gwen's. She'd been at Girton and Cambridge gowns were shorter and altogether sportier; and different! It elicited some comments in the early days, which reflected Jay's intention.

Through the archway between the admin block and the JCR lay the main college garden, although each building had its own quad as well. The only attraction for Jay lay in its retaining wall. Well, its external façade, to be precise. If you followed the South Bailey to the end of the JCR building and under the archway leading to Prebends then kenched sharply to the left there it was: a twenty-foot high, thirty-yard long bastion, ideal for climbing. The height was secondary. The best routes traversed the wall from left to right gradually increasing in severity and exposure as the steep ground below fell away to the Wear: ideal training territory and all the more attractive for being off-limits. The rock was sandstone – excellent friction but indifferent holds, with side-pulls de rigueur: ideal for developing technique. Routes at Crag Lough or in the Lakes always seemed a grade easier after the previous week's sustained finger-strengthening.

Elbow-strengthening was more convivial. Once a fortnight, the Mountaineering Club convened for a 'Smoker': an indoor meet at the Big Jug or the Dun Cow.

'New boy, eh?' Jay was ready to bridle. 'What're you having?' That was better!

'Pint of Exhibition, please.' And as his tall, smooth inquisitor shimmied through the crush to the bar Jay turned to his neighbour who was younger and seemed more approachable. 'Strewth! Who's the film-star, squire?'

'Oh that's Edrich, our president; everyone calls him Ed. He's okay when you get to know him. I'm Steyn, by the way, club secretary. And you are?'

'Jay Fincher. "Finch" to his mates! So what's job?'

'Well we're pretty informal. Whoever's around comes here or to the Cow. Then we plan our next meet, select routes, relive previous epics – that sorta thing. Mostly it's just an excuse for a few pints!'

That sounded all right, reflected Jay. Not that he needed an excuse. On the nights when he wasn't studying, which initially were most, he could be found in one of the town-centre pubs. Some were rough and encouraged the inevitable town v gown animosity exacerbated by the size of a city which was big enough to have plenty of pubs, but small enough to ensure they weren't 'separate.' Some of the Cuthberts circle whose periphery he frequented went out of their way to court trouble. His sort-of-mate Nige, for example, whose father owned a Pools company, reputedly provided his only son with an allowance of £160 a week (Jay's was about £8). His habit, when inebriated, of lighting cigarettes from the gas-fire with ten-shilling notes might have impressed his more sycophantic hangers-on; locals whose dads were either unemployed or down the pits didn't see the funny side. Nor was Tone, whose real name was Antonio but who insisted on styling himself 'Q,' likely to endear himself with his dismissive comments about Northerners, particularly when delivered in a Hampshire drawl which grew more pronounced in direct ratio to the number of bottles of Newky Brown he'd consumed. And Crawly – who lived in a cottage in Pelaw Wood with a constantly-shifting variety of strange companions – was just weird. Jay espoused eccentric: though as his big brother was wont to remark: 'A joke's a joke, but fuck a pantomime!'

Jay had gone to the trouble of cultivating some of the Durham lads by respectful conversation and standing more than his fair share of rounds. So he found himself apologising for his 'posh' friends. Particularly on the odd occasion they penetrated the Buffalo Head – a 'town' as well as 'gown' pub – which, by the end of his first term, had become his local. A long narrow passageway flanked just two rooms: a lounge at the front where he rarely sat and the bar where the card and shove-ha'penny tables – and, of course, the dart board – were. It was the only pub in town that served Federation, a brew normally reserved for working men's clubs. The Ordinary, which was okay if leavened with a dash of lemonade in the bottom – a 'pint-touch' – cost one and seven-pence; Special was one-and-nine. That was the weekend treat. Both were cheaper than the stuff Nige drank; but then Jay wasn't on eight grand a year!

Surprisingly, for a game where proficiency required a standard of hand-eye coordination not normally Jay's forte, he was good at darts. Especially singles: in doubles he'd lose concentration or faith in his partner or both. But he was even better at scoring. He'd regularly offer to 'chalk the board' and always had the score written up before the thrower had removed his arrows, let alone painstakingly computed his total. He wasn't flash about it; he couldn't help reflecting wryly that old Plug would've been surprised, though doubtless still unimpressed: so much for him getting a 'Nine' at Maths. Twat!

Entertainment in the JCR couldn't've been more different: poker and bridge – that first term to the accompaniment of endless Beatles LPs. There were two separate schools: the poker (and brag) players regarding bridge as an effete pastime for snobs, the bridge-players incredulous at the amount of money changing hands over a game as simple, yet brutal as poker. Bridge was played for prestige. Only Jay had a hand in both schools.

Judging by Chris's recent, albeit sporadic, letters from Hong Kong, Bridge was proving as useful in the wardroom as it was in the common room. Surprisingly, none of Jay's intake played and he found himself in the company of second and third-years, some of whom were good enough to make the college, and in one case, the university team. Augustine – Gus to his friends, including Jay who became his regular partner – was not especially bright academically but brilliant when it came to the finer points of contract. He taught Jay a new way to bid: 'Point Count,' named by its inventor Goren some fifteen years previously in the States but only recently in vogue over here. It seemed simpler than the Honours system his mum and dad deployed and far more accurate, being based on a mathematical approach which appealed to Jay and, he was certain, also improved his poker. They rapidly became JCR champs and their elevation to the college/university teams was only stymied by Jay's innate dislike of conventional clubs.

Though not night clubs, of course. He patronised the only one in town. The Caprice, which handily, was just round the corner from his digs. No one from Cuths went there and he enjoyed the buzz and the risqué if somewhat tacky surroundings. There was a square, parquet- floor surrounded by greasy-looking red plush couches (neither of which Jay frequented) and a small, raised platform for the band. Usually jazz: which was okay for background to the serious business. Three small gaming rooms – one for roulette and the others for craps and poker/blackjack – ringed the central area. Once he encountered his moral tutor, Dr Wallace, but after the initial embarrassment a mutual understanding ensured no further mention was made. What *was* made was money! Again, Jay demonstrated that any game where the opposition was the other players rather than the House could prove a reliable source of income. Only once, towards the end of term when the snow already lay thick on the pavements of Flass Street (where his digs nestled under the huge, stone viaduct carrying the London-Newcastle express trains) did he succumb to the roulette table. He won £34 in less than an hour. After that he stopped going: the subsistence gambler in him wisely cautioning that he could equally well lose that much next time and a month's allowance gone in an hour was hardly sound economics. Besides, by this stage the stakes in the JCR were frequently higher and the income more assured.

His weekly tally (on a blank note page at the back of the SRC diary) indicated his success: [1] £2/10/0 [2] 17/6 [3] £3/9/0 and so on. By the end of the Michaelmas term – during which he showed a loss in just one week – he'd amassed over forty pounds: equal to almost half his parental allowance (he didn't get a grant). 'Amassed' was of course a theoretical concept since it had all gone on beer and late-night Chinese meals at the Kwai Lam on Saddler Street, too conveniently opposite the Buff.

Meanwhile, there was his course: English Language & Literature. It had come as a bit of a shock to discover other students who were as widely read as he was. Mostly, they were a bunch of intellectual snobs (unlike him, of course!) and he had nothing to do with them outside lectures and seminars. By coincidence the only two with whom he did frequent the Dunelm (as the university's latest facility was predictably named) were Julia and Richard, the most scholarly. Richard had read all Shakespeare's plays, as had Jay; Julia had read all Shakespeare, including the poems, and all Dickens. What a swot! Two years older than Jay, she was an auburn beauty and always laughing and joking; so although she was already engaged to a young solicitor they had a lot of fun. Especially when they could shake off Richard.

'You go on ahead, Rich. Julia and I have got to see Birks.' (Dr Birkett was their American Literature tutor.) 'We'll catch you up in the Dunelm.'

Jay watched Richard leave the lecture room. Birks had already gone. 'Fancy tea and cakes in the refectory?'

'But you said we'd catch Rich up...'

'So?'

'Oh, go on then. But only if you promise not to rabbit on about Hemingway.' Jay had been arguing with Birks whose lecture had extolled the merits of Fitzgerald over those of his younger but worldlier compatriot. 'Why don't you like Fitzgerald anyway? He's a much better author.'

'He's a flowery poof! Hemingway's a man's writer!'

'What just cause he thinks in monosyllables! He's shallow.'

'Crap! He's like an iceberg – only one-eighth above the water.' Jay didn't attribute his simile, gambling that Julia wouldn't know it was Hemingway's own. 'His short stories are brilliant!'

Julia, who actually knew little of Hemingway, was impressed enough to shift to surer ground: 'Look at Gatsby. That's a brilliant short story, too.'

Not having read it, or anything else by Fitzgerald, Jay shrugged non-committally. Julia, all flash and sparkle, teased him. 'It's because you're too much like him. Gatsby, I mean. You're a young man from the provinces. And you've got a great capacity for wonder. You've even got the same Christian name!'

Jay was floored; but only for a moment. 'Well I know who I'd sooner meet for a pint, or ten!' he crowed, as if that were a clincher in any literary disputation.

Julia laughed, 'Oh, I'm sure that's a great accolade. Now, what about those cakes?' And she blew him a mocking but affectionate kiss.

Fifty-Three

Jill smiled reflectively. She was idling over a glass of tepid drinking-chocolate in Reg Dobson's café on Percy Street. She'd just started the second term of Year Two at the RVI and really ought to be moving, even though she wasn't on duty for another hour. But it was just too comfortable sitting reminiscing and, as usual, Reg was in no hurry for her to go, even though she'd already made her chocolate last an age.

The journey back had been like the World Cup – a game of two halves.

The first half had been distinctly uncomfortable. After the game finished the party had begun to disintegrate, although to be fair almost everyone was gracious to Jill and philosophical in defeat. The unknown neighbours had drifted off first, the men still apparently disputing England's third goal. The Spentolz family stopped on for a while, much to Jill's relief, although since there was now no excuse to share the armchair Adie reluctantly transferred to a separate one. Jill pouted sympathetically: it was a shame – she'd been looking forward to returning Adie's favours and was confident she could've given her friend as exciting an experience as she'd enjoyed. After a few glasses of strawberry wine however (in which Jill wisely declined to share) they decided it was time for them to be getting back too.

That just left the Schinklers. Mother and father began to clear away the debris; Wolfgang continued to sulk and Tomaz started to flirt with Jill, which only made things worse. Jill was relieved when, using the pretext of an early start the next day, she was able to escape to the solitude of her own room. She didn't expect Wolfgang to follow her and he didn't. Quite soon she was asleep.

The journey to the airport was the worst bit. Had he been less correct Wolfgang would've stayed at home but he insisted on escorting his guest to the safety of the departure gate. He started to get into the front seat of the BMW but a rebuke from Herr Schinkler condemned him and Jill to share the bench seat in the rear. They didn't speak much on the drive and after a while even their chauffeur's good humour deserted him and the car fell silent. Fortunately the traffic was very light and the journey took well under the two hours the conducted tour had consumed on the way. After they'd checked in her suitcase there was an excruciatingly embarrassing moment as Jill arrived at security and goodbyes became unavoidable. Herr Schinkler hugged her warmly and enthused about how she was always welcome. Wolfgang stood stiffly by. She thought he was going to click his heels and bow to her for a moment – as she'd seen him do to important customers in the gentlemen's outfitters where he worked – but at the last second he seemed to relent and held out his hand. When Jill took it reluctantly he raised it to his lips and briefly brushed them across her fingers: 'Lebewohl, Fraulein,' he intoned.

The second half was far better – no Wolfgang; and she was going home! Jill had finished *Under the Net* the day after the strawberry-doom. Whether it was the hangover or Jake's narration she wasn't sure, but she didn't enjoy it particularly. Still, it wasn't fair to judge an author on one book – as the lit twins would've advised – so she'd extricated the second Murdoch novel from her travel-handbag and settled down in Dusseldorf Departure Lounge Three (a far cry from Ponteland, but at least that was home) to while away the hour and a quarter to their scheduled departure. Like the first, it was a Penguin edition and should also have cost three-and-sixpence. Jill was canny over most purchases though, and once she'd discovered what she wanted to read she'd sought out the students' second-hand section where she'd picked up both volumes, nearly new, for four shillings.

The Flight from the Enchanter seemed appropriate in the circumstances! Not that Wolfgang had ever enchanted her – although he'd sought to, especially on their trip to the Lorelei – but it was certainly a relief to be getting away from him. Unlike Jake, Annette she identified with immediately: she was almost the same age and the first chapter found her deserting a school she disliked. True, Ringenhall Ladies' College was nothing like any establishment Jill had ever attended, but its headmistress, Miss Walpole, reminded her of Miss Sharples who could easily have put Jill off reading altogether. Admittedly, there weren't any chandeliers at Marsden Secondary but if there had been Jill would undoubtedly have sealed her departure by swinging from one, as Annette had so spectacularly done! She certainly didn't agree with Miss Walpole's rigid definitions of learning and curiosity: so far as Jill was concerned the latter was the very essence of the former. The Misses Walpole and Sharples would probably have got on famously.

By the time they embarked and Jill had settled into Seat 18A on the Boeing 727 she was taking off with Annette into the 'School of Life': a journey she felt infinitely better qualified than the protagonist to undertake...

The first term of her second year had been forgettable. She was living at home again, and whilst subject to few restrictions by parents who she rarely encountered, Jill was bored. Holy Cross did not have the buzz of Jesmond and she'd already decided she was going to find a flat to share. She mentioned this one Friday evening at the Engine. 'Well, that's a coincidence,' smiled Sue, 'Joyce and I are moving up to town. We'll keep you posted if we see anything suitable.'

Joyce had been promoted to the headship of a Newcastle RC infant school the previous term and Sue was due to take up a post as peripatetic adviser with the City's library authority. Jill was delighted for them: they both worked so hard, they deserved every success they got. She just hoped they'd come up with something that she and her friends could afford; preferably close to the hospital so they weren't incurring bus fares twice a day.

When she got home the following Friday her mam had a message: 'That Sue...' She pronounced it in a sneering tone to remind Jill that she didn't approve of lesbians. 'That Sue phoned. Could you meet her and her friend (again the snide intonation) at The Rose tomorra night – 'bout seven, she said. I divn't na why yer can't find some nice lad, instead of those two.' Jill didn't rise to the insinuation: she was used to it by now and it had long since ceased to irritate her.

'Thanks, Mam,' she trilled brightly, 'that's summat to look forward to!'

The following night Jill was smartly dressed. The Rose was a bit more up-market than the Engine and, besides, she liked to look her best for the lit twins who were always elegantly turned out. When she entered she noticed a few heads turn. Well, she smiled, the skirt was pretty short and the blouse virtually transparent. Be wasted on this lot anyway. She avoided the pub bore, got herself a bottle of Amber and a schooner and sat down trying to give the impression that she was waiting for someone and was not on the pull. Two lads on the table across the aisle started giving her the eye, sniggering to each other, and she was relieved when Joyce and Sue came in, arm-in-arm a few minutes later. The boys snorted their disapproval and stomped off to the games room.

Joyce bought two large glasses of Mateus Rosé (from a plastic wine box in the fridge) and another Amber for Jill and they all toasted each other's health. 'Good news, pet,' began Joyce, 'think you're going to like this. Well we hope so anyway.' Jill was all ears and Sue took up the dialogue.

'We've found just the place: a second-floor flat in a lovely Edwardian town house. It's in South Gosforth. There's just one snag: it's a bit too big for the two of us.' Jill was agog as Joyce interrupted.

'And we were wondering if you'd like to move in with us?' she said in a rush which, if it hadn't been her one-time teacher, Jill would've put down to nervousness. 'You'd have your own bedroom, of course. It's got a lovely big double bed in though. And we'd share the rest of the facilities.'

'Yeah,' concluded Sue, 'there's a grand airy lounge with a floor-to-ceiling alcove already lined with shelves – should be just right for a library. Then there's a really nice bathroom with a shower as well, a kitchen and – get this – a separate dining room.'

'It'd be just perfect for the three of us,' promised Joyce, 'Do say yes!'

Jill made up her mind instantly. It was, after all, what she'd hoped they'd suggest ever since they'd told her they were looking for somewhere more central. However, feeling Amberly-mischievous she decided to feign uncertainty. She took a full swig of her drink and rolled it round her mouth, puffing out her cheeks as if she was weighing up the pros and cons. Then when she saw how downcast the twins were beginning to look she gulped it swiftly down and burst out laughing: 'You should see your faces! Don't be daft: course I'll come. It'll be great. Thanks a bunch!'

'We'd have to ask you for a bit of rent but only like a peppercorn. We're aiming to move in after Easter. So you're welcome to join us then.'

Jill was delighted. It was a better prospect than some nurses' commune they couldn't really afford, and much more sophisticated. It made even the prospect of the next three months on Female Geriatric seem bearable.

Fifty-Four

Going down for that first un-Anglian Christmas felt strange. It wasn't home. It was simply where his parents had moved to – at Her Majesty's behest – just outside Chester. Jay judged the bureaucrats harshly: the DES (as the Ministry had now become, incorporating Science as well as Education) exhibiting the temerity to uproot his father from their idyllic Norfolk setting! In reality, Ray's superiors had been eminently reasonable, having extended the normal seven-year posting by three years whilst Jay completed his sixth-form schooling.

Eschewing the rail option (which would've consumed several pounds' worth of beer money and entailed changes at Leeds, Manchester and Crewe) Jay had shouldered his rucksack and trudged up to the Neville's Cross roundabout where the A1 traffic bottle-necked sufficiently to ensure a good spec. He was fortunate: no one else was waiting and he picked up a Mini that took him as far as Scotch Corner where another large roundabout led to the A66 over the Pennines. He'd waited only ten minutes and cursed a mere handful of drivers when a red E-Type drew up and although his sac only just fitted on his knees, restricting his view somewhat, he couldn't believe his luck: wait 'til he told Malc this one! They'd thumbed all over the country – though not together – and had a continuing competition over who could bag the best rides. The Jag-bloke was all right, too: quite young and turned out to be a bit of a climber so the next two hours had flown by before he turned off the M6. He was headed for Manchester, but if Jay walked across the motorway roundabout he'd be on the A556 which would take him straight into Chester. Subsequently he'd needed two more lifts but he still made it door-to-door in less than four hours. That'd take a bit of beating!

The new house was called 'Jedka.' Fortunately it had a number, too – 27 – so he wouldn't have to reveal, or worse employ, such a plebeian name. It was small by comparison with The Gatehouse, let alone The Lodge. It wasn't on a country estate either; but it was at the end of a cul-de-sac, and had large, beautifully-maintained gardens with a potentially lucrative four-lawn cut. It was strange having first choice of the three remaining bedrooms: he'd never missed his big brother so much. Unwontedly altruistic, he tried to think which room Chris would prefer and then chose the smaller of the two remaining. By the time he came down for the Easter vacation that choice would've been pre-empted, his father deciding that, since there were only two albeit large reception rooms downstairs, his study would benefit from a more elevated view.

Having neighbours was weird, although the people next door, the Jeynes, were quite young, and apparently regarded his father with awe. But they seemed nice enough. And the house opposite was a garden: well it fronted the main road so was a good fifty yards away and was shielded by a row of leylandii. (Oh brave new suburbia! where were the friendly bombs?) The couple there – the Whittinghams – were older; but apparently had a daughter who was in her first year at Nottingham and would be home soon. Probably turn out to be a right bag, thought a none-too-gruntled Jay.

When they'd lived in Norfolk the boys had amused themselves, just as Lady Veronica had forecast any tenant of hers would need to. But after a term at Durham Jay had become used to entertainment on a plate and was promptly on the lookout for nightlife. It was not totally unpromising: there were two pubs in the village, although initial reconnaissance revealed one to be full of old fogeys and the other to serve undrinkable Whitbread Tankard ale. However, Chester was only four miles and although the Tiger Cub Sports roared no more he spotted his reliable, if elderly Raleigh in the garden shed. His mother's redoubtable 'Chig' (an A35 successor to the original 'Chug'!) was parked next to the garage. The Wolseley only just fitted in the latter's narrow, cramped confines. So he wouldn't be short of transport; it was just a case of establishing where to.

'Fancy a pint tonight?' enquired his mind-reader dad the following Saturday. Jay had conducted a couple of unsuccessful recces into town during the week and jumped at the opportunity, although anxious lest it entailed a walk to one – or both – of the village locals. 'I discovered a road-house a few weeks back coming home from an inspection of the Girls' Grammar at Helsby. It's only about three miles away: serves Greenhall Whitley. The Black Dog: think you'll approve.'

It turned out okay: two large rooms – lounge and public bar – where the bitter was, unusually, the same price, and a small conservatory which contained a bagatelle table. Neither had encountered one before but both played snooker (although Jay had not inherited his father's expertise) so they gave it a go. Fortunately, it was quiet and the landlord was on hand to explain the rules. Like bar-billiards, the table was rectangular, but instead of mushrooms and scoring holes it had a semi-circular finish with nine shallow pockets set in the curved-part's surface, each painted with a neat, black numeral on the polished-ash.

They played for a couple of hours, Jay emerging a narrow winner by six rounds (of two sticks each) to five. It was still early but time for dinner, and easy-going as his mother was over most things being late for meals was not one of them.

'How many have you had?' enquired his dad.

Jay thought briefly, computing the pints of Greenhall's bitter: 'Six, I think.'

'Probably better if I drive back then. I've only had four Guinnesses.'

'Next time you come I'll let you have a couple of sticks on the bar table,' promised Charlie. He'd been watching their progress from the lounge window and was sufficiently impressed by Jay's promise to invest some tutor-time in him. 'You'll find it a tad harder – and a lot faster. Best table in the League,' he added proudly.

By the end of the holiday Jay was averaging sixty-two and his father, unschooled by Charlie, fifty-eight. It was just a shame it wasn't played anywhere else: Autolycus the Acquisitive could definitely sense money-making opportunities were it available back in Durham.

Laura Whittingham turned out not to be a bag at all. She was bright and sparky and pretty and she was reading English, too. She had a boyfriend in the village – Jay wondered how much longer that would survive – but he was a decent bloke and the three of them went out a few times for drinks in Chester. Since Laura would be back for foreseeable vacations they agreed to keep in touch. Not that letter-writing was Jay's forte. His failure to respond promptly to Caroline's missives had already cooled the ardour of their long-distance relationship. Caro was in the Lower Sixth now – sharp as a tack and heading for star 'A' Levels. According to Tom Hood in whose circle she now moved she'd also been out with a crowd of them to Autumn Balls and was being pursued relentlessly by Freddie Maidstone. Jay's reaction – to delay replying to her letters to indicate his disapproval – did not appear to be working. When he did call her from the Jedka 'phone over Christmas their dialogue was interested and polite rather than romantic. Caro said nothing about Freddie.

The car-port kept him busy, too. His father had concluded reluctantly that Chig was on its last wheels; and with his mother teaching at the local secondary modern school they could easily afford a replacement. There being no room for a second garage but space between the existing one and the elder-lined ditch that marked Jedka's boundary his father had requisitioned Jay's help in constructing a lean-to. It was basic: just white-painted wooden uprights and almost-horizontal struts fixed to the garage guttering, with a clear-Perspex, corrugated roof. But it was soon to house his mother's brand new Hillman Imp, which arrived in early January: pale green with the registration plate 'OMB 516 D.' Memorising number plates was still one of Jay's party-pieces (he could remember every car they'd had since BG 9835 at Ivy Bank) but for once his mother was first off-the-mark with her affectionate mnemonic: 'Our Mother's Bomb'! She didn't bother with the numbers but they were so easy ('5+1=6') Jay had them by heart instantly.

Best of all was a trip with his dad to Derbyshire. They were to meet up with John. 'John' was their father's private name (he was always formal in company) for Brigadier Sir John Hunt, CBE, DSO who'd retired from the Army after leading the first successful expedition to Everest and was now running the Duke of Edinburgh's Award. He'd enlisted Raymond, as chairman of the DES camping panel, to disseminate the decade-old Award more widely amongst English secondary schools. The two had become firm friends: Raymond admiring Sir John's integrity, energy and mountaineering achievements and John impressed by Ray's vision, drive and determination to bring the great outdoors to the less privileged. Ray Fincher was already responsible for two significant national initiatives. He was busy combining the activities of academic Field Studies and rugger-bugger Outdoor Pursuits into a new concept which he'd dubbed provisionally 'Outdoor Education.' And to ensure its lessons were given due weight he was devising an RPA – 'Record of Personal Achievement' – which promised to revolutionise the way less-able youngsters could incorporate their 'til-now-unrecognised experience beyond the classroom. And not just the less-able: their joint vision encompassed all strata of learning and experience.

The two had recognised the potential complementarity of their approaches and the weekend was designed to bring together practitioners from both schools of thought who would be proselytisers out in the big wide world of secondary education, and beyond. Fittingly, they were to meet not under the auspices of a university seminar but under canvas on Kinder Scout.

They'd arrived late on the Friday night and pitched camp in a rough, heathery field by Upper Booth on the south side of the moor. They could make out other tents but were not about to wander round trying to locate people by torchlight. There'd be time for reunions on Saturday. The plan was for Sir John and Ray to brief the potential regional leaders with two open-air presentations and then to mingle informally and respond to queries and other ideas on a group ramble up Edale Head and onto the summit of Kinder Scout. It wouldn't quite emulate the mass trespass of 1932 which had transformed the concept of the 'Right of Way' and in which – although they didn't know it at the time – both John and Ray had participated. But it was intended to pave the way for an educational initiative that was just as radical.

'My God, Ray, I might have known you'd be on bacon 'n' eggs whilst the rest of us survive on hard tack!' Sir John's grizzled, but handsome features poked through the outer flap of their prototype Vango Force Ten: 'Room for a little 'un, you old bugger?'

'John!' exclaimed Ray with obvious delight, 'course there is! Bacon butty? Come and meet my younger son.'

Jay had rehearsed meticulously: 'An honour and a privilege, Sir John. It's great to meet you.' He'd also taken the opportunity of including the family copy of *The Ascent of Everest*. On the title page opposite a full-colour print of Tenzing on the summit, his ice-axe proudly displaying the fluttering flags of Great Britain, Nepal, the UN and India was the inscription: 'Best Wishes, Jay. John Hunt. 12 January 1966.' It subsequently became his most treasured volume.

Fifty-Five

The move did not go smoothly. The lit twins had to vacate their Wallsend flat a month earlier than anticipated but couldn't get the keys to the new pad in Jesmond until the beginning of June. Until then, they were lodging with Joyce's sister in Tynemouth; an inconvenience for all. Even when they finally got installed, Jill was unable to join them until some indeterminate date in the summer; her mother having moved temporarily to Barnard Castle to care for a sick aunt. Her dad, who seemed unusually flustered by the arrangement, had insisted Jill remain at home to look after the household.

It felt like she was back to square one: commuting into town on the bus, coming back to prepare the men's teas if she were on a split-shift (the disruption of which she hated anyway) or leaving cold-plates in the fridge if she wouldn't be back until six. George and Al, who was apprenticed at Swann's as well, expected their tea at 4.30 except on a Friday when they'd call at the East End Club for a few pints and have whatever Jill had laid out for them when they got round to it. At least that suited her – she had every other weekend off and that meant Friday night at the A-Go-Go.

She'd been there a couple of years previously with Sally and the crowd from Eskdale Terrace. It had been her first foray into Newcastle nightlife and quite an adventure. The Animals were in their Geordie heyday and Alan Price's mate Georgie Fame was up from London. When Eric Burdon and the rest of the group took a break Alan acted as keyboard backing for Georgie who sang a medley of his Radio Caroline songs, finishing to tumultuous applause with a duet-version of 'Yeh, Yeh' which had topped the charts earlier that year. Not easily impressed, Jill had been as star-struck as the rest of the Eskdale groupies and had queued for ages afterwards to get her T-shirt signed in purple felt-tip by Alan and Georgie. It still had pride-of-place in her den, fixed securely to the hardboard insert with bright red, plastic-tipped drawing pins.

The days of the Animals had passed unfortunately – they were said to be going down well in America – but the music scene at the A-Go-Go was as vibrant as ever and Jill was a classy mover on the dance floor. Even though she was gyrating with a couple of other nurses she knew she'd already caught the attention of three blokes who were propping up the bar. As the music subsided temporarily the tallest of them strode over.

'Hi,' he began, 'I'm Stephen. Stephen Edrich. Can I…um…er…buy you a drink?' He flashed her a tentative smile.

The weird combination of self-assurance and modesty intrigued her – as if he knew he was good-looking (which he was, very) but was desperate for her to think so too. Naturally cautious, Jill gave no such indication. But she accepted his offer of a brandy and Babycham and, after consuming most of it in two gulps, his invitation to dance. Her expectations subdued by previous experience, she was delighted when he proved to be as accomplished as he was enthusiastic. For once she really enjoyed dancing with a boy; well, man, really – he must've been three or four years older than her (so, maybe almost as mature, grinned Jill inwardly). In between energetic exhibitions, which were greeted by good-natured ribbing from her fellow-nurses, she quickly established some background. He might strive for modesty but he was a man so, naturally, his favourite subject was himself!

He was twenty-three and had studied biology at Durham. He shared a flat with Alistair, a postgraduate archaeologist, in Kenton, just north of Nun's Moor. He was a medical rep with a big drugs company: Upjohn; and although – admirably – he didn't boast about it that meant he must have a car. Not that she was banking on it but Jill filed away the possibility of a free taxi later; Stephen wasn't drinking. She resolved that if he passed the 'smooch-test' he could drive her home.

Procul Harum's *A Whiter Shade of Pale* had been No. 1 for six weeks over the early summer and remained a late-night favourite. So Jill was unsurprised when she saw Stephen making a beeline for her before she succumbed to anyone else (not that she was about to, but he needn't know that). Like everyone she knew the words by heart; and didn't understand them. But she was prepared for a fandango with this attractive newcomer and was impressed when he held her close enough to demonstrate he was interested without stifling either her steps or herself. As the enchanting tune faded and she murmured: 'time for home…' she was relieved to hear him offer her a lift.

True it meant he would know where she lived but since it was her parents' home that shouldn't prove problematical and it wasn't as if she was ashamed of St Peter's Road, as she might've been had they still lived in Bewicke Street. Stephen didn't strike her as the sort to worry about such trivia anyway: another refreshing change after some of the snobbier undergraduates and medics she'd been unfortunate enough to encounter at RVI parties. He'd parked just round the corner at the Haymarket and as they walked down Percy Street he held out his hand gallantly enough for her to accept it. She was quite flattered when he made a point of unlocking the passenger door first but sat down demurely to ensure her already short skirt didn't reveal any more thigh than was unavoidable. Other than noticing the car was light green she paid it no attention until the change in his demeanour as they drew out of the car park suggested he was a man who took his driving seriously. Remembering that talking about cars came second only to talking about themselves she posed the appropriate query and was rewarded with a faintly bumptious: 'Ford. Cortina de Luxe. 1500 CC.'

Other than that, they drove in an easy silence until Stephen needed directions; and when they drew up outside No. 124 he immediately leapt out and scurried round to open her door. He walked her up the drive unexpectedly – it *was* two in the morning – and there was a moment's embarrassment as he was clearly undecided whether a goodnight kiss was in order. Jill liked that; and, standing on tip-toe gave him an affectionate peck on the cheek. They didn't arrange to meet again, but she'd already casually let slip that she might be in the Collingwood a fortnight hence.

That weekend Jill was in a quandary. For the first time she felt like talking about a boy she'd met; but, being at home and having no nursing confidante, she had no one to tell. Her mother was still in Barnard Castle as the mysterious-illness-situation showed no signs of ending. Jill wasn't unduly concerned about the aunt, whom she scarcely knew, but was finding her dad's lonely-moods hard to cope with. On balance she wished her mam was back though normally she was the last person Jill would confide in. The rest of the family were naturally out of the question. Which left the lit twins. Somehow Jill didn't think they'd receive the revelation with aplomb.

Back on the ward she took the first available coffee break to seek out Sally. They'd never been especially friendly but they'd developed the knack of always being able to take up where they'd left off, even after a hiatus of three or four months. Jill had long suspected she might be bi, so who better than Sally – who was openly so – to consult. To her relief Sally was completely relaxed and very supportive. First, being bi was only a big deal if Jill let it be or if some so-called friends found it a problem. Second, it was only one date, if that, so it was far too soon to decide whether she might have discovered a penchant for men to complement the one she clearly had for women. Jill should make sure she was at the Collingwood as planned; if she needed any moral support Sally would go with her. That way she'd get to judge how broad-minded Stephen was, too!

It made sense; ten days later they strolled into the lounge bar, dressed to kill. He wasn't there, and Jill construed her disappointment as confirmation that she really did want to see him again. She and Sally were on the Amber – it was still early – and when she went up to replenish their glasses the regular barman, who'd been down the cellar when they arrived, served them.

'You're Jill Walker, aren't you?' and when she nodded: 'There's a message for you from a bloke called Stephen. Came in here specially, last night. Said he'd had to go to Edinburgh on business but he'd be in by eight. Left a fiver for your drinks an all.'

By the time he did arrive the girls had made the most of the sub (although more than half of it was intact) and Jill was much more relaxed about meeting him again. As he sought them out in the now-crowded bar Sally let out a low whistle: 'Phwoar! Yer didn't say he were gorgeous, man Jill. I'm on first refusal if yer change yer mind, pet!' She winked to show it was only a joke, but a twinge of apprehension suggested how Jill really felt. On second sight Stephen *was* pretty good-looking!

He was tall – a bit over six foot, she reckoned – with lustrous black hair, swept back. She hadn't noticed his eyes in the alternating dim–disco-flashing-blindness of the A-Go-Go: they were large and olive-brown. He had generous lips and a ready smile that revealed even teeth. He was dressed well, too. Cream slacks over fashionable crocodile sneakers and a pale blue, slim-fitting shirt which showed off a well-exercised body, were topped by a navy-blue blazer sporting a Union Jack on the breast pocket. Subtle as a train crash, Sally asked him what it stood for.

'Sorry! Dressed to impress a client and didn't have time to change. I don't normally flaunt it. I'm in the Olympic fencing squad for Mexico City next year: it's our official insignia.'

Sally's response was typically over the top; Jill's perversely low-key, as if she met Olympic fencers most days of the week. Stephen noted it and was impressed and amused in equal parts. He'd already clocked Sally's provocative behaviour and approved of Jill's obviously liberal outlook. Here was a girl worth cultivating. He also realised he'd some catching up to do and, replenishing their brandy and cokes bought himself two pints of Exhibition. He wasn't showing off: it had been a long day, he was thirsty and – with his flat only five minutes' walk away – he most definitely wasn't driving.

He was good fun. A bit full of himself, like most blokes, but – unusually – well aware of it and given to self-deflating humour when he sensed he'd gone too far. He was also curious, and unlike most of the RVI crowd Jill hung around with, he seemed genuinely interested in her responses. Not that she revealed much; whilst Sal was there you didn't need to – she was indiscreet enough for three, and revelled in it. Within minutes of Stephen's badge-explanation she'd informed him that Jill was used to sportsmen: her brother swam and boxed for United Services and he, too, could have been an Olympian. Jill didn't mind that: these days she was proud of Rob and his achievements. But Sal also let slip that Stephen was a lucky man: Jill usually preferred girls. She was less pleased about that. She'd figured on Stephen being able to decide that for himself. Once she had for *herself*, of course...

The evening was progressing well and the party had moved on to the next-door pub. They'd established that Stephen's other great passion was rock climbing and, as if on cue, in came a bunch of lads from Northumbria Mountaineering Club. It didn't take a genius to work out that's why they'd gravitated to The Brandling. Jill was half-prepared for the evening she had in mind to fall apart as two of them came over and without even acknowledging her and Sal engaged Stephen in earnest debate about whether he was going to join them at something called the 'Peel Meet' the following Wednesday. Jill was prepared to be miffed that they hadn't been introduced when she realised that Stephen was deliberately not getting embroiled in climbing plans tonight. The interlopers didn't twig, however, and in the end Stephen had to get rid of them by announcing he'd catch up with them later as the three of them had a table booked at Falfino's for nine o'clock. It was the first either of the girls had heard of it but Jill was chuffed that Stephen had put them before his climbing mates. She was wondering whether he really had booked the restaurant and, if so, whether for three or for two. Ambivalence reigned: she'd much prefer it to be just the two of them, now that she was becoming more relaxed in his company; but she'd feel bad if they dumped Sally.

And then Trina walked in.

Jill knew she and Sal went back yonks and as she plonked herself down unceremoniously and virtually in Sally's lap the solution was obvious. Jill wasted little time speculating about whether Sally had arranged the tryst – kinda job-done-my-turn-for-fun – but the two of them were already engrossed when Stephen suggested quietly that Jill and he might go to dinner now, if that was okay. Sally waved them off absent-mindedly with the stock advice: 'Have a great time, hinny, and divn't do owt I wouldn't!'

If Stephen hadn't made all the arrangements in advance he must've been extremely well known at Falfino's. The maître d' greeted him like a long-lost friend and showed them to 'your usual table, Mista Edrich?' That turned out to be a discreet corner of the narrow room with a good view of the rest of the diners. Stephen ordered cocktails she'd never heard of and a bottle of burgundy without even consulting her. Still, he'd made it clear it was his treat and explained the steak tartare was a speciality. Jill reckoned he might know about fancy wines but she'd wager her knowledge of meat was better than his. She hadn't mentioned her mam was a butcher yet, though, so she kept quiet: the fillet steak had better be good!

It was; and so was the cheese board that followed. The Pommard went down so well they ordered another bottle and by the time she'd stipulated Cointreau-on-ice with her coffee Jill was feeling pleasantly mellow.

'So whadya do when you're not selling drugs?'

Stephen laughed, 'Well, the fencing you know about. Then there's birds.'

Jill looked at him quizzically, 'Hmm, nowt like being brazen about it!'

'No, no,' came the hasty rejoinder, 'I mean the feathered variety. I'm a member of RSPB.' Then, in response to Jill's puzzled look, *'Royal Society for the Protection of Birds*. Been going for ages – nearly seventy years. Your fault originally!'

'How d'you work that out?' Jill sensed a trap.

But it was just a chance to show off: 'Well it was founded to stop the barbaric trade in plumes for women's hats.'

'Not my style.'

'No, but I bet you'd look good in feathers!'

Jill snorted dismissively. Stephen tried to recover his ground: Only joking...what do *you* do when you're not ministering to the sick?'

'Um...well, when I'm on my own I read a fair bit. Plus I like going out with the girls from work.'

'What? Like Sally?'

'Yeah, 'owt wrong with that?' She hadn't meant to sound defensive but was relieved when Stephen just shook his head gently.

'Nothing at all. As long as you spare some time for me.' He smiled winningly and disappeared to sort out the bill. Jill was pleased to have revealed hardly anything about herself but she wondered a tad anxiously how the rest of the date would pan out. He'd mentioned how close his flat was and she anticipated being invited back for a nightcap. What else did he have in mind, though?

She needn't have worried: 'I've ordered a taxi for you. Should be here in ten minutes.' Jill was relieved and disappointed in even measure. She wouldn't have to fight him off later. But didn't he fancy her? When the taxi arrived – paid for in advance by Stephen – she had her answer as his arms snaked around her and pulled her close. He squeezed her affectionately and then kissed her tentatively on the lips. When she didn't demur he repeated the process rather more passionately. But before Jill could decide whether to reciprocate the taxi driver intervened.

'Howay, pet! Some of us have got a job t'do!'

Fifty-Six

Two letters awaited Jay on his return to Flass Street.

Anticipating bad news he opened the one from Caroline first. It drivelled on about school and social life in Bungay for several paragraphs before coming to the unpalatable point: she was going out with Freddie Maidstone.

Jay was furious. That Tom had forewarned him weeks back and he'd done nothing to retrieve the situation was irrelevant. He'd been stabbed in the back by his girlfriend and one of his supposedly best mates. Bastards! Bloody bastards!

He didn't bother unpacking; and overlooking his brother's Air Mail envelope he stomped off down North Street and into the town square. It was only four o'clock. Normally the pubs would've been shut but, this being a Saturday, the Market Tavern was open all day. It was a bit of a dive: not that that worried Jay who was comfortable in any premises, provided they were licensed. But following a run-in with some locals soon after he'd arrived it wasn't a pub he frequented. It had been one of those too-familiar occasions when Nige was flashing his cash and a couple of roughnecks from Chester-le-Street had taken exception. There'd been a bit of a ruckus and they'd only escaped by Jay flooring the more objectionable of the two and then persuading Nige to run before they'd regrouped.

All was quiet just now, however. He ordered a pint of Youngers and downed it in one. Then he bought another, plus two packets of pork scratchings, and slumped into a corner seat away from the bar. He was still simmering and hoped he wouldn't encounter any aggro: bound to get into a fight if he did. Meanwhile, rooting in his coat-pocket he discovered his dog-eared copy of RB Frere's *Thoughts of a Mountaineer* and settled down to read. Usually, if he was feeling low, the first few chapters which described the young climber learning the ropes (literally) would lift his spirits. With titles like 'The first soft notes' and 'The way of the Eagle' they were guaranteed to fire the imagination. Today, though, he read them without any of the normal exhilaration; they just helped – temporarily –

to fill the void. Similarly, three more pints of Youngers served only to dull his distress before he decided on a change of scene.

He didn't fancy the bonhomie of the Buff; it was opening time there now but he wasn't in the mood for darts or shove. The afternoon had crumbled into fuliginous dusk as he plodded dispiritedly across Elvet Bridge and down to the Half Moon. He remembered the first night he'd been in, just after he'd come up: eight pints of Exhibition and he'd still managed to walk back to his digs. Not bad: they'd've been impressed at the Tute! Eight pints tonight mightn't even slake his thirst.

It did, of course, and after visits to The Jug and The Dun Cow he found himself wandering up New Elvet towards Dunelm House. A sociable SRC was the last place he wanted to be so he tottered across the high-span of Ove Arup's Kingsgate Bridge and staggered up to the Bailey. He remembered subsequently reaching the JCR and ordering a pint and a whisky chaser: maybe two, or even three. But the next thing he knew was waking up in Gus's rooms with a pounding headache, a torn shirt (his parka had disappeared) and deep gouges in his brand new Churches.

'That'd be when you fell downstairs,' explained Gus sympathetically, 'before we managed to get you up here yesterday evening.'

So what time was it now? 'Three o'clock Sunday afternoon, old boy. You slept straight through – fifteen hours. Probably just as well, you were in a bad way when I found you. Lurching about, and pretty much incoherent.'

'Pretty much? What was I saying?'

'Something about, fuckin women…and bastard Maid…somebody.' Didn't make a lot of sense; girlfriend trouble, I presume?'

'You could say that, yeah! Thanks for looking out for me, Gus.'

Jay weaved unsteadily down the stairs and into the JCR to ironic applause from a small band of poker-players. He smiled weakly, looking round for his belongings. He wasn't that worried about his coat, just his Frere: it was a first edition and out-of-print. Irreplaceable!

The fortune of the exceedingly drunk had not deserted him, however. He'd not abandoned the parka in some unfrequented boozer but in the corner of the JCR nearest the bar door, his precious volume still securely lodged in its inside pocket. He slunk out ignominiously. Figuring it would be a good idea to line his stomach he stopped off at The Union and ordered pie, peas and chips plus a pint of milk. Two-and-six, registered Autolycus: just! He wolfed them down and set off back towards his digs. He was fine over Elvet and through the Market Place; it was only as he crossed Framwellgate Bridge that the cold air hit him. It had the reverse effect of sobering him up. He just managed to stagger across to the parapet before voiding his recent meal into the dusk-murky waters of the Wear. Then he resumed his journey, managed to avoid his landlady on the way in and careened upstairs for a second sleep-of-the-dead.

When he awoke he was lying fully clothed on his narrow bed. He tried to read his watch. As the hands came into focus he realised it was ten o'clock. Everyone would be out.

He re-entered his dingy room feeling cleansed. In body at least. The sun, suspended above the viaduct, streamed through the greasy panes and onto Chris's letter. It began with an apology. The pattern of the last fourteen months — all of which he had served on HM/Sub *Ambush* out in the Far East — had been of short spells on shore, usually in Singapore, interspersed by six-to-eight weeks under the South China Sea. They were troubled times in Indonesia and Chris was rarely at liberty to share much of his experiences and never to divulge his movements in the coming weeks, even when he knew, which, as navigation officer, he presumably did.

It was dated 28 December (the date of the Immortal Dinner, smiled Jay wryly, doubting if his big brother would recognise the allusion) and began by thanking Jay for his smashing Christmas present: a plain silver and onyx stud-box. It'd actually cost a fair chunk of Jay's recent winnings so he was pleased that, if unimaginative, it was apparently just the ticket.

'It's most useful, thanks, and the sort of thing one just wouldn't buy for oneself. I can never find cufflinks, and uniform buttons are constantly lost unless you keep them in one place. Which I can now!'

Jay felt retrospectively guilty. Chris's present to him — for birthday and Christmas combined — was a magnificent smoking jacket. It was made out of sybaritically-heavy Thai silk and could be worn as a scarlet coat, complete with ornate golden dragons, or inside-out as a jet-black kimono. Bit like Dr No, he recalled; savouring the memory of their attendance at the London Pavilion over three years previously. They'd had no pretensions to a World Premiere. Apparently HMS *Venus*'s captain had a sister who worked for Pinewood Studios and she'd managed to get him two tickets for the premiere. It wasn't his bag so he passed them on to Number One who happened to be on duty that weekend. He'd forgotten all about them until a few days before but had offered them to Midshipman Fincher, the only officer on shore leave that Saturday. Chris had rung home in a flap and, as luck would have it their dad was working in London on the Friday. He negotiated a day off school for a delighted Jay who borrowed Tom Hood's DJ for the occasion. Chris had worn full uniform and the pair of them had revelled in the crowds thronging Coventry Street, desperate to get a glimpse of the stars. Their angular determination had secured them a front-row spec and – perhaps noticing Chris's uniform – a grin from Sean Connery. Jay immediately regretted not bringing his copy of *Dr No* along. It was only a Pan paperback edition but Connery's signature would've allowed extensive dining-out amongst the Pokists. Even so, with the evidence of the programme to display Jay had made the most of the coup.

The letter continued with references to – but little detail about – recent more martial events:

'Incidentally, our captain, Charlie Baxter (who got his MBE for driving AMBUSH through all the action earlier in the year) stands a very good chance of his brass hat, as do one or two of the other COs. And, on a note of more personal celebration as of 00.01, 1 January 1966 I shall be Lieutenant (Submarines) in Her Majesty's Naval Service! But you may continue to address me as Sir!

'As you say it won't be long now, not much over four months. Just round the corner really. It's high time, too. With the departure of Peter Ling at Christmas I've been here as long anyone in the Division and in AMBUSH longer than all but the captain.

'I sold my car, by the way. Primarily to help me accumulate a bit of cash against my return though doubtless by the time I get back to England's green and pleasant I'll be as broke as ever. Especially since a trip to Japan is not entirely out of the question now that confrontation here seems to be easing off a bit.

'Well, kid, I must finish… I'm Duty and the sailors' needs must come first. Your loving brother, Chris.

'P.S. Thanks for the Zhivago – I'll endeavour to return it in due course.'

Six weeks of submarine-silence ensued, during which his pique at being dumped by Caroline gradually diminished in inverse ratio to the standard of his rock climbing. Local meets at Crag Lough and Ilkley clearly benefited from the Cuthbert's wall traversing and he trained hard – both on the wall and in the bar – in preparation for the highlight of the Epiphany Term's outings: the Langdale Meet. They were to stop in the FRCC hut at Raw Head.

Dad had told Jay a bit about the Fell & Rock on their journey back from Kinder Scout. The club first met in the Sun Hotel in Coniston: now one of his and Malc's favoured haunts. Their inaugural president had been Ashley Abraham, one of the two famous brothers who'd pioneered Lakeland crag-photography and climbing towards the end of the last century. He went up to the library at Castle Green and found a scruffy copy of Vol. 1 of the Journal deep in the stacks. You couldn't borrow books from that part of the library so he slid it down the front of his jeans and retrieved it back at his digs.

To encourage and foster under the safest and most helpful of conditions the exhilarating exercise and sport of Fell Rambling and Rock Climbing in the Lake District was the principal objective of the Club. Meritorious enough for me, thought Jay. He knew his father had talked about becoming a member but in spite of his experience and contacts had never managed it. Jay didn't aspire to membership: it was sufficient that DUMC were able to use the Fell & Rock huts, even if, like Raw Head, they were pretty basic.

There were only two blokes from his year in the recently revived university club: an obnoxious character called bizarrely but aptly Obnose and a young American called Skeet. He'd no intention of climbing with the former and the latter, with whom he'd developed an instant rapport, couldn't make it the first weekend in March. So he found himself in the company of one of the Club's notorious characters, a third-year Hatfield man named Bill Clarke. Bill, whose regular partner was President Ed, had a reputation for being a bit of a piss-head (which appealed to Jay) but a fine climber too, particularly skilled on snow and ice. As the president was on some jaunt in the Cairngorms, Bill would be happy to show young Finch the ropes. They got on well from the outset and having razzed off a couple of Hard Severes on Raven Crag on the Saturday celebrated appropriately that evening. Jay could remember getting down to Ambleside, but after a lost-count intake of Jennings's bitter could not recall how they got back. Nor how Bill had finished up being drunk-in-charge of a 'No Waiting' sign!

They sought more serious fare up in White Ghyll on the Sunday. Jay recalled his father's references to routes Brown and Whillans had put up there and hoped earnestly that Bill's hangover was as bad as his and they'd be content with something a bit less taxing. Fortunately, Bill agreed: they'd take alternate leads on Hollin Groove – it was only Severe.

It had been wet first thing but after breakfast and several prevaricating cups of Stygian coffee the sun came out. By the time they reached the sycamore in the bottom of the ghyll that signalled the start of the climb, it was warm and the route looked dry. Bill ran the first three pitches into one and then belayed. They were straightforward and enthusiasm by now fully restored Jay was happy to lead through and bridge up the eighty-foot, right-angled groove that gave the climb its name. Confidence sky-high in the aftermath he was persuaded by the silver-tongued Clarke that now was the time for his first VS lead – called, a tad ominously, 'Slip Knot'! Again Bill floated up the first corner to a withered tree in a thin crack just below the main overhang. Jay didn't fancy the latter at all and said so.

'Nah, don't worry kidda. It doesn't go up the overhang. It goes out to that rib,' and he pointed out across shattered rocks to the right.

'Oh right, thass ok then,' claimed Jay exuding a conviction he couldn't muster inwardly. He unclipped the belay and traversed delicately into the corner. The step onto the sliver was awkward and once on it he was immediately aware of the exposure: the rib was bottomless and the boulders of the ghyll-bed a hundred feet below. He was perched on a half-inch-wide ledge acutely conscious that his nearest runner was the far side of the rib and that he'd fall a good forty feet if he slipped. Most inopportunely the muscles in his left calf began to twitch and the vibration threatened to dislodge his tenuous stance. Jesus! He gulped, searching the crack above desperately for somewhere to slot a nut into. Then, just as he was convinced he was about to fall he found a perfect crevice. He jammed in the nut and clipped his rope into the karabiner. His face was paper-white and he was clammy with fear – but safe again.

His leg was still shaking though. Trying not to think about it, he hurtled up the steep wall above, too gripped to get any further protection in, and landed in a breathless heap on the steep grass at the top of the crag. As his heart-beat slowed to a speakable rate he hauled in the rope and shouted down to Bill the time-honoured falsehood: 'It's not too bad at all, mate! Climb when you're ready...'

Jay was reading his big brother's latest missive over a pint of Fed Special in the back room of the Buff. It was a bit confusing. Three months on he couldn't remember what he'd said before Christmas, though presumably it had included the lurid details of the Cuthbert's end-of-term dinner as it had provoked one of his brother's typically gentle put-downs: 'Without wishing to black cat, our New Year's party – just a memory now – involved the consumption of amounts of alcohol that would've cheerfully rendered the incumbents of Cuth's unconscious' and went on to describe various other up-country jaunts about which he was usually able to be a bit more open than on operational matters.

'I much enjoyed my excursion into darkest Malaya which though now rather dim and distant was nevertheless very pleasant, particularly the last seventy-two hours. These consisted of myself, an RAF pilot, an English girl from Seramban (a town near KL) and a Chinese girl from Penang roaring round Malaya in a British Racing Green TD that the girls had acquired but couldn't drive. A first class weekend was had by all, particularly myself who became much enamoured of one of the pleasantest and prettiest Chinese girls I've ever met.

'Apart from that there's not much to tell you. One undoubtedly gets into a rut out here and for that reason alone I shall be very glad to get back to England come May. Incidentally, my next appointment is to OLYMPUS. It's a very jazzy sub at present in refit in Pompey and likely to remain in S/M 1 which is the squadron that operates from there. Don't know much about the intended programme yet but if the grapevine is correct I'll be the Number One! I know that's much more rapid promotion than normal but a few of us have been involved in quite a show out here. Can't say anymore – I'll bore you with all the lurid details when we see each other. We'll be refitting until August after which there'll be the usual submarine workup from Faslane and then allocation to One's Squadron: probably the 3rd in the North.

'This would have horrified me a bit back – life up there being grim an' all – but now that the family lives in Chester it's probably no further away and it'd certainly be easy enough for a weekend or two in Durham to see what I'm missing in life! Keep the letters coming, kid: maybe they'll prove a factor in my own decision either to abandon the idea of university or to make a serious attempt at persuading one of the seats of learning that ex-U-boat officers are capable of assimilating the seeds of wisdom.' (Crapsville! snorted Jay. Learning maybe, not so sure about wisdom. Well not at Durham anyway – the most distinguished don in the Faculty was an absolute burke!) 'Plus there's Pose, of course' (his brother's friend of the family, English girlfriend). 'She might very well prefer a boyfriend who's a traditional scholar rather than a trained killer from the Orient!

'Then again, I'm still uncertain about whether to remain in the Navy but I doubt if I shall leave. You can say this is as short-sighted as you please but I'm doing a job which I enjoy and am reasonably well paid to do; and worse there is something about submarines which is like flying or exploring – once bitten, you've had it.

'S'pose I justify it in the following way – if the evolution of England and the world continues in the present pattern then I'm quite happy to assist this from the anachronistic position of a U-boat officer. However, if the changes are very drastic the qualifications for influence will be an ability to assess a situation and take decisions accordingly; and I reckon one has every bit as much chance of training oneself to do this in the Navy as one has at university.

'Anyway that's more than enough cod-philosophy for the moment. The good news is that our Malaysian amours said I could hang on to the TD for the duration! The better news is that I'll see you in two months, kid...'

Fifty-Seven

One Sunday afternoon when Al was out and Jill supposedly so, Aunt Cissie called. She was Dad's eldest sister and, so far as he had one, his confidante. Her chief claim to fame, so far as Jill was concerned, originated from a disgusting episode during a New Year party when she was quite small. Everyone was smashed and Jill watched – fascinated and horrified by turns – as her aunt puked into the sick-bucket and then realising she'd lost her false teeth in the process proceeded to grub around until she retrieved them and then shove them straight back in her mouth. Yuk!

Jill was in the den and only heard snatches of the conversation. They were enough, however, to establish that her mam was not nursing anybody: in Barnard Castle or anywhere else. She was shacked up in South Shields with the manager of the Tunnel Club; and had been these last three months. She was at work, but not at home. Jill, whose relationship with her mother had always been rocky, hated her with a renewed vengeance, which was exacerbated even further when she caught the sound of her dad sobbing. She'd never heard him cry before: indeed, it had never struck her that he might. Her fists were clenched in anger as she struggled to pick up Aunt Cissie's softer tones. She got the gist of it – if he wanted her back, all George could do was to be patient and Mary'd see the error of her ways soon enough. Then, even though he was in the right, he should welcome her home – but on his terms, whatever they might be.

Jill needed some air. She slipped noiselessly downstairs and out of the front door, crossing St Peter's Road to the cemetery. They'd been trimming the saplings and she grabbed one to run along the railings. Her mam had always been 'a bit flighty' but nowt as serious as this. Angry as she was with her, Jill couldn't help hoping she'd return, mainly for her dad's sake, but also for her own. It was so frustrating when they'd only recently started to get on that much better.

The railings gave way to a low wall above which the ragwort stuck up like golden spears. Jill vented her fury, slashing them down indiscriminately. Then she realised with dismay that they'd given way to sunflowers and she'd just lopped off three smiling faces. She stopped abruptly, close to tears. They were her favourite flowers and she'd destroyed them out of anger. What was she thinking?

Lying was a fault she tried really hard to eschew, and she resolved forthwith to tell Joyce and Sue about Stephen. Much as she wanted to be honest she didn't want to burn her bridges. She liked them both as friends and knew she had an awful lot to thank them for. Additionally, she still fancied Sue to bits and didn't want to perpetuate pangs of unrequited lust. She'd just have to confess as openly and as sensitively as she knew how and hope that they could all remain friends. Unexpectedly, it was Joyce who paved the way.

She'd suggested they meet in The Millstone, which was only round the corner from their new place in South Gosforth. They could have a bar snack and Jill could slip round and see the flat afterwards. Joyce said nothing about moving in; almost as if she'd interpreted the long delay as indicating that Jill might've had second thoughts and needed some room for manoeuvre. That made life easier. It was Sunday lunchtime and crowded, but they managed to get a table – the prerequisite for ordering lunch. There seemed to be quite a few families in: not a regime Jill was used to, but it made for a more informal atmosphere. The conversation was stilted, but only for a few minutes. They soon got back into their usual topics – books and authors, holidays and professional life, including Jill's prospects at the RVI and beyond.

'In case you're feeling awkward about not moving in, don't be,' announced Joyce firmly. 'We've gathered things are a bit fraught at home,' she added diplomatically. Of course, Joyce's nephew was a barman at the Tunnel Club: no secrets there!

It was very tempting just to go along with the excuse. It was true, as far as it went. But Jill was determined to tell them the whole truth, not just a convenient part of it. So she took a deep breath and explained: 'Yeah, it is all a bit tricky right now. But it's not just that. I've met someone. A boy – well a man – called Stephen.' She almost faltered when she saw Sue's eyebrows arch dramatically but before her courage failed her, Joyce chipped in.

'Well that's lovely, pet. We're so pleased for you. Aren't we, Sue,' and before the latter could do anything but nod in agreement she continued: 'So, come on, tell us all about him. Where did you meet him? What's he like? What does he do?'

Greatly relieved, but still concerned about what Sue's real reaction was, Jill plunged into far more detail than she'd normally have divulged, halting only when interrupted by expressions of approval. Her uncharacteristic garrulousness gradually subsided as she concluded rather lamely: 'I'm so glad you're pleased. I thought you might be upset – y'know, about the flat.' It was the closest she came to any deception but it was immediately seized upon by Sue when Joyce went to settle the bill for their lunch.

'I always knew this would happen. Not that I'm not pleased for you, pet. I am. But it doesn't change anything as far as we're concerned. We'll all still be friends. And you and I will always be special, if you ever change your mind. About this Stephen, or any other man.'

It couldn't've gone any better, reflected Jill that evening back at St Peter's Road. Just shows the value of being honest. There was a difference between honesty and transparency, though. She hadn't mentioned the lit twins to Stephen and she didn't see any immediate need to.

Mam finally returned that July, with her tail between her legs. She would relinquish the job at the Tunnel Club: they could manage without the wage. What with George and Al bringing home good money from Swann's, her own promotion to manager at Watson's and Jill chipping in with treats from her nursing salary the Walkers were better off than they'd ever been. And in a fit of magnanimity (guilt, more like, reflected Jill) Mary even promised to spend some of her previously-secret savings on a new family car. George would be the driver, of course (a blatant falsehood as although he *could* drive, their dad's ineptness had so far made him reluctant even to fly solo in the Herald, let alone chauffeur the rest of them). They'd all be able to take trips up the coast. She'd even run Jill into the RVI when she was on night shifts (don't expect that to last long, sniffed Jill).

In spite of Jill's cynicism, however, her mam did make an effort over the next few months, and she and George did take some trips out together. Every other Sunday to begin with, they'd go to the Maurie, or the lounge of the Labour Club (women weren't allowed in the bar, of course), returning around three when Mary would actually cook dinner for the family. Jill and Al were expected to join the feast – invariably a roast, fresh from Watson's – if they were at home. However, with regular weekend shifts to excuse her; and wanting to spend more time with Stephen, Jill hardly ever made the Sunday get-together. It was a failing which her mam was wont to hold against her.

By the autumn she was seeing Stephen most weekends she wasn't working. Having shelved moving in with the lit twins it was a relief to get out of the house. In spite of the miles he covered for Upjohn during the week, he was always willing to take her on a run up the coast or inland to the villages towards Kielder. He was teaching her to drive (her mother had offered soon after her return but Jill had circumspectly declined), and as the Cortina was easy to master she was progressing well. Twice they went up to Holy Island (she still didn't mention the lit twins) and, ever keen to improve her self-taught knowledge of birds, Jill was learning how to recognise them by their calls alone. She could distinguish the cries of sea-birds quite quickly: it was the smaller varieties – Passeridae, Paridae and Fringillidae, for example – she found difficult. Stephen's penchant for using their Latin names didn't help but as a trained biologist the generic terms were presumably more familiar to him. Still, it was all new stuff and, if he grew a little too precious, she would tease him about his lack of literary knowledge. Not only did it not extend to Shakespeare; he appeared to read very little and his few book shelves were apparently stacked only with ornithology and mountaineering volumes.

Fifty-Eight

The knock on Jedka's front door was firm, authoritative even.

> 'Oh they had to carry Harry to the ferry
> Oh they had to carry Harry to the shore
> And the reason that they had to carry Harry to the ferry
> Was that Harry couldn't carry any more
> Oh, St Cuthbert's, Oh St Cuthbert's...'

Jay was half-humming, half-singing the Cuthbert's drinking song as he ferried his luggage up to his bedroom, having returned from Durham the day before. But the rest of the chorus was curtailed by a louder rap.

His parents were in the lounge, so he answered the summons.

A tall, heavily-built policeman stood in the porch, the pips on his shoulders indicating he was an Inspector. Bit senior for a social call, puzzled Jay, anxiously dredging his memory for any misdemeanour that could have brought the Constabulary to their door. He couldn't think of anything and by now the Inspector was enquiring after his father. He invited him into the hallway, just as his dad emerged, looking equally bemused. The two of them repaired to the lounge, leaving Jay to resume unpacking his trunk. Several trips later it occurred to him that whatever the long-arm-of-the-law wanted he was taking his time over it: must have been here a good twenty minutes.

He was just about to take the last elbow-cradle of books upstairs when his father and the police officer came out, both looking grim. The latter departed and his father said gravely, 'Need to talk to you, son. Let's go up to the study.' Jay wondered what could be so serious they couldn't discuss it in front of his mum, but he was used to his dad's discretion and fell in behind him as they made their way upstairs.

'It's terrible news, I'm afraid. The worst. Your brother's dead. Killed in a car accident. Some idiot joy-riding in an MG. The driver's ok apparently...' he added superfluously. 'I need to get back to your mother.

I expect you'd like some time on your own. We'll talk again later.' And he departed, leaving Jay ashen and trembling.

The evening deepened. At first Jay could still see the tear-blurred, dark green tips of the leylandii, but they gradually merged into an all-pervading gloom.

He didn't close the curtains, or switch on the light.

He cried for ages, finally flinging the tears aside like a spaniel shaking water from its coat. He swallowed hard and took a series of deep breaths, trying to compose himself.

Chris couldn't be dead! Not his big brother! Plod must've got it wrong. That was it. Must be the other bloke. The driver. Tomorrow they'd get the true version... The straw he sought to cling to sank. Panting sobs consumed him once more and the tears welled up again. He tried, but couldn't hold them back.

Much, much later, it seemed to Jay, his mother came into his bedroom. He was lying in the dark, crying silently. She came over and sat on the bed. They didn't speak for some time. Jay gradually became more aware of her presence. She was crying too. It felt like she didn't know what to say.

Putting her arms around him she sobbed tearfully, 'It doesn't mean we'll love you any less, darling. You'll always be special, too.'

Then she withdrew leaving Jay to reflect bitterly: like hell I will. Chris was the only one who really mattered...ever...

The following morning was cold and blustery, but Dad announced a 'walk would do us good.' Jay wasn't sure who the 'us' included but decided that unless specifically *excluded* it meant him. He'd lain awake most of the night, sobbing fitfully and turning over his mother's assurance. He'd reached a provisional judgement: she meant what she said, and he'd be harsh to pretend otherwise. On the other hand, she'd never be able to understand how second-class he'd always felt. But he wasn't about to mention it as he couldn't see what possible good it would do. He suspected he'd always feel that way. After all, however complimentary Chris had been about his little brother's supposedly-superior intelligence, it was small comfort. Chris was basically a nicer bloke; plus he was taller, better-looking, had a more attractive personality and lived an altogether more glamorous life. A dashing Naval Officer destined for great things.

Well, until now.

Jay wasn't surprised when his mum didn't join the outing. She'd been crying off and on ever since they'd all struggled to force down a silent breakfast. A walk wouldn't help. Besides, she explained, she'd some 'phone calls she felt impelled to make. And at least he could ask his dad some of the questions that had been nagging him. Was Plod absolutely certain it was his brother? Was the MG the same one the Malaysian girls had leant Chris 'for the duration'? If so, why wasn't Chris driving? And who was the mysterious 'joy-riding idiot'? Why had Chris been killed when the other bloke was apparently okay? Why him?

Such queries were not about to be resolved, however. They walked along the canal bank in silence and Indian file for around four miles, the false-spring wind and rain lashing into their faces. Then they turned around and trudged back. His dad never spoke during the two-and-a-half hours they were out. He was pretty sure it wasn't intentional; but he couldn't help thinking a dead son meant more to his father than a live one.

An interminably-desperate fortnight dragged by...

Then it was Easter; with sod all chance of resurrection...

His parents were involved in a protracted argument with the naval authorities over the return of Chris's remains. For some reason which no one would explain the Navy would only fly his ashes, not his body, home. His parents were hugely distressed, but as far as Jay was concerned it made little difference. His brother was dead: why did it matter whether his body or his ashes were buried?

He hadn't reckoned with the urn, though...

His dad drove the ageing Wolseley immaculately. Normally, Jay would've had the AA book out checking the route and garnering fresh facts about any new towns they were to pass through. But he hadn't the heart; and certainly didn't anticipate sharing any knowledge with his co-passengers. The motorways passed in a blur, with only a minimal hold-up as they joined the A5 and picked their way around the north of Birmingham. Then, after a mercifully-anaesthetised M1 they were in central London where they were to meet a senior officer from the submarine service who would hand over the parcel.

Jay had given no thought to what form such a parcel might take but was unprepared for sitting on the back seat with only a bright-turquoise Singaporean Airlines plastic bag for company. They were due to drive up to Norfolk where the funeral would be conducted the following day by Ken Lewen. That was something, at any rate; Jay had always liked the worldly vicar from his time in the choir onwards. The Hoods would be there (he wondered how he'd feel about seeing Fliss but knew it wouldn't be the time or the place) and no doubt most of the village (well, the high element anyway). When his mother had fallen asleep and he judged his father was preoccupied with the busy A12 around

Colchester, Jay surreptitiously unzipped the bag. The urn was smooth and cold. Engraved on the dull-gold steel was the inscription: 'Lt CJ Fincher, RN.'

Fifty-Nine

He'd promised her a steak as good as her mother's. Mary had now met him several times and pronounced him 'Alreet.' It didn't help that, much to Jill's disgust, she would flirt with him and whether through susceptibility or diplomacy Stephen would return the compliment, goading her mother onto even more brazen behaviour. God knows what would've happened if they'd been left alone together; Jill made sure they weren't. Her father, on the other hand, didn't think much of his daughter's new boyfriend, finding him flash and over-familiar (he called him 'George' the first time they met). When Stephen came to tea Mary would go out of her way to procure the finest T-bones which she'd serve him with chips, onion rings and fried eggs: a feast which her father rarely received, even these days. So Stephen knew that when he made the boast one evening over drinks in The Brandling he'd have to fulfil it.

The pharmacist in Bellingham was one of Stephen's clients. So although it was a Saturday he could combine business with pleasure and get paid petrol money for Jill's driving lessons. They'd set off first thing and by coffee-time Stephen's promotion of Neo-Medrone ('for acne'), Kaomycin ('don't ask') and Neo-Cortef ('inflammation in your lugholes') had been completed and they were seated in the corner of Bistro Napoli. It was the only 'Italian' establishment in the village although any local would tell you that 'Napoli' was actually Geordie Mitchell. He'd been on holiday to Sorento a couple of years previously and had come back 'with aall this Eyetie shite!' Jill smiled when she heard the pretension exploded but the strong aroma of espresso leavened any criticism: the coffee was excellent, Italian or Geordie.

Stephen had been lauding his selling powers. They were no doubt persuasive, if the rest of his silver tongue was anything to go by. But Jill's exaggerated yawns suggested he should change the subject. 'If you'd like to stay over tonight,' he garbled rapidly, 'we could go over to Durham first thing. There's a college tournament at Maiden Castle. I'm fencing for Northern Universities. It starts at nine, so it'll be over by soon after lunch. Only if you'd like to, of course...'

Jill had been expecting such an overture for a while and had determined her response. She pointed out she'd need to call over home to get some clothes. She was slightly alarmed when Stephen let slip that Alistair was away for the weekend – attending an archaeological symposium at Vindolanda – and then reassured when he added that she could have the spare room. Nevertheless, it would be a first; she was nervous. So far he'd behaved impeccably but all that time alone together – and on his own territory – might prove too much for his self-discipline. Still, if Jill kept her wits about her she was confident nothing untoward would transpire. Unless she discovered she wanted it to of course.

The evening started inauspiciously. They'd just broached the Amber in the Collingwood when an RVI crowd breezed exuberantly in on the tail of a doctors' party. Jill knew most of them: Stephen, with his medical rep connexions, a lot of the others. They got separated for a while, and with the celebrations in full flow Jill drank considerably more than intended. She was confident Stephen would be his usual circumspect self, however, and would take control once they left for the flat. Unfortunately, he'd got a tad carried away as well and the two of them were pleasantly merry by the time they swayed up the stairs to Flat Three in Morpeth Court.

Jill inspected her surroundings with interest. First, she checked that there was indeed a spare room and, on locating it, enquired pointedly whether she could install herself for later. Reassured by having commandeered her own patch, Jill wandered through to the living room to be greeted by Stephen, in a chef's apron, proffering her a large schooner of chilled amontillado. She'd had sherry before, of course, but not so elegantly served nor in such generous quantities: so much for staying sober.

Resolving to make the one drink last until dinner she began to scrutinise the books. Stephen's were in short supply: birds, rocks and fencing amounted to a shelf and a half. But Alistair's tomes were everywhere. The rest of the bookcase was full of individual plays from the New Cambridge edition of Shakespeare together with a collection of Victorian poets – mostly Tennyson, Browning, Rossetti and Arnold: not her cup of espresso at all! There was a separate bookcase for archaeology studies and piles of periodicals, magazines and journals on every available flat surface. Stephen even had to clear the table they were to dine on. Jill offered but was told that Alistair didn't take to anyone interfering with his arcane collection. Stephen would have to be careful to replace them in the correct place subsequently. Resigned, Jill opted for Arnold and relaxed with *Dover Beach* and the amontillado until the chef announced that dinner was served.

Stephen had not exaggerated: the steaks were excellent – bloody and tender just as her mam would've prepared them – and accompanied by a surprisingly delicate looking side salad; helped down with a bottle of burgundy: 'Vosne-Romanee' announced Stephen rather pompously. They ate largely in a silence which was testimony to the quality of the food rather than any embarrassment, and it was only when they'd both tidied their plates (like the Spratts, suggested Jill giggling) that Stephen offered to explain a bit about fencing. Jill didn't expect to remember much of it but recognised the instruction as the price for dinner and tried to look interested.

'How about I start with the weapons?' Stephen began suggestively. 'There's three: foil, epee and sabre, my favourite. The foil's the lightest. You can thrust it at any part of the upper body, back and front: so!' And grabbing a steak knife he leapt to his feet to demonstrate, snagging the table cloth as he did so and almost depositing the crockery on the relocated pile of Alistair's archaeology journals. 'I'd show you properly but all my kit's packed ready. Anyway, you have to use the tip. If you touch with any other part it doesn't count and you just carry on.

'The epee's similar. But you can aim for the whole body. Plus you can move your feet more. So!' He lunged forward at an imaginary opponent. Very athletically, conceded Jill. 'And you don't automatically get penalised if you collide. Though you would if you obviously meant to.

The sabre's different altogether. Much more swashbuckling – touch of the Errol Flynn – that's what I like about it. Your footwork's even more important, just like climbing,' and he elaborated with some fancy steps, once again designed to impress. 'Plus it's more of a cutting weapon so you can score a hit…'

'A very palpable hit?' Jill interrupted and when he looked blank added: 'Hamlet – it comes in the fight scene right at the end of the play.'

Stephen looked nonplussed and continued: 'Well, as I was saying… you can use the side of the blade, and its edges. But only on the upper body – like the foil.'

It was Jill's turn to be confused. 'I think I've got the differences between the swords. But what's the point? No pun intended!'

'Well it's to beat your opponent, obviously. When you get in first it's an attack. If he defends successfully by deflecting your blade it's a parry. There's a lot more to it – like ripostes and remises and reprises. The junior bouts are first so we can watch them and I'll explain it all better then; it'll be clearer when you see it in action.'

Jill wondered whether it would indeed make any more sense, but smiled graciously: 'I'm sure it will.' She couldn't help feeling the whole demonstration had been to show off Stephen's physique. Initially, she'd quite admired it but as his ego burgeoned she began to be turned off.

Stephen cleared away the plates that had narrowly survived the fencing lesson, and then enquired about a second course. The instruction and the wine had taken their toll. They didn't bother with any sweets but at Stephen's insistence opened another bottle of burgundy. He dimmed the lights and put on a record. 'Ravel's Bolero,' he announced rakishly, confirming Jill's suspicions. By the time he remembered coffee she was ready for bed. 'Alone!' she muttered with unnecessary emphasis at which Stephen looked pained and said he'd just clear up and would see her in the morning bright and early.

No doubt the day had dawned bright, it was beautifully sunny now, but that was more than could be said for either Jill or Stephen. Neither woke before nine, when they were due to have been at Maiden Castle. Stephen, having finished off the burgundy in a fit of pique and frustration was in no fit state to drive, let alone fence competitively. Annoyed more with himself than her, he was nevertheless inclined to take it out on Jill, implying that her bad influence had kept him up too late. Just in time he anticipated her justifiable indignation and shifted his ground: 'Well, not to worry. It was my fault. Tell you what, the next weekend you're off we'll go down to Durham anyway and you can meet some of my friends there.'

Sixty

It was a late sunny afternoon in June. More than a year after his brother's death Jay now had days, sometimes two or three in succession, when he realised Chris had not pervaded his thoughts.

He had just hitched up from London where he'd spent an enjoyable couple of days with his dad. They'd stopped at The Ivanhoe and taken in *Wait until Dark* at The Odeon in Leicester Square. Then they'd had a couple in Old Compton Street, rounding the evening off with a sumptuous dinner at his dad's favourite Soho restaurant, Nik's Havajah. The following morning, whilst the department summoned his father, Jay explored Carnaby Street, buying two shirts so outrageously camp he doubted if he'd ever have the nerve to wear them in Durham. One was bright red replete with black zigzags, the other pale green but plastered with garish flowers. Jay regarded them as ironically symbolic, reflecting that for all the talk of 'permissive society' this was about the closest he'd come to it!

Now, strolling up the Bailey, he heard the alluring sound of chinking coins and made his way into the JCR. It was a leisurely post-exams game with none of the frenetic betting that had recently led to their senior tutor imposing a temporary ban on all card games after Nige had lost £110 to Crawley in a single bet. They'd both been bragging, of course, and neither would back down; but when it transpired that Crawley's winning hand was only Jack-high, the cat-calls and ironic applause revealed that even the assembled crowd concluded things had got out of hand. Received wisdom was that whilst Nige could afford it, if it had been the other way round Crawley would've been destitute. It occurred to no one that the debt might remain unpaid if that'd been the outcome, as obviously Crawley wouldn't've expected to be let off. In the event, Nige merely shrugged: 'Oh well, easy come, easy go,' and disappeared up to his rooms. He rejoined the still-shocked brag circle five minutes later and counted out Crawley's winnings in crisp fivers. No one had ever seen that much on the table and the silence had a mix of awe and envy when Dr Stuart had walked in.

There was no way of explaining away the situation: hence the ban.

That'd been more than a month ago, and the brag school had calmed down a bit since. There was maybe fifteen shillings on the baize and just about to scoop it up – with a king-flush – was *Il Presidente*.

'Wanna come to the Lakes, Jay?'

'Sure, Ed,' he responded, wondering when he could fit it in. 'When?'

'Oh, 'bout half an hour.'

'Great! I'll get my gear.'

They'd met properly the previous Rogation Sunday, just two months after his brother's death. Jay had been climbing well that day – on the near-vertical dolerite of Crag Lough – and they'd hooked up to do three VSs. They'd climbed a few times together since, mostly as part of a DUMC meet. Ed was a better climber than him but not so much better that Jay couldn't follow anything Ed could lead: a sure recipe for a successful climbing partnership. They only met on the rocks. Ed lived in Newcastle, had a full-time job, and, more significantly, his own car.

By 8.30 that evening they'd rendezvoused with Club stalwarts Steyn and Whitts in Patterdale, and after an hour or so in the White Lion were ready to pitch camp. Ed and Whitts had other ideas, however: the forecast was good and if they drove round tonight they could be on Scafell Crag early the following morning. They stopped briefly in Ambleside to fill up and Ed, claiming he was knackered, suggested Jay might like to drive. Coming from a semi-professional (Jay wasn't sure what he did for a living but knew it involved driving) that was a compliment. Though, on second thoughts, it probably just meant Ed wanted to see if he was any good. All went well up and over Wrynose; then, at the summit of Hard Knott Ed sprung it on him: 'D'you know how to heel-toe?'

It was a technique he'd heard his father outline once to Chris and involved using the left foot conventionally for the clutch with the right heel poised over the brake and the right toe over the accelerator so that on a steep downward incline you could brake and blip the accelerator simultaneously as you double-de-clutched to avoid crunching the gearbox on the non-synchromesh lower ratios. Jay said he knew how in theory.

'Well you're about to find out in practice. The other side of the pass is much steeper than Wrynose and I'm not havin those buggers catch us. Steyn fancies himself as a bit of a rally-driver so you'll have to go as fast as you can. You'll have learned before we reach the bottom. Or we won't reach it!'

It was just the sort of challenge that appealed to the reckless side of Jay's nature: firmly in the ascendancy these days. Not only did they make it but they razzed off the others and reached Wasdale Head in time for a pint. When the second car didn't arrive for a full seven or eight minutes, Jay felt his stock soaring; which seemed vaguely significant. He'd never admit it, of course, but Ed's opinion of him was not totally irrelevant. Not that he wasted much time on self-analysis. ('Even to understand oneself is not a human right,' according to Iris Murdoch, he recalled. Though he still preferred Pope 'Know then thyself, presume not God to scan/The proper study of mankind is man...')

In the early months he and Pose – telephonically – had formed 'CONCH' – the 'Cociety for not-creeping-into-holes,' and had promised to support each other and not get all I-am-a-rockish. It didn't work. She was in London, he was in Durham and when he discovered that she, too, had found somebody new it compounded the bitterness he still felt about Caroline's betrayal. *Sounds of Silence* became his favourite album. Besides it was a natural climbing anthem: rocks felt nowt – and nor would he, provided he didn't let anyone get too close. He wasn't prepared to blame such anti-social tendencies on his brother's death; though he conceded privately that it probably hadn't helped. It was just the way he was.

As forecast, the next morning dawned dry and bright and after a dubious fry-up of black-pudding-bacon-and-eggs they'd toiled up Brown Tongue and Hollow Stones to find themselves under the intimidating black-brows of Scafell's Central Buttress. The climbs went brilliantly. Jay led Whitts up his first serious big-crag climb. He'd seen the FRCC guide: 'Botterril's Slab – 140 feet. Very severe (delicate). Rubbers. 100-foot rope suffices...but 120 feet is needed to reach a really good belay.' And delicate it certainly was, not to mention extremely exposed in the upper reaches – how the hell had they put that up in 1902? Ed and Steyn, meanwhile, had conquered the much more serious, indeed redoubtable, Central Buttress (or 'CB' as it was known to all proper climbers) – 'Combined tactics and rope engineering almost essential on the Flake Crack.'

Their endeavours would be rewarded by a second night, not under canvass, but in the relative luxury of the Tranearth hut. There was some friction when Ed initially refused to 'go to the pub with you dressed like that.' But Jay dug his heels in and the general consensus seemed to be that if he wanted to look like a tool that was up to him. True, everyone else was in climbing gear, or at best jeans; but the two-piece hounds-tooth Austin Reed suit (cut-down for him by Gieves & Hawke in Chester) had belonged to Chris and Jay wasn't about to remove it just because the rest of the world thought he should. Besides, he'd show 'em...

An hour and four pints later Jay carefully removed his purple-silk-lined jacket, hung it on the only spare hook in the bar of the Black Bull and issued a challenge to the entire company. He would take on anyone: 301 – best of three – loser buys the ale. It was risky as several of the club, including Ed, were handy players. But he wasn't so much confident as certain: he'd teach 'em to mock his brother's sartorial elegance. Two hours later with four pints drunk and eight lined up on the bar, he hadn't lost a single game. Instead of triumphantly downing his spoils, however, he paused and melodramatically let a silence develop. Then, when he was certain he had everyone's attention he snapped his darts-case shut, retrieved his jacket, straightened his tie, glared at Ed and stalked out of the bar. In the morning, still in his suit – and only partly as an apology – he 'made a debonair breakfast for four with just the nineteen eggs.' The quote came from that year's *DUMC Journal* and featured further tributes:

'The return journeys are becoming noted for Steyn's singing and (Please note that this is a warning) Clarke's jokes. At the "Fleece", an incredibly suave, sleek Fincher is first out of the coach and before, yes readers, before ordering his pint, with a deft flick of the right hand his darts are neatly studded (all three) in the treble 19. By this time the bar is packed: Mays mumbles paternally whilst drooling pie crumbs down his beard and "Just the 174" comes from the dart board, indicating that Bell and Thomas are once again being burnt off by the dynamic duo of Fincher and Clarke...'

Jay liked that – except for the claim that his darts would take precedence over a pint. Gross calumny!! But it just went to show: legends spring not from conformity!

The funeral had been an anti-climax. Jay had imagined a packed St Mary's and a suitably jingoistic valedictory from Ken Lewen since, somehow, word had got round that the submarine having been recently involved in the Indonesian conflict Chris had been killed in action. Or perhaps – still knowing little more of the circumstances – Jay had imagined that. Either way he'd expected more of a fuss. True the Hoods were there in force, and most of the gentry, including Ray's erstwhile golfing cronies, the Hedhams, resplendent in the dusted-down uniforms of, respectively, an Air Commodore, a Brigadier and much to Jay's satisfaction a captain in the Royal Navy. The *Senior* Service! But the interment of the ashes in a small clearing near the lych-gate had been a very low-key affair. The lowering skies didn't encourage attendance and only a handful of people had come out to the plot. With a shock, Jay realised they included Caroline who, to his relief, had shown the good taste to come on her own. There being no wake he got to speak to her briefly afterwards.

'Hadn't expected to see you,' he offered in a neutral tone.

'Hope you don't mind. Just wanted to be here for you.'

Jay softened, 'Appreciate that. Thanks.'

'Can we meet up whilst you're here?'

'Don't see why not. If I can beg some wheels. I'll 'phone you.'

Then the Finchers repaired to Brooklands where the Hoods had insisted they stay. At one stage during the proceedings he'd found himself alone with Fliss who'd murmured sympathetic sentiments to him and put her arms around him affectionately. But it was the cuddle of a favourite auntie, not a once-upon-a-lover, and had left Jay unmoved. Fliss seemed to sense as much and there had been no further contact.

They were to stop a second night so the following morning Jay borrowed Tom's Austin Cooper and drove across to Wortwell, unsure of the reception he'd receive. He needn't've worried. Colonel Tillotson, correct as ever, nevertheless welcomed him warmly enough whilst Ranji was bubbling over with nervous hospitality. Caroline followed them down the steps, waited 'til the parental greetings evaporated and then simply wrapped her arms around him and held him for some moments in a reassuringly tight, affectionate embrace. They all went through to the parlour where the Colonel first offered his condolences ('Fine young man, great loss to the service') and then quizzed Jay politely about life at Durham. Ranji, meanwhile, busied herself making coffee then, when it had percolated, poured them each a mugful and ushered her husband out into their sitting room.

It was as if they'd never been apart, certainly never fallen out. Their talk was warm, verging on intimate, and on the spur of the moment Jay suggested they go out for dinner that night as he was returning to Cheshire the following day. The best place around was The White Hart, eight miles up the valley in Scole. 'Do you remember Jenny Dent?' enquired Caroline animatedly, 'she's head waitress there. If I give her a bell I'm sure she'll get us a good table.' She disappeared into the hallway only to re-emerge a couple of minutes later. 'All done! We're expected at half-seven for eight. She says she'll look after us herself.'

Jay was concerned how the news would be received back at Brooklands but, again, he needn't've been. His mother murmured absent-mindedly, 'That's lovely, darling, you two'll have such a lot of catching up to do.' It occurred to Jay that he'd probably never bothered mentioning that he and Caroline had split up six months previously; there hardly seemed any point now. His father and Roger Hood had gone off on a long walk, and were aiming to take in the Greene Man on the way back. Jay speculated over whether his father would be more forthcoming with his friend than he had been with his son and decided that he probably would be, but not much. Tom was a bit miffed but still offered the further loan of the Cooper, whilst Fliss clearly saw her principal duty as looking after Muriel.

The Hart was a splendid old coaching inn; Charles II was reputed to have stopped there for breakfast almost 300 years earlier but these days it was more renowned for its mixed grills. Knowing their reputation for gargantuan portions the erstwhile sweethearts decided to have a starter each and then share a 'Yeoman's Grill,' reckoning that one portion of steak, lamb chop, liver, kidneys, bacon, mushrooms and tomatoes topped off by a fried egg – well, two – on chips would be easily enough for both of them. Jay made a bit of a fuss of consulting with the wine waiter before ordering a 1961 Clos de Vougeot (which was what he'd intended all along).

'I never meant to hurt you, Jay. It was just you were so far away. I didn't know when I'd ever see you again. I missed you like hell. I was lonely.' And then when he didn't come to her rescue: 'And you know I've never liked to be tied down.'

'Yeah, I know. But Freddie, for Chrissakes! The bloke's a div: just because he's got a fancy accent doesn't make him superior.'

'And how long d'you think it took me to find that out? I only went out with him twice. If you'd read my letters you'd've known that.'

'Well, I guess so,' he conceded: ''fraid I never was much good at correspondence.'

The Yeoman's Grill arrived and for some time the only exchange was of nods and smiles of satisfaction. It was excellent, but a good job they'd only ordered the one! Conversation resumed over coffee and Martell VSOP.

'I was chuffed you came yesterday.'

'I was there for you…you know that. I thought it all went well though. Well…you know…as well as could be expected.'

'Yeah, I guess so. Didn't really know what to expect… I mean, yer know, it was nice so many people turned out. But…'

'But what, love?' risked Caro.

'Well, they all seemed to be there for Mum and Dad. I felt kinda left out.'

'That's why I came… Still special friends?'

'Still friends, I guess…yeah, yeah…course we are. Special.'

They ended in companionable silence (a distant memory of 'fellowship' stirred, but he wasn't sure you could include girls in the portmanteau). Jay settled the bill, remembering to thank Jenny and offer a tip to the communal collection box. Out in the car park they lingered briefly, Jay uncertain whether 'special friends' equalled kissing. He decided not and opened the passenger door of the Cooper. He knew Caroline liked that: she'd told him soon after they'd first started going out together that she admired a boy with good manners. It had never struck Jay as owt special: his father had always opened doors for his mother so naturally it was the proper thing to do.

He drove back quickly but not recklessly (as he might have done had the Cooper been his and he'd been on his own: he'd only had a couple of pints and half-a-bottle of burgundy, after all; well, and that double brandy). At The Manse he smiled inwardly, recalling his brother's pebble-spraying panache in the MGA and opted, instead, for a softly-softly entrance. They sat talking quietly for a few minutes before Caroline signalled it was time for him to go by leaning across and kissing him tenderly on the lips. He returned the compliment and they hugged warmly, agreeing to make greater efforts to keep a special friendship alive in future.

Sixty-One

When Stephen promised her a trip to Durham to meet some of his friends, Jill assumed it would be for drinks and a meal.

And when Ed proposed bringing his girlfriend down to the indoor meet that Thursday night, Jay thought nothing of it. Several of the lads brought their 'spice' to the Dun Cow. He'd meet them there about 8.30; before that he'd be in the Buff.

Jill had resolved to dress up, but not over. You never knew with Stephen. Sometimes you'd finish up at The Dolce Vita, other times in some dive on Wallsend High Street. Not that she minded; Jill was nothing if not flexible. Still, if these were new friends she was meeting it would've been nice to know. She might even have asked him but he'd been working up in Glasgow for the first three days of the week and the only confirmation she'd had that they were actually going was a 'phone message passed on by her mam: 'It were that Stephen. He's a canny lad, mind. Yer could do a lot worse, hinny! Said he'd pick yer up boot seven. An divn't be late.'

Still none the wiser, she'd plumped for a modishly short black skirt and a tight, beige, polo-necked pullover that showed off her figure without making her look a tart. She'd gone to some trouble with her make-up; but no more than if she'd been meeting the lit twins down The Gosforth Park. It would have to do.

Jay didn't worry much about his appearance. He was going down the Buff and then onto the Cow with the usual Thursday-night crowd. His black jeans chose him, secured with the Fascist belt Chris had once coveted, together with a bright orange shirt. As an afterthought, knowing it would irritate Ed, he knotted a black silk scarf around his neck. Then he stuck his darts in his back pocket and strolled off down the Bailey. He'd had a good week on the baize so, as a treat, he bought himself a pint of Fed Special and settled down to a session of shove with Cec, the landlord. After a while a couple of the locals came in to play darts so he chalked the board and then played the winner. He was on form – always handy when his climbing-partner was in the offing – and was still on the board when Ed walked in with his latest bird on his arm.

Holy Moses! What a corker! Comprehensively thrown, he tried to pretend he hadn't seen them, which was difficult in the cramped bar. Shit and derision: she was dazzling! For a second he thought they'd met before but they couldn't have, surely? He'd've remembered. He'd never seen anyone remotely as pretty.

Jill parked her bag on a stool and adjusted her skirt. She took in the room with a lighthouse glance, clocking the boozers propping up the bar as well as the quartet engrossed in their dominoes. She hoped the silk-scarf playing darts was not one of Stephen's friends. He looked vaguely familiar but if he was trying to make an impression he was failing miserably.

Jay just couldn't take his eyes off her.

He thought: she's stunning! Absolutely fuckin gorgeous...

She thought: what a prat!

Lightning Source UK Ltd.
Milton Keynes UK
UKOW04f1211130515

251444UK00002B/4/P